P9-CKR-320

# Secretly Yours

**By Tessa Bailey**

*Secretly Yours*

BELLINGER SISTERS

*It Happened One Summer* • *Hook, Line, and Sinker*

HOT & HAMMERED

*Fix Her Up* • *Love Her or Lose Her* • *Tools of Engagement*

THE ACADEMY

*Disorderly Conduct* • *Indecent Exposure* • *Disturbing His Peace*

BROKE AND BEAUTIFUL

*Chase Me* • *Need Me* • *Make Me*

ROMANCING THE CLARKSONS

*Too Hot to Handle* • *Too Wild to Tame* • *Too Hard to Forget*
*Too Close to Call* (novella) • *Too Beautiful to Break*

MADE IN JERSEY

*Crashed Out* • *Rough Rhythm* (novella)
*Thrown Down* • *Worked Up* • *Wound Tight*

CROSSING THE LINE

*Riskier Business* (novella) • *Risking It All*
*Up in Smoke* • *Boiling Point* • *Raw Redemption*

LINE OF DUTY

*Protecting What's His* • *Protecting What's Theirs* (novella)
*His Risk to Take* • *Officer Off Limits*
*Asking for Trouble* • *Staking His Claim*

SERVE

*Owned by Fate* • *Exposed by Fate* • *Driven by Fate*

BEACH KINGDOM

*Mouth to Mouth* • *Heat Stroke* • *Sink or Swim*

STANDALONE BOOKS

*Unfixable* • *Baiting the Maid of Honor* • *Off Base* (with Sophie Jordan)
*Captivated* (with Eve Dangerfield) • *Getaway Girl* • *Runaway Girl*

# Secretly Yours

a novel

TESSA BAILEY

AVON
*An Imprint of* HarperCollins*Publishers*

FIRST EDITION

*Designed by Diahann Sturge*

*Chapter opener illustrations © baza178/Shutterstock*

Library of Congress Cataloging-in-Publication Data has been applied for.

ISBN 978-0-06-323898-5 (paperback)
ISBN 978-0-06-323902-9 (hardcover library edition)

22 23 24 25 26 LBC 5 4 3 2 1

*For Kristy*

*A genuine friend, longtime encourager, and powerful advocate.*

*Thanks for the decade of laughs and truth telling.*

*I'm down for another one.*

# Acknowledgments

They say to write what you know. And if I know two things, it's wine and an identity crisis, so *Secretly Yours* is well within my wheelhouse. This book is best paired with whatever makes *you* happy, whether it's a perfectly aged Cabernet or a milkshake. Speaking of milkshakes, I'm going to try and not lay this on too thick, but you, reader, are the thing that makes *me* happy. I appreciate your voices, emails, and social media posts. I appreciate you even if you're one of the quiet ones. Thank you for giving me the confidence to keep doing this. Thank you, as well, to my steadfast and talented editor, Nicole Fischer at Avon, Holly Rice-Baturin—publicist of my dreams and perpetual ray of sunshine—and the wonderful and valued Naureen Nashid. Much gratitude to my agent, Laura Bradford. Eternal love to my husband, Patrick, and daughter, Mac.

# Secretly Yours

# Chapter One

Hallie Welch tipped down one corner of the comics section and peered across Grapevine Way, her stomach sinking when yet another group of locals bypassed Corked, her favorite, sleepy little wineshop, in favor of UNCORKED—the new, flashy monstrosity next door that advertised hot sauce and wine pairings in the window. The exterior of UNCORKED was painted a metallic gold that caught the sun and blinded passersby, giving them no choice but to stumble inside or risk vision loss. From Hallie's position on the bench, she could see through the front window to their state-of-the-art wine fountains and wall of stinky cheeses, the cash register lighting up like a pinball machine.

Meanwhile, the peeling white wrought-iron tables in the front courtyard of Corked sat empty and forgotten. Hallie could still see her grandmother at the far-right table, a modest glass of Cabernet sitting in front of her. Everyone would stop to say hello to Rebecca as they passed. They would ask her what flowers were in season and which bulbs were best to bury in the soil a particular month. And even though she was always reading a bestseller, she would carefully lay her silk-tasseled bookmark in the crease and give them her undivided attention.

The newspaper in Hallie's hands sunk lower, crumpling slowly at the vivid memory and eventually landing in her lap.

On the front patio of UNCORKED was a literal dance floor and a disco ball hanging from the eaves. It spun all day long, casting light refractions all over the sidewalk and turning people into apparent zombies who preferred wine out of a vending machine. At night, that ten-by-ten square patch of wood was packed to the gills with tipsy tourists, their purses full of overly pungent Rochefort, no one sparing a thought for Corked next door. Or outraged at the mockery of their very name by the overzealous newcomers.

When the shop opened a month ago, Hallie almost felt sorry for the young couple from downstate. Poor dears, sinking their hard-earned money into a gimmick. It would never attract the loyal Napa locals who honored tradition and routine. She'd been wrong.

UNCORKED was thriving. Meanwhile, Lorna, the sweet elderly owner of Corked, didn't even emerge at sunset anymore to light the candles on her outside tables.

Hallie looked down at the shatterproof wineglass in her purse. She'd been bringing it into Corked for tastings every day this week in an attempt to support the failing institution, but she needed a better game plan. Continuous day drinking had started off fun, but the days were beginning to blur together, and she'd found her car keys in the microwave this morning. Supporting Corked with only the help of a couple friends wasn't going to keep her grandmother's favorite table from vanishing off the sidewalk. And it needed to stay there. Far too many pieces of her grandmother seemed to float away into the wind lately, but not that table. Not the place Hallie had gone with Rebecca every single Sunday evening since high school and learned the art of gardening. It had to stay.

So, all right. Time to play offense.

Very carefully, Hallie folded up the funnies and tucked them beneath her arm. She scanned the sidewalk for any friends or clients, then walked briskly across the street toward UNCORKED. They'd added two potted ficuses on either side of their door, beautifully pruned into the shape of an ice cream cone, but there would be no brownie points awarded to the UNCORKED crew for proper plant maintenance. Not even for lush, well-loved greenery. And if Hallie Welch, proprietor of Becca's Blooms and St. Helena's premier gardener, didn't warm up to someone for diligent care of a plant, that's when they'd really pissed her off.

Besides, the plants weren't her current focus.

She paused outside of UNCORKED and eyed the disco ball, shifting in her rubber slip-ons.

*Here comes trouble,* said her grandmother's voice, drifting in somewhere from the great beyond. How many times had Rebecca taken a look at Hallie and said those words? Hundreds? Thousands? Now, in the reflective window of UNCORKED, she could see how her grandmother might make that prediction based on her facial activity.

Two round spots of color on her cheeks.

A firm set to her chin.

Expression . . . diabolical?

*Let's go with "driven."*

Mrs. Cross, owner of the coffee shop across the street, walked out of UNCORKED with a bottle of some celebrity's wine in hand and a paper bib around her neck that read *Sip Sip Hooray* on the front. She skidded to a stop and bowed her head guiltily upon spotting Hallie. "I don't know what happened," started Mrs. Cross, quickly tearing off the bib. "I let them add me to their text alerts just to be polite and this morning . . . I woke up to a message about wineglass rims dipped in chocolate and my feet just sort of brought me here for the three o'clock session."

"How was the wine?" Hallie asked, feeling winded. *Another one bites the dust.* "Robust, with a betrayal aftertaste, I'm guessing."

Mrs. Cross winced—and had the nerve to lick some chocolate from the corner of her mouth. "Sorry, hon." She slunk past Hallie and into the crosswalk, clutching her bottle of duplicity. "Have to run. I'm working the evening shift . . ."

Hallie swallowed and turned back to the disco ball, the glaring light forcing her to squint.

After a too-short second of debate, she retrieved a piece of bark that had been used to pot the nearest ficus—and reached up, jamming it into the top motor of the disco ball, halting the eyesore's next revolution. Then she bolted.

Okay, maybe "bolted" was an exaggeration. She jogged.

And she quickly realized she was not dressed for fleeing the scene of her first act of vandalism.

Rubber shoes were for plodding around in soil and grass, not for potentially being chased by the 5-0. Her colorful woven cross-body purse slapped against her hip with every step, her array of mismatched necklaces bouncing up and down in solidarity with her boobs. She had a teal scrunchie in her pocket, which she'd planned to use later to fashion a blond knot on top of her head while working. Should she stop and put her hair up *now* to make running easier? Curls were flying into her face, fast and furious, her gardening shoes making an embarrassing *squawk* with every step. Crime clearly didn't pay.

When a familiar face stepped into her path on the sidewalk, Hallie almost collapsed with relief. "Without asking me any follow-up questions, can I hide in your kitchen?"

"Fuck sake, what have you done now?" asked her friend Lavinia, donut artist and British transplant. She was just about to light a cigarette, a sight that wasn't all that common on Grapevine Way in St. Helena, but lowered the lighter to her thigh when she saw Hallie rushing toward her in a flurry of necklaces, curls, and frayed jean shorts. "Behind the standing mixer. Be quick about it."

"Thank you," Hallie squeaked, catapulting herself into the air-conditioned donut shop, Fudge Judy, speed walking past a group of gaping customers, and pushing through the swinging door into the kitchen. As advised, Hallie took a spot behind the standing mixer and embraced the opportunity to finally pull her curls up into a bun. "Hello, Jerome," she called to Lavinia's husband. "Those bear claws look beautiful."

Jerome tipped his head down to observe Hallie over the rim of his glasses and offered a slightly judgmental hum under his breath before going back to glazing donuts. "Whatever this is, don't drag my wife into it this time," he drawled.

Well used to Jerome's gruff, no-nonsense demeanor, Hallie saluted the former detective from Los Angeles. "No dragging. Message received."

Lavinia blasted into the kitchen, the smell of Parliaments trailing after her. "Care to explain yourself, missus?"

"Oh, nothing, I just sabotaged a certain disco ball outside of a certain wineshop." Hallie slumped sideways against the wall. "We had another defector. Mrs. Cross."

Lavinia looked disgusted, and Hallie loved her for it. "The one who owns the coffee shop? These hoes ain't loyal." She mimicked Hallie's posture, only she leaned against her husband's back, instead. "Well, I know where I *won't* be buying my afternoon coffee."

"The one you pour half into the garbage and replace with whiskey?" Jerome inserted, earning himself an elbow in the ribs.

"I knew you would understand," Hallie said, reaching a hand toward Lavinia.

"Oy. 'Course I do." The other woman grimaced. "But even I can't do any more daily wine tastings at Corked. Yesterday I gave away three dozen free donuts and told the postman I love him thanks to a Beaujolais buzz."

"Yes." Hallie replayed the whine of the disco ball grinding to a halt and her subsequent getaway jog. "I'm starting to think the daytime alcohol consumption might be affecting my behavior in a negative way."

Jerome coughed—his version of a laugh. "What's the excuse for your behavior *before* you started attending daily wine tastings?" he wanted to know. He'd turned from the glazing station and leaned back against the metal table, his deep-brown arms crossed over his barrel chest. "When I was on the force, we would have called this an escalation."

"No," Hallie whispered in horror, gripping the strap of her bag.

"Leave her be, Jerome," Lavinia scolded, swatting her husband on the arm. "You know what our Hallie has been through lately. And it is distressing to watch everyone migrate over to

UNCORKED like a big lot of lemmings. Too much change, all at once, innit, babe?"

Lavinia's sympathy caused a pang in Hallie's chest. God, she loved her friends. Even Jerome and his brutal honesty. But their kindness also made Hallie feel like the sole upside-down crayon in a box of Crayolas. She was a twenty-nine-year-old woman hiding behind a standing mixer after committing disco ball sabotage and interrupting the workday of two *normally* functioning people. Her phone buzzed incessantly in her purse, her three thirty appointment, no doubt, wanting an explanation for her tardiness.

It took her a full minute to fish the buzzing device out of her packed purse. "Hello?"

"Hallie! This is Veronica over on Hollis Lane. Are you still planning on landscaping my walkway this afternoon? It's past four o'clock now and I have early dinner plans."

Four o'clock? How long had she been brooding across the street from UNCORKED, pretending to read the same Nancy and Sluggo comic strip over and over? "That's fine. Go ahead and take off. I'll be over to get started soon."

"But I won't be home to let you in," explained Veronica.

Hallie opened her mouth and closed it. "Your garden is outside, right?"

"Yes, but . . . well, I should be here to *greet* you, at least. The neighbors should witness me acknowledging your arrival, so they don't think you're trespassing. And—oh fine, maybe I wouldn't mind supervising a little. I'm very particular."

There it was. Hallie's personal kiss of death.

A client wanting to control the flower narrative.

Her grandmother had been patient with that sort of thing, listening carefully to a customer's demands and gently guiding them over to her camp. Hallie didn't own a pair of kid gloves. She could produce beautiful gardens bursting with color and life—and she did. All over St. Helena. Keeping the name Becca's Blooms alive in the spirit of the grandmother who had raised her from age fourteen. But she didn't have a method to her madness. It was all gut feelings and mood planting.

Chaotic, like the rest of her life.

That's what worked for her. The madness kept her busy and distracted. When she sat down and tried to get organized, that's when the future seemed too overwhelming.

"Hallie?" chirped Veronica into her ear. "Are you coming?"

"Veronica, I'm so sorry for the inconvenience," she said, swallowing, hoping her grandmother couldn't hear her from heaven. "With it being late June and all, I'm afraid my schedule is bursting at the seams a little. But I have a colleague in town who I know could do a fabulous job on your garden—and he's much better at interpreting a specific vision than I am. I'm sure you've heard of Owen Stark, seen his name around town. I'm going to call him as soon as I hang up and have him give you a ring."

Hallie ended the call a moment later. "Well, my evening is free now. Maybe I'll go knock over a convenience store."

"Do steal me a pack of smokes while you're at it, babe," Lavinia requested without missing a beat. "And some antacids for our Jerome."

"Anything for my accomplices."

Jerome snorted. "I'd turn you in to the police in a heartbeat," he said, turning back to his bear claws, dusting them with powdered sugar.

*He doesn't mean that,* Lavinia mouthed at Hallie.

Hallie gave her friend a wry look. Truthfully, she didn't blame Jerome for being annoyed with her. This wasn't the first time she'd hidden behind the standing mixer. Come to think of it . . . had it even been a full month since the last time? On opening day at UNCORKED, she might have pilfered a few of the flyers being circulated around town. And by a few, she meant she'd canceled all of her appointments and snuck around, taking them out of store windows. On the final leg of her quest, she'd been caught by an overdressed manager in a tweed suit and little round glasses. He'd chased her half a block.

She should stop worrying so much about things she couldn't change. If she'd learned anything growing up with a vagabond for a mother, it's that change was inevitable. Things and people and even traditions were often there one minute and replaced the next. But her grandmother wasn't going to be one of them. Rebecca was the ship's rudder of her life. In which direction would Hallie go without her?

Hallie forced a smile onto her face. "All right, I'll leave you to it. Thanks for harboring me." Because she knew herself too well, she crossed her fingers behind her back. "I promise it's the last time."

Lavinia doubled over laughing. "My God, Hallie. I can see your crossed fingers in the stainless steel fridge."

"Oh." Face heating, she sidestepped toward the rear exit. "I'll just see myself out—"

"Wait! I forgot. I have news," Lavinia said abruptly, speed walking in Hallie's direction. She slung their arms together and pulled her into the small parking lot that ran behind the donut shop, as well as the rest of the stores on Grapevine Way. As soon as the screen door of Fudge Judy slapped shut behind them, Lavinia lit another cigarette and hit Hallie with the kind of eye contact that screamed *this is big news*. Exactly the kind of distraction Hallie needed to stall her self-reflective mood. "Remember that tasting you dragged me to a few months back at Vos Vineyard?"

Hallie's breath hitched at the name Vos. "Yes."

"And remember you got sloshed and told me you've been in love with Julian Vos, the son, since you were a freshman in high school?"

"Shhhh." Hallie's face had to be the color of beet juice now. "Keep your voice down. Everyone knows who they are in this town, Lavinia!"

"Would you stop? It's just you and me here." Squinting one eye, she took a long pull of her cigarette and blew the smoke sideways. "He's back in town. Heard it straight from his mum."

The parking lot seemed to shrink in around Hallie, the ground rising up like a wave of asphalt. "What? I . . . *Julian?*" The amount of reverence she packed into the whisper of his name would have been embarrassing if she hadn't hidden behind this woman's standing mixer twice in one month. "Are you sure? He lives near Stanford."

"Yes, yes, he's a brilliant professor. A scholar with a case of the tall, dark, and broodies. Nearly your first snog. I remember everything—and yes, I'm sure. According to his mum, the hot prodigal son is living in the guesthouse at the vineyard for the next several months to write a historical fiction novel."

A zap of electricity went through Hallie, straight down to her feet.

An image of Julian Vos was always, always on standby, and it shot to the forefront of her mind now, vivid and glorious. His black hair whipping right and left in the wind, his family vineyard like an endless maze on all sides of him, the sky burning with bright purples and oranges, his mouth descending toward hers and stopping right at the last second. He'd been so close she could taste the alcohol on his breath. So close she could have counted the black flecks in his bourbon-brown eyes if only the sun hadn't set.

She could also feel the way he'd snagged her wrist and dragged her back to the party, muttering about her being a freshman. The greatest tragedy of her life, right up until she'd lost her grandmother, was not landing that kiss from Julian Vos. For the last fifteen years, she'd been spinning alternate endings in her mind, occasionally even going so far as watching his history lectures on YouTube—and responding to his rhetorical questions out loud, like some kind of psychotic, one-sided conversationalist. Though she would take that humiliating practice to the grave.

Not to mention the wedding scrapbook she'd made for them in ninth grade.

"Well?" prompted Lavinia.

Hallie shook herself. "Well what?"

Lavinia waved her smoking hand around. "You might bump into the old crush around St. Helena soon enough. Isn't that exciting?"

"Yes," Hallie said slowly, begging the wheels in her head to stop spinning. "It is."

"Do you know if he's single?"

"I think so," Hallie murmured. "He doesn't update his Facebook very often. When he does, it's usually with a news article about space exploration or an archaeological discovery—"

"You are literally leaching my vagina of moisture."

"But his status is still single," Hallie laughed. "Last time I checked."

"And when was that, if you don't mind me asking?"

"A year, perhaps?"

More like a month, but no one was counting.

"Wouldn't it be something to get a second chance at that kiss?" Lavinia poked her in the ribs. "Though it'll be far from your first at this stage of your life, hey?"

"Oh yeah, it'll be at least my . . ."

Her friend squinted an eye, prodding the air with a finger. "Eleventh? Fifteenth?"

"Fifteenth. You got it." Hallie coughed. "Minus thirteen."

Lavinia stared at her for an extended moment, letting out a low whistle. "Well, Jesus. No wonder you have so much unspent energy." She stubbed out her cigarette. "Okay, forget what I said about bumping into him, you two-kiss pony. Happenstance isn't going to work. We must arrange some kind of sly meeting." She thought for a second, then landed on something. "Ooh! Maybe check the Web and see if Vos Vineyard is having another event soon. He's bound to be there."

"Yes. Yes, I could do that." Hallie continued to nod. "Or I could just check in with Mrs. Vos and see if her guesthouse needs some new landscaping. My waxed begonias would add a nice pop of red to any front yard. And who could turn down lantanas? They stay green all year."

". . . Hallie."

"And of course, there's that late-June discount I'm offering."

"You can never do anything the easy way, can you?" Lavinia sighed.

"I'm much better at speaking to men when I'm busy doing something with my hands."

Her friend raised an eyebrow. "You heard yourself, right?"

"Yes, pervert, I heard," she muttered, already lifting the phone to her ear, excitement beginning to skip around in her belly when the line started to ring. "Rebecca always said to look for signs. I just canceled that biweekly job with Veronica on Hollis Lane for a reason. So I'd be open for this one. Potentially. I might have Napa running in my blood, but wine tastings aren't my element. This is better. I'll have my flowers as a buffer."

"I suppose that's fair enough. You're just having a little look at him."

"Yes! A tiny baby of a look. For nostalgia's sake."

Lavinia was beginning to nod along with her. "Fuck me, I'm actually getting a little excited about this, Hal. It's not every day a girl gets a second shot at kissing her lifelong crush."

Exactly. That's why she wasn't going to overthink this. *Act first, reflect later.* Her credo worked out at least half the time. A lot of things had far worse odds. Like . . . the lottery. Or cracking open a double-yolked egg. No matter what happened, though, she'd be laying her eyes on Julian Vos again. In the flesh. And soon.

Obviously, this course of action could backfire. Righteously.

What if he didn't even remember her or that night in the vineyard?

After all, fifteen years had passed and her feelings for Julian in high school were woefully one-sided. Before the night of the almost-kiss, he'd been blissfully unaware of her existence. And immediately afterward, she'd been pulled from school by her mother for an extended road trip to Tacoma. He'd graduated soon after, and she'd never seen him again in real life.

A blank look from the man who starred in her fantasies could be a crushing disappointment. But her impulsivity had gotten worse since the loss of Rebecca in January, and it was too tempting to throw herself into one of her unknowns now. To let the chips fall where they may without reasoning through her actions first. A little niggle beneath her collar warned her to stop and slow down, take some time to think, but she ignored it, her spine snapping straight when Corinne Vos's crisp, almost amused-sounding voice curled in her ear. "Hello?"

"Mrs. Vos, hello. It's Hallie Welch from Becca's Blooms. I do the landscaping around your pool and refresh your porch every season."

The slightest pause. "Yes. Hello, Miss Welch. What can I do for you?"

Hallie held the phone away so she could gulp down a breath for courage, then settled the screen once more against the side of her face. "Actually, I was hoping I could do something for you. My waxed begonias are just stunning this year, and I thought some of them might look beautiful around your property . . ."

# Chapter Two

Julian Vos forced his fingers to move across the keyboard, even though the plot was going off the rails. He'd set aside thirty minutes to write without stopping. Therefore, thirty minutes needed to be completed. His hero, Wexler, who had time traveled to the past, was now musing over how much he missed fast food and indoor plumbing of the future. All of this would be deleted, but he had to keep writing for another thirty seconds.

Twenty-nine. Twenty-eight.

The front door of the guesthouse opened and closed. Julian kept his eyes glued to the cursor, though he frowned. On the screen of his desktop, Wexler now turned to his colleague and said, "No one is scheduled to be here this afternoon."

His timer went off.

Julian slowly sat back in the leather executive chair and allowed his hands to drift away from the keyboard to rest on his thighs. "Hello?" he called without turning around.

"It's your mother." Her crisp footsteps moved from the entryway to the hall beneath the stairs, which led to the back office overlooking the yard. "I knocked several times, Julian," she said, coming to a stop in the doorway behind him. "Whatever you're writing must be quite engrossing."

"Yes." Since she didn't specifically ask *what* he was writing, he assumed she wasn't interested and didn't bother elaborating. He turned the chair around and stood. "Sorry for the wait. I was completing a thirty-minute cycle."

Corinne Vos cracked a small smile, briefly unearthing the lines around her eyes and sides of her mouth. "Still sticking to your tight schedules, I see."

Julian nodded once. "All I have in the fridge is sparkling water," he said, gesturing for her to precede him out of the office. Deleting words was part of the writing process—he'd read extensively about drafting methods in *Structuring Your Novel*—but his mother didn't need to see Wexler waxing poetic about cheeseburgers and toilets. The fact that Julian was taking a break from teaching history to write fiction was already providing her with more than enough amusement. He didn't need to add fuel to the fire. "Have a glass with me?"

She inclined her head, her gaze ticking briefly over his shoulder to the computer screen. "Yes, please. Sparkling water sounds fine."

They relocated to the kitchen in silence, Julian removing two slim glasses from the cabinet and filling them up, handing one to his mother, who hadn't taken a seat. Not wanting to be impolite, Julian remained standing, too.

"How is this place?" Corinne asked, tapping her row of Sacramento-green nails on the glass. They were always painted the same shade, to match the Vos Vineyard logo. "Comfortable?"

"Very."

"Are you sure you wouldn't rather stay up in the main house?" With a bemused smile, she swept the kitchen with a look. "We have food there. A staff to prepare it. Without those things to worry about, you could focus more on writing."

"I appreciate the offer, but I'd rather have the quiet." They sipped in silence. The watch on his wrist ticked. Not audibly, but he could feel the gentle drift of the second hand as it rounded the midnight-blue face. "Operations are running smoothly at Vos?"

"Of course. Why wouldn't they be?" Corinne set her glass on the counter with a touch too much force and folded her hands at her waist, pinning him with a look that made him oddly sentimental. It called to mind the times his sister, Natalie, got them into trouble around the vineyard as kids. They would return home to find Corinne waiting at the back door with a pinched forehead and instructions to clean themselves up for dinner immediately. By no means could his family be termed close. They were simply related. They carried the weight of the same last name. But there were instances in the past, like showing up at the back door just before dark covered in mud and sticks, when he could pretend they were like every other family. "There is something I want to speak with you about, Julian, if you have a moment."

Mentally, he deducted fifteen minutes from his next writing sprint and added it to the final one of the day, bringing him up even. Right on schedule. "Yes, of course."

Corinne turned her head and looked out at the acres sitting between the guesthouse and the main one. Land filled with row after row of Vos grapes. Lush green vines wrapped around wooden posts, pops of deep-purple fruit warmed and nurtured by the Napa sunlight. More than half of those support posts had been there since his great-grandfather founded the vineyard and the distribution side of Vos Vineyard in the late fifties.

The other half of those pillars had been replaced after the wildfire four years prior.

Also known as the last time he'd been home.

As if he'd recalled that hellish week out loud, Corinne's attention snapped back to him. "It's summer in Napa. You know what that means."

Julian cleared his throat. "Enough wine tastings to turn St. Helena into drunk Disneyland?"

"Yes. And I know you're busy here and I'm not trying to interrupt. But there is a festival coming up in just under two weeks. Wine Down Napa. It's a ridiculous name, but it draws a lot of attention from the media, not to mention a crowd. Naturally, Vos will have a significant presence there, and it would look good, in the eyes of the press—and the Valley as a whole—if you were there. Supporting the family business." She seemed fascinated by the crown molding. "If you could be there from seven to nine in the evening, that should suffice."

The request gave him pause. Namely, because it was a request from his mother, and Corinne didn't make those. Not unless there was a very good reason—especially with favors pertaining to the vineyard. She took great pride in managing the operation solo. Still, he couldn't shake the feeling something was off. "Does the family business *need* some additional support?"

"I suppose it wouldn't hurt." Her expression didn't change, but there was a flicker in the depths of her eyes. "Nothing to be alarmed about, of course, but there is a lot of competition in the Valley. A lot of new flash."

In Corinne terms, that was tantamount to admitting to trouble. What degree of trouble, though? Julian didn't know, but the subject of the winery had been closed to him four years ago. Forcefully. By his father. Still, he couldn't very well *ignore* the buried note of distress in his mother's tone, could he? "What can I . . ." He cleared his throat hard. "Can I do anything to help?"

"You can be present at the festival," she said without missing a beat, a smile returning to her face.

Given no choice but to back away from the subject for now, Julian dipped his chin. "Of course."

If Corinne was relieved, she showed it only briefly by dropping her clasped hands and shaking them out. "Wonderful. I would tell you to mark it on your calendar, but I suspect it's the first thing you'll do when I leave."

Julian smiled tightly. "You're not wrong."

Maybe the one thing the Vos family could be counted on to know about each other was their individual quirks. Their faults. Corinne hated relying on anyone but herself. Julian needed an airtight schedule. His father, though gone now, had been obsessed with cultivating the perfect grape to the point that everything else fell to the wayside. And his sister, Natalie, was never not scheming or planning a prank. Good thing she was off terrorizing the population of New York City, three thousand miles from Napa.

Leaving his glass on the counter, Julian followed his mother to the door.

"I'll let you get back to it," she said briskly, turning the knob and stepping into a wash of sunshine. "Oh, before I go, there may be a small commotion outside later today, but it's nothing to concern yourself with."

Julian drew up short, a vision of his stopwatch app vanishing like mist. "What do you mean by a *small* commotion? There is no such thing."

"I suppose you're right." She pursed her lips. "It'll just be a commotion."

"What sort?"

"The gardener. She'll be dropping by to plant some begonias."

Julian couldn't hide his perplexity. "Why?"

Brown eyes, very similar to his own, flashed. "Because I hired her to do so."

His laugh was short. More like a scoffing exhale. "I couldn't care less about flowers, and I'm the only one here to look at them."

They both stopped and visibly straightened themselves. Arguing was beneath them. They were civilized. They had been taught to grin and bear their way through anger, to not give in to the urge to win. Victory meant everyone walked away half satisfied, relieved to get back to their own separate world.

"What time is she arriving?"

Did the corner of Corinne's mouth jump a little? "Three o'clock." She smiled and stepped onto the porch, descending one step. Two. "Approximately."

Julian's eye twitched.

He loathed the word "approximately." If he could remove one word from the dictionary, it would be "approximately," followed by "nearly" and "somewhat." If this gardener gave only ballpark arrival times, they were not going to get along. Best to stay inside and ignore her.

Should be easy enough.

THE GARDENER ARRIVED with five minutes left in his writing sprint.

What sounded like a truck crunched to a stop in the pebbled driveway, the rumbling engine falling silent. A squealing door slammed. Two dogs started to bark.

Sorry, make that *three* dogs.

Jesus. Christ.

Well, if they needed something from him, they would all have to damn well wait.

He wasn't even going to break concentration to look at the time.

But considering he'd started this thirty-minute writing session at four o'clock, he assumed it was nearing four thirty—and that made this gardener a grand total of an hour and a half late. That was so late, it didn't even constitute late. It was a full-blown absence.

He would be letting her know it. Just as soon as his timer went off.

"Hello?" called an extremely cheerful voice from the driveway, followed by a chorus of excited barking. "Mr. Vos?"

Julian's fingers almost stopped on the keyboard at being called Mr. Vos. At Stanford, he was Professor Vos. Or simply Professor.

Mr. Vos was his father.

For the breath of a second, the motions of his fingers grew stiff.

He typed faster to make up for the stutter. And he kept right on going when the front door of the house opened. "Hello? Is everyone decent?" Something about the voice of this gardener—and apparent trespasser—tugged at his memory, but he couldn't quite land on the face that matched. Why the hell did she need to enter the home when his garden was outside? Had his mother hired this person as payback for not coming home for four years? If so, the torture was effective. His blood pressure rose with every creak of her footsteps down the hallway. "I'm here to plant your begonias . . . *Boys! Heel!*"

If Julian wasn't mistaken, that was a pair of paws resting on his shoulders. The cold, wet muzzle of another canine snuffled at his thigh, then tried to dislodge his fingers from the keyboard.

Briefly, Julian's gaze fell to his stopwatch. Three more minutes.

If he didn't finish the session, he wouldn't relax all night. But it was hard to concentrate when he could see the reflection of a yellow lab in the computer monitor. As if sensing Julian's attention, the animal rolled over onto his back on the rug, tongue lolling out.

"I'm so sorry to interrupt . . ." came the bright, almost musical voice behind him. "Oh, you're just going to keep going. Okay." A shadow fell over a portion of his desk. "I see. This is some kind of timed session." She shivered, as if she'd just found out he was a phantom haunting the premises, rather than someone who simply valued minutes and their many uses. Perhaps she should take note. "You cannot stop . . ." she said slowly, her presence warming his right upper back. "Until the stopwatch runs out, or you won't earn your glass of whiskey."

Wait.

What?

Oh, Jesus. Wexler was voicing the thoughts inside of Julian's head again.

And the gardener was reading over his shoulder.

Finally, the timer went off, sending the dogs into a howling competition.

Julian pinned his phone's red timer button with his index finger, took a deep breath, and turned slowly in the executive chair, preparing the rebuke of the century. In the history department at Stanford, he was known for being particular. Exacting. Rigorous. But when it came to censuring students, he let his grades do the talking. He didn't have time for *extra* lectures after hours. When a student requested a meeting, he accommodated them, of course. As long as they scheduled in advance. God help the ones who showed up unannounced.

"If there is some reason you've decided to enter my home without permission, I would love to hear it . . ."

He finished turning.

Right there in front of Julian was the single most incredible pair of breasts he'd ever seen. Julian wasn't the type to gawk at women. But these breasts were just below his eyeline, mere inches from his face. There was simply no looking away. God help him, they were spectacular. Big, to put it bluntly. They were big. And displayed rather prominently in a baby blue T-shirt, through which he could make out the polka dot pattern of the gardener's bra.

"Is it true?" asked the breasts. "That you won't let yourself have a drink at the end of the day unless you write for the full thirty minutes?"

Julian shook himself, searching desperately for the irritation he'd felt pre-breasts, but he couldn't seem to locate it very easily. Especially when he looked up and finally met the gardener's sparkling dove-gray eyes and something, very unexpectedly, jolted in his midsection.

*God. That's a smile.*

And a whole lot of chaos.

Blond corkscrew curls rioted down to her shoulders, but a lot of them stood on end, pointing east or west, like broken couch springs. She had three necklaces on, and none of them matched. Gold, wooden, silver. The pockets stuck out of the bottom of her jean shorts and . . . yeah, he really needed to keep his attention above her neck, because her bold curves were demanding to be acknowledged and he had *not* been invited to do so. A lot like she hadn't been invited into the guesthouse.

Still. She was full-figured and hiding none of said figure.

There was something about the enthusiastic enjoyment of her body that made his own start to harden. Julian's realization that he was becoming aroused caused him to sit up straighter and cough into a fist, searching for a way to regain control of this insane situation. Three dogs were now licking themselves on the rug of his office and . . .

Something about this young woman was very familiar. *Very.*

Had they gone to school together? That was the likely explanation. Napa Valley might be large, but the inhabitants of St. Helena were a close-knit bunch. Around here, vintners and their employees tended to remain local forever. They passed on their practices to future generations. Just this afternoon, while on his daily run, he'd come across Manuel, the current vineyard manager whose father emigrated from Spain when Julian was in elementary school. Manuel's son was only twelve, but already he was learning the trade so he could take over for his father one day. Once wine seeped into the lifeblood of a family, it tended to stay there. Similarly, wine ran in the veins of most locals. With the exception of newly minted tech millionaires purchasing vineyards for bragging rights, there wasn't a lot of turnover in residents.

Certainly, however, if he'd gone to school with this now-gardener, he would remember.

She was nothing if not memorable.

Why was the sensation in his belly telling him he should know her *well,* though?

It would be better to proceed as if this was their first meeting, just in case his perception was off, right? Weren't men always trying to pick up women by claiming to know them from somewhere? Or was that just his colleague Garth?

Julian stood and extended his hand. "I'm Julian Vos. Nice to meet you."

The light in her eyes dimmed distinctively, and he suspected, in that moment, that he'd already fucked up their acquaintance. His stomach soured at the way she blinked rapidly and renewed her smile, as if putting on a brave face. Before he could claw his way back and ask why she struck him as so familiar, she spoke. "I'm Hallie. Here to plant your begonias."

"Right." She was short. Several inches shorter than him. With a sunburned nose that he couldn't seem to stop staring at. More appropriate than her incredible breasts, he supposed. *Stick with the nose.* "Did you need something from me?"

"Yes. I do." Now she seemed to be shaking herself free of whatever was happening in her head. Why did he feel as if he'd disappointed her? Furthermore, why did he want to discern her thoughts so badly? This unpunctual woman and her hounds were interrupting his work, and he still had one more thirty-minute session before his workday ended. "The water that leads to the hose outside is turned off, since no one has been living here. I'll need it to water the begonias after they're planted. You know? To really welcome them home? There should be a handle in the cellar or maybe in a laundry room . . . ?"

He watched her hand mimic the motion of twisting a knob, noting the abundance of rings. The dirt under her nails was from gardening, no doubt. "I have no idea."

She flicked a curl out of her eye and beamed a smile up at him. "I'll go have a look."

"Please. Be my guest."

A beat passed before she turned, as if expecting more from him. When he didn't deliver, she whistled at the dogs, bringing the trio of them to their feet. "Come on, boys. Come on." She coaxed them down the hallway with vigorous scratches behind their ears.

Without realizing right away what he was doing, Julian followed them.

Everything about her movements drew the eye. They were harried and controlled all at once. She was a walking whirlwind, knocking into her dogs, apologizing to them, and turning in circles, searching for the handle of this faucet. In and out of rooms she went, muttering to herself, surrounded by her pack of animals.

He couldn't look away.

Before Julian knew it, he'd followed Hallie into the laundry room, finding her on hands and knees, trying to wrench a circular piece of metal to the left, her dogs barking as though delivering encouragement or possibly instructions.

Had this house really been dead silent five minutes ago?

"I've almost got it, boys, hold on." She groaned, strained, her hips tilting up, and the blood in his head rushed south so quickly, he nearly saw double.

One of the dogs turned and barked at him.

As if to say, *Why are you just standing there, asshole? Help her.*

His only excuse was being thoroughly distracted by the lightning jolt of energy she'd delivered to his space in a matter of moments. And yes, also by her attractiveness—an odd cross between radiant pinup girl and unkempt earth mother—and being distracted by her appearance wasn't appropriate at all. "Please get off the floor," Julian said briskly, unfastening the buttons on the wrists of his dress shirt and rolling up the sleeves. "I'll turn it on."

When she scooted back and stood, her hair was even more disarrayed than before and she had to tug down her ridden-up jean shorts. "Thanks," she breathed.

Was she staring at his forearms?

"Of course," he said slowly, taking her spot on the floor.

In the reflection of the handle, he could have sworn she was smiling at his bent-over form, specifically his ass, but the image was probably just inverted.

Unless it wasn't?

Shaking his head over the whole odd situation, Julian gripped the handle and wrenched it left, turning until it stopped. "Done. Do you want to check it out?"

"I am," she said throatily. "Oh, the hose? I—I'm sure the water is on now. Thank you."

Julian came to his feet just in time to watch Hallie tornado her way out of the house, her canine admirers following her with utter devotion in their eyes, their nails clicking over his hardwood floor until they disappeared outside. Silence descended hard.

Thank God.

Still, he followed Hallie.

No idea why. His work was waiting.

Maybe because he felt this oddly unsettled feeling, like he'd failed a test.

Or perhaps because he'd never answered her question.

*Is it true? That you won't let yourself have a drink at the end of the day unless you write for the full thirty minutes?*

If this young woman was blunt enough to ask a stranger about his habits, there was a good chance she would have several uncomfortable follow-ups, which he didn't have the time or inclination to answer. Yet he continued to the porch, anyway, watching as she lowered the gate on her white pickup truck and started to unload pallets of red flowers. The tiny woman who barely reached his chin staggered under the weight of the first load of flowers, and Julian lurched forward without thinking, the dogs yipping at his approach. "I'll carry the flowers. Just tell me where you want them."

"I'm not sure yet! Just set them down on the lawn. Where that line of shrubs begins."

Lifting a pallet of flowers, Julian frowned. "You're not sure where they're going?"

Hallie smiled over her shoulder. "Not yet."

"When will you decide where they should go?"

The gardener dropped to her knees, leaned forward, and smoothed her hands over the turned brown soil. "The flowers more or less decide for themselves. I'll move them around in their individual containers until they look just right."

Julian didn't exactly love the sound of that. He stopped a few feet away, trying and failing not to notice the strands of frayed, white denim lying on the backs of her thighs. "They will be an equal distance apart, I assume."

"Maybe on accident?"

That did it. His mother was definitely punishing him. She'd sent him this curvaceous gardener to throw off his concentration and flaunt his need for organization. Detailed plans. A schedule. Relative sanity.

She laughed at his expression, stood, and chewed her lip a moment. Brushed her hands down the worn-in lap of her shorts. Was she blushing now? Back in the house, he could have sworn she was cataloguing his physique. Now, however, she ducked past him, almost as if too shy to look him in the eye. The mini blond hurricane returned to the truck for a canvas bag full of tools, then picked her way back across the yard in his direction. "So," she started on her way past him. "You took a break from teaching to write a book. That's so exciting. What made you decide to do that?"

Finally, he set down the tray of flowers. "How did you know?"

Trowel in hand, she paused. "Your mother told me."

"Right." He didn't know what to do with his hands now. They were too dirty to put in his pockets, so he just kind of stood there looking at them. "It's something I'd always planned to do. Write the book. Though the occasion came sooner than I expected."

"Oh. Why?"

Hallie knelt straight down into the dirt, and his stomach turned sideways. "Can I not get you a towel or something?" She threw him an amused glance but didn't answer. And, in a way, Julian supposed he was stalling. He didn't know how to answer her question. Why was he back in Napa, writing the book sooner than expected? His answer was personal, and he'd spoken it out loud to no one. For some reason, though, the idea of telling Hallie didn't make him feel uncomfortable. After all, she was casually digging away in the dirt, instead of waiting on his answer as if it would be some monumental revelation. "I changed the order of my ten-year plan slightly after . . . well, my colleague at Stanford, Garth, had something of a mental breakdown."

She set down the trowel. Twisted her butt around in the dirt to face him, cross-legged.

But her undivided attention didn't throw him off or make him wish he hadn't started down this path. Her knees were caked in soil. This was as low pressure as it got.

"Normally I would be teaching through the summer. I've been going year-round for some time now. I wouldn't . . . know what the hell to do with a break."

Hallie's gaze flickered past him to the sprawling vineyard, and he knew what she was thinking. He could come home to his family's nationally renowned vineyard on a break. No. It wasn't quite as easy as that. But that was a far different conversation.

"Anyway, toward the end of the spring semester, there was a commotion during one of my lectures. A student ran down the hall and interrupted my lesson on the geographical conceptions of time. They asked me for assistance. Garth had . . ." The difficult memory had him rubbing at the back of his neck, remembering too late that his hands were dirty. "He'd locked himself in his office. And he wouldn't come out."

"Oh no. Poor guy," Hallie murmured.

Julian gave a brief nod. "He had some personal issues I wasn't aware of. Instead of dealing with them head-on, he'd taken on a heavy course load and . . ."

"It was too much."

"Yes."

One of the dogs approached Hallie, nuzzling her face. She received the lick, absently patting the animal on the head. "Is he doing better now?"

Julian thought of the relaxed phone conversation he'd had with his colleague three days prior. Garth had even laughed, which had relieved Julian, while at the same time filling him with a certain envy. If only he were as resilient and quick to get on the road to recovery as his friend. "He's taking some much-needed time off."

"And . . ." She picked up her trowel again and started creating a completely new hole. As far as he could tell, she wasn't even finished with the first one. "The situation with Garth made *you* want to take a break as well?"

A rock formed in his throat. "We've been teaching the same length of time," he said briskly, leaving out the fact that he wasn't without his own—unacknowledged—personal issues. Many of which had to do with their current surroundings. Memories of the tendons in his throat constricting, a weight pressing down on his chest. The dizziness and inability to find roots in his current surroundings. Julian determinedly shuffled aside those thoughts, returning to the matter of Garth. "We had the same course load with very little leeway. Stepping back just seemed like the wise thing to do. Thankfully, I'd left some flexibility in my schedule."

"Your ten-year plan."

"That's right." He looked back at her truck, noting the bright blue-and-purple script reading *Becca's Blooms*. "As a business owner, surely you have one."

She rolled her lips inward and gave him a sheepish look from her position in the dirt. "Would you settle for a one-hour plan?" Her hands paused. "Actually, scratch that. I still haven't decided if I'm picking up dinner from the diner or Francesco's on the way home. I guess I have a ten-minute plan. Or I would if I knew where these flowers were going. Boys!"

The dogs descended on her, snuffing happily into her neck. Almost like she'd called them over with the express purpose of derailing her train of thought.

"Who is Becca?" Julian asked, wincing at the slobber left behind on her shoulder. "Your truck says Becca's Blooms," he explained a little too loudly, trying to drown out the odd pounding of his pulse. He'd never seen anyone so casually muddled in his life. In the dirt with her flowers and dogs and no plan.

"Rebecca was my grandmother. Becca's Blooms was established before I was born. She taught me how to garden." She tilted her head a little, didn't meet his eyes. "She's been gone since January. Just . . . heart failure. In her sleep." A shadow moved across her features, but she brightened again quickly. "Now *she* would have put your flowers an equal distance apart."

"I'm very sorry," he said, stopping when he realized she'd planted three big gatherings of red blooms and their accompanying greenery. It had happened so quickly and organically as they spoke, he didn't even notice. Stepping back, Julian framed up the plantings with the house and found she'd sort of . . . anchored the empty spaces in between the windows with flowers. Like filling in gaps. Did she do it unconsciously? There seemed to be a method here that he couldn't decipher. Still, the spacing was way off-kilter and already she was positioning the next one *way* off to the left, prompting a throbbing behind his eyes. "Would you mind just putting it closer to the others? You're right on the brink of a semicircle. If I tilt my head. And squint."

A lot like in their initial meeting in his office, he sensed her disappointment even though she kept right on smiling. "Oh." She bobbed her blond curls. "Sure."

"Never mind."

The words were out of his mouth before he realized he'd spoken.

But she'd already put the flowers closer to their counterparts. Patted the dirt around them and turned on the hose to give them some water. And now she was gathering her things, sliding the trowel into a pocket it hadn't been in earlier, if he recalled correctly. The dogs were circling her, sensing their imminent departure, dancing on their paws.

Yes, they were leaving.

Thank God. Right? Now he could get back to work.

What time was it, anyway?

Had he actually *lost track* of the minutes since Hallie's arrival?

Julian was so startled by the rare possibility that Hallie was halfway to the truck with her fan club before he realized it. "Bye, Julian," she called, tossing her tool bag into the open cab of the truck and prying open the creaking driver's-side door, stepping back so her dogs could pile in. "Good luck with the book. It was really nice to see you again."

"Wait." He froze. "Again?"

She started the truck and drove right out of his driveway without answering.

They'd met before. He knew it. Where? How?

The stillness that fell in the wake of Hallie's hectic presence eventually reminded Julian that he had a purpose for being in Napa. The cursor was blinking on his screen inside. Time marched forward. And he couldn't spare any more thoughts on the pinup earth mother or the fact that she was extremely pretty. She'd caused a disruption to his routine, and now it was over.

He should be grateful.

No, he *was.*

Perhaps he'd been momentarily fascinated by someone so wildly different from him, but on a regular basis? That kind of disorder in another person would drive him up the wall.

"No, thank you," Julian said to himself on the way back inside. "Not happening."

# Chapter Three

Hallie pushed her cart down the outdoor aisle of the nursery, tapping the skip button on the music app with her thumb. Next song. Next song. She'd gone through everything from Glass Animals to her nineties hip-hop mix and couldn't seem to settle on anything today. After seeing Julian Vos again the afternoon before, she was caught between songs about unrequited crushes, letting go of the past, and hot tub orgies. In other words, she was a tad confused.

She stopped pushing the cart and stooped down to pick up a bag of potting soil, adding it to her cart with a grunt and continuing on. Oh, fifteen years later, Julian Vos was still gorgeous. *Beyond* gorgeous, really, with his ropey forearms and perfectly groomed black hair. Those same bourbon-brown eyes she remembered, in all their intensity and intelligence. She'd actually forgotten how much he towered over her five-foot-three-inch frame.

And that *butt*.

That butt had aged like a Cabernet. Full-bodied and—she assumed—delicious.

Neither Julian nor his backside had remembered her, however.

It surprised Hallie how much him forgetting that night crushed her. Sure, she'd always carried a torch for him. But until yesterday, she wasn't aware of exactly how bright it burned. Or how much it would suck to have it snuffed out by his foggy memory.

And his exact oppositeness.

Yes, he'd always been studious and structured. She should not have been surprised when he asked her to relocate the begonias. But apparently she'd created some idea of Julian Vos in her mind that wasn't technically real. The man from her dreams who connected with her on a molecular level and could read her mind? He didn't exist in reality. She'd built him up into a fantasy that would never play out. Had she been measuring men with the Julian Vos yardstick for fifteen years? Who could measure up to a figment of her imagination?

Although, some stubborn part of her brain refused to accept that he was flat-out stodgy with a side of arrogance. There was a reason she'd crushed so hard on him during freshman year of high school, right? Yes. As a senior, he'd been nothing short of brilliant. A shoo-in for valedictorian. A track-and-field star. A local celebrity, by virtue of his last name. But those weren't the only qualities that had attracted Hallie.

No, on more than one occasion, she'd witnessed him being *good*.

At the one and only track meet she'd ever attended, he'd stopped running during a four-hundred-meter dash to help up an opponent who'd fallen and twisted his ankle, thus sacrificing his own opportunity to win. As she'd held her breath in the stands, he'd done it the same way she'd observed him doing everything else. With quiet intensity. Practical movements.

That was Julian's way. He broke up fights with a simple line of logic. He'd have his head buried in a book while the senior girls swooned over him from a distance.

Hallie had traveled all over the West Coast by that point. On the road, traveling from gig to gig with her mother. She'd met thousands of strangers, and she'd never encountered anyone like Julian Vos. So at ease in his good looks and rich with character. Unless her fourteen-year-old mind had truly embellished the finer points of his personality? If she was asking herself that question, it was probably time to let the crush go.

Later tonight, she'd remove the bookmark of his YouTube lectures. She'd smooth out the dog-eared page containing his senior yearbook photo. In order to blot out the memory of their almost-kiss, she'd probably require hypnosis, but the recollection of his head dipping toward her, the fiery sky blazing all around them, had already begun receding at the edges. Her chest hurt over the loss of something that had been her companion for so long. The only constant besides her grandmother. But feeling stupid for nursing a crush on someone who didn't even remember her?

Yeah, that stung a lot worse.

She knelt down and admired a flock of honeydew-green zinnias. No way she could pass them up. Later today—she couldn't remember what time—she was landscaping the front yard of a summer home, preparing it for the arrival of the owners who lived in Los Angeles the rest of the year. They'd requested lots of unique colors—and that was an ask she didn't mind in the slightest—

"Well, if it isn't the talented Hallie Welch."

The familiar voice brought Hallie to her feet, and she smiled warmly at the young man with ginger hair approaching her from the opposite direction. "Owen Stark. What on earth are you doing in the nursery buying flowers out from under me? It's like you own a competing landscaping business or something."

"Oh, you haven't heard? So sorry you have to find out this way. I am your competition. We are mortal enemies."

She narrowed her eyes at him. "Pistols at dawn, Stark!"

He slapped a hand across his chest. "I'll alert my second."

They broke into mutual laughter and traded places so they could see what the other had picked up. "Oooh, I'll have to grab some of those succulents. Their popularity refuses to wane, doesn't it? I like them for window boxes."

"I've got a client requesting them along his walkway. White stone."

"Low-maintenance special. Table for one."

Owen chuckled and fell silent. Hallie gave him a smile on her way back to her own cart, trying not to notice the way he catalogued her features, the piercing blue of his eyes softening along with his expression. She liked Owen, a lot.

Surely a better match for Hallie didn't exist anywhere in the world. On paper, at least. They were both gardeners. They could talk flora and fauna until they were blue in the face. He was kind, the same age, good-looking.

There was nothing *not* to like.

But she might as well admit that Owen Stark had fallen victim to the Julian Vos barometer. *That* and . . . Owen would fit into her life seamlessly. He'd make perfect sense in a way that was too perfect. A relationship with Owen would be natural. Expected. The person who coined the term "settling down" probably had this exact kind of partnership in mind. And settling down meant . . . this was it.

She'd be a gardener from St. Helena and would remain one for the rest of her life.

Did she want that? Her heart said yes. But could she trust that feeling?

When Hallie came to live with Rebecca, she had taken a deep breath for the first time ever, her grandmother's routine grounding her. Giving her a firm place to settle her feet. To stop spinning like a top. Without Rebecca's anchoring presence, though, she was picking up speed again. Whirling. Worrying she'd only belonged in St. Helena because of Rebecca and now . . .

Owen cleared his throat, alerting Hallie to the fact that she'd drifted.

"Sorry," she muttered, attempting to focus on him. Consider him.

Maybe next time he asked her out, she would say yes. And she would wear a dress and perfume, hire a dog sitter, and take it seriously this time. She could see it was coming, too. Owen popped a tablet of gum into his mouth, chewed a moment, and exhaled at the ceiling. Oh, this was serious. He was going to go for a steak house.

Why had she left the dogs at home? They were always the perfect excuse to bolt.

"Hallie," Owen started, red infusing his cheeks. "Since it's Friday and all, I was wondering if you had plans for—"

Her phone rang.

She sucked in a thankful breath and snatched it up, frowning down at the screen. Unknown number. So what? She'd even take a telemarketer over agreeing to a steak house date and hours of personal conversation with Owen.

"Hello?" Hallie chirped into the phone.

"Hallie."

Her stomach dropped to the ground like a sandbag. Julian Vos? Julian was calling her?

"Yes. It's me." Did her voice sound unnatural? She couldn't decipher her tone over the sudden babble of white noise in her ears. "How did you get my number?"

"I googled 'Becca's Blooms in Napa' and there it was."

"Oh right." She wet her dry lips, searching desperately for something witty to say. "So important to have that internet presence."

Nope. That wasn't witty.

"Who is that?" Owen asked, not so quietly.

"Who is that?" Julian asked, too, after a beat.

*Client,* she mouthed to Owen, who gave her an understanding thumbs-up. To Julian, she said, "I'm at the nursery buying materials for a project later today. I ran into my friend Owen."

"I see."

Seconds ticked by.

She checked the phone to see if they'd gotten disconnected. "Are you still there?"

"Yes. Sorry." He cleared his throat, but the sound was muffled, as if he'd briefly placed a hand over the receiver. "I'm distracted by the gopher holes in my yard."

Her blood pressure spiked at the utterance of a gardener's least favorite words. Except for maybe "weeds" or "crabgrass" or "do you take personal checks." "Gopher holes?"

Owen winced with sympathy, turning away to peruse a plastic shelf of mini cactuses.

"Yes, at least three." She could hear footsteps, as if he'd walked to the window to look out over the green expanse of lawn and the sun-drenched vineyard beyond. "One of them is right in the middle of the flowers you planted yesterday, which made me think you'd dealt with something of this nature before. Do you have a way of convincing gophers to move on? Or should I call pest control?"

"No need for that, I have a mixture I can use to . . ." The seal busted on her laughter. "Convince them."

He made a considering sound. "You're taking issue with my word choice?"

"Not at all. I'm picturing a formal negotiation. Once the contracts are signed, we'll shake his little paw. He'll pack his tiny suitcase and promise to write—"

"You're very entertaining, Hallie." Briefly, she heard a ticking, as if he'd lifted his watch closer to his face. "I'm sorry, I only have five minutes for this phone call. Are you able to make it over or should I just try and flush him out with the hose?"

"God, no. Don't do that." She cut a hand across her neck, even though he couldn't see her. "You're only softening the soil and making it easier for him to dig."

Owen shot her a horrified glance over his shoulder. *Amateur,* he mouthed.

"I have a job this afternoon, but I can swing by afterward," she said to Julian.

"At what time?"

"Whenever I finish."

Julian's breath released in her ear. "That's extremely vague."

How could it be so painfully obvious that someone was all wrong for her, yet his deep voice, and the very fact that he'd called her at all, was causing a mudslide in her stomach? It made little to no sense. Her lingering crush made her feel like a silly, naive teenager. While at the same time, the anticipation of seeing him again made Hallie almost light-headed.

So she would let herself go to the vineyard once more, even at the risk of extending this infatuation longer than it should have ever gone. But she wasn't going to jump over hurdles for him. Oh no. At this point, her pride was on the line with this non-remembering fool.

"Vague is all I've got, I'm afraid." She stared into the eye of an iris for moral support. "Take it or leave it."

He was going to tell her to shove it. She convinced herself of that distinct possibility as the silence stretched. The Vos family had money coming out of their ears. They could find someone else to resolve their gopher issue at a moment's notice. Julian didn't necessarily need her.

"I'll see you later, Hallie," he sighed. "God knows when."

"Why?" she blurted.

"Excuse me?"

Why couldn't she just have said good-bye and hung up the phone like a regular person? Owen was looking at her strangely. As if maybe he realized this wasn't a normal client call and was growing more curious by the moment. "Why do you want *me* there, specifically, for gopher negotiations? It obviously bothers you that I can't give a formal time."

"That's a very straightforward question for someone so committed to being vague."

"I'm not . . . committed to . . ." Was she committed to being vague? "Please just satisfy my curiosity."

"Is your friend Owen still there?"

Was he? She glanced up, passing a tight smile to Owen, who was definitely attempting to eavesdrop. "Yes, he is. Why?"

"Just satisfying my curiosity." She could almost hear the ticking of his jaw. Was he . . . annoyed at her being somewhere with another man? No. No way. That didn't track—not even in the slightest. "Very well. Yes, I want you, specifically, to come back and intervene with the gopher. When you left yesterday, you said, 'It was really nice to see you again,' and the fact that I can't remember how or where we met has shot my concentration to hell."

"Oh." Well. She hadn't been expecting that. In fact, she'd been under the impression he was relieved to see her go and couldn't care less about greetings and salutations. "I'm sorry. I didn't realize it was going to be such a big deal."

"I'm sure it wouldn't be. To most people."

Hallie thought of the meticulous way he stacked his lecture notes. How precisely he rolled up his shirtsleeves. The way he couldn't stop writing until the time ran out. "But you need things organized and tidy. Don't you?"

He expelled a breath. "That's right."

That's all this was. Julian didn't want to see her again because of an attraction or because he enjoyed her company. He simply needed their acquaintance tied up in a neat little bow so he could go back to his manic typing sprees.

Maybe she needed their relationship, however casual, tied up, too.

The gopher wasn't the only one who needed moving on.

"All right." She swallowed the object in her throat. "Maybe I'll tell you how we know each other later."

"Vague."

"Bye, Julian."

When she hung up the phone, Owen gave her a questioning look. "That was a weird conversation," he chuckled.

"Right?" She pushed her cart past him slowly. "Gophers put everyone on edge."

Metal rattled behind Hallie, signaling that Owen had turned his cart around so they could walk in the same direction. Normally that wouldn't bother her. Not at the nursery, anyway, where colorful flowers shot up out of the dirt everywhere she looked, acting as bright little buffers. But before the call from Julian, Owen had been on the verge of asking her out. And she'd been resigned to saying yes. Now, though? Now she hesitated. Once again, because of Julian Vos.

Man, she really needed to get Professor Forearms out of her head, once and for all. She wasn't being fair to herself. Or to Owen, for that matter.

"Owen." Hallie stopped the cart abruptly and turned, looking him right in the eye. Which seemed to stun him. "I know you want to ask me to dinner. On an actual date. And I want to say yes. But I need a little time." Julian's intense bourbon eyes blinked in her mind, but instead of stalling her speech, they gave her the impetus to push forward. "That's asking a lot, considering how much space you've given me already. If you say no, I'll understand."

"I'm not going to say no." He scrubbed at the back of his head. "Of course I'm not. You take your time." A beat passed as he sobered. "I'm just asking you to take me seriously."

His words hit her like stones. "I will," she said, meaning it.

# Chapter Four

Hallie may have been vague about her timing, but her arrival resounded like a fireworks show. The growl of her truck engine cut out, followed by the slam of her rusted door. One dog started woofing and his buddies joined in solidarity, announcing the entrance of their queen.

Julian sat at the desk in his office printing out an article about a sundial that had recently been unearthed in Egypt. He planned on reading it tonight before bed for research purposes. His hand paused on the way to the printer, and he slowly leaned sideways, looking past his computer monitor to the yard beyond. And when her blond corkscrews—tied up in a white scrunchie this time—came into view, his mouth went bone-dry. A very disconcerting reaction to someone who played fast and loose with arrival times had caused him stress all goddamn day. Coupled with the fact that he'd lost hours of sleep last night trying to figure out how they knew each other? Suffice it to say, his attraction to her was an irritant.

One he hoped to forget about after tonight.

He just needed this one little loose end knotted, and he'd get back to sleeping and working and concentrating as usual.

According to his mother, as a child, he'd suffered from anxiety. *Nervous episodes,* Corinne had called them, the one and only time they'd had a discussion on the topic. No one had a clue if his anxiety was precipitated by a certain event or if he'd just been born with dread in his bones, but at age six he'd started seeing a therapist.

Doctor Patel gave Julian the gift of schedules. To this day, an organized list of times and activities was the tool he used to control his anxiety. Simply put, it worked.

Right up until the vineyard fire four years ago, anyway. For the first time since childhood, he'd lost his grip on structure, because time meant nothing in a fire. Since that weekend, he'd kept the schedules even tighter than before, refusing to have another slipup. Another leak through the cracks. Garth's mental break was a wake-up call, the impetus to take a rare step back and reassess.

Prior to the fire, Julian had returned to St. Helena every August at the outset of grape harvesting season, staying at the vineyard for a month and making sure the annual process ran smoothly, after which he'd return to Stanford in the fall to teach. Even from a distance, he consulted on matters pertaining to the winery. But no longer. Maybe if Julian had taken a breather at some point, he could have avoided what happened after the damage was wrought by the flames. His father might have continued to trust him to help run the vineyard, instead of dropping it all on his mother and hightailing it to Italy.

A bone seemed to grow sideways in his throat.

*Focus on the problem at hand.*

This young woman whom he'd apparently met at some point in the past was poking at the careful net he'd constructed around himself. He probably shouldn't have called her back here. It had been a risk. He'd weighed the threat to his sanity against the reward of knowledge—and fine, the damn urge to see her again—and surprisingly, the risk column had lost.

He was paying the price now.

The howling dogs were distracting enough, but nowhere near as sidetracking as her. Even though early evening had arrived, the sun was still going strong in the Napa sky. Orange rays settled on her like loving spotlights, giving her cheeks a youthful glow. Did she *ever* stop smiling? Her lips always seemed curved, as if she were holding on to a secret—and she was, he reminded himself. That's primarily why he'd called her over, instead of just making the homemade gopher-repelling mixture himself (really, the information was one quick internet search away). Not to lust over the silhouette of Hallie's curves.

"Jesus Christ, pull it together," he groaned, dragging a hand down his face and pushing away from his desk. He tucked in his chair and straightened the wireless keyboard before turning and striding for the front of the house. Yes, he'd lost sleep last night for more than one reason. Trying to unearth a forgotten memory was how it started. But all that thinking about the bubbly blonde and her tight T-shirt had led to something very different. Twice.

When was the last time he'd masturbated *twice* in one night? Had to be in high school. And even back then, he couldn't remember being so . . . vigorous about it. While lying facedown on his stomach, no less. He'd been forced to throw the sheets into the washing machine in the middle of the night and move to one of the other bedrooms. A humiliating turn of events if he'd ever heard one. Really, calling her back here was incredibly stupid.

What if this visit didn't give him closure? Would he try to see her *again*?

Back in Palo Alto, he purposefully dated women who *didn't* occupy too much headspace. Women who kept tight schedules and didn't have a problem coordinating them for things like dinner or sex or a work function. Hallie wouldn't even ballpark her ETA. If they spent significant time together, they'd be fitting him for a straitjacket within a week. So yes, get the closure and go back to work. The plan was firm.

A lot like he'd been last night.

Disgusted with himself, Julian pried open the front door, closed it behind him, and descended the steps onto the driveway. Then he hooked a right to the yard, where Hallie sat cross-legged in front of the freshest gopher hole, shaking up something in a large plastic bottle. "Hello there, Professor," she called, her voice echoing slightly through the vineyard.

The dogs ran over to greet him, yipping and snarfing at the air. He patted their heads, one by one, watching helplessly as they slobbered all over his pant leg. "Hello, Hallie." One of the dogs nudged Julian's hand until he scratched him properly. "What are their names?"

"The yellow lab is Petey. My grandmother was a big fan of the original *Little Rascals.*" She pointed at the schnauzer. "That's the General. Not General. *The* General, because he bosses everyone around. And the boxer is Todd. I can't explain it—he just looks like a Todd."

Julian leaned back to study the boxer. "That's eerily accurate."

She breathed a laugh, as if relieved to be in agreement. He liked it, as well. Too much.

*Stick to business.*

He nodded at the plastic bottle. "What's in the formula?" As if he didn't already know.

"Peppermint and castor oil. They hate the smell."

She shifted onto her knees and dug some cotton balls out of the pocket of her jean shorts. They were lighter today. More faded. Meaning the material clung like underpants to her backside, while the sun stroked the worn denim in burnished gold. Her top wasn't quite as tight today—fortunately or unfortunately—but finger streaks of dirt were directly over her breasts, as if she'd wiped her hands off on them, palms chafing right over her nipples. Up and down. Feeling herself up in the front yard of some suburban hamlet, knees twisting in the dirt.

*This is getting embarrassing.*

While watching Hallie soak the cotton balls, he tamped down his attraction as much as possible, attempting to focus on more practical matters. Like getting himself untangled with this person. "Tell me how we know each other, Hallie."

She'd started nodding halfway through his demand, obviously expecting it—which he didn't love. Being predictable to her made him itchy. "I never said we knew each other. I just said it was nice to see you again."

Yes. That was correct. They didn't know each other at all. And they wouldn't.

Why did that only intensify the itch?

"Where have we seen each other, then?"

A blush rode up the side of her face. For a moment, he thought the sunset was responsible, but no. The gardener was blushing. And involuntarily, he held his breath.

"Okay, do you remember—" she started.

Hell broke loose before she could finish.

As soon as Hallie dropped those fragrant cotton balls into the gopher hole, the sucker peeked his head out the other end. Just like that. A real-life game of whack-a-mole, only with a gopher. And the dogs lost their ever-loving minds. If Julian thought they were loud before, their excited barking was nothing compared to the screeches and yelps of alarm as they dashed toward the emerging gopher—who, wisely, took off running for his very life.

"Boys! No!" Hallie jumped to her feet and sprinted after all three dogs. "Come back here! Now!"

Julian watched it all happen in a semi-trance, wondering how his plan to have a bowl of soup and read the Smithsonian article he'd printed out had been so spectacularly derailed. He'd anticipated having a clear head for the rest of his stay in Napa, this blip from the past having been resolved. But, instead, he was now running toward this loud explosion of mayhem, worried Hallie might get in between dog and gopher and accidentally get bitten for her trouble.

Wow.

He really didn't like the idea of her being bitten.

Or slipping. In the mud. Risking an injury.

Because that's what was happening. In slow motion, she turned into a pinwheel of limbs and corkscrews, and then her butt landed soundly in the bank of dirt that skirted the front lawn.

"*Hallie*," Julian barked—great, now he was barking, too—and scooped her up from behind by the armpits. "Christ, you can't just take off half-cocked like that. What were you going to do if you caught them?"

It took him a few seconds to realize her entire body was shaking with laughter. "Of course this is when I choose to have the most embarrassing fall of my life. Of course it is."

Frowning at that odd statement, he turned her around.

Big. Mistake.

The sun on her face made everything surrounding them—the

endless sky, the rambling vineyard, and the streaks of clouds, all of it—seem inadequate. Something tugged inside of him like a thread. The shape of her mouth . . . their height difference. Was there even something familiar about her earthy scent?

A heavy object rammed into Julian's leg, followed by a second one. Todd inserted himself between Julian and Hallie, barking in quick succession. A crunching sound came from behind Hallie—and there went the gopher again, followed by Petey and the General.

"Boys!" Hallie shouted, running after them.

They chased the damn gopher right back into the hole.

Hallie groaned and threw her hands up in the air. "He'll probably leave sometime during the night when my beasts have gone. No way he'll be able to stand the smell for long."

He could still feel the smooth skin of her arms in his palms, so it took him a moment to recover enough to respond. "I'm sure you're right . . ." he started, curling his fingers inward to capture the sensation before it fled.

But she didn't hear him, because she was busy wrangling her three frantic dogs. In shorts caked with mud. One of her feet was slipping dangerously toward the gopher hole. If an ankle sprain wasn't imminent, then something else anarchic would probably take its place. His whole evening would be off now. She'd done this to him for a second time, and he needed to take it as a sign to keep away. Strict schedules stopped the floor from rising up and swallowing him whole.

He wouldn't survive the shame of that downward spiral again. The night of the fire, he'd held on to his mettle long enough to do what was necessary, but what followed had been enough to drive his family to four different corners of the earth, hadn't it?

Julian required order. Hallie was *dis*order in the flesh. She seemed to shun the very method he used to cope with anxiety. Yes, she was beautiful and lively. Clever. Fascinating.

Also? So completely wrong for him that a sitcom writer couldn't make it up.

Why was he so interested in her thoughts and actions, then?

Or if this Owen character was really just a friend or a boyfriend of some description.

It made little fucking sense.

A vein throbbed behind his eye. He longed for pencil and blank paper, something simple that he could focus on, because being near Hallie was like staring through a kaleidoscope while someone twisted it really fast.

"Julian, is everything okay?"

He opened his eyes. When had he closed them? "Yes." He noticed the awkward way she stood, as if the mud on her shorts was beginning to harden. "Come on." He moved past her toward the house. "We'll get you something clean to wear."

"Oh, no, it's fine," she called to his retreating back. "I more or less go home in this condition every day. I usually strip in the backyard and hose myself down." Then, to herself, "Don't overshare or anything, Hallie."

*Don't think about rivulets of water coasting down her ripe body. Don't do it.*

Setting his jaw, Julian held the door for Hallie, who ambled past awkwardly, attempting to hold the denim away from her thighs. When the dogs tried to follow her into the guesthouse with paws that looked chocolate-dipped in mud, Julian pointed a stern finger at the General. "*Sit.*"

The schnauzer's butt hit the ground, tail wagging in a blur. The boxer and the lab followed their buddy's lead, plopping down at the base of the stairs and waiting.

"How did you do that?" Hallie whispered behind him.

"Dogs crave leadership, just like humans. It's in their DNA to obey."

"No." She wrinkled her nose at him. "They want to eat snails and howl at fire trucks."

"They can be trained *not* to do those things, Hallie."

"But you're forcing them to deny their natural urges."

"No, I'm preventing mud from being tracked into the house."

They looked down simultaneously to find she'd left four footprints just inside the door. With a tinge of pink in her cheeks, she toed off her rubber shoes and nudged them as close as possible to the door, leaving her barefoot on his clean hardwood floor. She had sky-blue nail polish on her toes, daisies painted onto the biggest nails. "If you tell me to sit, Julian Vos, I will kick you in the shin."

A strange lightness rose upward in his sternum, stopping just beneath his throat. A twitch of his lips caught him off guard. Did he . . . want to laugh? She seemed to think so, didn't she? The way she watched his mouth, a sparkle appearing in her eyes at his rare show of humor. Suddenly he was a lot more aware of their location—inches apart in a house glowing with late-afternoon sun—and again he encountered a tug of recognition but couldn't find the source.

God help him, he was too distracted, unable to look at her without his attention straying to her mouth, wondering if she kissed as wildly and without rhythm as she did everything else.

Probably.

No. Definitely. And he would hate the unpredictability of it. Of her.

Right.

"I'll get you that shirt," he said, turning on a heel. Though he didn't see her move farther into the house, he sensed that she would meet him in the kitchen, the heart and focal point of a home, not that he used it for much besides preparing turkey on whole wheat, soup, and coffee. Inside the bedroom, he hesitated for a moment at the dresser, observing himself in the mirror. Hair in disarray from his fingers, tightness surrounding his eyes and mouth. He took a long breath and looked down at his watch.

6:18 P.M.

The back of his neck clenched, so he filled his lungs one more time and mapped out a new schedule. At six thirty, he would eat and read his sundial article. At seven, *Jeopardy!* Seven thirty, shower. Then he would make some notes about tomorrow's writing plan, have them ready to go on his desk in the morning. If he kept to this schedule, he'd let himself have a glass of whiskey.

Feeling more in control, Julian took a folded gray shirt out of the top drawer. One with the Stanford logo silk-screened onto the pocket. As predicted, thank God, he found Hallie in the kitchen. But she didn't lift her head when he walked in because she was frowning down at something on the granite island in the center of the room. What did she find so offensive about his stack of mail? He'd had his correspondence forwarded to the vineyard for the summer, but the postal service was slow to begin the switch, meaning he was mostly receiving junk at this point.

She pinched one such advertisement between her finger and thumb, turning it over, letting out a distressed sound at whatever was on the back. "Wild Wine Wednesday . . ." she muttered. "'Let us blindfold your party and ply you with wine. Guess the vintage correctly and win a trip to the cheese wall.' I *hate* how fun that sounds."

"Beg pardon?"

"UNCORKED." She blinked rapidly, as if to keep moisture from forming in her eyes, and Julian experienced an uncomfortable pinch in his chest. "The newest wine bar sensation in town."

He set the Stanford shirt in front of her, an offering he hoped would prevent whatever was happening to her emotionally. "You don't like this new place," he guessed.

And then he died a little, because she used the Stanford shirt to dab at her eyes.

When there were perfectly good napkins within reach.

"Well. I've never been inside. I don't know the owners *personally* or anything. They might be lovely people who don't realize they are robbing a sweet old lady of her livelihood."

"Explain what you mean."

"Corked is right next door. A quiet little wine bar owned by Lorna. It has been there since the late fifties. My grandmother and I used to spend hours sitting at the white wrought-iron table outside. It was our spot. Lorna would give me a wineglass full of grape juice, and my grandmother and I would solve crossword puzzle clues or we'd plan gardens together." She looked down at her fingers for a few seconds. "Anyway, the whole shop is empty now because UNCORKED moved in beside it. They have a twenty-four-hour disco ball outside and endless stunts to attract tourists. The worst part is they *specifically* named their shop as a play on Lorna's bar and made a mockery of it. No one seems to mind, though. Lorna has quiet, intimate tastings without the fanfare. How is she supposed to compete with Adult Spin the Bottle?"

Her eyes took on a sheen that worried him, so he reached for a napkin and handed it to her, sighing when she used the shirt again, instead. "You're very upset about this. Are you close with Lorna or something?"

"She was closer to my grandmother, but yes, we're friends. And we've gotten a lot more friendly since I started attending daily wine tastings to offset the UNCORKED effect."

The corner of his mouth tugged. "Day drinking is always the solution."

"Said no one ever. Even in Napa." For a beat, she appeared almost thoughtful. "It has definitely made me more prone to committing petty crimes."

He waited for her to say she was joking. She didn't.

With a big inhale, she let the shirt unfurl down onto her lap. "I'm just going to change into this outside before I hop into the truck, so I don't get mud anywhere." With one last glance at the wineshop advertisement, she backed out of his kitchen. "Any *more* mud, I should say."

His plan had been to get Hallie out the door quickly, so he could start checking things off his to-do list for the night, but when she started to edge out of his kitchen, an anxious ripple in his stomach surprised him into saying, "Do you want a drink?" Totally normal to offer. He was just being a gracious host. "I have wine, obviously. Or whiskey."

He might even need two whiskeys himself tonight.

Could he drop the strict limits he placed on himself enough to allow that indulgence?

The offer of a drink had visibly surprised her, too. "Oh. I don't know." She considered him a moment. A long moment. As if she was trying to make some important decision. About him? What was it? "I better not," she said softly. "I'm driving."

"Right," he said, finding his throat was going dry. "Responsible of you."

She hummed, nodding at the mostly full bottle of Woodford Reserve whiskey sitting by the stove. "You should have one, though. A gopher in residence might even earn you two." She hesitated on the threshold of his kitchen, this wild-haired gardener with muddy shorts and a vendetta against a wineshop. "What would you have to do to earn two?"

His head came up quickly.

Because he'd been wondering that exact same thing.

How did she . . .

And then he remembered. Yesterday. When she'd walked into his office and read over his shoulder and asked afterward, *Is it true? That you won't let yourself have a drink at the end of the day unless you write for the full thirty minutes?* He'd never answered her question, but she'd held on to it. Was she that curious about his habits?

Julian had never told anyone about his goal-setting system. It would probably sound completely idiotic out loud. But he got the sense . . . well, he couldn't help but feel as if she were leaving for good, never to return, so what harm would it do to reveal this part of himself? She'd slipped onto her butt and cried in front of him in the space of twenty minutes. Maybe a part of him hoped admitting to his peculiar behavior would make them even. Make her . . . feel better.

Which was troublingly important to him.

"I only have two drinks at the end of a semester. The rest of the year, I allow myself the whiskey if I've checked the day's boxes." He'd been right. It did sound idiotic out loud, but it was how he remained glued together. Time had always been the stitches running through the fabric of his life, and he had nothing but gratitude for the structure it afforded him. "For instance, if I arrived everywhere on time. To class, to meetings. If I completed my workload and planned for the following day. Cleared my inbox. Showered. Then I have the drink."

She stared at him. Not judgmentally. Just taking it all in.

"I've adjusted my routine for the summer . . ." he added unnecessarily, just to fill the silence. "I guess you could say I'm in vacation mode."

An abrupt giggle snuck out of her mouth.

And satisfaction plunged from his neck down deep into his belly.

He'd made her laugh. Yes, but now she just looked a little . . . sad?

"Julian, I don't think there are two more different people in this whole world." Again, she didn't say those words as a judgment. More of a musing. Or an observation. "Do you?"

"No," he felt forced to admit. "I don't."

Oddly, that didn't mean he wanted her to leave.

His gaze ticked between Hallie and the UNCORKED advertisement. "They really named their store UNCORKED and moved in right beside a shop called Corked?"

She threw up her hands, as if relieved to finally have someone's attention regarding the matter. "*Yes.*"

"I'm surprised the local business association allowed that."

"I've emailed them on seven separate occasions. My last one was in all caps!"

He hummed, not totally surprised to find his fingers twitching.

"What are you thinking about?" she asked slowly, turning slightly to glance over her shoulder. "You look like you're trying to visualize a new backsplash."

He almost said nothing and walked her to the door. But he'd already outlined the mind games he played with himself. What was the sense in holding back now? After all, he weirdly, confusingly, wasn't quite ready to let her leave. "I don't like when things are out of order like this. A shop moving in and presenting a direct threat to the business next door should not have been allowed to happen."

"I agree."

He *especially* didn't like the whole situation making Hallie cry, but he'd leave that part out. "When things are unfair or disordered, I tend to . . ."

"What?"

"I have something of a competitive streak. A small one. For instance, last year a *Jeopardy!* contestant gave their answer after the buzzer and was given credit. It didn't seem like a big deal at the time, but he went on to win Final Jeopardy with a margin of one hundred dollars. You see, a small breach in fairness can cause a snowball effect." He paused to gauge her reaction, deciding she looked more curious than judgmental. "A lot of us contacted the show and suggested . . . rather strongly that the other contestant be allowed to compete again. They relented."

"Oh my gosh." She rocked back on her heels. "You're a *Jeopardy!* groupie. I always wondered, who are these people? Who feels so passionate about holding this game show accountable? It's you."

He scoffed. "There are thousands of us." Seconds ticked by. "Hundreds, at least."

She very visibly bit down on a smile. "What does this have to do with UNCORKED?"

The offer to help sat right on his tongue, but he couldn't do that. Helping would mean spending more time with her, and he'd already decided that was not a good idea, despite the fact that he couldn't seem to stop prolonging their acquaintance. Hadn't she been on her way out the door a few minutes ago? He'd been the one to stop her. "You might not be able to stop UNCORKED from operating, but you can help the underdog compete."

"You're saying that jamming bark into their disco ball isn't a solution?"

"What?"

She pressed her lips together, eyes twinkling. "Prank calls are out, too?"

"Hallie, my God. Have you been prank calling this new wine store?"

"Yes," she whispered. "You are the type to sit down with Lorna and find ways to save money. Or revamp her brand. My approach is less logical, more reactionary. Like I said, we are the two most opposite people in the world."

"You don't think I could prank call someone?"

What in the actual hell was coming out of his mouth now? His competitive streak was humming, sure. But Hallie obviously thought he was stodgy and boring, and for some reason, he couldn't let her leave with that impression of him. Even if it was true.

He'd never placed a prank call in his life.

"No, I don't think you could," she responded, studying her nails. "Julian Vos, St. Helena wine royalty, prank calling a local vendor? Unheard of."

That did it. Now he had no choice. "Very well." He unearthed his phone from his back pocket, smirking when she slid the advertisement across the island in his direction, propping her chin on a bent wrist and pursing her lips, clearly skeptical that he would go through with it. And really. Why *was* he engaging in this behavior? To impress this woman he had no business spending time with? Or was it actually just to make her feel better after she'd cried?

Because even minutes later, the knot underneath his collar remained very opposed to her crying. She was too . . . jubilant. Too bright for that.

This woman should be happy at all times. He was intelligent enough to know that one person could not be responsible for another's happiness. Not completely. But he found himself wondering what it might be like to fill that role for Hallie. In another life, obviously.

A full-time giver of Hallie Smiles.

Suddenly he valued his teaching tenure a lot less.

*Stop being ridiculous.*

"Put it on speaker," she said, her doubtfulness beginning to lose ground.

Doing as she asked, he raised an eyebrow at her and dialed the number.

Her mouth fell open.

A young man answered after the fifth ring. "Hello, this is UNCORKED." Music blared in the background. "We'll get you drunk and tell you you're pretty."

Julian and Hallie traded a withering look. It struck him that this one little act of rebellion had turned them into teammates of sorts. Temporarily, of course. "Yes, hello," he said briskly. "This is the health department. I'm afraid I have some very bad news."

A pause dragged itself out. "The health department? Why . . ." Sputtering. "Bad news?"

"Yes, we're going to have to shut you down."

It appeared Hallie's legs were no longer working. Hands slapped over her mouth, and the upper half of her body fell across the island for support. "Oh my God," she wheezed.

"What are we being shut down for?" whined the gentleman.

"It's the disco ball." Hallie's sides started to shake with laughter, making it nearly impossible to keep a straight face. Or his cold, dead heart from doing the cancan. "According to section fifty-three dash M of the health code manual, you're in direct violation of the public's right to avoid bad dancing."

A sharp curse. "Another prank call? Are you working with that woman—"

"Yes." Julian hung up, neatly setting down his phone. "And that's how it's done."

Still unable to subdue her laughter, Hallie laid a hand across her chest. "That was . . . like . . . the Cadillac of prank calls." Pushing off the island, she looked at him as if through fresh eyes, before shaking herself slightly. "Thank you. With the exception of the friends I've dragged into this rivalry, I've felt pretty alone in my outrage."

He'd made her feel less alone. On top of provoking one of her Hallie Smiles.

*It feels like Christmas morning.* People were always saying that, but he could never relate, because opening presents with the Vos family had been a quiet and hurried affair.

He could understand that phrase better now.

"It's no problem," he said succinctly.

They nodded at each other for an extended moment. "Well,

you have my word that I will never again make fun of the *Jeopardy!* message board warriors."

His lips jumped. "Then I suppose my work here is done."

As soon as he said the words, he sort of wanted to take them back. Because she appeared to interpret them in a way he hadn't intended. As in, *time to go.*

With a nod, she said, "Bye, Julian." She passed him on the way out of the kitchen, leaving soil and sunlight lingering in the air. "Have those drinks. You definitely earned them."

All he could do was incline his head stiffly, turn, and follow her to the front door.

He watched through the screen as she reunited with the howling and yipping dogs, who celebrated her existence all the way to her truck. He traded a long look with her through the windshield when she climbed into the driver's side and slowly realized she'd never told him how they knew each other. Or where they'd met.

The tick of Julian's watch reached his ears, distracting him, and his chest grew tight enough to make his vision narrow. How awry had his schedule gone since she showed up? He had no clue. In an attempt to center himself, he pressed his ear to the ticking watch on his wrist and forced himself to concentrate on minutes. The next few hours in front of him. He couldn't change the ones behind him.

And he didn't want to, either. Wouldn't take back a second he'd spent with Hallie. Unfortunately, starting now, he wasn't sure it would be wise to spend any more.

But maybe, in the name of closure, he'd take one more look at the Becca's Blooms website before bed . . .

# Chapter Five

Hallie stared across the table at Lavinia without really seeing her.

Around them, conversations swelled in the dining room of Othello, her favorite St. Helena bistro. They'd already done serious damage to the breadbasket and were awaiting a family-style plate of spicy butter garlic shrimp with linguine. Naturally, they'd gone with a white wine pairing, and, Lord, it was never a good sign when they ordered a second bottle before the main course made an appearance. They may have cut back on day drinking, but they obviously had no qualms with doing so at night.

For the life of Hallie, however, she couldn't stop lifting the glass to her mouth. She'd crafted a new state of being. Bewildered drunkenness. In turn, Lavinia's current state of being was more like irritated anticipation with a side of sloshiness, but she'd imbibed far less than Hallie. So, clearly, there was a first time for everything. Such as drinking a Brit (who'd once been a Gorillaz roadie) under the table.

Or getting a glimpse at the real, adult version of her teenage crush . . . and liking that peek way too much.

Hallie forced herself out of a trance and looked around. Once upon a time, being a regular at a restaurant had been a new experience. She'd enjoyed the process of becoming one. Loved walking into the candlelit Italian bistro and having everyone know her name. Lavinia always sat with her back facing the kitchen; Hallie took the wall. But her grandmother had been around to make normalcy seem . . . well, normal. Now the repetition of coming here made Hallie feel jumpy in the absence of her grandmother's anchoring presence.

With a long, steadying breath, Hallie fell back in her chair, taking the glass of wine with her. She downed half and pushed aside her one-third life crisis for now. It had been twenty-four hours since she last saw Julian, and she still hadn't recounted the impromptu hang to her best friend, despite a serious amount of pestering and prodding.

"Come clean, Hallie Welch, goddamn you." Lavinia leaned in over the candlelight. Close enough to feel the heat on her chin, yip, and flinch away. Maybe they'd both had too much wine. Was this their second bottle or third? "I'll start smashing dishes. Don't think I won't."

"Okay, okay, okay." Hallie set the glass down on the table, holding up a finger when the waiter set the massive steaming bowl of pasta between them. Both women sighed as the savory aroma hit them like culinary crack. "Pasta presentation never gets old."

Lavinia threw an exaggerated chef's kiss at the swinging kitchen door. "Our deep and undying admiration to the chef."

"I'll let him know," the amused waiter said, skating away.

"Oy, don't forget that second bottle. Or third?" Lavinia called after him. Loudly.

"They love us here."

Hallie used the provided silver tongs to settle a heaping portion of pasta onto Lavinia's plate, laughing when she rolled her finger for more.

"Go on, then. Didn't have a single donut all day so I'd have extra room for this."

"You got it." Hallie forked up some more, sighing as a waft of fragrant steam hit her in the face. "Okay, before this pasta coma collides with my wine coma, I'll spill." She took a centering breath, as if preparing to impart very sensitive information. It was obvious Lavinia was expecting juicy news. And that left her wide open to be messed with. "Me and Julian did something pretty . . . intimate."

"You shagged him." She put her arms up in the shape of a V, whooping at the ceiling mid-chew. "Jerome owes me twenty bucks. I *knew* you had it in you, Hallie."

Hallie's mouth opened and closed on a sputter. Was *she* the one being messed with now? "You placed bets with your husband? On whether or not I would . . . would . . ."

"And I won." An eyebrow waggle from Lavinia. "You and I both did, from the sounds of it."

"You didn't let me finish." Indignation warred with amusement, leading to Hallie giving Lavinia a very pointed look that didn't quite stick. "We engaged in the intimate act of *prank calling*."

Lavinia's face lost any trace of mirth. She pretended to signal the waiter. "Excuse me. Garçon? I'd like to order a new best friend." Her eyelids punched shut. "Prank calling? *Really?*"

"Yes." Hallie fanned herself. "Best I've ever had."

"There wasn't even a grazed tit? Or an itty-bitty peck?"

Hallie dug into her pasta with more gusto than necessary, thanks to her overwrought and underserviced hormones. "Nope."

"But did you *want* a little bit of action from him?"

No use in pretending. "Since I was fourteen."

"Then why didn't you make a move, babe? I raised you better than this!"

It was a totally valid question. Women *had* to make moves on men these days, or everyone on planet earth would be single. Her attraction to Julian Vos had always been off the charts, and yesterday . . . well, she'd sensed interest. Right? The way he sort of regulated his breathing in her presence wasn't a figment of her imagination. More than once she'd definitely noticed his attention dip to lower parts of her anatomy. Mainly, her mouth. Like maybe he was thinking of kissing her. But nothing. And she had an inkling as to why.

"We are extremely different people. I think I might even unnerve him a little?"

"Hallie." Lavinia pushed aside her plate and leaned forward. "A history professor doesn't sound like a man who operates carelessly or without a lot of thought."

"Meaning?"

"Meaning the attraction can't be one-sided or he wouldn't have created an excuse for you to return to the house."

She gestured with her fork. "There was a gopher—"

Lavinia interrupted her with a groan. "Men don't ask for assistance without being under extreme duress. *Unless* they are setting aside that pride in the name of a woman."

Hallie considered that. She thought of the way Julian had called her to handle the gopher issue when he absolutely could have created the mixture himself. The way he watched her with an almost reluctant fascination. How he'd followed her from the house and down the stairs, like he was barely aware his feet were moving. It all added up to attraction, didn't it?

Maybe she *should* have made a move?

Lavinia regarded Hallie, drumming her nails on the tablecloth. "You're still carrying that torch. Either extinguish it or fan the flame."

"Fan it? To what end?"

"To *your* end, if you're feeling adventurous."

"Someone needs to cut you off." Hallie realized she was squinting in order to keep the image of her friend from doubling. Probably because she'd been punctuating the end of every sentence with a gulp of wine. "Imagine *me* dating a history professor. Ridiculous."

Lavinia pushed out her bottom lip. "You've still got a mad crush, don't you, babe?"

"Yes." Remembering those intensely curious bourbon eyes and how they sparked with rare humor during the prank call, Hallie's chest squeezed. "It's a hard fascination to explain, but... ugh, Lavinia, I wish you could have seen him in high school. He once tutored one of our classmates—Carter Doherty—who'd been struggling to pass physics. I suspect some difficulties were happening at home, but whatever the case, he'd decided to drop out. But Julian wouldn't let him. Tutored him all the way from a failing grade to a B. And never took any credit. The only reason I knew about it is my grandmother gardened for Carter's family and witnessed Julian showing up on their doorstep every Tuesday." She'd swooned right there on the kitchen floor when Rebecca told her, refusing to budge until dinnertime. "Spending time with him last night made the crush worse, even while it forced me to see we're completely different."

"You're horny *and* pragmatic now."

"Yes. Does that officially make me a grown-up?"

"Afraid so. That's what the wine is for."

Hallie slumped. Took a deep breath. "All right. Well, he's only here to write the book, and he'll be leaving again. I'll just brazen my way through any future encounters. And when he's gone, I'll force myself to stop comparing everyone to him—"

"You mean comparing Owen, yeah?" Lavinia popped a shrimp into her mouth. "Give him the green light and you'll be a fall bride, if that's what you want. The man is lovestruck for you."

Guilt flip-flopped in Hallie's belly. "That's why I owe it to him—or any other man who I might see in the future—to not be hung up on a ridiculous crush. It's gone on way too long."

Lavinia pursed her lips, twirled her pasta. "Then again . . ."

"Oh no. Don't give me 'then again.'"

"Then again, you owe it to yourself to really make sure there is nothing there. Between you and Mr. Vos. You're in heat over a prank call. Imagine if you actually kissed the son of a bitch."

Hallie sighed. "Believe me, I've thought about it."

Lavinia fell back into her chair and settled her wineglass on her pasta-filled belly. "You should write him secret admirer letters or something. Get all this angst off your chest before you end up walking down the aisle toward Owen with a bridal bouquet of regrets."

Hallie laughed, trying not to let it show how thickly her heart was beating over those three little words. *Secret admirer letters.* The romantic inside of her sat up, stars twinkling in her eyes. God, what a unique chance to express the feelings she'd been carrying around half her life without the risk of embarrassment. "Where would I leave the letters?"

Lavinia hummed. "He runs through town every afternoon. He passes the donut shop at two eleven, like clockwork. And he cuts down the trail on the corner of Grapevine and Cannon. No one else uses that path because it leads to Vos property. You could find a tree stump or something to . . ." Her friend straightened in her chair. "You're not taking this *seriously,* are you?"

"No." Hallie shook her head so hard, a few curls fell across her eyes, forcing her to shove them back into place. "Of course not."

"Me and my big mouth." Lavinia sighed. "You don't have to make this complicated. Just tell the man you like him and see what happens. Or is that *too* easy?"

"You think baring fifteen years' worth of feelings would be easier in person?"

"All right, no. Not technically, but . . ." Slowly, Lavinia set down her glass, visibly taking time to gather her thoughts. "Look, I know I encouraged you to see him again. But I want you to stop and think before getting yourself into a tangle, Hallie. You know I love you to death, but . . ." She paused. "Since we lost Rebecca, you've been a little more quick to wreak havoc where none is necessary."

Hallie nodded. Kept right on nodding until the back of her neck was too tight to continue.

While on the road with her mother growing up, Hallie had felt like a slot machine. Drop in a coin, pull the lever, and pick a new adventure. A new persona. Clean the slate. Her mother was as ever-changing as the wind, and she took Hallie with her, inventing new stories, new identities in the name of fun.

Hallie recalled that itchy feeling right before her mother pulled the metaphoric lever, and it felt suspiciously like her current, restless state. The state she'd been in since January. And constant, restriction-free movement was the only way to smother it these days. Or ignore it, rather. "Thanks for being honest," she said, finally, to her expectant friend.

Lavinia reached across the table to lay her hand on top of Hallie's. "Let's put the ol' letter-writing nonsense to bed, shall we?"

"I've read it a story and tucked it in," Hallie said, firmly ignoring the excited static licking at her nerve endings. "Good night, bad idea."

"Thank fuck," Lavinia said, raising her wineglass.

Hallie reached for her own glass and found it empty. Blinking away the increasing blur, she poured herself another glass. A final one, she vowed.

Absently, she wondered how late the stationery shop stayed open these days.

Wouldn't hurt to check on the way home, right?

Surely her Uber driver wouldn't mind a detour.

Barbed wire wrapped around Hallie's skull and it appeared to be tightening with a full twist every five to eight seconds. She walked into Corked, which hadn't yet opened for the day, and draped herself over the dusty, timeworn counter, burying her head in folded arms.

Knowing laughter approached, and then Lorna patted her forearm with beautifully aged fingers, her cinnamon-and-dish-detergent scent drifting down to Hallie and providing her with a small sense of comfort. Quite a feat considering the circumstances.

"One cure for cobwebs coming right up," sang the elderly woman, her footsteps carrying her behind the counter. "Overextended yourself last night at dinner with Lavinia, did you?"

"It was a special occasion."

"What were you celebrating?"

"Saturday night." She tried to smile at the older woman, but the action juiced her brain like an orange. "Please, Lorna. My Advil is lost somewhere in the wilds of my house. Either that or the dogs buried it in the backyard. I come begging for mercy."

Lorna clucked her tongue, hummed to herself. "You don't have to beg." She fiddled in the cabinet beneath the register a moment, before setting down twin blue pills on the counter in front of Hallie. "You should be right as rain in forty-five minutes."

"That's ambitious, but I will attempt to manifest that outcome." Pills dry swallowed, Hallie stood up a little straighter and focused on the sweetly smiling woman beside the antique brass register. One of her grandmother's best friends. If she closed her eyes, she could see them sitting together, heads bent over a crossword, giggling like teenagers over a whispered joke. "How . . ." She cleared the emotion from her throat, glancing around the quiet, dusty shop. "Has business been any better?"

Lorna's smile remained in place, her head ticking slightly to the right.

She said nothing.

Hallie swallowed, shifting in her seat. "Well, have no fear. I'm sure this hangover will be cleared up by the two thirty tasting. And it's well past time to restock my whites—"

"The last thing you need is more wine, dear. I'm a big girl. I can handle no one showing up for a tasting." Chuckling, Lorna reached out and squeezed Hallie's hand. "Would I like to see this place packed like the old days? Of course. But I'm not filling the register with your hard-earned money, Hallie. I'm just not doing it." She gave Hallie a final pat. "Rebecca would be proud of you for trying to help."

Tears pricked the backs of Hallie's eyelids. Didn't Lorna realize she was being partially selfish? Not only did this place hold a million special memories for her, but . . . Hallie needed it to *remain*, this piece of her grandmother. The more Rebecca faded into the past, the more anxious and rudderless Hallie started to feel. This place, her routine, *everything* felt foreign without Rebecca's stalwart presence. Like her life belonged to someone else.

"Will you at least bag me up a Pinot—" The bell over the entrance dinged, and Hallie's heart leapt hopefully in her chest. "Oh! A customer . . ." Her excitement faded when she saw the man who entered. The tweed-suited, round-glassed manager from UNCORKED sporting a very brisk, very harried smile on his face. She recognized him from the afternoon she'd gone around town removing their grand opening flyers and he'd chased her half a block.

"Hello." Just inside the door, he clasped his hands together at his waist and threw a pitying glance at the sparsely stocked shelves. "I'm from UNCORKED next door. And I hate to do this, but we have two bachelorette parties coming to the afternoon tasting and our supply delivery truck was delayed. We are low on wineglasses, if you can believe it. The party got a little out of control last night, and there was some unfortunate breakage. Would you happen to have a dozen or so we could borrow until tomorrow?"

Lorna was already rising from her seat, eager to help. "Of course. I'm sure I can spare a few." She crouched down to survey her supplies behind the counter. Hallie hopped up to assist before Lorna could lift something too heavy, helping her settle a box of rattling glass onto the counter. "I have two dozen here. You're welcome to half."

The young man in tweed sauntered forward, peeling back the cardboard flaps and extracting one of the glasses, holding it up to the light. "These must be the emergency stash. Not exactly high quality, are they?"

Lorna wrung her hands. "Sorry about that."

"No, no. Don't apologize," laughed Tweed Twit, the disingenuous nature of it causing acid to climb the walls of Hallie's throat. "Well, I guess I have no choice. I'll take whatever you can give me." The manager wasn't even looking at them. He was craning his neck to observe the line forming in front of UNCORKED. "Are you able to spare the full two dozen? It looks like we need the glasses a tad more than Corked," he said absently.

"Oh. O-of course." Hastily, Lorna slid the box across the counter. Hallie was too stunned by the sheer audacity of Tweed Twit to offer assistance. And she remained open-mouthed in shock as the manager lifted the glasses with a hurried thank-you and scurried back out the door.

Hallie's entire body was racked by hot tingles and second-hand embarrassment. Her face was hotter than the sun's surface, and her throat? Good Lord. Was she transforming into a werewolf or something?

"That . . ." She could barely speak around the cluster of sticks in her throat. "He cannot get away with that."

"Hallie—"

"I'm going over there."

"Oh dear."

This was bad. She knew it the moment she stepped onto the sidewalk and cool air practically sizzled on her skin. This was not a disco-ball-sabotaging level of righteous indignation. It was far worse. This was Hulk-level irritation, and it needed an outlet. A dear, sweet old lady, an institution of the community, had been brazenly belittled to her face by Tweed Twit, and Hallie's anger demanded satisfaction. What form would it take? She had no idea. Which should have been a signal to return to the safety of Lorna's shop and regroup, but instead, she found herself ignoring the protests of people in line and yanking open the front door of UNCORKED, the scent of blue cheese and chocolate hitting her in the face.

"Why don't you wine about it?" sang the robotic automatic door greeting.

"Shut up," she said through her teeth, seeing UNCORKED for the first time from behind enemy lines. Unlike the soft, homey feel of Corked, this place was a study in bad lighting. Neon signs that said HELLO GORGEOUS and GOOD VIBES ONLY cast a tacky glow on the endless rows of wine bottles that appeared to be purchased based on the aesthetic of their labels, rather than the quality of the contents. Unfortunately, there were cushy ottomans begging people to sit and lounge for an afternoon and polish off forty-dollar cheese plates. It was clean and new, and she hated it.

*What exactly are you doing in here?*

At the moment, she was kind of hovering between the door and the counter, the customers who'd made it inside staring at her curiously, along with the register person. A bead of sweat rolled down her spine. She should go—

Tweed Twit's voice reached her then. He strode behind the counter with Lorna's box, giving the register person an exasperated smile. "Scrounged up some glasses from the old folks' home next door. I should probably take them in back and clean them first. There's probably a decade of dust caked on the rims."

Hallie's adrenaline spiked back up, and she glanced around through the red haze, attention landing on the cheese wall. Each block had its own shelf, backlit by pink lighting. Little silver dishes extended out with samples arranged in neat rows, sort of like human feeding troughs. And she was already moving toward it, turning her shirt into a makeshift apron and piling the cheese samples into it by the handful.

This was it.

Grand Theft Gouda would be the crime that finally brought her down.

"Hey!" That was Tweed Twit. "What are you doing?"

Focused on her mission, whatever the hell it was, Hallie didn't answer. She just needed some sort of compensation for the chunk the manager had taken out of Lorna's pride. Was it silly? Probably. Would Hallie regret this? Almost definitely, but only because it wouldn't help Lorna in any way. Not really.

She ran out of room in her shirt apron and started stuffing cheese samples into her pockets.

"*Hey!*" The manager came to a stop beside her and started slapping at her hands, but she blocked him with her back. "Call the police!" he shouted over his shoulder. "This . . . Oh my God, it's the same girl who stole the flyers a few weeks ago!"

Uh-oh.

Jerome was right. This was textbook escalation.

Hallie made a break for it.

Tweed Twit was faster. He blocked the exit. She turned, searching for a back door. All of these places had them. It would empty into the alley, just like Fudge Judy. And then she would . . .

what? Hide behind the standing mixer again? Would she even be able to avoid the fallout this time? Her temples started to pound, the sounds of the wineshop turning muffled. Her face stung. Some of the cheese chunks plunked to the ground.

And then the craziest thing happened.

She locked eyes with Julian Vos through the glass window of UNCORKED.

He had a brown paper bag in one sculpted arm, and she recognized the convenience store logo. He'd gone grocery shopping. Julian Vos: *He's just like us!* The professor's attention dropped from her face to the mountain of assorted cheese blocks in her shirt apron, and he popped out his AirPod, a single black eyebrow winging up.

Slowly, Julian's gaze drifted over to the manager—who was simultaneously yelling at her and shouting orders to the person behind the counter—and his expression darkened. One long stride and he was inside UNCORKED. Leaving a chorus of complaints in his wake from people in line, he very effortlessly took command of the whole establishment without saying a single word. Everyone stopped and looked at him, somehow knowing his arrival was important. This man was a bystander of nothing.

The only person who didn't notice Julian entering UNCORKED was Tweed Twit, who continued to demand she pay for the ruined cheese, listing the crimes she'd committed against the wineshop like broken commandments.

But his mouth snapped shut when Julian stepped in front of Hallie.

"You're finished yelling at her now." Hallie couldn't see his face, but based on the clipped delivery of his words, she imagined his features were tense. "Don't ever do it again." He turned and glanced at her over his shoulder. Indeed, with his Very Serious eyebrows and jawline, he resembled a gallant duke come to rescue a damsel in distress. Well, call her Princess Peach Toadstool, because she welcomed his services. "Hallie, please go outside where this man can't shout at you anymore."

"I'm fine right here," she whispered, her belief in chivalry rising like the dead in an old zombie movie. Not even the threat of being bitten by a walking corpse could have convinced her to miss what was happening here. Julian defending her. Taking her side without getting both sides of the story first. Just being all-around wonderful. *God,* he was wonderful.

Tweet Twit sputtered. "She stole our cheese!"

"I can see that," Julian said with forced calm, turning back to the red-faced man. He lowered his voice to such a level that Hallie almost didn't hear his next clipped words to the manager. "You're still not going to yell at her anymore. If she's upset, I'm upset. I don't think you want that."

Hallie . . . was finding religion. Is that what was happening?

*Am I ascending to a higher plane?*

Whatever was happening on his face must have convinced the manager that ticking Julian off should be eliminated from his chore chart. "Fine, I'm done yelling, but we're calling the police," the manager said, snapping at the counter person.

"You're going to call the police over cheese samples?" Julian asked slowly. Hallie looked down at his butt—she couldn't help it, not when he was using the snobbish professor tone of voice—and, God, the way it tested the seam of his jeans almost made her drop the hunk of Parmesan that she'd been secretly planning to keep for herself. "I don't think that would be wise. Number one, that would upset her, too, and we've already established I'm not a fan of that. And two, you'd have to press charges. Over cheese. Against a local. I don't think the other locals—your customers—would like that very much, do you? We both know I wouldn't."

Heaven looked suspiciously like a cheese shop, but surely her personal cloud was around here somewhere. Could she book an angel-guided tour, perhaps?

"She stole our flyers out of shop windows and . . . yeah, I think she might have broken our disco ball?" Uh-oh. Hallie's stupor popped like a bubble, and she peeked around Julian in time to see the manager throw up his hands. "She's a menace!"

Hallie gasped.

"You're probably right," Julian drawled.

She gasped a second time.

"But if you say another word about her, I'll break a lot more than your disco ball."

Tweed Twit blew a raspberry in his outrage. "I can't believe this—" He stopped cold and squinted up at Julian. "Wait a minute, you look familiar."

Julian sighed, transferring the paper bag to his other arm. "Yes." He kept his voice low. "You must be familiar with Vos Vineyard."

"Vos Vineyard? Not really. We don't stock anything from those dusty-ass has-beens."

Hallie almost threw the block of Parmesan at the store manager—and it was definitely a big enough chunk to deliver a concussion. Did he really just say that out loud to Julian? The secondhand embarrassment she'd experienced for Lorna roared back now in his honor, flushing her skin and making her wish she'd stayed in bed this morning, like a good little hungover soldier. For Julian's part, his reaction was not what she might have expected. Instead of getting angry over the insult to his family business, he merely looked . . . perplexed. Curious.

"Dusty-ass has-beens?" he repeated, brow furrowing. "Why would you call—"

The manager cut him off with a finger snap. "No, wait. I know why you're familiar. You were in that alien documentary! What was it called . . ."

Julian was already turning on a heel, ushering Hallie out of the store with his free hand. "And that's our cue."

"Wait!" called the overdressed twentysomething. "Can we take a selfie?"

"No," Julian said flatly.

"What alien documentary is he talking about?" Hallie whispered up at Julian's set chin.

"Quiet, cheese thief."

"That's fair," she muttered, plucking the Parmesan out of her apron and taking a bite.

As soon as they were outside the shop and moving at a brisk pace down the sidewalk, Julian asked a question Hallie really didn't want to field. "Why did he speak that way about the vineyard? Was it an unpopular opinion or the consensus?"

Hallie gulped. "If I answer, will you explain the alien documentary?"

His sigh could have withered an oak tree. "Deal."

# Chapter 6

They were the adult version of Hansel and Gretel. Except, instead of bread crumbs, they were leaving crumbles of Manchego in their wake. Somehow Julian wasn't surprised by this turn of events. Of course he'd stumbled upon this captivating, lunatic woman who inspired him to make prank calls stealing cheese from a local establishment. What *else* would she be doing?

He couldn't quite locate the wherewithal to be exasperated with her, however. Who could be upset over anything when she was smiling? Not him. Especially when two very prominent emotions were crowding everything else out.

Number one? He was pissed the hell off. Wanted to go back into UNCORKED and knock some teeth out of the manager's head, which was unlike him in every way. He wasn't a violent man. He'd been in a few scrapes as a teenager, but he'd never experienced that hot surge from his belly to his throat before, like he'd felt when he'd seen Hallie being yelled at through the window. Who could shout at this . . . human sunflower? *None of my business,* his head tried to tell him. But his gut compelled him to storm inside and stand between her and any sort of negativity. *Not on my watch.*

Number two? An encroaching sense of dread tightened his arm around the sack of groceries. *Dusty-ass has-beens.* Those words cycled from one corner of his brain to the other, back and forth, so unlike the phrasing he was used to hearing describe Vos Vineyard.

Institution. Legendary. A cornerstone of the industry.

They stopped at a trash can, where Hallie rid herself of countless cheese samples, though she stubbornly held on to the Parmesan. "Before I tell you anything," she started, squaring her shoulders and taking a deep breath that did nothing to settle his nerves. "I want you to know that I, personally, do not share any negative opinions about your family's vineyard. Case in point, I just knocked over that cringey wine nightclub because it's stepping on the toes of my beloved old stomping grounds. I value tradition and history—those are both words I would use to describe Vos. It's part of St. Helena. But it, um . . . well, in recent years, some might say . . ."

The dread deepened. "Don't soften the blow, Hallie. Let's have it."

She nodded once. "The fire was a setback to a lot of established wineries. They tried to recover, but the pandemic came along and knocked them out. Now there is a flood of competition from the buyers of those turnkey wineries. They've come along and modernized their operations, found new ways to lure in the crowds. And Vos . . ." She wet her lips. "According to what I've heard, it's still in recovery mode, while all the new kids are expanding, bringing in celebrity spokesmen, and conquering social media."

Bolts twisted on either side of his jugular. He'd found his mother's request that he attend the Wine Down Napa festival a little odd, but he didn't anticipate this. How bad were things? And . . . was he still so unwanted in the family business that she wouldn't even ask for his help in a desperate situation? Yes, his father had made it very clear he didn't want Julian's influence on the vineyard. But his mother? Maybe she had even less faith in him than he'd realized. After his humiliating behavior after the fire, could he blame her?

"My mother mentioned none of this," he managed.

"I'm sorry." Hallie offered him the Parmesan, lowering it back down to her side when he declined with a curt head shake.

"I'm more of a goat cheese type."

She did a double take. "Okay, Satan." She nudged him in the ribs to let him know she was joking, and he barely resisted catching her wrist, keeping her hand there. *Near.* "If it makes you feel any better, I got extremely drunk last night on a bottle of Vos Sauvignon Bl . . ."

She trailed off, her face losing some of its rosy color.

"What's wrong?" he asked, concerned. Just how much had that scrawny manager upset her? "I'm going back in there," he growled, wheeling back toward the shop.

"No!" She caught his elbow, stopping him. "I'm . . . I'm okay."

Clearly that wasn't true. "Too much Parmesan?"

"No, I just . . ." Suddenly she seemed unable to look him in the eye. "I just remembered I forgot to tip my Uber driver from last night. And he was really good. He even waited for me while I made a stop."

Why did she sound almost winded by the oversight?

"You can tip after the fact."

"Yes." She looked right through him, glassy-eyed, her color high. "Yes. I can. I will."

"Does this hangover have anything to do with the decision to burgle cheese?"

"No." She visibly shook herself, but her color was slow to return, voice slightly unnatural. "Maybe a little. But it didn't help matters when the Tweed Twit walked into Corked like an entitled troll and made off with two dozen wineglasses, claiming UNCORKED needed them more."

"Ah." Irritation snaked through him all over again. "I'm extra glad I didn't give him a selfie."

"Speaking of which." They walked down the sidewalk while Hallie tried and failed to tuck the cheese block into the front pocket of her jeans. Honestly, she was a constant jumble. And he couldn't seem to take his damn eyes off her nonetheless. "What alien documentary?"

"It's nothing," he responded briskly.

"No way it's nothing." She laughed, and he was relieved to see her looking less pale than a moment ago. "Also, you promised an explanation, Vos. I demand satisfaction."

A corner of his lips tugged. "Yes, I'm aware. I just don't like to talk about it."

"You just caught me committing a robbery. Give me something."

He grew momentarily fascinated by her cajoling smile. Hungover or not, she still had her glow, didn't she? Her brand of discombobulated beauty. And a lot like the first two times he'd been in the presence of Hallie, the pressure of his schedule seemed to have receded. But it tried to roar back into focus now, demanding he regroup. His watch became heavier on his wrist, minutes flying by without being accounted for. "Right, I'll explain. But I have writing to do . . ."

She blinked at him, and he nearly leaned in to get a better look at the black circle around her irises. Is that what made their color so . . . distracting? He could take half an hour, couldn't he?

Might as well face facts. Hallie was a stick of dynamite to his peace of mind, and he couldn't seem to adhere to his plans when she was around. Especially when she tilted her head one way and squint-smiled up at him, the sun basking in that crease in the middle of her bottom lip. And the fact that he was noticing these details in lieu of the ticking clock meant something was seriously wrong with him.

"Why are you looking at me like that?" he asked.

"I was just thinking the morning could have turned out a lot different," she said. "If you hadn't intervened, that is. Thank you. That was pretty heroic."

What was the odd feeling in his middle? Heroic he was not. Yet he couldn't help but covet Hallie thinking of him that way. To have this woman smile at him was some sort of celestial reward he didn't know he'd been missing. When was he going to get enough of it? Soon, hopefully. This couldn't very well be *sustained*. "No one should ever yell at you."

She blinked. Was she breathing faster now? He wanted to know. Wanted to get close and study her and mentally file away the patterns of her behavior. The pathways to her Hallie Smiles.

"Th-thank you," she responded, finally. Quietly. As if she couldn't get the breath for much more—and it was little wonder why after her altercation with the manager.

He should really go back in there.

Would have. If she didn't beam a grin at him and turn in the direction of the path that would lead to Vos Vineyard. The path he *would* have already gone down if this unruly woman hadn't dragged him from his routines in such an adorable—no, criminal—way.

"I still want to know about the alien documentary."

"I suspected as much," he muttered, ignoring his watch. "A few years ago, I was asked to be part of an untitled documentary film. A *student* film. I assumed it was a semester project, something they would be turning in for a grade, so I didn't read the fine print on the release form." He shook his head over such uncharacteristic negligence on his part. "They asked me to speak on camera about the timekeeping methods of the ancient Egyptians. I was not aware that my theories would, in a roundabout way, support their belief that aliens are responsible for influencing certain time-measuring devices. They got a B minus on the film, but somehow it was picked up by Netflix, and now I'm an unwitting participant in an alien documentary. My students find it all very amusing."

"And you clearly do not."

"Correct." Reluctantly, he added, "It's called *Time Martians On*."

She slapped a hand over her mouth, then let it drop, giving him a sympathetic look. "Sorry, but that's extremely clever."

"I suppose it is," he admitted. "Unfortunately, I was not. And now I'm on film talking about a very important subject and they've edited it in such a way that I appear to be . . . *very* passionate about the existence of aliens."

Looking ahead, she said something under her breath. It sounded like *How did I not know about this?* He must have heard her wrong. And then he got distracted by the way a dimple appeared in her cheek when she tried to bury a smile. It was adorable, really, and he had the insane impulse to fit his thumb into it.

"You're lucky I don't have Netflix or I'd be watching that sucker tonight with a bowl of popcorn."

"Don't have Netflix?" He couldn't hide his shock. "Their documentary section alone is worth the membership, *Time Martians On* notwithstanding."

"Oh no," she deadpanned. "I can't believe I'm missing out on all that excitement." Whatever his expression—he guessed it was affronted—it made her giggle, the sound making him swallow thickly. "Oh, come on. There are worse things to be passionate about," she said. "At least it wasn't a Bigfoot biopic."

The giggling was over, then? "That's the only silver lining."

"Oh, I don't know." Amusement spread across her face, and a corresponding ripple went straight through him. "It was kind of nice watching Tweed Twit get starstruck in the midst of his tirade against me."

They'd reached the beginning of the trail leading to the vineyard. He needed to wish her a good rest of the weekend and be on his damn merry way. But he hesitated. The full half an hour hadn't passed yet. Changing his plan of action twice in one morning would throw him off even more, wouldn't it? Yes. So he might as well keep talking to her. And ignore the relief sinking into his gut.

"Where did you go to high school?" He asked the question without thinking about it. Because he was genuinely curious, not just making the necessary small talk as he tended to do with women. He needed to know where a woman like Hallie sprang from.

A few beats of silence dragged out. Very briefly, her smile dimmed, and his stomach dropped with it. "Napa High," she said, continuing on without giving him a chance to process that bombshell information. "You would have been three years ahead of me, I believe. A cool senior." Her shoulder jerked. "I'm sure our paths didn't cross very often."

But they obviously had.

And he'd forgotten? *How?*

Who wouldn't remember every detail of Hallie?

*This* was why she'd been disappointed in him the first time they'd met. Now he'd made the blunder twice. He'd be terrible at the job of full-time provider of smiles for this woman.

"I'm sorry, I didn't realize—"

"Stop." Cheeks red, she waved off the apology. "It's fine!"

Uh-oh. Not fine. Definitely not fine. He needed to get that smile back on her face by the time they parted ways, or he wouldn't sleep tonight.

"Let me guess," he said, equally determined to find out more about her. For reasons that couldn't possibly be wise. "You were in drama club."

"Yes. But only for a week. Then I tried playing the trombone in the marching band. For a month. Then I got a pair of nonprescription horn-rim glasses and joined the newspaper. And that was only sophomore year." She looked into the distance at the rows of grapes on his family's property, the sun bathing the earth in gold. Bathing her in gold. Her cheeks, her nose, the wild ringlets buried among the bigger curls on her head. "By junior year, my grandmother had gotten ahold of me. Helped me settle down."

"I can't imagine you ever settling down, Hallie."

Her eyes shot to his. Probably because of the way he said her name. Like they were in bed together, tangled up in damp sheets. He could visualize them there so easily. Could feel himself liking what they did there. Loving it. To such a point that coming back down would be difficult. His *reaction* to her was flat-out difficult. It was too much.

"Um . . ." She wet her lips. "Well, she had a way of reining me in. Or maybe I just felt at home with her and I could relax. Focus. I'm a little untethered without her around. If she was there this morning for the cheese show, she would have said something like, 'Hallie, all that glitters is not gold' or 'an empty vessel makes much noise,' and I would have sighed or maybe even argued with her, because not every situation can be summed up with a proverb. But I probably wouldn't have felt the need to steal cheese in the name of justice, either. Maybe I've been wrong all along and those proverbs are golden. Or at least a way of saving bail money." She took a much-needed breath. Interested as he was in what she was saying, he'd actually started to get worried. "It's terrible how you only realize these things when it's too late."

"It is. My father . . . he hasn't passed or anything and God knows our relationship was never perfect. But I often find myself discovering meaning in something he told me, right out of the blue. It'll just be relevant." He went on speaking without considering his words. Odd behavior for him. Normally everything he said out loud was weighed and measured beforehand. "Your grandmother sounds like someone worth missing."

He didn't realize he'd stopped breathing regularly until a smile formed on her mouth again. Again, he had the sudden urge to touch, to stroke her cheek, so he slipped his hand into the pocket of his shorts.

"Thank you. I like that. And she is."

They just kind of looked at each other, her face turned up to the sun in deference of his height. Maybe he should stoop down slightly so she didn't get a crick in her neck?

"She never quite pushed me as far as she'd hoped. Or she left before she could. The library . . . you know the town library? They'd been asking her to landscape their courtyard for years. She kept saying no. She asked *me* to do it, instead. It would be the biggest project I've ever taken on. The one that required the most commitment. I think . . . I don't know, she wanted me to realize my potential to knuckle down and nurture something. The topper on her master-plan cake." She shook herself as if embarrassed she'd been speaking for so long. As if he wasn't praying she'd continue. "Wow, I've definitely taken up enough of your time. You came into town for a quick stop at the store and ended up sympathizing with a burglar." Abruptly, she held out her hand to him for a shake. "Friends, Julian?" When he didn't take her hand right away, she shifted right to left. "I appreciate what you did for me this morning, but wow . . . it really did make it obvious that we should probably be the kind of acquaintances that wave at each other in the store, right?"

Yes. That was true. Totally true. That didn't mean he enjoyed parting ways with her. Didn't like it last time, either. But if it had to be done—and since it did—he definitely preferred it happening as friends. Unfortunately, she was a friend he suspected he'd be thinking about to the point of distraction for a long time. "Right . . ."

Finally, he took her hand.

"Would it make you smile if I gave you my Netflix login?" He was actually saying this out loud. "So you could watch *Time Martians On* with popcorn?"

The slow grin that spread across her face made the entire world feel brighter.

"I think that would elevate you from friend to hero. Twice in one day."

*How in God's name* did he forget being in the same place at the same time as her?

She must have been dressed up for Halloween at the time. Or been wearing a potato sack that covered her head to toe. Those were the only explanations he could muster.

"Then I'll text it to you," he said, shaking her hand. "Enjoy."

Hands dropping to their sides, they hesitated a moment, then turned and walked away. And Julian continued down the path, not glancing at his watch even once. He was too busy (a) texting Hallie his login and password, double- and triple-checking his punctuation and briefly considering a flower emoji, because it reminded him of her. And (b) replaying the last hour of his life and trying to figure out how the whole Hallie business had been so completely peculiar and off-beat, while also . . . dangerously exhilarating.

However, when he saw the white envelope sticking out of a tree stump ahead—an envelope with *his name* looping across the front—he had a feeling the day was about to get even more peculiar.

And he was right.

"OH JESUS!" HALLIE cried into the phone. "Oh *Jesus*. You're not going to believe this."

"Quiet down. Someone has stabbed me through the fuckin'

eye with a high heel," Lavinia screeched back, clearly neck-deep in her own hangover. "What has you in a state?"

"Lavinia, I want to die."

"Me too, currently." Her friend's voice was now muffled by a pillow. "I'm suspecting for a different reason. State your business or I'm hanging up."

"I wrote the letter," Hallie scream-whispered into the phone, just as she reached her truck. She threw herself inside and slammed the door, her pulse frenetic, stomach roiling. "I wrote Julian a secret admirer letter last night after dinner and I left it for him to find. I wrote it in the back of an Uber. I'm pretty sure I even asked the driver for advice and he said don't do it. Don't do it, crazy passenger. But I did. I left it for him on the jogging path, and unless it blew away, he's in the process of finding it *right now.*"

"I can't believe you did that. You swore you wouldn't."

"I can't be expected to make promises under the influence of pasta and wine!"

"You're right. I shouldn't have trusted your word." A couch groaned in the background. Lavinia's voice was clearer when she spoke again. "There's no way to do damage control?"

"No. I mean, I didn't sign my name, obviously. I think, anyway?"

"That would seriously defeat the purpose of a secret admirer letter."

Her phone dinged to signal a text message. Julian's Netflix login.

He'd saved her from a troll in tweed, rekindled her belief in good deeds and noble men, made her heart beat like it had finally remembered how, *and* given her his Netflix password—which was "calendar," by the way—and in return, she'd word-vomited her admiration of him in a torrent of compulsiveness.

"I can't even remember what I wrote!" Hallie dropped her forehead onto the steering wheel. "Please tell me the morning dew blurred the ink or the whole thing blew away. Please tell me that's possible and Julian Vos isn't reading my drunken ramblings right now."

Lavinia's pause lasted a beat too long. "I'm sure it blew away, babe."

"No way I'm that lucky, huh?"

"Doubt it." There was a muffled voice in the background. "Got to go. Jerome needs help with the rush. Keep me posted, Shakespeare!"

Hallie took a deep breath and let the disconnected phone drop to her lap, staring into a void. What was she going to do?

Nothing. That's what. Sit tight and hope. That if the letter didn't get caught in the wind, nothing she said in those paragraphs could identify her. For all she remembered, she might have actually labeled the envelope with her home address. *God.*

Okay. Tomorrow she was scheduled to be back at the Vos guesthouse to do some planting. She'd just have to remain in the dark until then—and then she'd either be granted a reprieve. Or her feelings for Julian would no longer be her innocent little secret.

# Chapter Seven

Julian stared down at the letter, his eyebrows dangerously close to being swallowed up by his hairline.

*Dear Julian Vos,*

*Oh my God. I can't believe I'm really doing this.*

*You get one shot at life, though, right? Have to pull that trigger!*

*Okay. Seriously, though. I think you're wonderful. Really, truly wonderful. I've been dying to get that off my chest for a very long time, but I didn't have the guts. You've always been so quietly kind, never lording your name over anyone or acting superior, you know what I mean? Just a real down-to-earth fellow with brains to burn and a big, secret heart.*

*I wish I'd told you all of this a million years ago, because when you feel something, you should just say it! You know? I don't want you to think I'm creepy (of course you're going to think I'm creepy, I mean, look what I'm doing), but way back when, in days of yore, I witnessed your character when you didn't think anyone was watching and it really inspired how I've treated other people throughout my life. Mostly! I'm not perfect. Sometimes I hang up on telemarketers. But I hope you're happy and healthy and headed for the kind of happy future you deserve. I used the word "happy" twice there, sorry, but you get up what I'm putting down.*

*Okay! This was great. Let's do it again sometime. Maybe you'll write back? You're never too old for a pen pal. I'm sure that's the generally held belief on the subject.*

*Secretly Yours*

Julian lifted his head. "What the fuck?"

A secret admirer letter?

He turned the envelope over in his hands, searched the back of the paper for some sign of the prankster's identity—because that's definitely what this was. A prank. But there were no clues to point him in the direction of the person apparently trying to mess with him.

Who the hell had written it?

Who knew about his habit of taking this shortcut between home and town?

A lot of people, he supposed. Anyone he jogged past on Grapevine Way in the afternoon. Shop owners. Or people who lived in the residential houses closer to the top of the path. It could be any number of women. Or men.

He shook his head, scanning the lines one more time. Nobody wrote secret admirer letters these days. Contact was made through social media, almost exclusively, right? This had to be some kind of joke at his expense, but why? Who would go to so much trouble?

As soon as Julian arrived at the guesthouse to find his sister loitering in the driveway, the mystery solved itself. "Wow. How long have you been in town? An hour?" He waved the letter. "Barely made it off the plane before kicking off the psychological warfare?"

He didn't buy her confused expression. Not for a second.

"Uh. Thanks for the warm welcome," Natalie said, skirting the bumper of her hatchback. Rented, based on the window sticker. "Tone down the emotion before this family reunion gets embarrassing." Sauntering toward Julian, she eyed his letter as if she'd never seen it before. "Yes. It is I, the prodigal daughter. I would give you a hug, but we don't do that sort of thing . . ." Her smile was tight-lipped. "Hi, Julian. You look well."

The way she said it, with a hint of measuring concern in her eyes, made the back of his neck feel tight. The last time they'd been together in St. Helena, on the soil of Vos Vineyard, was never far from his mind. The smoke and ash and shouting and flames. The worry that he wouldn't do what needed to be done in time. He could taste the acrid burn in the back of his throat, could feel the grit that seared the backs of his eye sockets. The hundred-ton weight pressing down on his chest, making it impossible for him to breathe in the smoky air.

Natalie scanned his face and looked away quickly, obviously remembering, too. How he'd lost his composure in a way that was so physical, he could only remember it happening in snatches of sound and movement. One moment he'd been capable of thinking critically, helping his family, and the next, when he knew Natalie was safe, he'd simply gone dark. He'd retreated into the sooty house, closed himself in a back bedroom, and gone to a place where he was comfortable. Work. Lessons. Lecture notes. When he came up for air, days had passed while he'd been in a state of numbness. Leaving his parents and Natalie to deal with the fallout from the fire. Unacceptable. He'd never go to that place again.

"What are you doing here?" he asked, a little too sharply.

Her chin snapped up. Fast. Defensive. With her face to the morning sun, he catalogued the differences since the last time they saw each other. Natalie was younger than him by three and a half years, making her thirty now. She had his mother's ageless complexion, black hair down past her shoulders, messy from the wind constantly moving through the valley, although she continuously tried to smooth it with impatient palms. She'd arrived dressed for New York City, where she'd moved after attending Cornell. In black dress pants, heels, and a ruffled blazer, she could have walked straight off Madison Avenue into the front yard.

As for *why* Natalie was in St. Helena, Julian expected a practical explanation. She was in town on business. Or here to attend the wedding of a colleague. He definitely wasn't expecting the reason she gave him instead.

"I'm taking a break from work. A *voluntary* one," she rushed to add, picking lint from the sleeve of her jacket. "And if I have to stay in the main house with our mother, I'm pretty sure we'll fight enough to invoke the apocalypse, so I'll be crashing here with you."

The muscle directly behind his right eye had begun to spasm. "Natalie, I am writing a book. I came here for peace and quiet."

"Really?" Genuine, surprised pleasure crossed her face before she hid it behind amusement. "My brother, a novelist? Very impressive." She studied him for a moment, visibly evaluating the information. "Who says I'm going to mess with your process?" She pressed her lips into a line, seemingly to suppress a laugh. "You call it your process. Don't you?"

"That's what it's called." He folded up the prank letter, already planning on tossing it into the trash can as soon as he walked inside. "And it's your track record that says you'd mess with it."

Natalie rolled her eyes. "I'm a grown woman now, Julian. I'm not going to throw a kegger on your front lawn. At least not until I lull you into a false sense of security." When a rumbling sound started coming from his throat, she reached for the rolling suitcase waiting behind her on the driveway. "Oh, come on, that was a joke."

He watched in disbelief as she dragged the suitcase up the stairs, letting it smack loudly into each wooden step. "Natalie, there has to be somewhere else you can take a break."

"Nope."

The screen door snicked shut behind his sister, her heels tapping toward the kitchen.

Julian followed her, nearly wrenching the door off its hinges in the process. This couldn't be happening. Fate was determined to fuck him over. This guesthouse had been sitting empty for four years, and suddenly *both* of them were back? And at the very same time, it had also been imperative to plant begonias? The women in his life were dead set on derailing his goals. At this very moment, he was supposed to be in the shower, preparing for the second half of his writing day.

Julian arrived in the kitchen and watched his sister remove her jacket, hanging it neatly on the back of a chair. Thank God, at the very least, they had tidiness in common. Their father hadn't tolerated anything less growing up. When Natalie and Julian were younger, the driving force in Dalton Vos's life had been crafting wine better than his father. To make the vineyard twice as successful and rub it in the face of his estranged old man. And when Dalton succeeded, when he'd been showered in accolades and become the toast of Napa, being better than his father wasn't as satisfying as he'd hoped. Nor did he have a son he found capable of bestowing his legacy upon. The fire was the final blow to Dalton's invincibility, so he'd signed over Vos Vineyard to his ex-wife as a parting gift in the divorce and moved on to the next project, leaving this one behind for Corinne to assume.

As badly as Julian wanted to believe himself nothing like Dalton, there were similarities, and he'd stopped trying to fight them. Did he resent anyone who interfered with his plans? Yes. Was he competitive? Perhaps not as much as Dalton, but they both craved perfection in every one of their undertakings. In a way, he'd even followed in Dalton's footsteps and abandoned the vineyard for the last four years.

Just for a very different reason.

Clearing the discomfort from his throat, Julian moved to the coffeepot and pressed the on button, the sounds of it warming up filling the quiet kitchen. "Afternoon caffeine boost?"

"Count me in."

While removing mugs from the cabinet, he observed his sister, taking note of the bare ring finger on her left hand and raising an eyebrow. At Christmas, she'd emailed him and Corinne to inform them of her engagement to "the Tom Brady of investing."

Had it been called off?

Natalie caught him noticing her lack of hardware and glared. "Don't ask."

"I'm going to ask."

"Fine." She hopped up onto a stool and crossed her arms, mimicking his earlier posture. "There's no law that says I have to answer."

"No, there isn't," he agreed, getting the milk out of the fridge and trying desperately not to panic over the minutes as they slipped away, one by one, right through his fingers. As soon as he drank this cup of coffee and squared the Natalie situation away, he would tackle his afternoon schedule. In fact, he would add extra writing time to put himself ahead. Julian's shoulders relaxed at that reassurance. "I don't know a lot about the financial sector, but I know it's too competitive in New York to simply take a break."

"Yes, it's part of the doctrine. You don't leave New York City finance unless you die or get fired, right?" She gestured to herself. "Unless you're a unicorn like me and you're valuable enough to earn some leeway. I'm a partner at my firm, Julian. Stop hunting. I just wanted a vacation."

"And you came *here*." He paused for emphasis. "To relax."

"Is that not what people do here? In the land of endless wine?"

"Other people, maybe."

Her arms dropped heavily to her sides. "Just make the coffee and shut up."

Julian gave her a dubious look before turning back around and doctoring the mugs with milk, plus one sugar for Natalie. Unless she'd changed her order in the last four years, that's how she took it. When he set it down in front of her and she sipped without comment, flicking him a reluctantly grateful glance, he guessed her ideal formula remained the same.

It surprised Julian that he experienced a tug of comfort in that. Knowing the way his sister took her coffee. They weren't close. Twice a year, they exchanged emails to wish each other a happy birthday and a merry Christmas. Unless his mother needed to inform them of the death of a relative, their line of communication was pretty inactive. Shouldn't she have contacted them about her engagement being called off? With three thousand miles between them, he never stopped to wonder about his sister's personal relationships. But now, as she sat in front of him clearly trying to outrun something, the lack of knowledge was a hole in his gut.

"How long are you staying?"

The mug paused on the way to her mouth. "I don't know yet." Her attention slipped over him. "Sorry. I know unquantified time gives you heartburn."

"It's fine," he said stiffly.

"Is it?" She stared into her coffee. "Last time we were here—"

"I said it's fine, Natalie."

His sister's mouth snapped shut, but she recovered quickly. Even faster than he could begin to feel guilty for being harsh. "So . . ." She took a deep breath and exhaled, somewhat unevenly. "Have you had any heartwarming encounters with our mother yet?"

"Perhaps not heartwarming," Corinne said from the kitchen entrance, arrival unannounced. "But positive and productive. That's what we aim for here, isn't it?"

Julian noticed the barest flash of hurt in Corinne's eyes. Over his sister arriving without warning? Or her offhanded sarcasm about their heartwarming relationship? It wasn't like his mother to be, or at least appear to be, upset over anything. Natalie and Julian's stiff upper lips were genetic, after all. After his conversation with Hallie this morning, it was easier to notice a chink in Corinne's armor, however. Not only now, but the last time she'd stopped by, too.

Was the vineyard in trouble? Would Corinne let the family business fade into obscurity, rather than request a helping hand? He was almost afraid to ask. To find out if she had the same use for him as Dalton. Namely, none. Sure, she'd asked him to participate in a festival, but that was far from hands-on. That was merely for the cameras.

"Since you're here, Natalie, I'll extend the same invitation I made to Julian. Wine Down Napa takes place in a week. A little Vos representation won't hurt. Will you be in St. Helena long enough to attend?"

No movement from Natalie, save a thick swallow. "Probably."

Corinne processed that information with a tight nod. "Lovely. I'll make sure you're issued a badge." She folded her hands at her waist. "Please try and remember the wine at these events is mainly for the paying attendees, Natalie."

"There it is." Natalie laughed, sliding off her stool and batting at the wrinkles in her pants. "It only took you forty-five seconds to put me in my place." Julian's sister split a venomous look between him and his mother. "I'm thirty now. Can we all get past the fact that I rebelled a little bit as a teenager?"

"A little bit?" With a bemused expression, Corinne tucked

some hair into the bun at the nape of her neck. "A little rebelling doesn't land you in rehab at seventeen."

Color infused Natalie's cheeks. "Yes, well, I landed on my feet at Cornell, didn't I?"

"Not without some strategic maneuvering."

"I'm . . ." Natalie's head of steam was diminishing quickly. "I made partner last fall."

Corinne eyed the suitcase. "And how is that going?"

"That's enough," Julian said firmly, his coffee mug hitting the island. "Natalie shouldn't have to explain her presence in her own home. I'm . . . sorry I made her do that. It ends now."

Natalie's head swiveled toward him, but he didn't meet her eyes. For some reason, he didn't want to see her surprise that he'd defended her. Once upon a time, it would have been a given. They might not be confidants or the closest of siblings, but he'd offered quiet support for his sister. At school, at home. Hadn't he?

When had he let that part of their relationship fall by the wayside?

His sister was obviously going through something serious, and he found it impossible to turn a blind eye to that now, as he'd been doing more and more since they'd each left St. Helena. Hadn't he been so wrapped up in his world that he'd missed the warning signs with his colleague Garth? One day they were discussing quantum theory in the hall, and the next, Garth was locked in his office and refusing to communicate with anyone outside. It didn't appear that Natalie was on the verge of a breakdown, but he should pay attention.

Be more present. More empathetic.

*I witnessed your character when you didn't think anyone was watching and it really inspired how I've treated other people throughout my life.*

Unexpectedly, that line from the secret letter popped into his head, and he mentally scoffed it away. The whole thing was a prank—and he wouldn't think about it a second more. It wasn't the letter that had inspired him to step up for Natalie.

Was it Hallie and the way she staunchly defended the owner of Corked, by fair means or foul?

Thinking of the gardener, he immediately caught a whiff of her soil and sunshine scent. Had it been lingering in the kitchen since Friday night or was that his imagination? What had that impulsive, curly-haired bundle of energy done to him?

Why couldn't he stop thinking about her?

Julian ordered himself back to the present, where his mother and sister were eyeballing each other across the kitchen. Yes, the Vos family had their share of issues—and he was far from the exception.

"Was there anything else either of you needed?" Julian asked, tight-lipped. "I need to shower and get to work." He glanced at his watch and felt his pulse accelerate. "I'm already forty minutes behind schedule."

Natalie staggered dramatically, gripping the handle of her suitcase. "The keeper of time hath spoken! To be idle is to smite his holy name."

Julian gave her a dead-eyed stare. His sister smiled back, which was odd and unexpected. All because he'd intervened with their mother?

Corinne cleared her throat. "I only came down to let Julian know the gardener will be back tomorrow."

The dueling spikes of relief and alarm in his chest were disturbing to say the least. "She's coming back here, then."

"Yes, I spoke with her on my walk over." Oblivious to his imminent coronary, Corinne gestured to the side of the house facing the vineyard. "I like what she did with the begonias. The guesthouse is visible on the vineyard walking tour, you know. I should have made more of an effort to give it some exterior charm before now."

"Is there no one else you can hire to plant some flowers?" Even as Julian posed the question, he wanted to take it back. Badly. Didn't they agree to be friends, despite the sour taste the word put in his mouth? Someone else digging in the front yard would just be . . . wrong. Very wrong. But the thought of Hallie coming back and taking a Weedwacker to his itinerary unnerved him a great deal. Unnerved *and* excited him. Made tomorrow seem far away.

In other words, nothing made sense anymore.

"There is one other gardener in St. Helena. Owen something, I believe?" Corinne checked the screen of her phone. "But I've already hired the girl."

So Owen was *also* a gardener?

Someone with her exact interests. Were they really friends? Or friends with benefits? Or had Hallie simply referred to Owen as her friend to be professional, when the man was actually her boyfriend?

*Jesus Christ.*

A few brief meetings and she'd already put him in a tailspin.

"Fine. I'll deal with her," he growled, a surprising wave of jealousy curdling the coffee in his stomach. "Is there anything else?

Would you perhaps like to send the high school marching band over to practice outside my window?"

"That's all," Corinne said simply. Then to Natalie, "Welcome home."

Natalie inspected her nails. "Thank you." She wheeled her suitcase out of the room toward the guest room on the opposite side of the kitchen from Julian's. "See you two around."

"Good-bye," Corinne called breezily on her way out of the house.

Leaving Julian standing alone at the counter with a ruined schedule and another visit from the ultimate distraction on the horizon. Why couldn't he wait? "Fuck."

# Chapter Eight

Hallie shifted the truck into park in Julian's driveway, heartbeat wild as a jackrabbit's. There he was, stretching in the front yard. Deep, long movements that had her head tilting to the right unconsciously before she realized it. Wow. She'd never seen those kind of shorts before. They were gray. Loose sweatpants material that stopped just above the knee, a drawstring hanging down over the crotch. Which had to be why her eye was continually drawn there. Among other places. He could have cracked walnuts with those thigh muscles. Squeezed grapes in those butt cheeks. They were on a vineyard, after all.

"You should be locked up," Hallie muttered, forcibly closing her eyes.

A full day had passed since she'd last seen him and—good news—she hadn't been slapped with a restraining order yet. Which was generous of Julian, assuming he'd even found the letter in the first place. But that was the thing—*she had no idea.* And as the queen of avoidance, she would rather not know. Sneaking around for the rest of her life sounded so much easier.

Why did he have to be standing outside? She'd timed her

arrival with the end of his run, hoping she could do her planting while he was in the shower and skedaddle again before he ever knew she was there. Now he was watching her through the windshield with that impeccably raised eyebrow. Because he knew she'd written the letter and found her cutely pathetic, like a puppy? Because he couldn't believe the audacity of her, to show up after such a humiliating display of drunken affection? Or had the Napa winds been in her favor yesterday morning and the letter was halfway to Mexico by now?

*Act natural.*

*Stop smiling like you just got your tax return.*

*You're still waving. It's been, like, fifteen seconds of gesticulation.*

In her defense, Julian was sweaty—and that would turn a nun's head. His white shirt was sodden, straight down the middle, plastering the material to his chest. With the sun beating down on him, she could see through the white cotton to his black chest hair and the hills and valleys of muscles it decorated. God almighty, celibacy was no longer working out for her. At all. A virgin in heat is what she'd become.

She could no longer delay getting out of the truck to face her fate. The dogs were in doggy daycare today, so she couldn't even use them as a diversion. A few words out of his mouth and she would know whether or not he'd found and read the letter, right? Maybe he was even accustomed to women professing their admiration of him and this would be no big deal. They could laugh about it! And then she could go home, curl up, and die.

Hallie alighted from the truck on shaky legs, lowering the rear gate.

"Need some help?" he called.

Did he mean the psychiatric kind? If so, that would indicate he'd read her confession.

Hallie peeked over her shoulder to find him coming toward her with his usual commanding grace, expression inscrutable. Even in her nervous state, every step this man took in her direction turned a screw in a different location. Deep, deep in her belly. Between her legs. Just above the notch at the center of her collarbone. Was her distress obvious to the naked eye? It didn't appear so, since he continued to come closer instead of calling an ambulance.

As soon as she was alone with her phone, she would google, *How Horny is Too Horny?* Those search results ought to be interesting.

"Hi, Julian," she sang. Too loudly.

"Hello, Hallie," Julian said seriously, scrutinizing her closely. Wondering if she was the secret admirer? Or perhaps being fully aware of it already? For all she knew, she'd signed her actual name at the bottom. "What are you planting today?"

Oh. Oh, sweet relief. The wind blew the letter away.

Either that or he was being extremely kind.

Those were the only two options. Obviously he wasn't *interested* in her now, thanks to the sloppy admission. This man would only respond to a sophisticated approach to romance. A colleague introducing him to a young professional at a gala. Something like that. Not a spewing of infatuation scrawled in the back of a spiral notebook. And that was fine, because they'd agreed to be friends, right? Yes. Friends. So thank God for the Napa winds.

"Your mother asked for color, so we're going with some flannel bush," Hallie said. "Those are the yellow flowered plants you see in the bed of my truck. I'm going to come back tomorrow with some Blackbeard Penstemon, too."

"This is going to be an ongoing, long-term project." He nodded once. "I see."

"Yes." The tightness at the corners of his mouth made her heart sink down to her knees. "I know you're working. I won't make a lot of noise."

He nodded again. The wind tripped around them, blowing a curl across her mouth, and he surprised Hallie by reaching for it. She held her breath, lungs seizing almost painfully, but he stopped, drawing his hand back at the last second and shoving it into his pocket with a low curse. "And what are we going to do about you?"

*Breathe before you pass out.* "Me?"

"Yes." That word hung so long in the air, she swore she could see the outline of those three letters. Y-E-S. "You're more . . . disruptive to me than the dogs," he said, almost so quietly that she didn't hear him. "Hallie."

That grinding snap of her name was the equivalent of fingertips raking downward over her breasts. Was he admitting to being attracted to her? Like, out loud? Between that and him almost touching one of her curls, she was in imminent danger of passing out from sheer shock and happiness. "I can't do anything about that. Sorry," she whispered. "However, I am not sorry that I spent last night watching *Time Martians On*. So, you really believe the government is hiding an entire extraterrestrial colony in New Mexico?"

"I do *not* believe any such thing," he murmured, leaning closer. So close she was beginning to grow dizzy. "As I said, they were very liberal with the editing button."

"You're definitely on a watch list, nonetheless," she breathed.

He hummed in his throat. "Did it . . . make you smile? Watching the documentary?"

How could one man be so magnetic? "So much that my face hurt afterward."

A muscle popped in the history professor's cheek. His right hand flexed at his side. And then he forcibly withdrew from the intimacy of their conversation. So abruptly that she almost staggered under the sudden absence of it. "Good." He looked back toward the house, speaking after a few beats of silence. "I apologize for my mood. My sister, Natalie, has become my new roommate. At this rate, maybe it would be better if I rented office space in town."

She swallowed her disappointment. "Maybe it would be."

His attention slid down to her mouth and away, leaving her pulse rapping in her temples. Drunk or not, she'd meant every word of her letter. Her attraction to Julian Vos was twice as potent as before, when he'd been just a memory. A two-dimensional person on the internet. Then he'd gone and delivered a top-notch prank call and saved her from the Tweed Twit. Now she couldn't stop wondering what else he was hiding under the surface.

She *wanted* to know.

Unfortunately, he found her presence disruptive.

Where was the lie? But did he find her distracting in a sexy way? If so, he clearly didn't *want* the distraction. Or perhaps . . . the temptation.

Lord, to be a temptation to Julian Vos. She'd throw out her entire bucket list.

As soon as she got around to making one.

Was it possible she *did* tempt him? The way he continued to catalogue different regions of her body, seeming to get stuck on the area just above her knees, made her wonder if the answer was yes. Unless this burdensome horniness was playing tricks on her. Entirely possible. Lately she'd been finding the angles of her gardening hoe more and more charming.

Flirtatious, even.

A gardening tool could never make her heart race like this, though. The way it had done when he stood up for her at the scene of her—totally justified—UNCORKED crime.

*If she's upset, I'm upset.*

Hallie found herself staring into space at the oddest times, repeating those words. Wondering how seriously he'd meant them or if he'd just been trying to defuse the situation as quickly as possible. It scared her how much she wished for the former. Wished for a man this good and honest and valiant to care about her feelings. Enough to not want them hurt.

She waited for Julian to leave, to go back into the house—and he seemed on the verge of doing so at any second, but he never made the move. Simply continuing to study her as if she were a riddle. "So . . ." Hallie cleared the rust from her throat. "Natalie's visit wasn't planned?"

He scoffed, crossed his wrists at his back. "No. God forbid anyone have a plan."

Ouch. She was definitely not a sexy distraction to him.

"Hey, look at me," she said with determined sunniness. "Here before the kickoff of your fanatical writing sessions."

His eyes narrowed slightly. "Did you plan that?"

"Uh . . . no." That would mean she'd been paying way too close attention. Heh. "My day just kind of started . . . earlier than usual. A squirrel in the backyard set off a howling event before the crack of dawn, and I figured since I was already awake, might as well plant some things."

"And so," he said in a very professorial tone, "without the squirrel's intervention . . ."

"I'd have been here around dinnertime." She hefted one of the larger bushes, taking a moment to smell a yellow bloom. "Between noon and seven, at least."

"You're a menace." He took the bush from her hands, jerked his chin at the rest of the lot, as if to say, *I can take another one.* "No, Natalie showed up out of the blue. We didn't know she was coming in from New York." Grooves formed on either side of his mouth as he glanced back toward the house. "*She* didn't seem to know she was coming."

"Didn't say why?"

"A break from work. No further details."

Hallie hid a smile, but he caught it and raised a questioning eyebrow. "Is it gnawing at you?" she asked. "The vagueness of it all."

"That smile suggests you've answered your own question." Again, his gaze dipped to her mouth, but this time it lingered twice as long. "Then again, you're usually smiling."

He'd noticed her smile?

"Unless I'm masterminding a cheese heist," she responded, breathless.

"Yes, unless that," he said quietly, brows pulling together. "That man hasn't gone near you again, has he?"

His dangerous—almost protective?—tone of voice made her fingers dig into her palms. In a way, he'd claimed her as a responsibility. Someone to look out for. Because that was just so totally Julian Vos, wasn't it? Everyone's hero. Champion of men. "No. I haven't seen him."

"Good."

Trying and failing not to feel flustered, Hallie picked up the other bush, and they walked toward the front yard, side by side, their shadows stretching on the grass to highlight their difference in height. The companionable feeling of carrying plants with Julian made fizz pop in Hallie's bloodstream. Man, oh man, she had it so bad. For a split second, she even felt a niggle of regret that he wouldn't see the letter. God knew she'd never have the courage to say those words in person.

"Um." She swallowed. "Your mother must be thrilled to have both of her children home, though."

A humorless laugh. "I guess you could say it's complicated."

"I know a little about complicated relationships with mothers."

Her gait faltered slightly. Did she just bring up her mother? Out loud? Maybe because she'd been having digital, one-sided conversations with Julian's face on YouTube for so long, she'd forgotten this one was real? Or perhaps talking to him in person seemed surprisingly easier than it was when she fantasized about them riding through a misty vineyard on horseback. Whatever the cause, she'd said the words. It was done. And she certainly didn't expect him to turn with such rapt attention. As if she'd shocked him with something less than teasing or small talk about flowers.

"How do you know?" he asked, setting down the bushes. He took hers and put it on the ground, as well. "Does your mother live in St. Helena?"

"She grew up here. After high school, she ran away to Los Angeles. That's where I was . . ." Her face heated, definitely turned red, and he watched it all happen with a small, fascinated smile. "I was conceived there. Apparently. No further details."

"The vagueness of it all," he said, echoing her earlier words.

"Yes," she said on a big breath. "She tried raising me on her own. We came here, from time to time, when she needed to recharge. Or long enough to soften up my grandmother into loaning her some money. Then we'd be off again. But by the time I reached high school, she finally admitted I would be better off here. I still see her every couple of years. And I love her." Hallie wished she could rub at the discomfort in her throat but didn't want him interpreting the action. Or chalking it up to pain that had been building over a lifetime. "But it's complicated."

A low grunt from Julian. "Why do I get the feeling you've given me the CliffsNotes?"

"Maybe I have. Maybe I haven't." Hallie tried to smile, but it wobbled. "The vagueness of it all," she tacked on in an almost whisper.

Julian stared at her long enough that she started to fidget.

"What?" she finally prompted.

He shifted, drawing those long fingers through his hair, still sweaty and windswept from his run. "I was thinking, in order to make this an even exchange, maybe I should give you the CliffsNotes version of why the Vos family, or what's left of it in Napa, is complicated."

"What's stopping you?"

Mystified eyes flickered over her face, her hair. "The fact that I've completely lost track of time. And I don't do that. Not around anyone but you, apparently."

Hallie had no idea how to respond. Could only stand there and savor the information that she made this man forget the most important component of his world. And how . . . that could either be a great thing or literally the worst possible thing.

"Makes me wonder how long you could make me . . ." He dragged that bottom lip through his teeth while seemingly transfixed by the pulse on her neck. "Lose track of time."

That pulse sped up like a sports car on an open road. "I have no idea," she murmured.

He took a step closer, then another, a muscle bunching in his cheek. "Hours, Hallie? Days?" A raw sound ground up from his throat, one hand lifting to run a single finger down the side of her neck. "*Weeks.*"

*Do I just jump him now?* What was the alternate option? Because her thighs were actually trembling under the onslaught of his full intensity. That exploring gaze. His deep, frustrated tone of voice. Before she could fully convince herself they were talking about the same thing—sex, right?—behind her, a shout went up from the vineyard and they both turned, watching the tops of several heads move down the horizontal rows, all gathering in one place.

She turned back to Julian and found him frowning, his chest lifting and falling a lot faster than usual. "Looks like they're having a problem," he said hoarsely, clearing his throat. After that, he seemed to hesitate, those long fingers flexing. "I should see if they need help."

Nothing happened. He didn't move. The shouting continued.

Hallie shook herself free of the lingering need to get up close and personal with the apparent game-changing invention of sweatpants shorts. Did he seem uncertain about walking into his own family vineyard? Why? "I can come with you," she offered, not sure why. Only that it felt like the right thing to do.

Those eyes cut to hers, held, as he inclined his head. "Thank you."

When Hallie and Julian approached the group of men—and one woman—among the vines, every head swiveled in their direction. Conversation ceased for several seconds.

"Mr. Vos," blurted one of the men, the tan of his cheeks deepening. "Sorry. Were we being too loud?"

"Not at all, Manuel," Julian said quickly, flashing him a reassuring smile. Silence fell again. So long that Hallie looked up at Julian and found his jaw in a bunch, his eyes wandering over the rows of grapes. "It just sounded like something was wrong. Can I do anything to help?"

Manuel looked horrified at Julian's offer. "Oh no. No, we have it under control."

"The destemmer is broken again," the woman said, giving Manuel an exasperated look. "Damn thing breaks once a week." Manuel buried his head in his hands. "What? It does!"

"Does Corinne know about this?" Julian asked, frowning.

"Yes." Manuel hedged. "I can fix the destemmer, but we're already short-staffed. We can't lose one more person out here. These grapes need to come off the vine today or we won't stay on schedule."

"Corinne is stressed enough," said the woman, whipping a handkerchief from her pocket and swiping sweat from her brow. "We don't need another delay."

"My mother is stressed," Julian responded tightly. "That's news to me."

Just like yesterday, when she'd informed Julian of the slow decline of Vos Vineyard, Hallie could see that he truly had no idea. He'd been kept completely in the dark. Why?

“I can call my son home from summer school—” started Manuel.

“No, don’t do that,” Julian broke in. “I’ll pick the grapes. Just show me where to start.” No one moved for long moments. Until Julian prompted Manuel, the apparent vineyard manager. “Manuel?”

“Uh . . . sure. Thank you, sir.” He stumbled in a circle, making a hasty gesture at one of the other men. “What are you waiting for? Get Mr. Vos a bucket.”

“I’ll take one, too,” Hallie piped up automatically, shrugging when Julian gave her a measuring look. “I was going to spend the day in the dirt anyway, right?”

His attention flickered down to her knees. “I think you mean every day.”

“Careful,” she returned. “Or I’ll pinch your grapes.”

Manuel coughed. The woman laughed.

It was tempting to go on staring into Julian’s eyes all day, especially now, when they were sparkling with that elusive humor, but Manuel gestured for them to follow, and they did, trailing behind him several yards into the vines. “This is where we left off,” Manuel said, gesturing to a half-picked section. “Thank you. We’ll have the destemmer up and running in time for the grapes to come in.”

“No need to thank us,” Julian said, hunkering down in front of the vines. He stared at them thoughtfully for a moment, then glanced back at Manuel. “Maybe we could sit down later and you could let me know what else around the vineyard needs attention.”

Manuel nodded, his shoulders drooping slightly with relief. “That would be great, Mr. Vos.”

The manager left, and they got to work, which she would have done much faster if Julian Vos wasn't kneeling beside her in sweaty clothing, with a bristly jaw, his long, incredible fingers wrapping around each grape and tugging. Lord, did she experience that tug everywhere.

*Hide your gardening tools.*

"The quality of these grapes is not what it should be. They've overcropped," Julian said, removing a cluster of grapes from the vine and holding it out to Hallie. "See the lack of maturation in the cane? They weren't given room to breathe."

His professor voice sounded so different out in the open like this, as opposed to pumping from her laptop speakers. "Hey, I just drink the wine," she murmured, wetting her lips. "I don't know the intimate details." He had the nerve to smirk at her while adding the grape cluster to his bucket. "You are one of those professors who gives a test review that covers nothing that ends up being on the actual test, aren't you?"

His gaze zipped to her, with something close to surprised amusement. "The entire body of material should be studied."

"I thought so," she drawled, trying not to let it show how flushed and sensitive his attention made her skin. "Classic *Jeopardy!* enthusiast move."

He chuckled, and she couldn't help but marvel at how different he looked in this setting. At first, he'd been tense, but he relaxed the longer they moved down the row in tandem, plucking grapes from their homes. "What did you do after high school?" he asked her.

"Stayed right here. Went to Napa Valley College. By then, my grandmother had already made me a co-owner of Becca's Blooms, so I needed to stay close."

He hummed. "And did you have professors like me in school?"

"I doubt there are any professors *exactly* like you. But I could usually tell on the first day of a semester which classes I would be dropping."

"Really. How?"

Hallie sat back on her haunches. "Cryptic comments about *being prepared*. Or understanding the *full scope* of the course material. That's how I knew their tests would try to trick us. Also that they were most likely sadists in their spare time."

His laughter was so unexpected, Hallie's mouth fell open.

She'd never heard him laugh before—not like that. So rich and resonant and deep. It appeared he'd startled himself, too, because he cleared his throat and quickly returned his attention to the vine. "It's safe to say you would have dropped my class."

She shifted on her knees beside him, still awash in the sound of his laughter. "Probably."

Yeah, right. She'd have sat front and center in the first row.

"More likely, I would have dropped you the tenth time you showed up late."

Now it was her turn to smirk. "Actually, I managed to make it to most of my classes on time, obviously with some exceptions. It was . . . easier back then. My grandmother wasn't a strict person, but she'd cross her arms and look stern while I set my alarm. I made the effort because I couldn't stand disappointing her."

The rest of her explanation hung unspoken in the air between them.

Showing up on time no longer mattered, because she had no one to disappoint.

No one but herself.

That thought made her frown.

"It helps me to write my schedule down, too," he said. "I would have liked her."

"What happens when you don't write down your plans?" she asked, surprised to see his fingers pause midair, the line of his jaw turning brittle. "Do you still . . . keep them as usual? Or does not seeing them on paper throw you completely off track?"

"Well, I definitely didn't have picking grapes on my schedule today and I seem to be doing fine." In one fluid motion, they crab walked to the right and continued picking. The action was so seamless, they traded a fleeting look of surprise, but neither one of them addressed their apparent grape-harvesting chemistry. "Schedules are vital to me," he continued a moment later. "But I'm not totally thrown off by a deviation. It's more when things sort of . . . move beyond the bounds of my control that I don't . . . maintain the course."

"I hope you're not revealing your rage-control problem while we're alone in the middle of this vineyard."

"Rage control," he scoffed. "It's not like that. It's more of an attack of nerves. Followed by sort of the opposite. I just . . . check out. In this case, I did it when my family needed me most."

Panic attacks. That's what Julian was getting at. And it was telling that he couldn't call them by their proper name. Was he simply irritated by something he saw as a weakness or was he in denial?

"That must be why your colleague's breakdown affected you so much," she said, worried she was overstepping, but unable to help it. Not when they were side by side like this, hidden from the rest of the world by six-foot vines, and she wanted so badly to know the inner workings of his mind, this man she'd been fascinated by for so long. He was nothing like she expected, either, but his flaws didn't disappoint her at all. They actually made her less self-conscious. Less . . . alone in her own shortcomings.

"Yes, I suppose so," he said, finally. Just when she thought the subject was closed, he continued, though the words didn't seem to come naturally. "My father's head would explode if he knew I had my hands on these grapes," he muttered. "He doesn't want me anywhere near the operation of the winery. Because of what I just told you."

It took her a full ten seconds to grasp his meaning. "Because of . . . anxiety?"

He cleared his throat loudly by way of answering.

"Julian . . ." Her hands dropped to her bent thighs. "That's the single most ridiculous thing I've ever heard in my life."

"You didn't see me. That night. The fire. What came after." He used his shoulder to wipe away a bead of sweat, remaining silent for a moment. "He's well within his rights to ask me to keep a distance. This morning, the destemmer breaks down, tomorrow there will be a lost shipment and an angry vendor pulling out. This is not for someone with my temperament, and he did the hard thing by pointing it out."

"What happened the night of the fire?"

"I'd rather not, Hallie."

She tamped down her disappointment. "That's fine. You don't have to tell me. But, look, you handled the broken destemmer just fine. You filled the need as efficiently as you do everything else." Okay, it sounded like she'd been paying way too much attention. Sort of like a secret admirer might? "Or, at least, that's how you seem to me. Efficient. Thoughtful." She swallowed the wild flutter in her throat. "Heroic, even."

Thankfully, he didn't appear to pick up on the notes of swooning admiration in her voice. Instead, a trench formed between his eyebrows. "I think my mother might need help. If she does, she's not going to ask for it." He pulled down a grape cluster, studying it with what she could only assume was an expert eye. "But my father . . ."

"Isn't here." She nudged the bucket toward him. "You are."

He scrutinized Hallie. And went right on looking until she felt her color rising. He seemed almost surprised that getting the worry off his chest hadn't been a waste of time.

When the quiet had stretched too long, Hallie searched for a way to fill it. "It's funny, you know? We're both shackled by these parental expectations, but we're dealing with them in totally opposite ways. You plan everything down to the minute. The very *peak* of adult responsibility. Meanwhile I . . ."

"You what?" he prompted, watching her closely.

Hallie opened her mouth to offer an explanation, but it got stuck. Like one of those king-sized gumballs, trapped behind her jugular. "I, um . . ." She coughed into the back of her wrist. "Well, I guess unlike you, I'm kind of self-destructive, aren't I? I calmed down a lot for Rebecca. *Because* of her. Don't get me wrong, I've never been well organized. Never owned a planner in my life. But lately, I think maybe I've been *intentionally* getting myself into messes . . ."

Seconds passed. "Why?"

"So I don't have to slow down and think about . . ." *Who I am now. Without Rebecca. Which version of myself is the real one.* "Which style of necklace to wear," she said on a laughing exhale, gesturing to the eclectic collection around her neck. There was no chance he was buying the way she made light of their discussion, but thankfully, he just studied her in that quiet, discerning way, instead of prodding her to elaborate. She couldn't even if she wanted to. Not with these troubling revelations still so fresh in her head. "I guess we better finish up," she muttered. "I have a few other appointments today that I'm considering keeping."

"There you go. Already turning over a new leaf," he said quietly, humor flickering in his eyes—and something more. Something that had his lids growing heavy, his focus sinking to her mouth. The notch of her throat. Her breasts. She would normally take offense to that, except when this very disciplined man checked her out inappropriately, as if he couldn't help it to save his life, her vagina was the opposite of offended.

If she leaned a few inches to the left, they would? Could? Kiss?

Weren't they about to kiss when they were interrupted? Or had she imagined it?

Despite her sad lack of make-out partners throughout her life, she could tell he was considering it. Very. Strongly. They'd given up any pretense of harvesting grapes, and he'd wet his lips. Holy shit. This had to be a fever dream, right?

She'd had plenty of those starring this man.

"If I regret one thing about not having a direct hand in making wine at this vineyard . . ." He leaned in, letting out a long, heavy breath into her hair. "It's that I can't watch you drink a glass of Vos wine and know my efforts are sitting on that tongue."

*Oh my God. Oh my God.* Goose bumps made their presence known on every inch of her skin, her blood turning hot and languid. Definitely not a dream. She couldn't have come up with that line to save her life. "I mean . . ." Her voice wobbled. "We could pretend."

"As friends, right, Hallie?" His lips brushed her ear. "Is that what you suggested to me?"

"Yes. Technically."

"My friend who I think about at night in her polka dot bra. That friend?"

Wow. New fave undergarment.

*Focus.* Don't get pulled under. There was a reason she'd suggested friendship, right? Yes. "You need control and punctuality." His teeth closed around her ear, bit lightly and licked the spot, leaving her moaning, her fingers itching to rub her sensitive nipples through the front of her shirt. "I'm like a leaf blower to those things."

"Oh, I'm well aware. I wish I could remember that when I look at you."

Hallie's ears echoed with the beats of her twisting heart. How could she do anything but kiss this man who was equally incredible in the past and present? How?

She turned her head slightly to the left, and his mouth skated across her cheek, getting closer. This was it. Finally. She was going to kiss Julian Vos, and he was even better than her memory. But there was something about the setting that tugged hard at her memory. The last time they'd almost kissed was right here in this very vineyard—a moment that had ruined her forever. And he didn't even recall it. *Still.*

Didn't she have more pride than to pucker up after he'd implied without words that she was so forgettable? Yes. She did. Not to mention . . . she was reeling a little bit after her trip down Self-Discovery Lane. Her frame of mind was scattered. Enough to act in character and do something she might possibly regret. Like give in to her attraction to Julian while her disappointment over his lack of memory still jabbed sharply upward beneath her skin. After acknowledging the root of her recent behavior, she was too aware of those faults to indulge them now. If he just *remembered* her, maybe she could justify turning her head that final inch.

Meeting his parted lips with her own.

But while he regarded her with enough lust to power Canada, there wasn't any of the recognition she needed to make this okay. Furthermore . . . she didn't know if she wanted to be this man's leaf blower. Any kind of relationship with her would be bad for him, wouldn't it? Even if it was strictly physical. Did she want to be bad for him?

"I better go," she said, questioning her decision more with every passing second, especially when the fingers of his left hand curled in the dirt. As if restraining himself from reaching for her. "See you soon, Julian."

"Yes," he rasped, visibly shaking himself. "Thank you for the help."

"Of course." Hallie started to pick her way down the row, but hesitated, looking back to find the professor watching her from beneath two drawn brows. The last thing she wanted was to walk away and leave things awkward or heavy, when talking to him had unlocked something big. When he'd shared so much with her in return. "Hey, Julian?"

"Yes?"

She hesitated for a beat, before blurting, "Abraham Lincoln had anxiety. Panic attacks ran in his family."

His expression didn't change, but he shifted slightly. "Where did you learn that?"

"*Jeopardy!*," she answered, smirking.

A laugh crashed out of him. That was two in the space of one afternoon. She held it to her chest like a cozy sweater, sort of wishing she'd let go of her pride and kissed him after all. What was she going to do about her feelings for this man? "You watch?" he asked.

She turned and walked away, calling over her shoulder, "I've caught it once or twice."

His chuckle was lower this time, but she could feel his gaze on her back, following her out of the vines.

JULIAN FELT DIFFERENT when he walked into the guest room bathroom late that afternoon. Not bothering to turn on the light, he stopped in front of the mirror and observed himself streaked in dirt and sweat from hours spent harvesting grapes. The sun's muffled shine through the frosted glass window backlit his body, so he could barely see his own shadowed expression. Only enough to know it was unfamiliar. A cross between satisfied at having sunk his fingers into the soil of the family land for the first time in years . . . and haggard with hunger.

"Hallie," he said, floating her name into the silent bathroom.

He thickened so fast in his briefs that his dirt-caked hands curled into fists on the sink. Squeezed. With a jerky motion, he turned on the faucet, and after adding several pumps of soap, he scrubbed the earth from his palms, knuckles, forearms. But even watching the soil circle the drain reminded him of the gardener and her dirty knees. Hands that always looked fresh from planting something. The polka dot bra that remained pristine and protected inside of her shirt . . . and how she'd look stripping it off after a long day.

"Fuck. Not again."

Even as he issued that denial, his teeth were clenched, his

breaths coming faster and fogging up the mirror. His brain didn't issue an order to shove down the waistband of his filthy sweatpants shorts, his hands simply knew beating off was inevitable when the polka dot bra came into play. God, the irony that something so frivolous could literally make him pant was galling—but his dick didn't care. It strained free of his waistband, and he gripped it hard, biting off a moan.

Apparently Julian wasn't half as evolved as he'd believed himself to be, because his fantasies about Hallie were increasingly sexist. In a way that was unforgivable. This time, she was stranded on the side of the road with a flat tire and no idea how to change it. She almost definitely had that knowledge in real life. Did his dick want to hear it? Hell no.

It just wanted that reward of Hallie sighing in relief as he wrestled the spare tire out of her trunk and jacked up her vehicle, dogs and all.

*No, wait, the dogs are at home. It's quiet, except for the sound of him tightening the lug nuts. She leans against the truck in nothing but that polka dot bra and jean shorts, watching him work and smiling.*

*Christ, yes. She's smiling.*

Julian groaned while mentally picturing those unbelievable lips spreading into her cheerful grin, propping a forearm against the mirror and burying his face in the crook of his elbow, his opposite hand moving in hard strokes, the base of his spine already beginning to gather and jolt. It wasn't even funny how hard he was going to come. How hard he climaxed *every* time he gave in to his infatuation with Hallie.

Infatuation.

That's what this was.

Infatuation was why, in his fantasy, *he imagined her running to him, throwing her arms around his neck and thanking him breathlessly, her tits barely contained inside the bra now. Just bare and bouncy against his chest, her hand exploring the front of his pants, her eyes widening with appreciation at the length of him, her frilly bra just kind of disintegrating into the ether of his daydream. Along with the jean shorts. Still smiling.*

*She was still smiling as he took those generous tits in his hands and guided them to his mouth, one at a time, sucking her hardening nipples and listening to her whimper his name, her fingers clumsily yanking down his zipper.*

*"Please, Julian," she purred, jacking him off, mimicking his increasingly frantic movements over the bathroom sink. "Don't make me wait for this."*

*"As long as this isn't out of gratitude for changing your tire," he rasped back, making a pitiful attempt to prevent his fantasy self from ditching ethics altogether. "Only because you're hot for it. Only because you want it."*

*"I want it," she moaned, arching her back against the truck. "No, I need you."*

*"I give you what you need, do I?"*

*"Yes," she whispered, twisting a blond curl around her finger. "You make me happy."*

*Lights out.* No matter where the fantasies started, he knew only precious seconds were left when she said those words. *You make me happy.* His harsh inhales and exhales filling the bathroom, he mentally *stooped down, lifted her naked body against the side of the truck, and entered her with a grunt, watching her face transform with total euphoria—this was his dream, after all—her pussy pulsing, gripping him nice and tight. Slippery. Heaven. "Such a good girl. So fucking wet," he praised in her ear, because even the imaginary version of this woman deserved worship, especially when he was driving into her so hard, the encroaching orgasm putting him on that desperate edge. "If this was real life, sweetheart, I'd take better care of you than this."*

*"I know," she gasped, her curls and tits and necklaces shaking, moving with her, part of her. "But it's a dream, so be as rough as you want."*

*"As if I could help it when you make me feel like I'm going to fucking die at any second. Unless I'm inside you. Unless I'm as close as possible to that smile, that voice, your . . . sunlight."*

Julian choked on that truth into the crook of his elbow, stroking fast enough to break the sound barrier, picturing Hallie's legs around his hips, her head thrown back in a throaty call of his name, her pussy cinching up with an orgasm, their mouths latched together while he joined her with a final ram of his hips, impaling her maddening body to the truck.

*"I'd make you come just like this. Hard and wild. That's not a fucking dream, do you understand me?"*

*"Yes," she said on a shaky rush of breath, still trembling against him, even while she blinked up at him with a sweep of eyelashes. "Just like I'm making you come right now."*

A sizzle in his loins was followed by a trap door opening, all of the pressure and sexual frustration escaping. He dug his teeth into the muscle of his forearm, the tension that had been coiling leaving him in sharp waves while he still thought of her. Those eyes and breasts and filthy knees.

Julian couldn't stop thinking of her when it was over, either—

and he was beginning to wonder if a moment's peace from the captivating gardener was nothing more than wishful thinking.

THAT EVENING, HALLIE walked into her house and stopped just inside the door, seeing the mess through fresh eyes. It hadn't always been like this. Not when Rebecca was alive. Not even immediately following her death. Sure, Hallie's heartbeat naturally spelled out the word "clutter" in Morse code, but the disorganization was nearly a hazard now. Precarious stacks of mail and paperwork. Laundry that would never see the inside of her dresser. Dog paraphernalia galore.

Her mind was still stuck in the vineyard with Julian, replaying their conversation over and over.

*I'm kind of self-destructive, aren't I?*

*I think maybe I've been* intentionally *getting myself into messes . . .*

*So I don't have to slow down and think about . . .*

Anything, really. Wasn't that the truth? As long as the whirlwind of trouble continued to spin, she wouldn't have to figure out how to move forward. And as who? As Hallie, the dutiful granddaughter? As one of the many personalities crafted by her mother? Or was she a version of herself she hadn't truly gotten to know yet?

Only one thing was for certain. When she was talking to Julian in the vineyard, she didn't feel as alone. In fact, everything inside of her had quieted and she'd seen the source of her problem, even if she had no earthly clue how to solve it. The strict control Julian kept on himself had grounded her, too, in those stolen moments . . . and she wanted more of them.

It took Hallie a good fifteen minutes to find the notebook

she'd purchased in the stationery shop, thanks to the General partially burying it in the backyard. And another ten minutes to locate a pen that wasn't out of ink. She started off writing a to-do list, but stalled out almost immediately after writing *Clean Out Refrigerator* and *Cancel Subscriptions for Phone Apps You Are No Longer Using.* What she really wanted was to be back in the vineyard, talking to Julian. There was something about his directness, the intent way he listened, and his own willingness to admit his flaws, that made it so easy to dig into her own. To see them clearly.

After today, she was pretty sure Julian was attracted to her. They could talk about personal things like they'd been having heart-to-hearts their entire lives. But she'd been living with her feelings for Julian so long, it was almost hard to be around him knowing his couldn't measure up. It was so impossible, she'd actually suggested they be friends only, just to avoid that potentially painful speech from him.

But here, in her letters, she could let her admiration pour out, almost in a therapeutic way.

And so, instead of being responsible and outlining a way out of #thatclutterlife, she found herself turning to a fresh page.

*Dear Julian . . .*

# Chapter Nine

Julian ran extra hard the next afternoon.

He'd woken with purpose that morning. Plowed through four writing sprints, made himself a protein shake, and now he was focused on beating yesterday's running time.

Yes, that was the plan—and he'd be sticking to it.

Unfortunately, his feet had other ideas. When Julian spied the line outside of UNCORKED, the loitering mass of people blocking the entrance to Corked, he jogged to a stop and frowned. At them. At himself for once again being unable to stay on schedule.

Initially, the unfairness of UNCORKED's success had gotten under his skin. They were making a mockery of the long-standing shop next door and, frankly, insulting the whole process of wine tasting by turning it into a stunt. A thumbing of the nose at the wine industry wouldn't normally bother Julian, except that *everything* these assholes did bothered him now.

Because they upset Hallie.

He loathed her being upset. The real version of her *and* the fantasy version.

She should always be smiling. Simple as that.

Was there something he could do about this?

Back in high school and even slightly beyond, he'd been more inclined to reach out a helping hand to those who needed it. He'd gotten involved. Tried to make himself useful. Somewhere along the line, he'd become focused on his own agenda, never glancing right or left.

Hallie's passionate defense of Corked had really brought that into focus, and he couldn't seem to continue on his merry way this afternoon. If Hallie could burgle hundreds of dollars' worth of cheese, he could certainly make his presence known.

In the process, perhaps he could help Corinne. And Lorna.

After he'd finished picking grapes yesterday, he'd invited Manuel into the guesthouse for coffee and . . . yeah. Suffice it to say, the manager had pulled off Julian's blinders. Corinne was doing an admirable job of maintaining the winery, but quality had begun to fall by the wayside in favor of expediency. Vos Vineyard needed money, so they churned out wine, but the superiority they once claimed had been slowly waning.

His mother had not asked him for help. Maybe that was in deference to his father's wishes or perhaps she didn't have any faith in Julian, either. Whatever the reason, he couldn't stay on the sidelines and watch his family legacy fade into obscurity. Nor did he want his mother carrying this load by herself when he was willing and able to pitch in. Was Hallie's refusal to let UNCORKED bully her friend's shop responsible for this head of steam?

Yes. In a way, perhaps it had reminded him that legacy was important.

Maybe there was a way to give Vos Vineyard a boost *and* make Hallie happy in the process. The possibility of a Hallie Smile over something he did made his pulse knock around.

Refusing to let himself hesitate any longer, Julian made his way through the line of tipsy tourists who would probably benefit from sitting out their next tasting, and walked into Corked. He was greeted by soft music and lighting, and a woman with a lined, smiling face behind the register. She couldn't quite manage to hide the fact that he'd startled her by simply walking in.

"Hello," sang the woman, who had to be Lorna. "Are you . . . here for the tasting?"

"Yes," he lied briskly, perusing the shelves, relieved and maybe even slightly prideful to see a wide selection of Vos wines for sale. "What is on deck today . . . ?"

"Lorna. This is my shop." She emerged from behind the counter, fussing with her hair. "To be totally honest with you, I didn't think anyone was showing up, so I haven't even set up glasses." She rushed to the back of the store, clearly excited to have some life within the shop's walls. "Choose any bottle you want and we'll crack it open. How about that?"

Julian nodded after her, continuing his trip up and down the aisles, circling back to the front of the store. Behind the register was a black-and-white picture of Lorna as a young woman holding hands with a man outside on the sidewalk, the Corked storefront in the background. The man was her husband, most likely. Both of them looked so optimistic. Proud. Ready to take on the future. No inkling that someday a disco ball would be stealing their business. No wonder Hallie was fighting the decline of Corked so fiercely.

That sealed it. He was going to be the best customer this woman ever had.

As he waited for the older woman to set up two glasses and produce a corkscrew from her apron, Julian selected a Vos Vineyard

Cab from 2019. Ideas to aid Lorna formed, one after the other. Some bigger than others. But he thought it best not to overwhelm the woman all at once.

She poured him a half glass of wine, and he took a brief moment to mourn his productivity for the rest of the day. "Thank you. Are you joining me?"

"Don't mind if I do," she said, eyes twinkling.

Yes, it was becoming quite clear why Hallie felt the need to rob and vandalize in this woman's honor. Kindness rolled off her in waves. "Great." He sipped the wine, holding it on his tongue for several counts before swallowing. "Wonderful. I'll take three cases."

She almost spat out her wine. "*Three cases?*"

"Yes, please." He grinned. "I'll pay now and pick them up later, if that's all right." Seemingly in a daze, she took the American Express he handed over, but like any smart businesswoman, she beelined for the register before he could change his mind. "With an established shop like this, you must have local regulars."

"Lately, everyone seems so busy. And it has become increasingly easy to order wine online." Her tone retained its pep, but he could see wilting beneath the surface. "I do have some loyal customers, though, that refuse to let me down."

"Oh? Who might those be?" Good God, he was fishing. "Maybe I know them."

"Well, there's Boris and Suki. A lovely couple that come in every other day for a bottle of their favorite Shiraz. There's Lavinia and Jerome—they own and operate Fudge Judy and make the most *delicious* Boston cream pie donuts. But I'd have to say my most loyal regular is the granddaughter of one of my dearest friends, God rest her soul. A local gardener named Hallie."

Lorna brightened. "Actually, she's close to your age. A bit younger, maybe."

Yeah. No mistaking that his heart had picked up speed. "Hallie Welch?"

Lorna ripped the credit card receipt with a flourish. "That's her! Did you go to school with Hallie, then?"

Sore spot prodded, he hid a grimace. Why could he not *remember*?

"Yes. High school." He took a casual sip of his wine, set it down, twisted the stem. "She's doing some gardening work for my family at the moment, actually. Small world."

"Oh my, isn't that a coincidence?" laughed Lorna over the register, her lips turning down at the corners after a beat. "Poor girl took it very hard when Rebecca passed. I don't think she knew up from down. Came to the funeral in two different shoes and everything."

The sensation of having his chest stomped on was so visceral, he actually looked down to make sure nothing was there. Hallie in mismatched shoes at a funeral, not knowing up from down, made him feel very helpless. Was she better now? Or just better at hiding her grief?

"Of course, she does have some very good friends to see her through. She's joined at the hip with Lavinia. And of course there's that lovely Owen—but I doubt you know him, he moved here about—"

"Owen. And Hallie. Have they . . ." He relaxed his grip before he could snap the stem of the wineglass. "Dated?"

The older woman went right on smiling, clearly unaware there was a shiv to his throat. "Yes, I think they have. Casually, though." She spoke in an exaggerated whisper out of the corner of her mouth. "Although I think Hallie is the one who keeps putting on the brakes."

"Oh." Tension escaped him like air leaving a balloon. "Interesting." He barely restrained himself from asking Lorna *why* Hallie continued to put on the brakes. Did Owen have any annoying habits? Did he double dip, perhaps? Any reason to validate Julian's irrational dislike of the man would be welcome. But he'd gone far enough with this line of questioning. Going any further would be considered stalking in at least twenty states.

No more inquiries about Hallie. But . . . the whole making-her-smile thing was still on the table, wasn't it?

"Lorna, do you happen to have business cards of any kind?"

"I'm afraid not. I've always relied on foot traffic. It used to be enough to have a sign outside that said 'free wine tasting.'"

"As it should be." He twisted the glass right to left. "I would be happy to make you up some cards. Maybe . . ." It had always been rare for him to drop the Vos name, but there was no way around it in this instance. "My family owns a vineyard here in St. Helena. Maybe we could give cards for Corked out to our visitors. If they bring in the card, ten percent off their first bottle? Does something like that sound agreeable to you?"

"Your family owns a vineyard?" She handed him back the credit card, along with his receipt to sign. A blue pen. "Isn't that nice. Which one?"

He coughed into a fist. "Vos Vineyard."

Lorna lurched against the tasting table, nearly upsetting the open wine bottle. "Vos . . . Are you the son? Julian?" Her mouth opened and closed. "I haven't seen you in years. Forgive these old eyes, I didn't recognize you." She shook her head a moment. "And you would really offer to hand out cards for me?"

Julian nodded, grateful she didn't seem inclined to make a huge deal out of his last name. "Of course." She chewed her lip as if waffling. Perhaps scared to be hopeful? So he added, "Your shop is a landmark. If you haven't been here, you haven't been to St. Helena."

The older woman's eyes sparkled at him. "You're damn right."

That competitive streak of his was ticking like a metronome. "Actually, I'll take a few bottles to go now." He winked at her. "In case I get thirsty on the walk home."

Which is how Julian found himself in the neighboring yoga studio eight minutes later, handing bottles to the men and women emerging from class. "Lorna sent these," he explained to the sweaty and confused people.

They traded perplexed glances. "Who?"

"Lorna," he said again, as if they should know. "From Corked. Next door. The longest-standing wine store in St. Helena. No trip to Napa is complete without it." He smiled at the girl behind the counter. "I'll drop off some business cards for you to hand out."

When Julian left the yoga studio and restarted his watch, his shoulders were lighter. He continued down Grapevine Way for a while, past the health spa and several cafés. As he got farther from the center of town, the shops he passed were more for the locals. Pizzerias and a dance school for children. A car wash and a donut shop named after Judge Judy, which he could not find fault with. And that's where he turned right and cut down the wooded path leading to Vos Vineyard. Another three-quarters of a mile and he'd be at the guesthouse. Sure, he had a slight wine buzz, but he wouldn't let it postpone his shower, and then it would be straight to work—

Up ahead, a square, white object, totally out of place among the greenery, snagged his attention. Julian stopped so abruptly, his sneakers kicked up a dust cloud.

No way. Not again.

Another envelope. With his name on it. Stuck in the crack of a tree stump.

Standing in the center of the path, he looked around, positive he'd find Natalie hiding and snickering behind a bush. Apparently she hadn't gotten the prank out of her system yet. But she must have come and gone a while ago, because he was quite obviously alone there, no sound save the afternoon breeze sweeping down off the mountain. What kind of bullshit had his sister written this time?

Shaking his head, Julian plucked the letter out of the stump—and immediately noticed the handwriting was the same as last time, but more controlled. And the further he got into the correspondence, the more it became clear Natalie had *not* written it.

Dear Julian,

There is something so easy about an anonymous letter. It puts less pressure on both of us. There is less fear of rejection. I can be totally honest, and if you never write back, at least I let out the words that have been trapped in my head.

They're your problem now—sorry.

(Forget what I said about less pressure.)

When you run down Grapevine Way in the afternoons, a solitary figure on a mission, I wonder how you feel about your solitude. If it's the same *way I feel about being alone. There's so much space to think. To consider where I've been and where I'm going. I wonder if I'm who I'm meant to be or if I'm just too distracted to keep evolving. Sometimes it's overwhelming. Do you ever get overwhelmed with the silence or are you as content in the solitude as you seem?*

*What would it be like to know you completely?*

*Does anyone know you completely?*

*I've been loved by someone for all my faults. It's a wonderful feeling. Maybe you want that for yourself. Or maybe you don't. But you're worthy of it, in case you're wondering.*

*This is getting too personal coming from a stranger. It's just that I don't truly know you. So I can only be honest and hope something inside you . . . hears me.*

*I'm sorry if you found this letter strange or even terrifying. If so, please know that I meant the opposite. And if nothing comes from this, your main takeaway should be that someone out here thinks about you, in the best way possible, even on your worst day.*

*Secretly Yours*

Julian finished the letter and immediately read it again, the tempo of his pulse increasing steadily. This letter was nothing like the last. It was more serious in tone. Earnest. And despite the oddness of finding a letter on his jogging path, he couldn't help but respond to the wistful tone woven into the words. No way Natalie wrote this, right? He couldn't imagine his sister taking an emotional deep dive like this, even for a joke.

The envelope was bone-dry, meaning it hadn't been there since last night. The morning dew would have dampened it, at the very least. Although noon had come and gone, Natalie was asleep when he left for the run, plus there had been two empty wine bottles on the kitchen counter, neither of which he'd had a single glass from. He supposed his sister might have battled through a hangover to prank him—she'd never lacked dedication. And she would have had opportunity, since he'd run for nearly half an hour, plus his pit stop at Corked.

Maybe he just *hoped* Natalie hadn't been the one to write the letter, because the damn thing had unexpectedly struck a chord with him. It was written by the same person who penned the last letter, meaning their interest was romantic in nature.

*What would it be like to know you completely?*

The closer he got to home, the more that question circled his head.

*I wonder if I'm who I'm meant to be or if I'm just too distracted to keep evolving.*

Four years had passed since he'd been home, and he'd barely registered the length of time. Not until he'd arrived in St. Helena to find his mother keeping the winery's troubles a secret. His sister going through a crisis, and he didn't even know the barest details. What if his coping mechanisms weren't helping him anymore?

What if keeping rigid schedules was harming him . . . and his relationships, instead?

Julian entered the house and immediately strode toward his sister's room.

She was asleep. Sprawled out, an empty wineglass on the floor near her dangling hand.

When the scent of alcohol hit him, he closed the door again with a wince.

If she'd left the house this afternoon with all of the alcohol in her system, she would have either burst into flames or passed out somewhere along the trail.

Which meant he actually had a secret admirer in town. The first letter had been real. Should he write back?

*Jesus.*

He should forget about the letters. Cast them aside as a disruption. But he continued to think about the questions she'd posed in the second one. He'd read the letter only twice, and he could already mentally recite it, word for word.

How odd.

*What if Hallie is my secret admirer?*

No. Impossible. She was not a serious romantic interest, despite the amount of time he spent fantasizing about her, leading to an embarrassing amount of breaks being taken from work to relieve himself of sexual frustration.

*Julian, I don't think there are two more different people in this whole world.*

Hadn't she said those very words? Not to mention, she'd been the one to suggest a relationship based purely on friendship. He'd never met a more bluntly honest person. If she was his admirer, she would simply tell him, wouldn't she? She didn't lie about her faults—no, she practically bragged about showing up late and flying by the seat of her pants.

Or her annoyingly tight cutoffs, as it were.

Whoever was on the other side of these letters, there would be no writing back, despite his being reluctantly intrigued. Something about establishing communication with this person didn't sit quite right—but exploring that too deeply could come only at his own peril, so Julian quickly stuffed the letter back into his pocket with the intention of forgetting about it.

Again.

# Chapter Ten

If Hallie leaned just so to the right and stretched, she could see Julian through his office window. Working diligently, with his ticking stopwatch and rigid shoulders. The sky was clouded today, so the lamplight from the house spilled across the grass, highlighting the mist in the air. It was definitely getting ready to rain. She should absolutely get going. But she wouldn't have this view of Julian Vos and his cleft chin from home, so she risked the inclement weather by planting extra slowly, spreading the soil with slow-motion hands.

Their eyes met through the glass, and she quickly looked away, pretending to be enthralled by the blooming stem of a snapdragon, while her belly continued to take one long skydive. Had he found the second, decidedly more coherent letter? She'd been working in the guesthouse garden for two days and they hadn't spoken, so she couldn't get a read. But he definitely hadn't written back. She'd checked. And that couldn't be a good sign, right?

Maybe he'd marched her letter directly to the police and asked them to handle it. Maybe they were forming a task force right now. Find and eliminate the rogue secret admirer before any more men were forced to read about feelings.

Thunder rolled loudly overhead.

Once again, their gazes danced toward each other through the mist-covered window, and he raised a very sharp eyebrow. As if to say, *Do you not have a weather app on your phone?*

Or eyeballs?

Finally, he lifted a phone to his ear. She assumed he had to take a call until her own phone started vibrating in her back pocket. "You're calling me from inside?"

He hummed, and the low sound was like a soft shock down her spine. "Shouldn't you be wearing a jacket? Or maybe calling it a day altogether, considering it's about to pour?"

"I'm almost done. These lilacs just can't decide where they want to be." Julian's head fell back on his shoulders, eyes imploring the ceiling for sanity. "You know I can see you, right?"

Despite Julian's frustration, his lips tugged. "Maybe you could try something new and space out the flowers evenly—"

"This just in: they want to be directly behind the daisies."

His laugh was like the sizzle of water on a hot stove. There was something intimate about it. About the storm and his lamplit window. "Are you enjoying yourself?"

"Maybe a little." She fell forward on hands and knees, securing the lilacs in place and patting the earth around the edges. "I don't mind working in the rain, actually. The one responsible thing I've done recently is buy a waterproof phone case. Did you know there is no dog slobber damage clause in the Apple contract?" The raindrops on the window didn't quite obscure the twitch of his lips. "If you need to get back to writing, we can hang up."

"No," he answered, as if involuntarily. "How is Corked doing these days?"

Hallie paused and studied Julian. Was he really not going to take credit for buying three cases of his own family's wine? Apparently not. He was frowning at the computer screen, no sign of the good deed visible in his expression.

She'd skidded into Corked for the afternoon tasting, only to find that Julian had not only stopped in and had a glass of wine with a thoroughly charmed Lorna, but he'd dropped enough cash to pay this month's rent. As if she needed another reason to send him love letters—of which there would be only two. Two, tops.

Unless he answered.

Which he definitely didn't seem inclined to do.

Maybe a third would nudge him?

"Corked is doing slightly better than usual, actually. Lorna has more of a spring in her step the last couple of days, which is nice to see," she said breathily, her hands working the earth. "I'm not sure why, though. She's been very tight-lipped. Maybe she landed an investor. Either that or she's got a boyfriend."

He studied her through the window, trying to either determine if she was joking or perhaps deduce whether or not she'd been made aware of his generosity. When she only kept her features schooled, he cleared his throat. "And this makes you . . . happy? Lorna having more spring in her step?"

Did he appear hopeful, or was that her imagination? "Yes. It does."

"Hmm." Apparently the topic was dismissed, because he leaned forward to look up at the sky and shifted in his chair. "There is going to be a downpour any second now, Hallie. Come inside," he said, without thinking. "I don't want you cold."

Her hands paused slightly at his deeper tone.

She looked up, their eyes latched, and her oxygen grew scarce. Did he have any idea how his caring affected her? It was a glimpse at the man beneath. The man she'd always known was there, but who had been buried in his adulthood. Not so deep that she couldn't see it. Couldn't wish to dig and dig and wrap herself in his uniquely refined kindness.

"Do I need to come out there and get you?" he prompted.

Mother Nature sent thunderheads rolling across the sky above them. Or maybe that turbulence was moving straight through her, reverberating in her bent thighs and tightened tummy muscles. She was the human version of a plucked tuning fork. Bottom line, if she stood up right now, her arousal might not be visible . . . but she couldn't guarantee it. Who could hide *this* potent a feeling? Better to stay crouched, maybe drown in a flash flood.

"Very well," he clipped, hanging up before she could . . . what? Tell him not to bother coming to collect her? Was she really going to pretend that she didn't want to go inside his house to wait out this romantic rainstorm?

A screen door opened in the distance, and her heart accelerated, beating even faster when Julian came into view. Just in time for the sky to make an ominous tearing sound and condensation to begin falling in a spiky deluge.

"Come on," he said, reaching down to take her hand, his warm palm sliding against hers, his fingers compressing around hers, leading to what felt like an electrical charge straight to her hormones. Leaving her tools to fall where they may, she allowed herself to be pulled along the front path and into the cool, dry interior of the house.

Julian guided her into the kitchen and stopped, looking down at their joined hands, his thumb ever-so-slightly brushing over the pulse at the small of her wrist. Could he feel it pounding like McConaughey on a pair of bongos? Did she want him to? Ultimately, a muscle popped in his cheek and he let her go, retreating to the opposite side of the island like last time, with his hands propped wide, dress sleeves rolled up to his elbows. Oh Lord, the forearms. There they were. In her fifteen years of fantasizing about this man, she'd definitely neglected one of his best features. Going forward, she needed to do better.

She opened her mouth to make a joke about Californians never being prepared for rain. But she stopped short, a flash of cold running up her arms. There on the marble counter sat the envelope containing the secret admirer letter.

No.

*Both of them.*

They were in a neat stack, naturally, with a brass duck paperweight on top.

Oh Lord. He'd gotten them. Both letters. Read them with his eyes and brain and forearms. They sat between them like an accusation. Was she too blindsided by her crush to realize she'd just walked into a confrontation? Her pulse picked up. She needed to figure out what was going on here and fast.

"Is Natalie home?" she asked, glancing toward the back of the house.

"No. On a date, I believe."

"Really? Good for her. In the rain and everything."

"Yes." He seemed to blink himself out of a trance. "She met someone at the gas station of all places. I don't understand how that happens. I've never had a conversation with anyone while filling my tank, but she seems to have built-in . . . what do my students call it? Tinder?"

"Her sixth sense is locating single people. That's an enviable skill."

His left eye twitched. "You wish you were better at asking out men?"

"Sure." Were they having the most ironic conversation possible considering the letters sitting beneath the mallard? Or had he intentionally led them here in preparation for a secret admirer intervention? "Don't you?" she managed through her dry throat. "Wish you were better at coming right out and telling someone that you're interested?"

He considered her from across the island.

Thunder boomed outside.

Though she couldn't see the lightning that came a few moments later, she imagined it zigzagging across the sky. Much like the veins in his forearms.

*My God, pull yourself together.*

"I don't usually have a problem with that," he said, narrowing his eyes.

There you have it, folks. Julian Vos didn't have any issues telling the opposite sex he was interested. Was this a gentle letdown? *Nice letters, but I'm into scholars who like to attend astronomy lectures instead of getting drunk and eating linguine.*

"My problem mostly comes later in the acquaintance," he continued. "When it's time to state my intentions. I worry they'll become attached when I have no intention of doing the same. I don't want to promise something and not deliver. That's worse than being . . ."

"Being what?"

"I don't know. Disconnected." He was beginning to look troubled. "I tend to remain disconnected with people, because it's easier to focus. On work. On keeping time. It's never bothered me until now. I never meant to become so unattached in all my relationships. Only romantic ones. But my sister. I don't know what's going on with her and . . ." He caught himself with a hard headshake. "Sorry, I shouldn't be bothering you with this."

"I don't mind." In fact, with his halting revelation still hanging in the air, she could barely stand the pressure in her chest. "You're worried about Natalie?"

"Yes," he answered succinctly. "She's always been so good about taking care of herself. Coming home would be a last resort for her."

"Have you tried talking to her about it?"

After a moment, he shook his head, those bourbon eyes finding her from across the island. "What would *you* say? To make her comfortable enough for that?"

It meant something that Julian was asking her this. The tentative manner in which he posed the question told her exactly how often he requested advice. Next to never. "I would tell her you're glad she's here with you."

Julian's spine straightened more than it already was. "That's it?"

"Yeah." Hallie nodded, folding her hands in front of her. "But before you say it, make sure you mean it. She'll be able to tell the difference."

His lips moved slightly, as if repeating her advice to himself.

This man. She'd been right about him. All along.

He was heroic.

Somewhere along the line, had he convinced himself of the opposite?

It took all of her self-control not to cross to the other side of the kitchen, go up on her tiptoes, and press their mouths together.

But . . . would that be unethical now? He was opening up to her without knowing she'd written him those letters. Letters he'd obviously read and kept.

His gaze shifted down to the letters briefly, then away. "Someone recently asked me how I feel about my solitude. They said, 'There's so much space to think. To consider where I've been and where I'm going. I wonder if I'm who I'm meant to be or if I'm just too distracted to keep evolving.'" A wild rush of butterflies carried through Hallie, winging up into her shoulders and throat. Did he just quote her letter from *memory*? "That made sense to me."

Oh dear. This wasn't an intervention.

He'd read the letters . . . and liked them. They'd resonated with him.

Hallie's first reaction to that was a burst of joy. And relief. This distant bond she'd always felt with Julian . . . maybe it wasn't a figment of her imagination after all.

"That makes sense to me, too," Hallie rasped into the kitchen, the sound of rain almost drowning her out. Wait. Now she was having a full conversation with him about the contents of her letter. That wasn't good. She'd never intended this, and she needed to come clean right now—

"Lately I've been wondering if I'm so trapped inside this need for structure that it's ceased to have any meaning at all," Julian said, looking just beyond her shoulder. "I haven't used minutes or hours on anything besides my job, and does that mean I've essentially . . . wasted some, if not all of it?" His attention fell to the note. "Maybe I haven't evolved, as this person says. Maybe I've been too distracted to grow, when I thought I was being so productive."

She related to that so hard, she almost reached across the island for a high five. "Sort of like, as you get older, you start taking on myriad responsibilities that make you an adult. But really, they're just distracting you from the things that matter. And then you've misspent your time, but there's no way to get it back."

"Exactly."

"When your colleague had his breakdown, you started to wonder about this?"

"Almost immediately. He should have been somewhere else. A healthier place for him. With his family. And then I thought, is this where I'm supposed to be?" He tucked his tongue against the inside of his cheek, examined her. "Do you ever lose sleep wondering if you're in the wrong place or timeline?"

*You have no idea.* "Sure," she whispered, wondering if he could read her mind. Maybe he could. After all, there was something magical charging the air in that moment, in the nearly dark kitchen with a thunderstorm rioting outside. Standing with this staid and private man while he confessed his inner turmoil. There was nothing she could do to stop herself from leaning into the intimacy. Going after it with both hands.

Not even her conscience, apparently.

"The first fourteen years of my life, I was on the road with my mother. We were never in the same place longer than a week. And my mom . . . she's kind of this beautiful chameleon. She likes to say midnight transforms her back into a blank canvas, like Cinderella and the pumpkin. She became whatever her current love interest wanted. If she changed bands, went from soul to country, she'd go from a lounge act to a cowgirl. She evolved constantly, and she . . . took me with her. On the road *and* on these makeovers. She redesigned me over and over. I was punk,

I was girly, an artist. She'd kind of impress these different identities on me, and now . . . sometimes I don't know if this is the right one, if this is actually *me*. It felt right when my grandmother was here."

Julian's gaze dipped to her multitude of necklaces. None of them made sense together, but she could never decide which ones to wear. Throwing them all on got her out of the house and away from the mirror fastest. The simple act of picking a piece of jewelry or restricting flowers to certain beds of soil felt like major decisions.

So she flaunted them, committing to everything and, thus, to nothing.

"Anyway," she said quickly. "For what it's worth, I think you're in the right timeline. You were there to help your colleague in a moment of need and it propelled you here at the same time as your sister, who also needs help. Not to mention the vineyard. That can't be an accident." A smile stretched her lips. "If you weren't in this timeline, who would the perpetually late, unsystematic gardener be driving crazy these days?"

For some reason, that drew his brows together.

And he started around the island. Toward Hallie.

Her breath came out in a short burst, and she couldn't seem to replace the expelled oxygen. Not with Julian looking at her like that, his jaw locked, each step purposeful, his gorgeous features arranged in a near scowl. He reached the closest corner of the island and turned. Continued. Then, oh Lord, he moved in close enough to Hallie that her head tipped back automatically to maintain their searing eye contact.

"I don't like being driven crazy, Hallie."

"I sort of noticed."

He propped his hands on either side of her on the island. Stepped closer. Enough that his body heat warmed her breasts, his jagged exhale stirring her hair. "I also spend a lot of time wondering who else you're driving crazy."

Hallie melted back against the island. In theory, she wasn't a woman who found jealousy attractive. At least, she didn't think so. No one had ever displayed envy where she was concerned. That she *knew* about, anyway. Still, she shouldn't like it. She also shouldn't like the smell of gasoline. Or cold pizza crust dipped in barbeque sauce, but explain the word "shouldn't" to her taste-buds. Explain "shouldn't" to the hormones that went absolutely wild at the knowledge that he'd spent his precious minutes and hours thinking about where she was.

And with whom.

*You can like it. Just don't reward him for it.*

"Keep wondering, I guess."

His right eyebrow went up so fast, it nearly made a *whoosh*ing sound. "Keep wondering?" A blast of lightning briefly turned the kitchen white. "That's what you're . . . giving me . . ."

When he didn't continue, she prompted him. "What's wrong?"

Several seconds passed. His chest started to move faster, up and down, his head ticking slightly to the right. Recognition slowly registered in his eyes, and he cursed low and sharp under his breath. "Your hair wasn't curly back then."

What was he talking about? She had no idea, although her pulse was beginning to zigzag, as if it knew something was coming. "Back when?"

"That's how we know each other." He eagerly traced her features with his gaze. "We went for a walk together in the vineyard. The night my sister threw that party."

She blinked rapidly, pulse kicking into an even faster gallop. "Wait, you . . . remember?"

Julian nodded slowly, perusing Hallie as if seeing her for the first time.

*This* decade, at least.

"My friend straightened my hair that night. She thought it made me look older." A corner of her lips jumped. "It fooled you. Until I fessed up to being in your sister's grade."

"Right." His mouth opened and closed. "I thought you had to be from a different school. I never saw you in the halls after that. Anywhere."

"My mother took me back on the road." God, she sounded like she'd been running on a hamster wheel. "It wasn't until you'd left for college that I settled into St. Helena permanently with my grandmother."

"I see." A shadow crossed his face. "I'm sorry I didn't remember. My sister threw that party without permission. Without planning or telling me first. I tend to . . ."

"What?"

This appeared hard for him to say out loud. "I've been known to check out after I lose control of a situation. It makes my memory spotty. Not to mention the alcohol I drank . . ."

Knowing what she did about him now, that made sense, though she suspected there was a much more elaborate explanation behind *checking out*. "You're forgiven."

A handful of heavy seconds ticked by.

"Am I?" Slowly, he crowded her closer to the island. Their chests pressing together, her head tipping back. Rain pounded the windows. "I'd like to be one hundred percent sure that you don't hold my cloudy memory against me." His breath stirred her hair. "I want to feel you forgive me. I want to taste it in your mouth."

*Mother Mary,* he had a way with words. "Maybe that's a good idea," she managed, legs almost losing strength completely. "For the sake of closure and all."

"Right," he rasped. "Closure."

And then his fingers were sliding into her hair. He rubbed her curls between the pads of his thumb and index finger, as if fascinated. His warm breath accelerated so close to her mouth, and it was a heady thing, their inhales and exhales matching, quickening, their gazes linking. Holding. His was glazed. Heavy. He looked at her mouth as though it would anchor him in a storm, and he went for it desperately.

Hallie's lower back flattened against the island, and he quickly moved with her, rubbing his thumb against her cheek, as if apologizing for coming on so strong. But he didn't seem capable of slowing down, either. He took rough pulls of her mouth, tilting her head sideways and taking deep tastes. Thorough and savoring. *My God.*

Their tongues plunged and collided, causing her to whimper and Julian to groan, and that sound raced in her blood like rocket fuel. In seconds, this had gotten completely out of control, and Hallie loved being punted straight out of reality. Craved the unpredictability of his mouth and the unexpected courses taken by his hands. His right one left her curls to scrub down her spine, just like he'd done in the vineyard fifteen years earlier, but now the man gripped fabric and pulled her body closer. Their bodies just kind of melted, like liquefied metal being poured into a mold. Curves fit into peaks, muscle flexed against softness.

"I like it when you're standing in one place," he growled,

breaking the kiss so they could suck down heavy pulls of air. "When you hold still."

"Don't get used to it," she whispered breathily.

"No?" His mouth opened on her hairline. "Would you like me to unzip these shorts so you can move better, Hallie?" She found herself nodding before he even finished posing the question. At the mere suggestion they get rid of the denim barrier between them, her shorts became unbearable. An offense. Looking her right in the eye, he lowered her zipper and shoved them down her hips, a *whoosh* followed by the material hitting the floor, the buttons making a metallic clink. After several breaths lost among the thunder, his hand curled around Hallie's wrist, guiding her own hand to her upper thigh. Higher, until her fingertips almost met her panties.

Sensations bombarded her. Julian's rain-and-spice scent. His quickening breaths near her ear. The chafe of his dress shirt on the cotton of hers. When his chest shifted to one side, then the other, it rubbed her nipples to life and electricity snapped out into her limbs.

"If you can't hold still . . ." He brought her fingertips another inch higher—and flush with her sex, her wetness evident through the material of her panties. "Make it count."

The ground rippled beneath her feet. "You want me to—"

"Touch yourself. Yes." His open mouth raked over her ear. "It's only fair, since I've been fucking my hand on a regular basis since you started working outside my window."

Was this *real life*?

How many times had she brought herself to orgasm while thinking about this man? Having him not only watch but *order* her to do it made her knees shake. Sensory overload. She kind of wished she'd imagined this scenario sooner. Wished she'd known long before now what it would feel like to have Julian slide a finger into the waistband of her panties and tug them down, slowly, to the tops of her thighs, exposing her sex to the storm-lit kitchen, then re-brace his hands on the island where he had her body pressed. Waiting.

Hallie bit her lip, fingers twitching—and that alone made him groan. Yes, this buttoned-up professor groaned even before she started tracing the damp seam of her flesh with her middle finger, raking that digit up and down until her folds parted organically. In need of more. She all but bloomed for him on a rush of wetness, her fingers gathering the moisture and spreading it over her clit, her gasp mingling with the sounds of rumbling thunder.

"Fuck me," he muttered into her ear. "You do this in your bed at home."

Not a question. A statement. So she didn't answer. Couldn't.

Her head fell back, neck strength depleted, fingers rubbing eagerly.

"Do you ever go to bed with those dirty knees, Hallie? Do you climb onto the mattress facedown and open those filthy knees wide in your sheets, like you do on the front lawn? God, I'd fucking pay to see it."

*Holy mother of...*

The words this man gritted out like a modern-day barbarian into her ear were not what she'd expected. Not what she'd imagined him saying for years and years while feverishly writhing in her bed. In her fantasies, Julian usually told her she was beautiful—and that had been enough to bring her to climax? God, how boring. He was giving her dirty *knees* talk. He'd pulled down her underwear and asked her to masturbate in his kitchen.

In the future, her spank bank was going to be lit.

But she didn't want to consider the future right now. There was only this man's harsh pants in her ear, those intense eyes locked on the actions of her fingers. Two of them now that speared wetly through her flesh to stimulate her clit and, really, it was *beyond* stimulated. If she gave it three seconds of concentration, she could peak, no questions asked.

Something else continued to circulate in her mind, though, preventing her from giving her pleasure full concentration. What he'd said. *It's only fair, since I've been fucking my hand on a regular basis since you started working outside my window.*

Okay, she'd fantasized about Julian going solo.

Her imaginary sex life hadn't been *that* boring.

Would she ever get another chance to see it live? This storm, the happenstance of being in his front yard when it started to rain and having this forced intimacy . . . there was a high chance it would never occur again. Her desire to watch Julian touch himself was more than just a desperate need to satisfy her curiosity or gather fantasy fodder for the future. She felt a bone-deep welling of responsibility, of need, for him to find satisfaction, too. If he didn't come with her where she was going, it wouldn't be as fulfilling.

"You, too," Hallie managed, moaning when his mouth stamped over hers. Not kissing. Just magnetized. Drawn instantly by the fact that she'd spoken. "Please."

A beat passed. Then, lips still clinging, he reached down and unfastened his belt, lowering his zipper. She saw none of it, but the metal zing alone was enough to make the muscles in her tummy tighten, her bare toes curling on the floor.

"I had to put this on my schedule. Right there on my notepad.

*Beating off to Hallie.*" His tongue traced her bottom lip. "I've already done it once today."

"You wrote those words down?" she said, gasping when he nipped at her jaw.

"No, I just wrote your name. My cock knew what it meant."

Leaning back slightly, Julian looked Hallie right in the eye and reached into the opening of his pants, grunting through his teeth, eyelids drooping over the first stroke—

And Hallie's orgasm blew in without warning. Like a door flying open during a hurricane. She whimpered, legs turning to jelly, and very nearly dropped into a heap on the floor. But Julian moved fast, supporting her with his upper body, his mouth heating her neck while his hand never stopped moving. Hallie had never wished more fervently for better camera angles in her life, because she couldn't see the way Julian guided his erection up into the juncture of her thighs. Not touching her. Just stroking himself faster, faster, into the opening between her legs, just above her tugged-down panties, their aroused parts never meeting. But she felt him *everywhere* nonetheless.

"Jesus Christ, this is out of control," he rasped into her hair. "I'm not in control."

"That's okay."

"Is it?"

She nodded, but he couldn't see the way she bobbed her head, not with his face buried in her neck. And then his free hand slid around to palm her backside, massaging it roughly in his hand—and her fingers turned slippery again. She began stroking her too-sensitive flesh, because there was no help for it. No stopping. No easing the twist of those deep, deep knots growing more complicated beneath her belly button, twining and snaring, urging her fingers to increase their pace. Their pressure. *Oh God, oh God.*

"Good, Hallie," he muttered thickly. "Is that pussy going to give it up twice?"

"Yes," she gasped.

He pressed his mouth to her ear. "God. The way you lost it when I wrapped my hand around my cock. I'll be thinking about it for years. Decades. How many times do you need to be on the schedule per day? Three? Four?" The swollen head of his arousal pressed flush to her mound and they both moaned, body jolting against body. Shaking. And when he ground himself there, against her fingers and, in turn, her clit, a second climax drew all of her muscles tight and let them go rapidly, leaving pulsations in its wake. The *throb throb throb* of release. "Jesus. You had to be so fucking sweet."

Julian crushed her against the island, his muscles coiling, his big shoulder pressing to her open mouth—and he jerked, groaning as he left warm moisture on her inner thigh. Two, three, four stripes of liquid heat, until he slumped against her, the sounds of the storm roaring back in along with the pounding of hearts.

For long moments, she could only stare off into space. In utter wonder.

Her first sexual experience with a man, beyond kissing, and it had blown her preconceived notions out of the water. She'd been right to be picky. Even without a lot of experience, Hallie somehow knew not all men would turn her on like Julian had just done. Nor would their pleasure make her own so much fuller.

And yet, as breathless and exhilarated as she felt, there was something in the air.

Something stirring.

Julian's hard body stiffened a little more with every passing minute, but he hadn't quite caught his breath. Not the way she had. And when he finally pulled away from her, it was more of a ripping apart than anything. Like a Band-Aid being torn from skin, it took a piece of her along with it. She caught a flash of thickly rooted flesh as he rearranged himself back in his pants, and then he paced to the other end of the kitchen, plowing a hand through his hair.

Several seconds ticked by while he said nothing.

It didn't take a genius to know he had immediate regrets.

For his hasty behavior. For letting his body make decisions for itself.

For engaging in something unplanned and spontaneous . . . when that was something he never did.

They'd agreed from the start that he was control and she was chaos—and he was obviously feeling the impact of that now, unable to look at her while fixing his clothes, that groove between his brows deeper than ever before.

Not only had she caused him to lose the control he needed so badly . . . she'd discussed the letters with him. Openly. As if she hadn't written them. Sure, the fact that he was quoting from *actual* correspondence was never said out loud, but she'd known. She'd lied by omission, hadn't she? She was given every opportunity to stop, too, and she didn't take it. Even now, when she had the chance to confess, she couldn't bring herself to do it, because he was visibly shaken by what they'd done. How would it help to tell him she was his secret admirer?

"I have to get home to walk the dogs," she said, sidestepping to yank the shorts up her legs and buttoning them with unsteady fingers. "The next phase of planting shouldn't be for a few days. Next week, most likely—"

"Hallie."

His hard tone propelled her toward the front door. "I really have to go."

Julian caught up with her at the door, curling a hand around her elbow and slowing her to a stop. They faced each other in the darkness of the entryway. "Listen to me for a second." His eyes went right to left, as if searching for an explanation. "I go from zero to a hundred in three seconds flat with you. I'm not used to it. Somehow I go from having boundaries for everything to burning them down. Something about you brings me to the edge of my comfort zone. In the past . . . look, my experience going beyond that boundary hasn't been positive."

"I'm messing with your inner compass and you want to keep it pointed north. It's fine. I totally understand." It *wasn't* fine. He was ripping her heart out. Why did she say that? "I really have to go."

As she spoke, he'd started pinching the bridge of his nose between his thumb and index finger. "Goddammit. Maybe that was too honest. But that's my other problem around you, isn't it? I talk to you in ways I don't talk to anyone else."

"I'm glad you're honest with me," she said with a catch in her throat. How did he say the exact right thing while simultaneously breaking her in two? "But sometimes the truth is just the truth and we have to accept it. We're too different."

Julian dropped his hand away, braced it on the doorjamb. He shook his head as if to deny it, but didn't. How could he? Facts were facts. "It's still raining pretty hard. You shouldn't drive." He started patting his pockets, coming up empty in an obvious search for his keys. "Please let me get you home safely."

She almost laughed. Like this wasn't awkward enough? "Look,

I can talk to my friend Owen about taking over the garden out front—"

"I'll have no one but you."

Hallie waited a beat for him to clarify that confusing statement, which seemed to indicate the opposite of what was happening here—a good-bye of sorts?—but he added nothing to that stern denial, the confusing, complicated man. Not wanting to give Julian a chance to find his car keys, she spun on a heel and jogged out into the rain. "Good-bye, Julian. I'll be fine."

As much as she wanted to leave without looking back, her gaze was drawn to him while backing down the driveway. *I'm sorry,* he mouthed to her. And she replayed his silent apology over and over on the way home, deciding to accept it and move on. Which would be a lot more difficult now that he'd exceeded her fantasies, both physically and emotionally, by about several hundred miles.

Unfortunately, their differences had never been more obvious. *I go from zero to a hundred in three seconds flat with you. I'm not used to it. Somehow I go from having boundaries for everything to burning them down.*

*Something about you.*

Julian needed planning and predictability, and she bucked those qualities like a rodeo bull. And she couldn't, in good conscience, continue to play Julian's imaginary girlfriend now that she'd missed her opportunity to reveal herself as the secret admirer. It wouldn't be right. Even she didn't have that much anarchy inside of her.

Time to put this crush behind her once and for all. Before she caused any more trouble.

# Chapter Eleven

Julian stood in the low-lit kitchen, drumming his fingers on the island, the sound weaving together with the tick of the clock to create a pattern of sorts. Even by his own punctual standards, he'd gotten dressed too early for the Wine Down Napa event this evening. Anything to avoid the blinking cursor on his computer screen. And memories of a certain energetic gardener gasping for air against his mouth. *Jesus.* He couldn't get the fucking taste of her out of his head. It stayed with him day, night, and every second in between.

Turned out, he'd almost kissed her once before. Fifteen years ago. That night, he'd drunk too much out of pure irritation with his sister. Vodka and anxiety had blurred the details of the evening. But ever since the memory resurfaced, details were returning. Vivid ones that made him question how he could have ever forgotten in the first place—even after checking out for a brief window of time afterward. Now? Julian remembered the fading light on her hair and the overwhelming urge to kiss her. The smooth skin of her back.

And the realization that she was a freshman, after which Julian was fairly certain he'd hustled her back to the party with his face on fire.

How did he misplace a memory that had the power to rock him now?

Julian didn't know, but it appeared that Hallie was determined to turn up once every decade and put cracks in his concentration. He couldn't fit his regular thoughts in between the ones of her moaning, thighs shaking with her orgasm. And what happened afterward.

What *had* happened afterward?

Still unclear. He'd been thrown the hell off, he knew that much. Normally, with a woman, there was an orderly physical progression from kissing to more. With Hallie, he'd operated on blind instinct, his body in total control, not his mind. Yeah, he'd been off-kilter when the fever cooled, trying to put his head back together. By the time he'd succeeded, she was halfway to the door.

Which was for the best, right? He'd been trying to convince himself of that for two days.

Obviously she was a danger to his control. Control he relied upon so he wouldn't aggravate his anxiety. With Hallie, he'd lost any sense of self-preservation and . . . took. Gave. Got lost. With her breath on his mouth and her green-thumb scent infiltrating his brain, he'd moved without conscious thought. If he'd wanted to keep touching her, if he'd wanted release, he'd had no choice. But coming down had been like crashing into a wall. His mind wasn't supposed to go offline like that. His impulses were meant to be . . .

Subdued.

Funny, he'd never thought of them that way.

Julian jerked his chin to the side, setting loose a series of cracks in his neck. Tension that continued to build with the passage of time since Hallie's hasty departure. Now Saturday night had arrived, and his mood was not the kind he should be unleashing on the general population, especially when representing Vos Vineyard, but what choice did he have? At least he could get away from the blank page taunting him in the office for a few hours.

Natalie trudged into the kitchen in stoic silence, dressed in all black, oversized mirrored sunglasses hiding her eyes. One might think they were on their way to a funeral, instead of an outdoor wine event on a fine summer evening in Napa. And Natalie could easily be the grieving widow, considering she'd only gotten out of bed for the day an hour earlier.

What *was* going on with his sister? Despite a rebellious phase in her youth, Natalie had turned into a Grade A overachiever once she'd gotten it out of her system. Once, after not hearing from her for a while, he'd checked her Facebook page and found she'd posted a Forbes article in which she'd been touted as a rising star in the world of investing. Add in her missing engagement ring and things had obviously taken a turn. But the Vos family operated on a need-to-know basis. They didn't exactly shoot the shit. Information was given out as needed and, more often than not, kept to oneself.

Why was that?

Growing up, he'd more or less assumed that sucking it up and handling a crisis alone, so as not to disappoint or inconvenience anyone, was normal. In college, he'd been shocked by his roommate's semiweekly phone call to his parents, during which he told them every piece of information under the sun, from his cafeteria meals to the girls he dated. Then, as a history professor, he'd witnessed the close relationships his students had with their parents, as well. On Family Weekend at Stanford, they showed up in droves wearing red sweatshirts and bearing care packages. They . . . gave a shit.

Perhaps not every family was close, sharing trials and triumphs as a matter of course. But based on the real-world data he'd witnessed with his very own eyes, families that cared about one another were more commonplace—and healthier—than his.

*I would tell her you're glad she's here with you. But before you say it, make sure you mean it. She'll be able to tell the difference.*

He cut Natalie a speculative glance, hearing Hallie's words in his head—far from the first time today. In fact, since she'd left Thursday night, braving a storm to get away from him, he'd been hearing the gardener's voice in his fucking sleep.

Natalie removed a flask from her purse, unscrewed the cap lazily, and tipped it to her lips. After a second gulp, she offered him the metal container.

"No, thank you," he said automatically. Why, though? Didn't he *want* a belt of whatever was in that flask? Yes. Obviously. He hadn't slept since Thursday night due to his brain's insistence on replaying every second of his interaction with Hallie on a torturous loop. "Actually . . . yes, I'll have some."

Natalie's eyebrows shot up behind her sunglasses, but she passed him the flask without comment. "Rough going on the book, big brother?"

He studied the opening of the container for a moment, trying not to make a mental list of all the reasons he shouldn't imbibe hard liquor at five o'clock. For one, he'd have to interact with the public on behalf of the family business—which might be in more trouble than anyone realized. And two, he desperately needed to get back to his book at some point. But if he had a drink this early, he would almost certainly have two, which would lead to lethargic thoughts tomorrow.

*Hallie running away from him into the rain, feelings hurt.*

"The hell with it," he muttered, tilting the flask to nearly a ninety degree angle, letting the river of whiskey warm a path down his throat and hit his empty stomach like a boulder. "I can already tell that was a terrible decision," he said, handing the whiskey back to Natalie.

She took another rip of the drink, then stuffed it back into her purse. "Evidently I'm rubbing off on you."

Normally, he would let that cryptic statement go without comment. Letting someone's bad mood go unaddressed was the standard. None of his business. Only, it was, wasn't it? "Why do you say that? Have you . . . made any bad decisions lately?"

"What?" Natalie did a double take. "Why are you asking me that?"

Apparently communing with one's family was harder than he thought. "For one, you slept until four o'clock in the afternoon. Now you're dressed like you're going to deliver a eulogy instead of shaking hands at something called Wine Down Napa."

"Maybe I'm eulogizing the grapes. Do you know how many of them had to die so people from Oklahoma can pretend they're getting an oaky aftertaste?"

*She would get along great with Hallie.*

That thought came out of nowhere and stuck like an arrow in his jugular.

Well, he might as well let that possibility go right now. Natalie and Hallie would probably never spend time together, unless one of these days Natalie actually went outside and introduced herself in the yard. After all, Hallie probably never wanted to see him again—and rightly so. How could one woman draw him in so intensely, while throwing him so far outside his comfort zone?

He rubbed at the throb in the center of his forehead. "I just wish you would tell me what has brought you back to St. Helena, Natalie."

"You go first."

Julian frowned. "I'm writing a book."

"'I'm writing a book,'" she mimicked. "If all you wanted was to write a book, you could have done it back at Stanford." Her fingers fiddled with the air. "Subtract two hours of gym time per week, eat your meals five minutes faster. There's your writing time. You didn't have to come to Napa to write Wexler's adventures."

He blinked. Shifted against the island. "How did you know my hero's name is Wexler? Have you been reading my manuscript?"

Did her color deepen? "I might have skimmed a page or two." She looked like she was considering reaching for her flask again. Instead, she threw out a frustrated hand. "How long are you going to leave him dangling over that stupid cliff?"

"You seem oddly invested," he sputtered, kind of . . . touched that his sister seemed concerned about old Wexler?

"I'm not," she said, waving him off. "Just, like . . . he has a grappling hook attached to his belt. In case you forgot."

He'd totally forgotten. "I didn't."

"No, of course not." She sighed, pursing her lips. Then: "Why did you make him blond?" His expression must have betrayed his utter puzzlement, because she elaborated. "Blond men are unrelatable."

A laugh came very close to sneaking out of him. That was happening more and more frequently lately, wasn't it? He couldn't remember his chest ever having felt this loose. But then why, around Hallie, did it get so tight again? "That sounds like theory, not fact."

"Nope. It's fact. Have you ever stood there talking to a man with white-blond hair and not speculated on his lifestyle? You can't *not* do it. It's impossible. You don't hear a single word coming out of his mouth."

"So you're saying I should make Wexler a brunette."

"Obviously, yes. Look. Blond men say things like 'hot tubbing' and they go hiking in Yosemite with the cool girl. I want to root for a guy who is unlikely to go on an adventure." She gave him a wry look. "Like you."

Julian made a sound. "I'll take the hair-color change under advisement."

"Great." She waited a beat. "So you are just going to own the unadventurous label?"

"No arguments there," he said briskly, nudging the brass mallard on the kitchen island. "Unless you count having a secret admirer as adventurous."

*"What?"* Natalie slapped a hand down on the marble. "No way. What? You are lying."

"Nope. They've been sitting right here. Maybe if I'd kept them in the wine refrigerator, you'd have found them." He grinned at her middle finger. "At first I thought you wrote it as a prank, but they're too . . ."

"There's sex stuff in them?"

"No. Nothing like that." Lines from the second letter drifted through his head. "They're just . . . more personal than one would get when pulling a prank, I suppose."

She raked both hands down her face, dragging the skin beneath her eyes farther than seemed wise. "Oh my God. I need to know everything."

"There is nothing important to share." Saying that made his stomach sour. Why did he have such a loyalty to this unknown person? Perhaps because, although he knew Hallie hadn't written those letters, some part of him secretly wished she had. Out of sheer masochism, he'd imagined her penning those words on the pages, and he'd sort of gotten stuck picturing her as the admirer. Which was nothing short of ridiculous and yet another way for the gardener to occupy his brain day and night. "I'm not going to write back."

"Fuck that. Yes, you are, Julian." She clasped her hands together beneath her chin. "Please let me help? I am so *bored*."

"No." He shook his head, the bitterness in his stomach turning even more acidic. "I'm here to work. I don't have time for some sort of ridiculous pen pal."

Natalie's shoulders slumped. "I officially hate your guts."

Guilt trickled in slowly. Why was he denying his sister something that might serve as a distraction from whatever was causing her to drink too much and hibernate in her dark bedroom? Anyway, maybe he *should* write back to the admirer. If for no other reason than to satisfy his curiosity. Obviously at some point he would have to put the gardener out of his mind. He could either do it now or when he inevitably returned to Stanford. If he could stop picturing Hallie when he read those words, moving on eventually would be a lot easier.

Still didn't feel right, no matter which way he sliced it. Damn, she'd gotten to him.

Although, writing the return letter didn't necessarily mean he had to *send* it. But having a mutual project might create an opening for Natalie to confide in him. He wanted that, didn't he? "All right, since we have some time to kill before we leave, you can help me write a response," he said grudgingly, already regretting the decision. At least until his sister started fist pumping her way around the kitchen, more animated than he'd seen her since she'd come home.

Forty-five minutes later, Julian and Natalie trudged up the path to the main house. Natalie walked to his right, freshly written letter in hand, rows of grapes extending out past her like outstretched arms into the evening. Light from his mother's windows beckoned ahead, crickets chirped in the near distance, and that elusive vineyard smell hung in the air. Kind of like a three-day-old floral arrangement. He'd forgotten how familiar it could be.

"Where are we supposed to leave the letter again?"

Julian bit back a sigh and pointed at the tree stump about twenty yards away, shaking his head when Natalie skipped toward it gleefully. He didn't have the heart to tell her he would come out later tonight and take it back. Nor could he regret the time they'd spent together writing the response. Such a simple activity had loosened something between him and his sister. Enough for him to pry?

"You mentioned that you're bored in St. Helena," he said slowly. "So why aren't you back in New York, Natalie?"

She finished tucking the letter into the stump, turned, and rolled her eyes. “I know. I’m intruding on your solitude.”

“No, I’m . . . I’m glad you’re here with me.” Her step faltered as they started up the path again, side by side. And Julian must have meant what he said about being glad, because she didn’t call him a liar. In that moment, he had the most pressing urge to tell Hallie what was happening. To call her right in the middle of it, although she probably wouldn’t even answer.

“I guess you could say that I’m . . . worried,” he tacked on around the goose egg in his throat. “About you. That’s all.”

Several seconds ticked past before she laughed, turned, and carried on up the path. “You’re worried about me? You haven’t called me in a year.”

His stomach sank. “Has it really been that long?”

“Give or take.”

“Well.” Following her, he clasped his hands behind his back. Unclasped them. “I’m sorry. I shouldn’t have let so much time pass.”

He felt her considering him from the corner of her eye. “I guess it’s not that hard to understand why. After everything that happened . . .”

“I’d rather . . .” He avoided looking at the vineyard. “Do we have to talk about the fire?”

“Do we have to talk about the fact that you were a total hero and saved my life?” She let out an exasperated laugh. “No, I guess not. I guess we can ignore the fact that you were incredible that night, but our father only saw what happened afterward. He had no right to judge you like that, Julian. To call you unfit to be involved with your family vineyard. He was *wrong*.”

Julian couldn’t unclench his jaw to respond. He could only

see images from that night. The nighttime sky lit up like something from the apocalypse, putting the people he loved in danger. People he was supposed to protect. Needles digging into his chest. His fingers curling into his palms and remaining that way. Stuck. Everyone watching him come apart.

That slow slide into nothingness afterward that he couldn't break free from, no matter how much he commanded himself to focus, to pull it together. No, instead, he'd gone dark. Left everyone else to sort out the mess while he navigated his mental fallout.

"It's my fault," Natalie said quietly.

That broke Julian out of his haze of discomfort, his attention whipping to the right. "What are you talking about?"

Even in the muted light, he could see the red staining her face. "If you didn't have to save me, if I hadn't put you through that, you wouldn't have lost it in front of him. I shouldn't even have gone into the shed. The fire was moving too fast—"

"Natalie. Don't be ridiculous." Realizing how harsh he sounded, he softened his tone. "You didn't do anything wrong. *Nothing* is your fault."

She made a sound, kept her face averted. "Could have fooled me. I mean, we weren't exactly the Tanner family to begin with, but we've barely spoken at *all* since then."

"I take responsibility for that. I should have been better about . . . being in your life. Obviously you've needed some—"

Natalie stopped walking abruptly, a glint in her eye that he could only interpret as dangerous. "Some what? Guidance? Advice?"

"I'm going to go with 'support.'"

A few degrees of tension left his sister, but her expression remained suspicious. She opened her mouth and closed it again.

Turned in a circle and looked out at the vineyard. "Okay, since you're so *deeply* concerned, Julian. I . . ." The corners of her mouth turned down. "I made a play on an investment and it tanked. Hard. Like . . ." Her tone turned choppy. "A billion dollars hard. I was asked—forced, really—to step down at the firm. And my fiancé . . . ex-fiancé . . . broke our engagement to save face." A lump moved up and down in her throat. "Morrison Talbot the *third* was too humiliated to be associated with me. And, of course, since I am no longer being paid, I was the one who moved out of the apartment." She splayed her hands. "So here I am. Half-drunk, talking shit about blond men and writing love letters with my brother. Wow, that really doesn't sound good out loud."

Julian couldn't hide his shock. She'd just been quietly living with this baggage since arriving in St. Helena? He didn't have a clue where to begin . . . what? Comforting her? He really should have clarified his goal before he started to question her. "Your ex-fiancé's name is Morrison Talbot the third and you're calling blond men unrelatable?"

Natalie stared at him blankly for long moments, but it only took Julian half of one of those moments to know he was not good at this. At least, until his sister burst into laughter. The loud kind that rang out across the vineyard and loosened that elusive something inside of him a little more. He started to think maybe—maybe—he would join her in laughing, but a voice sliced abruptly through the evening and cut off the sound.

"I had a feeling you weren't just home for a visit," his mother said, coming down the porch steps of the main house. Her features were backlit by the flickering lanterns hanging on either side of the front door and mostly hidden, but Julian swore a flash of hurt crossed his mother's face before she replaced it with a mask of indifference. "Well." She ran a hand along the loop of her silk scarf. "How long were you planning to wait before asking for money?"

His sister's spine snapped straight. Julian waited for her to issue a denial, to say that she wouldn't be asking for money—if for no other reason than pride—but she didn't. In the end, she looked their mother square in the eye and took a king-size pull from her flask.

"Lovely," muttered Corinne.

It wasn't lost on Julian that they were standing in the same spot—or close to, anyway—where the Vos family had been informed the fire was moving faster than originally predicted. Of course, they were minus one member. His father was in Europe racing Formula One cars. But *they* were here. They had problems to solve. Was he going to let an absent presence dictate how and when that was done?

No. Julian didn't think he would. What had four years of silence yielded, except for the three of them suffering alone, stubbornly refusing to turn to one another for support or solutions? "Corinne." He coughed into his fist. "Mother. Natalie isn't the only one who has been hiding something."

"What are you talking about?" Corinne snapped, quickly. Too quickly.

When he noticed the layer of panic in her eyes, he softened his tone. "The vineyard. We haven't quite made it back after the fire. Sales are down. Competition is fierce. And we can't afford to implement the changes that will make us viable again."

Natalie dropped the flask to her hip. "The vineyard . . . isn't doing well?"

"We are doing *fine,*" Corinne stressed, letting out a forced laugh. "Your brother was probably speaking to Manuel. Our manager is a worrier, always has been."

"Our equipment is malfunctioning and outdated. I've seen it with my own eyes. The public relations team is on permanent leave. We're behind on production—"

"I'm doing the best I can," Corinne hissed. "You think it was easy to be handed a burned-out vineyard along with divorce papers? It wasn't. I'm sorry it's not up to your standards, Julian." He started to argue that he wasn't blaming anyone, let alone her, but his mother wasn't finished. "Do you know I have to attend a luncheon next week in his honor? It's the twentieth anniversary of the Napa Valley Association of Vintners being formed, which I'll admit has done a lot of good in the region. He might be their founding father, but he's not even here! This place is falling into *disrepair,* and yet they want to celebrate the glory days. Your father trailblazed a path to them lining their pockets. They don't care that he abandoned this place and his family. He's still their hero. And I'm . . ."

"You're the one that kept the doors open, despite it all. I'm not blaming you for the decline. Please, I wouldn't do that. I'm asking . . ."

In the back of his mind, he could hear his father's voice echoing through the vines. *You've always been a fucking head case, haven't you? Jesus Christ. Look at you. Pull yourself together. Stick to teaching and just . . . stay away from what I've built, all right?*

*Stay away from the vineyard.*

Whether his father's assessments were true or not, he wasn't leaving his family to carry their burdens alone anymore. His father was gone. Julian was there. He could *do* something. "I'm asking to help, Mother. I know I'm not necessarily welcome—"

"Not welcome?" Corinne shook her head. "You're my son."

His throat muscles felt stiff. "I'm referring to what happened. And I understand if my input makes you uncomfortable, but frankly, that's too bad. You're getting it, anyway."

Corinne made a small sound, burying her face in her hands a moment. Just when Julian assumed she was working up the courage to ask him to remain detached from the business, she came forward with open arms and embraced him. For several seconds, he could only stare dumbfounded at his sister before she, too, came forward and wrapped her arms around both him and Corinne. "I did not have this on today's bingo card," Natalie sniffed.

"I'm sorry. To both of you." Apparently having reached her capacity for emotional displays, Corinne shifted free of the group hug. "It has been a long four years. I just . . . I never wanted either of you to feel unwelcome in your own home. You might have noticed I have a hard time admitting I need help. Or even . . . company."

"Well, you've got it now," Natalie crowed, hoisting her flask. "I'm never leaving!"

"Let's not get carried away," Corinne said, smoothing the sleeve of her dress.

Julian needed more time to process the revelations of the last five minutes. For now, he needed a distraction from the growing notch in his sternum. Remembering the small box stuffed into his jacket pocket, Julian removed the object, holding it out to Corinne. "This is only a small start, but I thought we could hand these out tonight at our table."

Corinne shied away from the white box like it might contain a garter snake. "What is it?"

"Business cards. For Corked on Grapevine Way." The two

women stared at him in expectant silence. "There is a new wineshop next door giving the owner, Lorna, some competition. I thought we could send some business her way. In the process, we're giving people an incentive to buy our wine. Here, look." He flipped open the top. "It's a small discount on Vos wine. Nothing major. But it's a first step toward selling the stock currently on shelves and making way for the new vintage. Wholesale orders will remain low until we clear what's already there—and there's a lot. Let's get the money we need to make this place whole again. It won't be restored overnight, but we have the framework, and that's half the battle."

His mother and sister traded an eyebrow raise.

"What brought this on?" asked Corinne while examining a business card. "Have you secretly been wanting to help all this time?"

Hallie. Making her happier. "Obviously, I don't have a stake in the situation. I just . . ." *Breathe easier when there is less of a chance of our gardener crying.* "Thought it could look good for the vineyard. You know, one local business helping another."

Though visibly skeptical, Corinne finally took the box and removed the top, sighing at what she revealed. "Well, at least they're not tacky."

"Thank you," said Julian, briskly.

"Wait. Did *you* design business cards for a local retail shop?" He nodded, prompting his sister to continue. "*And* you're getting secret admirer letters." Natalie looked down at the metal container in her hand. "I need to get out more."

"You *are* looking quite pale," his mother commented.

Natalie turned and let out a strangled scream over the rows of grapes.

Yes. Things certainly wouldn't change overnight. With them or the vineyard. But hell if they weren't at least pointed in the right direction now.

"We should go," Julian said, heading for the courtyard and driveway of the main house. "Wouldn't want to be late to Wine Down."

"You don't have to say it like that," his mother complained in a withering tone. "Sarcastically."

"He's not," Natalie interjected. "The name itself is doing all of the sarcasm heavy lifting. Do I have a minute to run inside and pee?"

Julian and Corinne groaned.

"Shut up," Natalie called over her shoulder, trotting back toward the house. Despite his exasperation, the night didn't feel like a total chore anymore. If he'd spent tonight working, he would have missed the revelation from his sister. Or these awkward family moments with Corinne that were semi-painful, but also . . . them. For so long, he'd been focused on making every minute productive. But perhaps his definition of "productive" was beginning to shift.

# Chapter Twelve

Hallie loved crowds.

Being able to hear everyone speaking at once but not make out a single word. The fact that all these people had dressed up and driven to the same location, all at once, for a special purpose. Crowds were a celebration of movement and color and trying new things.

For the second year in a row, she'd agreed to help Lavinia and Jerome behind the counter at Wine Down Napa. Convincing the festival committee to agree to allow a donut shop to display at the event had taken some fancy footwork, but the gooey baked goods were a huge hit the year prior, leading to a lot of stuffy connoisseurs walking around the massive tent with chocolate wings extending out from the corners of their mouths. Looking around the buzzing aisles of vendors, Hallie was pleased to see an even more eclectic mix this year.

Most of the displays were for local vineyards, and they were elaborate. Tasteful. Wine Down Napa didn't have the feeling of a typical indoor market. In true Napa style, the booths were constructed of polished wood. There was a step and repeat behind each one splashed with the vineyard's logo. Romantic lighting had been angled throughout the tent to create a dreamlike atmosphere, fairy lights twinkling on the ceiling, turning wineglasses into enchanted goblets. But in addition to Fudge Judy breaching the boundaries of wine world, there was an exhibit for gourmet dog treats and another for CBD gummies. They'd cast a wide net.

Ticket holders were beginning to arrive, journalists in press badges snapping pictures of people enjoying their first glasses of wine, angling the shots to capture the sprawling courtyard of the Meadowood hotel in the background. The air was sultry; orchestra music drifted down the mountain and through the tent on a light June breeze. And she couldn't help but remember her grandmother roaming the aisles slowly last year, saying hello to old friends and new, accepting pamphlets for vineyard tours to be polite.

Lavinia came up beside Hallie and gave her a gentle hip bump. "After weeks of designing the new, ultrarefined Merlot cruller, the Lucky Charms donut holes will probably be our biggest seller. Not even wine snobs can resist an artificially flavored marshmallow."

Hallie dropped her head to Lavinia's shoulder. "Especially when the CBD kicks in and they relax. Hopefully not enough to mistake the dog biscuits for donuts."

"Oh, I don't know. Could be entertaining."

They laughed, watching more and more people arrive in the tent, various levels of VIP access displayed around their necks. "So," Lavinia prompted. "We were in such a mad rush to get set up, I haven't had a chance to ask. What is the latest with our illustrious professor?"

Hallie blew out a breath, her gaze drifting over to the Vos Vineyard booth. No one had arrived yet, though they'd most likely tapped their in-house sommelier to represent them tonight. And even if Corinne Vos made an appearance, Julian definitely wouldn't be there. She'd assured herself of that for the last two days and still couldn't prevent the low sink of disappointment in her belly. "Oh, um . . ." She adjusted her Fudge Judy apron, heat creeping up the sides of her face. "The latest isn't really up for discussion. Not in polite company."

Lavinia reared back with raised eyebrows. "Good thing I'm not polite."

Hallie threw a pointed look at Jerome. "Later."

"Oh, come on, we both know I'm going to tell him, anyway."

"Good to know." They stopped to smile at two guests who wandered past looking down their noses at the donuts. They would definitely come crawling back after a few glasses of wine, though. "There might have been some . . . further intimacy. Not the whole enchilada. More like, I don't know, jalapeño poppers."

"You are speaking to a British woman in Mexican food terminology. Does not translate."

"Sorry. It's just that . . . honestly, I'm not really sure *what* happened in Julian's kitchen." She only knew her entire body started to tingle thinking about it. His breath on her neck, their mouths interlocked and panting. "Or if it was a-a . . . normal thing to do?"

Lavinia was agog. "Fuck off. He tried anal?"

"No!" Her cheeks were hot enough now to be fresh from the oven. "Not that."

"Oh, thank God." Lavinia briefly doubled over. "I was going to need a cigarette for this."

"It was more like . . ." Hallie looked around to make sure nobody was within earshot, then dropped her voice to a whisper. "The internet calls it mutual masturbation."

"Bloody hell, I do need that cigarette." Lavinia stared at her for a beat. *"What?"*

"I know."

Jerome approached his wife from behind, his default suspicious expression in full swing. "What's going on here?"

"I'll tell you later," Lavinia said quickly. "But in brief: it involves wanking." Without missing a beat, Jerome turned and moseyed to the other side of the booth. Lavinia shrugged defensively in the face of Hallie's sputtering shock. "I had to get rid of him so I can hear the rest of it, didn't I?"

Hallie slumped. "There is no rest of it. This time I'm really, *really* sure it was the last occasion we . . . do something both confusing and . . ." She tried to swallow, but her mouth was too dry, thanks to the sensual memories bombarding her. The way he'd ground his hardness there, the movements of his hand speeding up, his grunt of her name. ". . . arousing. Together."

"Yes, yes," Lavinia said, peering at her thoughtfully. "I can see you are definitely capable of saying no. Your nips aren't hard or anything."

"What?" Hallie looked down and saw the apron was definitely low enough to make out the outline of her nipples—and they were indeed bullet-shaped. Had they been anything but puckered and uncomfortable for the last two days? With a hasty yank, she tugged up the neck of the apron to cover the evidence. "No, really." She hesitated a moment, then blurted, "I wrote him a second secret admirer letter. Sober this time."

Lavinia rocked back on her heels. "No. You didn't."

"Lavinia, note my track record of complicating things. You know I did." She bit her lip. "And they were right there, in plain view in his Food Network–worthy kitchen. He *quoted* them at me, and I couldn't bring myself to tell him I'm the author."

Her best friend crossed herself. "Only God can save you now, Hallie Welch."

"That's a little dramatic." Nervous energy snapped in her veins. "Right?"

"What's a little dramatic?"

They both turned to find Owen standing at the front of the booth. At first, Hallie wondered if maybe the man was an evil twin. Or a doppelgänger. Since she'd only ever seen Owen in jeans and a T-shirt. Or shorts and gardening shoes. But tonight he wore pressed slacks and a tucked-in polo shirt, hair styled. And was that cologne?

"Owen. Darling." Lavinia recovered from the interruption first, leaning across the table to kiss Owen on both cheeks. "You look fabulous."

"Thanks." Rather adorably, he scrubbed at the back of his neck. "Same to you." His attention drifted to Hallie and stuck. "You look great tonight, too, Hallie. Really great."

She looked down at her outfit of choice, most of which was covered by the apron. Probably a good thing, considering she'd found it impossible to settle on an ensemble, so she'd ended up with a low-cut floral shirt tucked into a plaid, high-waisted skirt. At least her hair was in order tonight, curls tamed and loose around her shoulders. "Thanks, Owen—"

Her words cut themselves off. Because when she glanced up from her schizophrenic getup, there he was, directly over Owen's shoulder.

Julian Vos had entered the tent.

It was shocking to find out that she'd almost *slightly* gotten used to his presence—but only when it was just the two of them. In public like this? He was a Van Gogh in a gallery of children's finger paintings. He was quite simply incomparable. Tall and intense and handsome and attention-grabbing. Kind of impatient-looking, on top of it all. Every head turned at his arrival, as if they'd sensed a shift in the atmospheric balance.

He wore a starched white shirt totally devoid of wrinkles and navy blue slacks. A burgundy tie. Cuff links. He looked like the type of man who would wear those old-fashioned sock garters below the knee. And she'd touched herself in front of him. He'd done the same. They'd been completely weak in front of each other while the storm rampaged outside, and seeing him now, so composed and in charge, made the whole thing feel like a dream.

"Bet you'd have done anal," Lavinia said out of the corner of her mouth.

Thankfully, Jerome and Owen were engaged in a conversation about golf and didn't overhear. "Could you please never bring that up again?" Hallie implored.

"He'll be the one bringing it *up,* if you catch my meaning."

"Oh, don't worry. I do. You're as subtle as a chain saw."

Hallie ordered herself to stop staring at Julian, who was now crossing the tent with his mother and sister. And she failed. Everyone in the tent did. Vos Vineyard might be in need of an upgrade, but the first family of St. Helena moved like royalty and looked the part, too. Meanwhile here she stood in mixed patterns talking about butt sex.

She wouldn't change a thing. But the contrast only brought it home how utterly unalike they were.

None of that seemed to matter when Julian glanced over sharply, slowing to a stop when he saw her behind the Fudge Judy counter. *Oh my God,* her heart was going to beat right out of her body. It was magic, having this gallant, thoughtful man notice her from across a crowded room and stop dead in the middle of it all. Those times she'd opened up to him about her grief and one-third life crisis, she'd felt so utterly safe sharing with him. Did she imagine that bond?

No. She couldn't have.

In addition to the magic of being pinned by those whiskey eyes across the tent... was now lust. The urgent, frustrating kind she'd never experienced with anyone else. The kind she'd only half understood while mooning at him on YouTube, before his return to St. Helena. Beneath those lusty layers, though, was the wistfulness of regret.

Every time they connected, the *dis*connect between their personalities became a little more obvious, and what could be done about that?

"Hallie?"

Owen laid a hand on her arm, and she caught the barest change in Julian's expression. It clouded over, a groove fashioning itself between his brows. A muscle had begun to tick in his jaw when she finally managed to wrestle her attention away from Julian and focus on Owen. Who, apparently, had been addressing her to no avail for quite some time.

"I'm sorry. All this excitement..." Her laugh sounded strained. "I think I have wine envy."

Owen quickly set down the donut he'd picked up with the provided pair of silver tongs. "I'll get you a glass. What are you in the mood for?"

She could not let this man run around fetching her a drink when she was remembering how Julian's abdomen felt flexing against hers. "No, that's really okay, Owen—"

He was already off like a shot.

Hallie traded a guilty look with Lavinia, but they didn't have time to talk. The tent was quickly filling up and people wanted donuts. Mainly because, unlike last year, a lot of guests seemed to have brought their children. In the past, no one under the age of twenty-one had been admitted to wine-tasting events in Napa, but since the fire that damaged so much of the region, followed by the economic wrecking ball of the pandemic, St. Helena had slowly adopted more of a family-friendly image in the hopes of appealing to new visitors.

Apparently kids were the newest caveat.

And, in the case of Wine Down, the pitfalls of that decision quickly became obvious.

Children ran figure eights around the older clientele, their mothers receiving more than their fair share of judgment. The hosts of the event might have allowed children, but being that the beverage of choice was alcohol, there was nothing for the youngsters to drink or eat.

Except for the donuts.

That's how Hallie became the official babysitter of Wine Down Napa.

It started off with a single offer to watch the toddler of an overstressed mother while she went off and indulged in a glass of wine. Then a second family approached, inquiring about the professional childcare services, to which Hallie saluted them with her wineglass—and they left their child, anyway. Although Lavinia needed Hallie as an extra set of hands, the parents were buying donuts in gratitude, so they took the trade-off and booted Hallie in favor of the extra sales. Half an hour later, she had a football team of kids under the age of eight playing red rover on the field outside the tent and chomping on chocolate crullers.

She actually lost track of which one had eaten what. Or how many.

Now that, out of everything, turned out to be the biggest mistake.

Hopped up on an obscene amount of sugar, the kids decided they were thirsty.

"I want water!" announced one of the dinosaur-obsessed twins while picking a wedgie.

What was his name? Shiloh?

"Oh, okay," Hallie said, looking back toward the tent. There had to be water in there somewhere, right? "Um, everyone hold hands and let's go inside quietly and check—"

"MOM!" Shiloh screamed, running toward the tent, barreling through the flap—followed by the rest of the children, all shouting for their mothers.

"Wait. Guys, wait."

Hallie hurried after them with two empty donut boxes under her arms—whoa, empty?—but it was too late to prevent what happened next. She entered the tent just in time to watch the sugar-hyped kids fly around like pinballs. Wineglasses sloshed in the hands of VIP guests, and in two cases, tables were bumped, glass shattering and the hum of conversation grinding to a halt. Hallie stood just inside the entrance in a sort of trance, her gaze moving unerringly to Julian, who stood on the other side of the flabbergasted crowd, a glass of wine poised halfway to his mouth.

She could practically hear his thoughts out loud, they were so plain on his face.

Here was Hallie, once again proving herself a purveyor of chaos.

Barely fit to be among adults. And patently incapable of managing children.

Destruction in the flesh—now available for parties.

Julian lowered his glass, set it down, and just managed to steady a row of wine flutes on the Vos Vineyard display before they were knocked over.

Hallie winced and began chasing the wayward children. She was quickly joined by Owen, who gave her a sympathetic smile, which was a lot more comforting than Julian's steely-eyed judgment.

Like most times she was faced with an unpleasant truth about herself, she dodged it—and what else could that look in Julian's eyes mean except for exasperation?

*Forget about him and fix your mess.*

# Chapter Thirteen

*Owen has to go.*

There was already a crowd assembled, wanting to be entertained for the night. Why not make it a murder mystery? Everyone could take turns guessing who killed the redhead for continuously putting his hand on Hallie's arm. They'd eventually figure out it was Julian, or would perhaps take one look at his face and know straight off the bat.

God, he did not like the way they were laughing together. The way they sort of matched each other step for step, two very alike people on the same mission. Tame the maniacs who were currently blowing like miniature cyclones through the event, chocolate and sprinkles smeared across their chins and cheeks. The people sipping wine in front of the Vos table were complaining about the shoddy childcare—and he liked that criticism of Hallie even less than the sight of Owen staring at her curls as if eternally fascinated by their shape.

Actually, scratch that. He didn't like it less.

He simply liked none of this. Whatsoever.

Having her so close, looking so fucking beautiful, and feeling as if he wasn't allowed to speak with her. Had their last encounter been so bad that they weren't even on speaking terms anymore?

Her halting laugh reached Julian, and a tug started behind his collar. He'd missed that laugh. Had it really only been two days? Was he just supposed to never hear it again, even if embarking on any sort of relationship together would end in disaster?

No. That didn't work for him.

Julian didn't realize he was walking toward the emcee booth in the corner of the tent until he arrived there and held out his hand. "May I borrow the microphone for a moment?"

The emcee juggled the mike, clearly caught off guard by Julian's abrupt approach. He was thrown off, as well. What the hell was he doing?

*Joining the fray. Just because she's there.*

Refusing to question that disconcerting certainty, Julian raised the microphone to his mouth. "If I might have your attention, please?" He couldn't see anything but Hallie's blond head popping up from the floor, where she'd been trying to coax a crying child out from under a table—with *more sugar,* for the love of God. "I'm beginning children's story time now out on the lawn." He checked his watch automatically to register the time. "Please send them outside now. Pick them up at eight oh five. Thank you."

"Are we sure CBD doesn't get people at least buzzed?" Natalie asked as he passed. "I could have sworn you just said you were conducting a children's story time."

A bead of sweat trickled down his spine. "I did say that."

"Why?" she said, visibly astonished.

Julian started to brush off the question or give an unsatisfactory answer, such as, "I don't know," but he didn't want to take a step backward with Natalie. They'd formed a tenuous bond tonight. If he'd learned anything in that brief window of time, it was that having a relationship with his sister meant sharing potentially embarrassing things with her. "It's because of a woman."

Natalie's mouth dropped open. "*Another* woman?"

Jesus, when she said it like that, it sounded awful. "Well, yes. But . . ."

There was simply no way to explain that he'd cast the net of his interest in Hallie so far and wide that it had swallowed up his secret admirer. He'd wished them to be one and the same. Now they were inseparable entities.

"I don't get it." His sister sounded almost dazed. "You barely leave the house and there are two women on deck."

Julian scoffed. "That is hardly the case." She waited, saying nothing. More sweat slid down his spine. "It's complicated with Hallie. We aren't seeing each other. Nothing can come of it and we're agreed on the matter." Damn. Saying *that* out loud felt far worse than his sister's claim about him juggling two women. "It's just that when she's in trouble or experiencing any kind of distress, I feel somewhat . . . upset about it."

Natalie stared.

"That is to say, I feel as if I'm going to explode if the situation isn't fixed for her. When she isn't smiling, the world becomes a terrible place."

Several seconds passed. "Do you think what you're saying is normal?"

"Forget it," Julian growled. "Please continue to pass out the damn business cards for Corked. I'll be back in a while."

He strode out of the tent while unfastening his cuff links and tucking them into his pants pocket in order to roll up his sleeves.

It seemed like a best practice when dealing with kids. Wouldn't want to appear intimidating.

Brisk mountain air dried the layer of perspiration on Julian's forehead as he walked out of the tent. He stopped short when he found Hallie hustling a dozen youngsters into a half circle on the lawn—while Owen watched, his devotion to her clearer than a freshly washed windowpane. The other man turned at his approach, cautiously sizing him up.

Julian's sleeve-rolling movements became increasingly hasty. "Hello."

"Hi," Owen said back, taking a quick sip from his wineglass. "I'm Owen Stark."

Julian held out his hand. They shook. Quite firmly. He'd never really considered his height an advantage until the other man had to crane his neck slightly. "Julian Vos."

"Yes, I know." The redhead's smile didn't reach his eyes. "It's nice to meet you."

"Likewise." *State your intentions toward her, motherfucker.* "How do you know Hallie?"

Was it his imagination or did the bastard look a little smug? Yes, he was definitely the kind of man who would make a perfect guest of honor at a murder mystery. "We own competing gardening businesses in St. Helena." Of course, Julian had already known the answer to that. Apparently, he just wanted to torture himself by hearing this man speak with familiarity about the woman who occupied his every thought these days. "Someday, I'm hoping to convince her to join forces."

Now that was news. Or was it?

Owen's emphasis on *join forces* made it sound as if he meant something else—not business related. As in, a personal relationship with Hallie. Marriage, even. How close *were* they, exactly? And truly, what business was it of Julian's, when she appeared to want nothing to do with him anymore? He didn't know. But the gravelly grind in his chest was so unpleasant, it took him a moment to speak. "Maybe she doesn't want to be convinced or it would have happened by now."

"Maybe she needs to know a man is willing to play the long game."

*I guess I'm going to kill him.* Julian stepped closer. "Oh, is it a game to you?"

Hallie slid in between Julian and Owen, splitting a startled glance between them that quickly turned nonplussed. "Oh dear." Her hip brushed Julian's groin, and he had the most pressing urge to drag her up against him like a fucking caveman. "M-maybe we can continue this later? When we aren't under threat of mutiny?"

"That works for me," Owen said with a big, dumb smile, saluting with his wine.

"Absolutely," Julian agreed, keeping his eye on the other man as he went to the front of the semicircle. And then all he could do was stand there and absorb the absolute disarray that lay at his feet. Several children were sprawled out on the grass, coming down from their sugar highs with glazed eyes and twitching limbs. Sprinkles were trapped beneath fingernails and plastered to the corners of mouths. One of them was actually licking the grass, another trying to balance a small Nike sneaker on his head. Two girls fought over an iPad with twin expressions of violence. "Well, aren't you all just a mess? Your parents will have to hose you down before putting you in the car tonight."

A dozen pairs of eyes snapped in his direction, some of them startled.

Including Hallie's.

Maybe his greeting had been a little harsh—

One of the children—a girl—giggled. And then they *all* started to giggle.

"Our moms aren't going to spray us with a hose," she shouted, unnecessarily.

"Why not? You're all disgusting."

More laughing. One of them even pitched sideways onto the lawn. Was he doing all right at this? He'd spent exactly zero time around kids this young, but his college students definitely never laughed at him. They could barely be bothered to crack a smile. Not that he ever joked during a lecture. Time was a serious matter. Somehow he didn't think these kids would appreciate a talk on the impact of capitalism on the value of time.

"Why don't we talk about time travel?"

"I thought you were going to read us a story."

Julian pointed a finger at the interjector. "Disgusting *and* impatient. I'm getting to the story. But first I want to hear where you would go on a time-traveling mission."

"Japan!"

He nodded. "Japan now? Or a hundred years ago? If you hopped in your time-traveling machine and arrived in Japan in the year 1923, you might land in the middle of the great earthquake." They blinked up at him. "You see, all the events of the past are still . . . active. They remain in order of occurrence, existing in a linear path, beginning at a starting point and reaching all the way to this moment. Everything you're doing in this moment is being recorded by time, whether you realize it or not."

"Even this?" A boy in a San Diego Zoo shirt attempted a handstand, landing at an awkward angle in the grass.

"Yes, even that. Would anyone else like to tell us where they would go if they time traveled?" Several hands went up. As Julian got ready to call on someone, he happened to look up and catch the most fleeting expression on Hallie's face. One he wasn't sure he'd seen before and couldn't really describe.

What was it? Certainly not . . . adoration. He wasn't doing *that* well up here.

Still, it was hard to put any other description to her soft, dreamlike expression. The way she looked as if she were being held up only by a string.

He had to be misinterpreting the whole thing.

Or worse, what if that adoration was for Owen? Not him?

When Julian cleared his throat, it sounded like he'd just guzzled a handful of broken walnut shells. "All right, in keeping with the time-travel theme, on to the story." He clasped his hands behind his back. "There was once a man named Doc Brown, who built a time-traveling machine out of a DeLorean. Does anyone know what a DeLorean is?"

Silence.

Thankfully, the quiet carried over into the story, and the children remained seated on the grass, listening with only the occasional outburst of giggles or interruptions, until Julian finished. When he finally glanced up from his rapt audience, their parents were standing behind them holding little coats. And he was pleased to see that many of them were carrying the discount cards for Corked. Natalie must have worked overtime to put them in everyone's hands.

He watched Hallie slowly notice them, too, her gaze bouncing around to all the green-and-white cards. Then over at him. *That's right, sweetheart. I deliver for you.*

*I can't help it.*

"Okay, then. Story time has ended." He shooed the children away. "Go get hosed off."

They climbed to their feet in a way that reminded him of newborn giraffes. Most of them went straight to their parents. Julian was startled, however, when a pair of twins ran full speed in his direction and wrapped their skinny arms around his thighs. Hugging him.

"You're getting me dirty," he pointed out, surprised when his throat tugged. "Fine." He patted their backs. "Very good, thank you."

"Isn't that the guy from that alien documentary?" one of the parents mused out loud.

Julian sighed.

Finally, it was over. Thank God.

When the kids left, he didn't miss them at all.

Right.

Slowly, Hallie approached him, the beginnings of sunset creating a halo on top of her blond head. Over the course of his story time, she'd taken off her shoes, and her toes sunk into the grass now, tipped in all different colors. Red, green, pink. He could envision her sitting on the floor of a living room, trying to choose a shade, giving up and deciding a rainbow would give her the best of all worlds. When had that kind of indecisiveness started to come across as tremendously charming to him?

That mysterious look from earlier was no longer in her eye, and he wanted it back, wanted her to adore him again. How could he crave something that he'd obviously imagined?

"Thank you for doing that," she said to him, her soft voice mingling with the crickets, the music still coming from the wine tent. "You were great. I guess I shouldn't be surprised. They say kids are drawn to authenticity. You really nailed the genuine vibe, calling them disgusting and all."

"Yes." In the distance, he heard the grass-licker relating *Back to the Future* to his parents, and a weird clunk happened in his chest. "People say this all the time, and I never believe them. But did you notice the children were also kind of . . . cute?"

She pressed her lips together, clearly suppressing a laugh. "Yes, I noticed. Why do you think I was compelled to ply them with chocolate? I needed them to like me."

"I understand now," he admitted.

Hallie spent the next few moments staring down at her feet. Why? He had to stuff both hands in his pockets to keep from lifting her chin. Owen was watching them from the shadow of the tent, too, and, Christ, was Julian so selfish that he would sabotage her potential relationship with the gardener when he wasn't in a position to offer her one himself? No.

"Yes," he countered himself. Out loud.

Hallie's head came up. There. There were her beautiful eyes. "Yes, what?"

Pulse firing, he shook his head. "Nothing."

She hummed, narrowing her gaze. "Do you happen to know anything about those promotional cards for Corked that everyone was holding?"

He kept his expression neutral. If he informed her of their origin, he'd probably have to tell her about the new awning he'd ordered for Corked, too, and he didn't need to be told he'd gone overboard. He was well aware. And while a relationship with Lorna could help the vineyard, the true reason he'd intervened was standing right in front of him, with that perfect little crease that ran down the center of her bottom lip. That dimple in her cheek. "Promotional cards for Corked? I didn't notice."

"Really." She folded her arms across her tits, drawing his attention downward, and God almighty, the way the material of her shirt stretched over those generous mounds would keep him awake tonight. Already, he was mentally uncapping his bottle of lube, pressing his open mouth to the center of the pillow, and imagining her beneath him, naked, legs thrown over his shoulders. "How odd. I wonder where they came from."

If Julian told her, maybe she would kiss him. Or even come home with him. And fuck, that was tempting. But would he be leading her on? Yes, he wanted to make her happy. Yes, he wanted to eviscerate everything that caused her to worry and put an eternal Hallie Smile on her face. Every time he let himself indulge in Hallie, though, that out-of-control feeling threatened to topple him. He didn't know how to allow himself to . . . let go like that. It unnerved him. And he'd ultimately hurt her feelings—which was the exact opposite of what he wanted.

They were cut from different cloth. He craved order, and she was human pandemonium. Yet why was he beginning to have such a hard time remembering that? Maybe because those gray eyes were on him, her soft, round face brushed in sunset, her mouth so goddamn close, he could taste it.

"I thought of you earlier tonight," he said, without thinking, distracted by the dip of her dimple. "You were right about what to say to Natalie."

"Was I?" She searched his eyes. "You two had a heart-to-heart?"

"Of sorts, I suppose. The Vos version." There was no denying how good it felt to speak to Hallie like this. Just the two of them. He'd met women throughout his life who were logical and concise and regimented. Like him. Shouldn't it have been easier to open up to someone who operated the same way? "We . . . I guess you could say we bonded."

"That's amazing, Julian," she whispered. "Over what?"

Hallie wanted to be kissed. She was standing too close for him to draw any other conclusion. And when she snagged that full, creased bottom lip between her teeth and dropped her gaze to his mouth, he had to suppress a groan. Fuck it. There was no stopping himself. Two days without her taste and it was like being starved to death. "She helped me with a letter I've been meaning to write," he muttered, dipping his head—

Hallie straightened. "Oh." She blinked down at her hands. "Natalie helped you write a letter?"

Julian replayed his thoughtless words. What in the hell had he been thinking bringing up the secret admirer letter? He *wasn't* thinking. He couldn't keep his head on straight around Hallie. That was the problem. Why was he suddenly more desperate than before to go retrieve the letter from the stump before anyone could accidentally find it? Especially his admirer.

Jesus. As he stood there looking down into Hallie's face, the fact that he'd even temporarily left correspondence for someone else made him ill. But Hallie was waiting for an explanation, and he couldn't bring himself to lie. Not to her. "Yes," he said, praying the matter would be dropped immediately. "A secret admirer, if you can believe it. Writing back seemed like the polite thing to do, although it was more a way for me and Natalie to—"

"That's wonderful, Julian," she blurted. "Wow. A secret admirer. That's so old-school. Um . . ."

Wait. She wasn't letting him finish. He wasn't going to let the letter be found. It was important she understood that—

"I'm glad things turned a corner with your sister. I'm sure the fact that you're making an effort means the most of all. Not what I suggested you do." She took a step backward, away from him. "I better get back inside to see if Lavinia needs me."

"Yes," he clipped out, already missing her. Again. "But, Hallie—"

"Good night."

Why did he have a mounting sense of guilt over writing that letter? He and Hallie weren't dating. In fact, they'd specifically agreed *not* to form any kind of personal relationship. So why did he feel like he'd fucking betrayed her? No matter that he'd pictured Hallie's face while writing back to the secret admirer—the guilt remained.

"Hallie . . ." he called to her again, no clue what to follow up with.

Jesus Christ, he was nauseous.

"I'll be over sometime tomorrow to plant some dusty miller to really accentuate the lavender," she sang on her way back into the tent, thanking Owen for holding the flap open for her. "Thanks again for leading story time."

With a smirk for Julian, Owen followed in Hallie's wake.

Julian stared after the swinging canvas, winded. What the hell just happened?

And would anyone actually *miss* Owen if he disappeared?

When Julian reentered the tent, it took every ounce of his self-control not to pluck Hallie out from behind the donut booth and carry her back outside. To finish their discussion in a way that would end in her smiling. Why? It would only confuse this *thing* between them more. But it was a hell of a lot more preferable than leaving . . . their *thing* unsettled. This mental bedlam came part and parcel with Hallie, and yet, he couldn't stop going back for another helping.

Julian was just about to approach the donut booth when he spotted Natalie across the room. Since he'd gone outside for story time an hour earlier, his sister had clearly put the pedal to the metal on wine consumption and was now flirting with one of the wine vendors, a giant linebacker of a man in a *Kiss the Vintner* apron. As Julian watched, she made an attempt to boost herself onto the man's table in what she no doubt believed to be the ultimate seductive move. Until she slipped off—and would have landed on her ass if the linebacker's arm didn't shoot out from behind the table to steady her.

In Julian's periphery, he watched a photographer weave her way through the thinning crowd, her expression one of single-minded focus. The last thing the winery needed was a picture of drunk Natalie ending up in the gossip section of some wine blog. With a final frustrated glance toward Hallie, he hastened his way across the room, hoping to intercept his sister before she became internet fodder. But apparently his worry was all for nothing. The vintner noticed the photographer, too. At the last second, he maneuvered Natalie so his gigantic self was blocking the journalist from getting a decent shot.

"I'm telling you, August, it's impossible to hum while you hold your nose," Natalie was slurring when Julian reached them. "Try it."

Julian assumed this man would say something to humor or distract her, so he was surprised when the man actually pinched his nose and attempted the feat, flashing a navy tattoo in the process. "Son of a bitch," he rumbled. "Can't hum a note."

Natalie laughed long and loud. "You will remember this moment the rest of your life, August Cates."

"Yeah." Lopsided smile from the navy man. "Pretty sure I will."

His sister stared up at the man for an awkward length of time. "Are we going to make out?"

A flash of white teeth. "Cancel all my calls," he shouted over his shoulder to an imaginary secretary.

When Natalie took a step in the vintner's direction and the photographer finally found a better vantage point, that was Julian's cue. "Time to go, Natalie."

"Yep," she agreed without missing a beat, allowing herself to be dragged away by her brother. Although, Julian lost count of the number of times she looked back over her shoulder at her would-be make-out partner. "Forget gas-station guy. *That* man is the perfect rebound."

"Make that decision when you're clearheaded."

"I don't make good decisions when I'm clearheaded. That's why I'm in Napa, remember?" She pulled him to a stop while they were still out of Corinne's earshot. "How did things go with Hallie, for whom you would sacrifice your life but will not date?"

"Not well, if you must know."

She mimicked him, employing a British accent while doing it. Then she just kind of deflated all at once. "God. We are dysfunctional people, aren't we? Who unleashed us on the world?"

With perfect timing, their mother's most diplomatic laugh rang out while she raised a wineglass to the couple standing at the Vos booth. As soon as they departed, her smile dropped like an anvil from a ten-story building.

Natalie snorted. "I guess we have our answer."

Julian watched his sister rejoin Corinne behind the table, his attention straying back to the other side of the tent before he could stop it.

*We are dysfunctional people, aren't we?*

Perhaps Hallie was a wrench in the engine of his mental well-being, but was Julian the same to her? Or worse? He thought of the first afternoon they met, when he criticized her placement of the flowers and she'd lost some of her glow. Just minutes ago, she'd been soft and flirtatious, and he'd somehow ruined it. Again. Maybe he should be staying away from her because of the damage *he* could inflict. Because as much as she drove him crazy with her lack of plans and organization, he liked her. A lot. Definitely too much to be leaving letters for someone else.

With a spike in his throat, Julian rejoined his family behind the table, where they were preparing to leave. Logical or not, he needed to get that letter and destroy it. Tonight.

# Chapter Fourteen

It was well after midnight when Hallie, Lavinia, and Jerome drove down Grapevine Way, having packed up their Wine Down display and carpooled back to town. Shops were shuttered, though a few wine bars remained open, probably nearing last call. Along the road, ornate rooftop cornices were silhouetted by silver moonlit sky. Through the open back seat window of Jerome and Lavinia's catering van, she could hear the chirp of crickets carrying down the mountain and from nearby valleys and vineyards.

Jerome and Lavinia dropped Hallie off at her parked truck, and with an exchange of exhausted waves, they continued down the block to where they would unpack the catering equipment at Fudge Judy before heading home.

Hallie got into her truck and let her head loll back against the headrest. She should go home and climb into bed right now, surrounded by snoring dogs, but she made no move to start the engine. Julian had written back to his admirer, and try as she might, she couldn't seem to let it go. There was no way around it—she had to collect that letter. Now. Tonight. Under the cover of darkness, like a certified weirdo.

Teeth gritted, she pushed open the driver's-side door and hopped out, pulling her jacket tighter to her body to ward off the cool, misty air. She stole across the silent road, intending to cut through Fudge Judy's to their back alley, then down the road to Julian's jogging path. Having helped Lavinia and Jerome with catering events in the past, she knew they would be busy shelving items in the giant walk-in storage closet and would be none the wiser that she'd used the shortcut. Furthermore, any potential witnesses would assume she'd remained in the donut shop the whole time.

"Any witnesses? Listen to yourself," she muttered.

This whole activity was pointless—

Hallie stopped short in front of Corked.

Was that . . . a new awning?

Gone was the old, faded red-and-white-striped one. It had been replaced by a bold green one with scripted lettering. *Corked Wine Store. A St. Helena institution since 1957.*

Where did it come from? Between the rainstorm yesterday and preparing for Wine Down today, two afternoons had passed since the last time she'd stopped into Corked to visit Lorna. Apparently she'd missed the store getting a face-lift? Who was responsible for this?

Intuition poked and prodded at Hallie, but she didn't want to acknowledge it. Earlier as Wine Down . . . wound down . . . she'd gone on a mission to find the origin of the business cards, and lo and behold, everyone she spoke to claimed they'd been given out at the Vos Vineyard table. She'd already caught Julian buying pity cases of wine from Lorna. Then came the cards. And now this. A beautiful, crisp green awning that updated the struggling shop by several decades.

He'd done this, hadn't he? Bought Lorna an awning. Driven business her way. Put money in the register. What did all of it mean, and why, oh, why, did it have to make her heart pound like steel drums on a cruise ship?

This was not for her.

There was a *reason* he hadn't taken credit for any of this. He didn't want her to get the wrong idea. He was merely helping out a local business owner, not making some kind of dramatic romantic gesture, so the swooning had to stop. She should be ashamed of the fact that her knees were wobbling like chocolate pudding. If Julian wanted her as more than a onetime accidental hookup, he would have said so by now. God knew he was blunter than a baseball bat about everything else.

And he'd written back to the secret admirer.

*Hello.* Those were not the actions of an interested man.

Those were the actions of a man who'd perused the grocery aisle and said, *I think I'll take this reliable cauliflower, instead of the mixed bag of root vegetables I can't name.* She needed to get his lack of interest through her thick skull, collect his letter, and read it out of pure curiosity, then be done with this whole confusing mess with the professor.

With a final yearning look up at the awning, Hallie jogged down Grapevine Way toward Fudge Judy. She peeked in through the window, making sure her friends were nowhere in sight before she slipped in through the front door and went into the kitchen. Lavinia appeared from behind the stainless steel workstation and threw up her hands at Hallie's entrance, then slumped forward onto the waist-high table, clutching at her chest through a pink apron. "Fucking hell, I thought we were being robbed. What in the bloody hell are you at?"

Trapped, cursing herself for not taking the long way, Hallie shifted onto the balls of her feet. "I just thought I would go for a little moonlight stroll."

"What? *Where?*"

Why did her ideas always sound worse when they were spoken aloud? Like, every single one. "Down Julian's jogging path," she mumbled.

After a moment, Lavinia banged a fist down on the table. "He's written you, hasn't he?"

"Everything all right in there?" Jerome called through the door of the storage closet.

Hallie pressed a finger to her lips.

"All's well, love. Just bumped my elbow!" Lavinia reached back to untie her apron, a somewhat maniacal look in her eyes. "I'm coming with you."

There would be no stopping her. Apron removal meant business. "I'm not reading you the letter. It's private."

Lavinia rocked back on her heels, considering those parameters. "You don't have to read it to me word for word, but I want the general temperature."

"Fine."

"Going out for a smoke, love," Lavinia shouted, the door banging behind the two women on their way out into the alley. "How do you know he's written back?"

"He told me."

"He told you . . ." Lavinia drew out.

"Yes." She hugged her elbows tight, then realized she looked defensive, so she let them drop. "And yes, I realize that means he isn't interested in real-life Hallie. Only the Hallie from the letter. I'm just going to read his answer to satisfy my curiosity. That's all."

"I might trust you on that." Lavinia jogged to keep up. "If you hadn't sworn to me you wouldn't write these letters in the first place."

"Did you see the new awning on Corked?"

"Your ability to distract us from an actual problem is unparalleled, but I'll bite." Lavinia tilted her head. "A new awning? What happened to the red one covered in pigeon shite?"

"It's gone. And I think it was Julian who arranged it." Hallie snagged Lavinia's wrist and guided her down the private path leading to Vos Vineyard. "I traced those promo business cards for Corked to their table at Wine Down. That has him all over it, too, right? I realize this is all beginning to sound very Scooby-Doo."

"Ooh. I'm Daphne. She gets to shag Fred."

"You can have him. I have a healthy distrust of blond men."

"I don't want to trust him, I want to bang him. Where am I losing you?"

Hallie covered her mouth to muffle a laugh. "You aren't. The fact that we're sneaking around in the dark discussing sexual relations with a cartoon character—one who wears a sailor suit, no less—is exactly why we're friends."

They traded a wry smile in the moonlight. "Back to the case of the mystery awning, then. We think Julian is responsible."

"Yes." Hallie sighed, despairing over the zero-gravity sensation in her breast. "I could have walked away mostly unscathed if he wasn't prank call champion of the universe. If he didn't keep making these . . . these gestures that remind me why I was infatuated with him in the first place. Why I spent so long hung up on him."

Lavinia made a sound of understanding. "He's got you dangling from a fishing hook, all gape-mouthed and wiggly."

"Thank you for that flattering comparison." Hallie laughed, stopping in front of the tree stump, frowning. "This is where the letter should be. Wedged in between the crack."

"What a coincidence. That's right where you'd like Julian to be."

Hallie overcame her blush. "You're not totally wrong."

They each took out their phones and turned on the flashlights, searching the ground around the stump. "Could he have taken it back?"

Why was she dizzy with hope over that possibility? "No. Why would he do that?"

"Maybe he realized you're his dream girl—" Lavinia's beam of light landed on something white behind a brambleberry bush. "Ah, no. Sorry. Found it. Must have blown over."

"Oh," Hallie said, too brightly. "Okay."

She approached the envelope the way one might approach a lit puddle of kerosene and picked it up, commanding her stomach to stop pitching. "All right, so I'll just bring this home and read it."

Several seconds ticked by in the foggy stillness.

Hallie tore open the envelope.

"Exactly," Lavinia said, sitting down on the tree stump. "I'll be right here, awaiting any bread crumbs you choose to throw me."

She barely heard her friend's quip over the pounding in her ears. Pacing a few steps away, she shined her flashlight down at the letter and read.

**Hello.**

**I don't know where to begin. Obviously this is all quite unusual. After all, we are communicating as two people who know each**

other, but we have never met. It feels like we have, doesn't it? I apologize for talking in circles. It's not easy to expose oneself on paper and leave it out in a field where it could fall into the wrong hands. You were brave to go first.

In your letter, you mentioned having too much space to think. I always thought I wanted that. Lots of space. Silence. But lately it has become more of a force field to keep ~~you~~ people out. I've had it activated so long that anyone brave enough to come inside feels like an intruder, rather than what ~~you~~ they really are. An anomaly. A fork in the road of time. The thing that pulls me from distraction and forces me to become the next version of myself. And isn't it ironic that I teach the meaning of time for a living and, yet, I am staunchly fighting the passage of it? Time is change. But letting it move you forward is hard.

Enough about me. I am nowhere near as interesting as you are. I'll say this. I believe that if you're brave enough to write a secret admirer letter to someone, you're brave enough to evolve, if that's what you want. Maybe writing back will inspire me to do the same.

Sincerely,<br>
Julian

"Well?" Lavinia called from her stump. "What is the temperature?"

Hallie had no earthly clue. He'd gone way more in-depth than she was expecting. It reminded her of the conversation they'd had in the kitchen. Emotional. Honest. Only, this time, he'd had it with someone else. On one hand, his words had spread a balm over a wound inside of her. *You're brave enough to evolve.* On the other, it felt worse than if he'd asked to meet the mystery person. Or expressed serious romantic interest.

Tears pricked against the backs of her eyelids. "Um." She quickly folded the letter up and stowed it in the pocket of her hoodie. "I would say he's cautiously interested. Complimentary but not flirtatious. He leaves it open-ended for more correspondence."

When Lavinia didn't respond right away, Hallie knew her friend had picked up on the hurt in her tone. "Are you going to write him again?" Lavinia finally asked, quietly.

"I don't know." Hallie tried to laugh, but it sounded forced. "None of my impulsive decisions have resulted in actual pain before. Maybe that's a good sign to stop."

"I have a lighter in my pocket. Shall we go burn him at the stake?"

"Nah." Hallie turned, giving her friend a grateful look. "I hear they don't even have shrimp and garlic linguine in prison."

"I guess we'll let the lucky prick live," Lavinia muttered, pushing to her feet. Coming to stand beside Hallie, she put an arm around her shoulder, and they both stared out over the top of the vines. "You did something sort of brash, babe, but I have to tell you, I fucking admire you for taking a shot and doing something a little wild. Once in a while, a good thing comes from a shot of sudden bravery."

"Just not this time."

Lavinia didn't answer. Just squeezed Hallie's shoulders.

"This is a good thing," Hallie said slowly, watching her breath turn into fog. "I needed a wake-up call. Since Rebecca left us, I've fallen into this pattern of disorganized commotion. I don't want to acknowledge how bad it hurts to be alone now. And I don't know what happens next in my life. So I just . . . kept finding ways to avoid making decisions. To avoid being the Hallie I was when she was around, because it's too hard to do it alone." She closed her eyes and squared her shoulders. "But I can. I'm ready. I need to grow up now and stop making these . . ." She gestured to the stump. "Ridiculous choices. Starting tomorrow, I'm turning over a new leaf."

"Why not start tonight?"

"I need closure." Again, her gaze rested on the stump. "I need to tell him good-bye first."

THE LETTER WAS already gone.

Julian stared down at the stump with a pit in his stomach.

It was nearing one o'clock in the morning. They'd been home for an hour, but he'd spent it convincing Natalie to go to bed, instead of cracking open a bottle of champagne and playing an old version of Yahtzee she'd found in the hallway closet. As soon as he'd heard his sister sawing logs through her bedroom door, he'd booked it up the path to take back the piece of communication, but obviously he'd been too late. His secret admirer had retrieved the envelope while he was at the party. And he supposed that eliminated everyone who was there tonight. Why did that surprise him? Had he been holding out a small amount of dumb hope that his admirer was Hallie?

*Idiot.*

Why would she admire someone who was a rainstorm compared to her sunshine?

She'd been the one to point out they were too different and should only be friends.

He agreed, of course. Of course. He did.

Still. God, why did he feel so slimy? Despite the dropping temperature, the back of his neck was covered in sweat. He had no choice but to return home, carrying mounting senses of dread and shame behind him like chains, knowing he'd written back to a stranger while he was—let's face it—infatuated with someone else.

What the hell was he going to do now?

# Chapter Fifteen

Julian jogged down Grapevine Way that afternoon, his pace slowing when he spied the lazy-Sunday line of people on the sidewalk. But this time, they weren't waiting outside UNCORKED. They were patiently waiting their turn to get inside Corked. Others were emerging with bottles of his family's wine in their hands, tied up in ribbons.

He made a sound in his throat, nodded once, and moved at a faster clip to make up for lost time. After running more than a block, he finally allowed himself to smile. Finally acknowledged the somewhat unsettling flip in the dead center of his chest. Now that Lorna's shop was on an upswing, Hallie wouldn't worry anymore, right? She'd be happy.

Perhaps it wouldn't hurt to update some of Lorna's indoor displays. Have the floor buffed. That line of people might be there because of the deal on the business cards he'd handed out, but what about a long-term plan? For Corked and Vos Vineyard? Instead of working on Wexler's book this morning, he'd had a meeting with the bookkeeper and, with Corinne's approval, had shifted some of their financial priorities. This year would be less about producing stock and more about selling what was already on shelves. Once they had the revenue in place, they could make the necessary improvements to come back better than ever.

Julian was busy making calculations in his head when he ran past the stump.

He stopped so quickly, dirt kicked up in the air.

A new letter?

His immediate instinct was to keep jogging. *Don't pick it up. Don't open it.* Hallie was not on the other end of these notes. After last night, they seemed to be at even more distinct odds than before. Just two people who'd traded heavy personal secrets in a vineyard. Two people who'd completely lost their minds one night and pleasured themselves together in his kitchen. Who couldn't seem to stop colliding. He would almost certainly return to Stanford with the sense that he'd left behind unfinished business, but that couldn't be helped, could it?

He'd have to simply . . . live with it.

How?

They would never again have a conversation like the one they'd had the night of the storm. Or while picking grapes on his family's land. Exchanges he continued to replay over and over in his head, trying to make sense out of them being so different while finding it so easy to understand each other. So much so that when he'd written his letter back to the secret admirer, his words were almost a period on the end of his conversations with Hallie. It was hard not to crave a response to that, even if it wasn't coming from her.

The letter was in his hand before he realized he'd picked it up.

"Fuck."

Julian started running again, through the cool, twisting haze escaping down off the mountain. The sun broke through the mist in fragments and cracks, a rolling spotlight over different sections of the vines. Beneath his feet, the earth was solid, and Julian was grateful for that, because holding the letter caused anticipation and dread to war in his middle all the way back to the house. On the off chance Natalie was awake before two P.M. on a weekend, he tucked the envelope into his pocket on the way to his bedroom, making it there without incident.

After closing the door behind him, he stripped off his sweaty shirt and placed it in the hamper. Toed off his running shoes and paced the floor beside the king-size bed. Finally, he couldn't stand the unknown anymore. He took the letter out of his pocket and broke the seal.

*Dear Julian,*

*There was one part of your response that stuck out to me. That there are events or people in our lives that force us to become the next version of ourselves. Are we all constantly fighting that change to something new and unfamiliar? Is that why, no matter what we do in our personal or professional lives, somehow it's never done with full confidence? There's always the fear of being wrong. Or maybe we're afraid to be right and make progress, because that means change. And moving forward is hard, like you said. Scary. Lately, I think moving forward as an adult means accepting that bad things happen and there's not always something you can do to avoid or fix it. Is having that knowledge the final change? If so, what* *is beyond <u>that</u> bitter pill? No wonder we're digging in our heels.*

*As I'm writing this, I'm starting to wonder if the longer we fight change in ourselves, the less time we have to live as better people. Or at least more self-aware people.*

*I propose that we both do something that scares us this week.*

*Secretly Yours*

"Fuck," Julian said again, finding himself on the edge of the bed, without remembering exactly when he'd sat down. Once again, he was completely and utterly intrigued by this person's letter, and yet, he wanted to tear it up and burn it in the fireplace. Not only because he alternated between hearing the words in Hallie's voice and feeling immense guilt for reading it in the first place. But more so because the letter challenged him. He hadn't accepted or denied the challenge yet. Still, his veins felt like they'd been pumped full of static.

*Something that scares us.*

Julian left the letter on his bed, but mentally carried it into the shower. Then into his office, where he once again sat in front of the blinking cursor for hours. At some point, he heard Natalie stumble out of her room for sustenance, before going straight back in. Finally, he gave up attempting to concentrate on anything else and returned to his bedroom, picking up the letter and trying to find some sort of clue in the handwriting, something about the basic stationery and ink color that might identify the author. Maybe if he could just meet this person face-to-face, he could confirm whether or not that attraction ran both ways. For some reason, he hoped it wouldn't. But nonetheless, they could be friends, right?

Even though they'd only exchanged letters, he couldn't help feeling a sort of kinship with this person who was capable of identifying the worries he'd never been able to speak aloud.

Except with Hallie.

Maybe rather than writing back, he should go talk to *her*, instead.

Anticipation swelled so rapidly at the thought of seeing her, hearing her voice, that he dropped the letter. From a person he'd now willingly corresponded with. A person who was *not* Hallie. What the hell had he gotten himself into?

"I'M SORRY TO drag you away from your fan club," Hallie teased Lorna, smiling at her grandmother's best friend across the console of her truck. They drove through town Sunday afternoon, yielding for buzzed pedestrians every fifty yards or so, Phoebe Bridgers playing gently on the radio. "Are you sure about taking a lunch break?"

"Of course I am, dear. These old feet need a rest." Lorna smoothed the silk patterned scarf around her neck. "Besides, Nina has it under control." Before she even finished her sentence, she'd started laughing. "Can you believe I have an employee now? A couple of weeks ago, I barely had customers. Now I've hired part-time help just to keep up with them all!"

Hallie's chest expanded with relief. With gratitude. When she'd pulled up outside of Corked, patrons were gathered around her grandmother's white wrought-iron table with glasses of wine in hand, bringing it to life. Giving it purpose again. Keeping Rebecca's memory alive, at least for Hallie. And she owed most of this to Julian.

His name in her head was a simultaneous shot of adrenaline and a punch to the gut.

Was he writing back to his admirer again at that very moment?

*I propose that we both do something that scares us this week.*

Was he in the process of figuring out what scared him? At the very least, Hallie was in the process of checking that box today. Doing something uncomfortable. Fulfilling the challenge she'd laid down for herself and Julian by moving forward. She'd called Lorna about her trip to the library this morning and the wineshop owner had insisted upon coming along for moral support, despite the crowds that were now descending on Corked with Vos Vineyard discount cards and unquenchable thirsts.

"Lorna, I couldn't be happier for you." One of Hallie's hands left the wheel to rub at the euphoric pressure in her chest. "I could just burst."

"I didn't see it coming," breathed the older woman, staring unseeing out the windshield of the truck. "Then again, some of the best things in life happen when you least expect them."

Sort of like Julian suddenly showing back up in St. Helena to write a book? Or the professor somehow being the chivalrous hero that lived rent free in her memory, while also being completely different than she'd imagined for the last fifteen years? Yes, he might be the quietly studious man of her imagination, but he was also intense. A keeper of painful secrets. Funny and quick to find solutions. Protective. A million times more engrossing than the person she'd crafted in her mind, and she had no choice but to leave him with some final food for thought and move on. Which is what she should have done in the beginning, before getting in too deep. "What if you spend your whole life expecting one thing . . . and get another entirely?"

"I'd say the one thing you can expect in life are thwarted plans," said Lorna. "Fate keeps its own schedule. But sometimes fate drops a present in our lap, and we realize that if everything we'd arranged ourselves had gone according to plan, the gift from fate never would have arrived. Like you coming to live with Rebecca in St. Helena. All those attempts to get your mother on the right path didn't work out, but in the end, those struggles are what brought you here. Rebecca was always saying that. 'Lorna, what's meant to be will always find a way.'"

"She loved a good saying."

"That she did."

Hallie shifted in the driver's seat but couldn't get comfortable. "What if I only belonged here in St. Helena while Rebecca was alive? That's how it feels. Like I don't . . . know how to be in this place anymore. As just myself."

Lorna was quiet for a moment. Hallie could feel the shop owner gathering herself before she eventually reached out and laid a hand on Hallie's shoulder. "When you came here, this place changed, along with Rebecca. It rearranged itself to fit you, and now . . . Hallie, you are part of the landscape. A beautiful part of it. St. Helena will always be better for having you here."

When Hallie shook her head, a tear came loose and she swiped it away. "I'm a disaster. I'm flighty and disorganized and I don't know how to control my impulses. She was always around to help me do that. To know who I am. I was Rebecca's granddaughter."

"You still are. Always will be. But you're also Hallie—and Hallie is beautiful for all her flaws. Because the good things about you far outweigh the bad."

Until Lorna said those words to Hallie, she didn't know how badly she needed to hear them. Some of the density in her chest lessened, her grip loosening on the steering wheel. "Thank you, Lorna."

"I'm happy to tell you the truth any time you want to hear it." Lorna patted her shoulder one more time before taking her hand back. "What made you decide to approach the library today about the landscaping job?"

Hallie hummed. Took a deep breath. "I want to do something she would be proud of. But . . . I think, more importantly, I have to do something I'm proud of. I have to start . . . taking pride, period. In myself and my work. It has to be for me now."

Hallie pulled her truck up against the curb across the street from the white, U-shaped building, also known as the St. Helena Library. It stood by itself at the end of a cul-de-sac, sun-soaked vineyard vines spreading out behind the structure in endless rows.

This morning, while pondering the trip, she'd bitten her nails down to the quick.

It had been a long time coming. Some part of her never really expected to get there.

The courtyard of the library definitely needed greenery and color and warmth. As of now, it had none of those things. Just overgrown indigenous plants that would have been beautiful with a little maintaining and the addition of some perennials. It did have a big lawn in front, shaded by an oak tree. Two children sat on that lawn now, blowing bubbles with very little success, suds dripping off their wrists onto the grass. A smaller toddler nodded off in her mother's lap, their library books spread out around them.

Hallie couldn't help but think the library could be thriving, with a little care. If people drove past, the flowers would call to them like an invitation. Marigolds and sunflowers and water fixtures. But in order to do this particular job, she would have to come up with an exact blueprint, have it approved by the library manager, Ms. Hume, and *stick* to it.

With Rebecca there to guide her, Hallie would have had no problem with a plan. But she was a dress pinned to a laundry line in a windstorm these days, waving in every direction. Had the years she'd spent under her grandmother's wing been a waste, though?

No.

As soon as Rebecca left, Hallie had gone back to being indecisive and jumbled. But it didn't have to continue that way. She could do something spectacular, all by herself. She could be proud of herself, discombobulated chaos and all. She was the granddaughter of a community staple—a gloriously kind woman who loved routine and simple pleasures, like wind chimes on the back porch and teach-yourself-calligraphy kits. Hallie had settled down as much as she was capable, because it was important to her grandmother. She appreciated when Hallie tried, when she reined in her scattered focus and applied it to schoolwork or carried out a specific landscaping strategy. There was no one around now to appreciate those efforts.

No one but herself. That would have to be enough.

*I propose that we both do something that scares us this week.*

Taking on a huge project like this definitely qualified as scary. It was a job that would require structure, diligence, and a very particular librarian looking over her shoulder the entire time.

Was she up for it?

*Yes.*

Something had to give. Putting her anxieties on paper, writing letters to Julian, had been therapeutic. She could be totally honest about her fears and feelings. That honesty felt good. Authentic. But now she needed to be truthful with herself. To admit she'd been avoiding the library job, because she didn't believe herself capable of the focus it would take to complete a task so large. Rebecca believed in her, though. So did Lorna. It was time to take that faith and turn it inward.

Lorna nudged her in the ribs from the passenger seat. "Go ahead, dear. You can do it. I'll be waiting right here."

She turned to her. "Are you sure you don't want bottomless champagne brunch, instead?"

"Maybe next week." Lorna laughed, shooing her into opening the driver's-side door. "For now, I want to watch my best friend's wild-child granddaughter learn a lesson. That she doesn't have to change to suit anyone. Unless that anyone is herself."

They held hands for a moment; then Hallie blew out a slow breath, climbed out of the truck, and crossed the street.

The cool brass doorknob slid against her palm, and she opened the heavy library door. Just as she remembered, the place was bright and inviting on the inside. Stained glass windows lit the stacks in reds and blues, hushed conversations took place over laptops at the tables, and the distinctive scent of old leather and floor polish drifted out to greet her.

Ms. Hume's head popped up from behind the reception desk, her slender, deep-brown fingers pausing on the keys. She removed her glasses, letting them drop to where they were caught by a long, beaded necklace, and stood. "Hallie Welch. Rebecca told me you would show up sooner or later," she said, a smile tugging at her lips. "Are you here to apply for a library card or finally fix our garden?"

Hallie took a moment to reconnect with her grandmother. Like a whispered hello from somewhere beyond. Then she centered herself and approached the desk. "Maybe both. You wouldn't happen to have any self-help books on staying organized, would you?"

"I'm sure I can pull a few."

"They're for a friend, obviously," Hallie joked, matching the librarian's knowing smile. "As for the garden . . . yes, I'm ready. I thought we could discuss layout today and I could get started soon."

Ms. Hume arched an eyebrow. "*When* exactly?"

"Soon," Hallie said firmly, in that moment accepting that there were some things about her she could never change.

And that . . . maybe she didn't need to.

# Chapter Sixteen

The familiar rumble of Hallie's truck grew louder as it made its way down the driveway, and Julian stood, crossing his bedroom to the window. Sunset was beginning to deepen the Sunday evening sky to orange.

How long had he been sitting there, contemplating the letter on the floor?

And thinking of Hallie.

Not long enough to reach his limit, apparently, because he stared through the glass now, starved for the sight of her. The dogs dove free of the truck first, moving in streaks of fur toward the trees at the back of the house. Hallie didn't follow right away. She sat in the driver's seat chewing her lip, unaware that he could see her. That he could witness her indecision or nerves. About . . . seeing him? He hated that possibility as much as he could relate to it. Being around her always left him in a state of hunger and confusion. Regret, too, because he couldn't seem to stop fucking up and either leading her on or pushing her away.

Finally, Hallie hopped down from the truck, went around to the rear, and lowered the tailgate. Sunset spilled across her shoulders, turning her cheeks gold. She tipped her face toward the sky and closed her eyes to let the fading light kiss her features, and yearning plowed into his stomach. Hard.

*Something that scares us.*

Hallie would definitely be at the top of that list, but a man didn't scale Kilimanjaro on his first hike. And would he now be betraying the letter writer if he used the challenge as an excuse to go after what he—might as well admit it—wanted so goddamn bad, he was being tortured day and night by the thought of it? Her? Also known as the beautiful gardener trudging toward his garden in rubber boots, cutoff shorts, and a navy blue hoodie that hung off one shoulder.

In her arms, she carried a pot of what Julian assumed was the dusty miller she'd referred to at the Wine Down event. The dogs trotted over to escort her, sniffing at her elbows and knees. She greeted each of them by name, her voice fading into the evening light as she disappeared around the side of the house. And he moved like an apparition to his office so he could pick up the sound again, hear it in full effect. The silly baby-talk way she spoke to her pets that was beginning to sound totally normal to him. The soft expulsions of breath when she exerted herself or dropped to her knees in the soil. Her voice seemed to fill the entire house, warm and sultry and singularly hers.

Jesus, was he starting to sweat?

Julian was on the verge of returning to the bedroom out of pure necessity, to handle the situation arising in his pants, when his sister's voice joined Hallie's outside the office window.

He felt as if ice water were spilling from the crown of his head to his toes.

This wasn't good.

He didn't know *why* exactly it wasn't good, but it was decidedly not.

Last night at Wine Down, he'd been distracted by Hallie. Too distracted to be careful with his words. It was only after he'd said those revealing things to Natalie about his unyielding drive to make Hallie happy that he wished he could go back in time and cram a cork in his mouth. There'd been more than enough of the bottle stoppers around, after all.

He might have made progress with Natalie last night—they were working their way back to a better sibling relationship, slowly but surely—but unfortunately, she wouldn't know discretion if it bit her on the ass.

Julian moved at a fast clip toward the front of the house and blew down the steps, only slowing to a sedate walk when the two women came into view. They were smiling, Hallie introducing Petey, Todd, and the General to Natalie, who was still in night shorts and a Cornell T-shirt. "Aren't you all just the sweetest gentlemen? Yes, you are! Yes. You. Are."

What was it about dogs that made people talk like that?

The animals were eating it up, too, tails whipping like chopper blades.

They shocked the hell out of Julian by bounding over to him next, reacting with—dare he say—*triple* the enthusiasm they'd displayed for Natalie? He was oddly pleased by that. Did he have an undiscovered way with animals? He always assumed pets were for *other* people. People who chose to devote hours of their lives to caring for an animal instead of useful endeavors. Now, looking down at the guileless eyes of Todd, he wondered if being loved unconditionally wasn't useful after all. "Hello," he greeted them in a normal voice, patting them each on the head. They weren't satisfied with that, however, weaving through his legs until he scratched them behind the ears. "Yes, okay, you're very good boys."

"They are slobbering on your socks, Julian," Natalie said, looking at him curiously. "Hey, you . . . forgot to put shoes on? You?"

"Did I?" he murmured, looking down with a pinch of alarm. He'd never gone outside without his shoes before. There was a process to going outdoors, and he'd forgone it completely. The dogs were indeed getting strings of saliva all over the no-nonsense white cotton tube socks, and he would need to change them, but that delay didn't gut him like it might have before.

How odd.

He looked up to find Hallie watching him with a curious expression. "Evening," she said, bringing the dogs tangling back in her direction.

"Good evening, Hallie," he said, his tone deep and formal. And he had no idea why. Only that he wanted to reestablish their footing somehow. Everything between them felt off-kilter, and he was getting really tired of analyzing why their being in balance was so important to him.

Natalie, however, was only getting started.

She split a gleeful look between Julian and Hallie, rocking side to side on the balls of her feet, as if waiting for the starting gun of a race. "So, Hallie. I didn't put it together last night, but we went to St. Helena High together." She narrowed an eye. "You were the cool new kid for a while. At least until someone else's parents decided to move here and open a vineyard."

Hallie tore her eyes from Julian and beamed at his sister,

and his chest crunched like cans in a trash compactor. Jealousy brewed inside of him like a pot of dark roast.

Damn, did he want that smile directed at him, instead.

"That was me. Although I challenge your assessment that I was cool." Absently, she scratched the General under his chin, still smiling that delighted smile. If she could just glance at him once while it was on her face . . . "You were the one throwing the parties. I had the pleasure of attending one or two."

"So you've seen me topless," Natalie said conversationally, producing a withering sigh from her brother. "Good to know."

"They still hold up," Hallie commented, giving her chest an impressed nod.

"Thank you," Natalie returned, pressing a hand to her throat.

Julian, for his part, was dumbfounded. "For all intents and purposes, you've just met and you're already discussing your . . ."

"Oh boy, do you think he's going to say it out loud?" Hallie murmured out of the corner of her mouth. "Ten bucks says he doesn't."

"I can't bet against you. I'd lose and I'm too broke to pay up." She faced Hallie fully. "You wouldn't happen to need a firmly titted assistant by any chance?"

Julian slashed a hand through the air. "You are not working together."

Both female heads swiveled in his direction. One startled. One looking like a cat who was on her way to snuff out the family canary. "Why not?" Natalie drawled. "Are you worried we'd talk about you?" She propped her chin on her wrist. "What could there possibly be to discuss?"

Silence ticked by along with the pulse in his temple.

Hallie looked at him.

In reality, only three seconds passed while he tried to come up with the right words for his inconvenient fixation on Hallie, but it was long enough.

"Nothing to discuss," Hallie answered for him. For them. With color in her cheeks, she slid her attention back to Natalie. "And, sorry. You're overqualified, Cornell."

His sister shook a fist at the sky. "Dammit. Foiled once again by my sharp intellect."

They shared a fond laugh, visibly considering each other. "Listen, there is a rebound in this town that still needs to be bounded, and he has my name on him. Would you want to attend a tasting with me on Tuesday night? Wine crafted by a former Navy SEAL," she cajoled, waggling her eyebrows. "I'm sure he's got a friend. Or two, if you're into that sort of thing. Or maybe you already have a boyfriend you can bring? I don't mind being the third wheel—"

"Natalie," Julian said through teeth that could not be unclenched to save the world. "That's enough."

"Says who?" Hallie asked, pivoting to face him.

"Says me." *Idiot.*

For once, the dogs were silent.

His sister had the expression of an Olympian holding up a bouquet of roses.

"I didn't realize you spoke for me." Hallie laughed, her eyes bright.

"My sister is making trouble out of sheer boredom, Hallie. I'm just trying to prevent you from getting wrapped up in it."

Natalie reared back a little, looking genuinely hurt. "Is that what I'm doing?"

Hallie laid a hand on Natalie's arm, squeezing. The look of reproach she gave him was like a line drive to the gut. "Friends don't let friends go to tastings alone. Someone has to talk you out of buying in discounted bulk. Count me in. But . . ." She avoided his stare. "No plus one. Just me."

He battled the urge to drop to his knees and worship her.

"Are you sure?" Natalie cut her a sideways glance. "You're not just saying yes because my brother is being a tool?"

This time she looked him square in the eye. "I'd be lying if I said that wasn't a good forty percent of the reason."

Natalie nodded, impressed. "I respect your honesty."

What the fuck was going on? He'd lost his grip on this situation entirely. In the blink of an eye, his sister had become friends with Hallie. Friends who went drinking together in the company of Navy SEALs. Somehow *he* was the bad guy. But the real problem, the reality he did not want to admit to himself, was that he liked Natalie and Hallie forming a bond. It reminded him of the moment Hallie turned her face to the orange sky and he could hear the dogs barking in the yard, and it hit him like a wave of preemptive melancholia. He'd think of this someday. He'd think of all of it. A lot.

With a rough clearing of his throat, Julian walked on dirty socks back into the house, which really took the dignity out of it all, and stripped the soggy things off before setting foot on the hardwood floor. He threw them into the hamper, on top of his running clothes, and paced back to the kitchen, pouring himself a third of a glass of whiskey, cursing, and adding another inch. He slugged it back, then stood there staring down into his empty glass until the rumble of Hallie's truck engine brought his head up, just in time for his sister to storm into the kitchen.

"Are you a whole-ass moron, Julian?"

No one had ever asked him a question like that. Perhaps it had been implied by his father, but in a far more aggressive format. "Excuse me?"

Natalie threw up her hands. "Why did you let me let you write back to that secret admirer?"

A mallet swung and connected with his temple. "Hallie told you she knew?"

"In passing. Yes."

He came as close as he ever would to smashing a glass on the ground. "How does something like that get mentioned in passing? Couldn't you talk about the weather instead of swapping life stories after a five-minute acquaintance? *Jesus!*" he shouted. "I told you I didn't want to do it."

"You didn't tell me why!" She raked her fingers through her dark hair. "Oh my God, the way you spoke about her last night and now the chemistry and the angst." She threw herself backward into the pantry door, rattling it loudly. "*I'm going to die.*"

It was not good for whatever peace of mind he had left to have someone recognize the connection between himself and Hallie and say it out loud. Why was he suddenly winded? "You think I should pursue Hallie. Is that what I'm getting from your theatrics?"

Her eyes flashed with accusation. "I don't know if you have a chance with her now, secret-admirer-letter returner."

Was there a pickax buried in his chest? "You *begged* me to write that letter!"

She made a disgusted face, flashing him a middle finger. "You want to get tangled up in semantics, fine, but the point is, you blew it. She's a rare spot of sunshine, and you're committed to huddling in the shade." She paused. "Maybe I should write a book, instead of you. That was a sick metaphor."

Julian started to leave the kitchen. "Speaking of which, I'm going to work."

"You haven't written in a week. It's because of her, isn't it? You're all . . . tied in knots and full of woe like a T-Bird in love with a Scorpion. *Grease* is my comfort movie. Okay?" Her voice rose. "What is the issue with pursuing her?"

He spun around at the mouth of the hall. "She makes me feel out of fucking control," he snapped. "You've been that way your whole life, so maybe you don't understand why that would be undesirable to someone. She leaves things to chance, she's flighty, she doesn't think her course of action through from beginning to end, and chaos is the result. She comes with dirty footprints, and corralling dogs and sticky children, and tolerating lateness. I'm too rigid for that. For her." A low, distant ringing started in his ears. "I'd dim her glow. I'd change her, and I would hate myself for it."

Natalie's throat worked for a series of heavy moments, the room lightening and darkening with a passing cloud. "Learn to let go, Julian. *Learn*."

He scoffed, making his throat burn worse. "You say that like it's easy."

"It's not. I know, because I've done it in reverse."

That gave Julian pause, drawing him out of his own misery. In reverse? Natalie had gone from free spirit to . . . dimmed down? Fine, she'd quit her antics, buckled down, and gone to a prestigious college, worked her way up to partner at a major investment firm. But she wasn't anything like him. Was she? She was full of humor and spontaneity and life.

Unless there was a lot more happening under the surface. A lot he couldn't see.

She diverted her gaze before he could search for it.

"Come with us Tuesday night, Julian. Don't live with regrets."

Julian stared at the empty archway long after Natalie had vacated it, trying to remember how he'd gotten to this point, this edge of the cliff where leaping was necessary. He hadn't asked for this. Never wanted it. But now?

*I'm too rigid for that. For her.*

*Learn to let go.*

That advice had come across as flippant at first. It made sense to him, though. If he knew how to do anything, it was learn. Expand his way of thinking. He'd just never done so in the name of romance. With the intent of . . . what? Was he going after Hallie now? Pursuing her?

The very idea was absurd. Wasn't it?

They lived an hour and a half away from each other, leading extremely different lives. The fact that they were polar opposites hadn't changed one iota. Hallie still brought disorder with her wherever she went. And he . . . would dull all of that. He'd squash it. When they first met, he thought she needed to change. Learn to be punctual. More organized. He'd even been so arrogant as to critique her as a gardener and decide she could do with some symmetry training. Now the idea that she would change, even in the slightest, on his account made Julian feel seasick.

*Then learn.*

It would have to be him that changed.

Pursuing Hallie meant easing his grip on time management. It meant learning to exist without the constraints of minutes and hours. Living with paw prints on his pants and understanding that she would do inconceivable things like volunteer to babysit thirty children and stuff them with donuts. Or steal cheese in broad daylight.

Why was he smiling, dammit?

He was. He could see his reflection in the microwave.

*I propose that we both do something that scares us this week.*

Was it in bad taste to take the advice from his secret admirer and use it to suit his purposes with Hallie? Probably. But, Jesus, now that he'd given himself permission to go get her, a rush of anticipation started in the crown of his head, blasting down to his feet so swiftly, he had to lean against the wall.

Okay, then.

*My goal is to date her. My goal is to be her boyfriend.*

He could barely hear his own thoughts over the ruckus his heart was making.

And yes, he was going to try his damndest to stop stuffing everything in life into the parameters of a plan and a schedule. But not when it came to this. To her. He needed a plan for winning her, because something deep in the recesses of his chest told him this was too important to be left up to chance.

# Chapter Seventeen

Tuesday night Hallie stood in front of her full-length mirror in two different shoes, trying to decide which one looked better. She snapped a quick picture with her phone and fired it off to Lavinia, who promptly responded with: Wear the heels. But if you replace me as your best friend tonight, be warned that I will stab you with one.

Never, Hallie texted back, snorting.

She kicked aside some of the clothes and beauty products on her floor and found the lint roller, dragging the stickiness down her snug black dress to rid it of three varieties of dog hair. She stepped over the pile of rejected shoes and entered her en suite bathroom, leaving the lint roller in a place she probably wouldn't find it next time and—

Hallie straightened, her fingers pausing in the act of rooting through lipsticks to find the right shade of golden peach. Watching her actions as if they were being performed by someone else, she removed the sticky strip of dog hair from the roller, threw it in the trash, and replaced the essential tool for dog owners in the drawer, where she used to keep it.

She stepped back from the mirror and looked around, wincing at the clutter.

Now that she'd taken a big step in her professional life, tomorrow she needed to take a leap in her personal one—and rein in this house jungle. Or at least get a running start.

But first, she'd get through tonight.

Going to a wine tasting with Julian's sister was a terrible idea considering she'd resolved to move on. For real this time. Especially after the awkward scene that had played out in his front yard. He'd made it clear that they were incompatible and written a letter to someone else, so what gave him the right to decide what she did with her time? Or whom she spent it with?

The guesthouse garden was almost complete. She hadn't quite decided what she would use to fill the final spaces, but it would come to her. Hopefully on her next trip to the nursery—and then she could wrap up her responsibilities to the Vos family, bill the matriarch, and move on. No more secret admirer letters, either. They were just another ill-conceived part of her life. She'd acted on impulse, and where did it lead her?

To having him validate all of her feelings. The ones she'd held on to for so long. And those things were not good, because Julian remained unavailable to her. Nothing had changed. If she revealed herself to him as the author of those letters, he would probably be disappointed that she wasn't some like-minded scholar with a home filing system.

Maybe she would write the letters to herself from now on, instead of to Julian. They'd led her somewhere useful, hadn't they? She'd finally admitted that avoidance through chaos was harming her livelihood. Even her friendship with Lavinia, who had begun looking at her in that worried, measuring way. Hallie needed to turn onto a new path. A healthy one.

Hallie shuffled a few lipsticks into her makeup case and snapped it shut, suddenly looking forward to a cleaning spree in the morning. A fresh start. Maybe she would even pick a new wall color for the living room and do some painting. Peony pink or peacock blue. Something vivid that would serve as a reminder that she was not only capable of admitting her self-destructive habits, but of finding a way to correct her course while remaining true to herself.

With a nod, Hallie requested an Uber and spent the ten-minute wait saying good-bye to the boys, which led to another harried trip to the lint roller, but the snuffling snuggles were well worth it. She'd taken them to the dog park after dinner so they could run off any excess energy that might lead to her coming home to couch stuffing all over the floor. Now she put some extra food in their bowls and walked out the front door, clutch purse in hand, sinking into the back seat of the black Prius.

Julian must have given his sister Hallie's phone number, because Natalie had texted her that afternoon with an address to the apparently SEAL-owned winery, Zelnick Cellar. The place had a website, but it was under construction, and she'd never heard of it from anyone in town. She was curious, even if spending the evening with a Vos wasn't the wisest step on her road to separating herself from all things Julian.

Ten minutes later, the Uber stopped in front of a medium-size barn surrounded by wooden fencing. Flickering light shone from within, and she could see a small crowd standing around. She had to imagine they were locals, since she hadn't been able to find the tasting advertised anywhere on the Web. Was it entirely through word of mouth?

Tossing a thank-you to the driver, Hallie climbed out of the back seat and stood, tugging down the snug hem of her dress. She opened the flashlight app on her phone—getting a lot of use out of it lately, huh?—and did her best to navigate the dirt path leading to the barn while wearing skinny three-inch heels. The closer she got to the music and the crowd, the more well-lit the path became, and she slipped her phone back into her purse. Glowing white bulbs bounced up and down in the breeze, strung from high points of the barn. Was that the Beach Boys playing? This had to be the most casual wine tasting she'd ever attended. No doubt she'd overdressed—

Julian stepped into the barn entrance.

In a sharp, charcoal-gray suit.

Holding a bouquet of wildflowers in his hand.

Time slowed down, allowing her to feel and experience the over-the-top response of her hormones. They sang like tone-deaf preteens in the shower, screeching the high notes with misplaced confidence. Wow. Oh wow. He looked like he'd walked out of an advertisement for an expensive watch with too many dials. Or Gucci cologne.

Good. Lord.

*Wait.* Wildflowers were her favorite. How had he known?

Honestly, it tracked that they would be. But still.

She recognized the pink cellophane wrapping. He'd gone all the way to the nursery for that colorful spray. Who were they for?

Why was he here in the first place?

*Close your mouth before you start drooling.*

Salivating became even more of a possibility when Julian closed the distance between them, striding forward in that purposeful way of his. And when his head blocked the light coming from the barn, she saw determination and focus in the set of his jaw, the intensity of his eyes, the deep line of concentration between his eyebrows.

"Hello, Hallie."

The sheer depth of his voice, like the belly of a submarine scraping the ocean floor, almost had her backing away. Just dropping her purse and running.

Because what was happening here?

Without breaking eye contact, Julian picked up her free hand and wrapped it around the bouquet of wildflowers. "For you."

She shook her head. "I don't understand."

He seemed to be expecting that, because his expression didn't shift at all. He merely seemed torn over which part of her face to study. Nose, mouth, cheeks. "I'll explain. But first, I want to apologize for my behavior on Sunday. I acted like a jackass."

Hallie nodded dazedly. Was she accepting that apology?

Hard to say, when she was watching Julian slowly drag his tongue from right to left along his bottom lip, an answering clench taking place between her thighs. Something was different about him. He never failed to be entirely magnetic, but this was on a whole other level. It was almost *intentional.* Like he'd forgotten his filter at home.

"I'd like the opportunity to spend time with you, Hallie." His attention traveled downward, stopping at the hemline of her dress, that bump in his throat traveling high, then low, along with the register of his voice. When he reached out a single finger and traced the location where her skin met the hem, the air vanished from her lungs. "I want to . . . *date* you."

He packed so much bite into the word "date," there was no pretending it didn't have more than one meaning. Especially when his finger was just inside the hem now, teasing side to side to side, setting her legs trembling.

"You want to date me?"

"Yes."

"I still don't understand. What changed?"

Julian hooked his finger and dragged her close by the hem of her dress. Breathless, her head fell back so she wouldn't have to break eye contact. God, he was tall. Did he grow in the moonlight or did he just seem larger now that he'd apparently stopped withholding himself?

"Truthfully?" he asked.

"Yes, truthfully," she whispered.

Acute distress flickered briefly in his gaze. "I felt you slipping away from me. On Sunday in the yard." He paused, visibly searching for an explanation. "We'd left things up in the air before, but this was different, Hallie. And I didn't like it." He studied her closely. "Was I right? Have you slipped away from me?"

Under such intense scrutiny, there was no point in providing anything but the truth. "Yes. I have."

His chest rose sharply, shuddering back down. "Let me try and reverse that decision."

"No." She ignored how sexy he looked with that single professor's eyebrow hoisting into the air and let the word hang between them. Maybe the longer she left it there, the better chance she would have of actually *keeping* her resolve. Panicked by her slim odds, Hallie reminded herself that he'd written back to the other woman. Or what he *assumed* was another woman. He'd told a stranger deep, important things about himself, and that hurt, because he'd made Hallie feel like his confidant. Then he'd given that confidence to someone else.

Oh, she was the furthest thing from blameless here. Writing those letters had been deceptive and shortsighted. Part of the reason for distancing herself now was to leave her folly behind her, pretend she hadn't acted so impulsively, and enjoy the clean slate she planned to start writing on tomorrow. She could admit that. However, the sting of him leaving a letter on that stump continued to linger.

And last, but definitely not least, hadn't she proposed in her last letter that they both do something that scared them? For her, it was walking into the library and taking the landscaping job. For Julian, obviously it was her. She—this—scared him.

Hallie bit back the sudden need to knee him in the jewels.

"No?" he echoed Hallie, his fingertip pausing in its sensual travels beneath her hem, misery etching itself on his features. "I really have behaved poorly, haven't I?"

In all honesty, they both had.

So she couldn't answer with a yes. Not without being a hypocrite.

"What happened to us being wrong for each other?" she asked instead. "We decided that pretty early on, didn't we?"

"Yes," he said, moving his hand away from her with a visible effort, curling his fingers into a fist, and shoving it into his pants pocket. "It's come to my attention that I am far more wrong for you than the other way around, Hallie. You're nothing short of breathtaking. Unique and beautiful and bold. And I'm a goddamn idiot if I ever made you feel otherwise." She could feel in her bones how badly he wanted to reach for her in that moment. "I'm sorry. Every second we've spent together, I've been restraining myself. Trying to keep . . . to stay controlled."

"And that's not important to you anymore?"

"Not as important as you."

"Wow," she whispered, breathless. "Hard to fault any of these answers."

That fist came out of his pocket, and he shook it out, flexed his fingers and stepped forward to cup her cheek, his thumb tracing the cupid's bow of her upper lip. "I want to learn you, Hallie." His voice was low, imploring. "Let me learn."

*Oh my.*

A tremor coursed from her belly down to her knees, almost causing her to lose her balance. She might have, if the magnetism of his gaze wasn't holding her steady. Of course, when this man decided to be romantic, decided to try and woo a woman, the results were deadly. She'd just underestimated *how* potent his full effort and attention would be.

Also, if this was an inappropriate time to be turned on, someone needed to tell her vagina, because while standing with Julian in the swirling mist of the moonlit night, his breath bathing her mouth, belt buckle grazing her stomach, it took serious effort not to lick him. Just lick him anywhere she could reach. Maybe those cords in his neck or the forearms he was hiding underneath the sleeves of his suit—

"Everything you're thinking is right there on your face," he said, battling a smile.

Hallie took a step backward, losing the warmth of his hand, his breath. "I'm thinking about the wine I'm going to drink."

"Liar." He tossed a glance toward the barn. "And don't get your hopes up. It's terrible. If my sister wasn't in there, I'd suggest we make a run for it."

"Terrible wine?" She grimaced. "How badly does anyone *need* a sister?"

He laughed. A rich, rumbling sound that made the air feel lighter. “Come on.” He held out his hand to her. “We’ll spill it out under the table while his back is turned.”

“That sounds like the kind of plan I would come up with.”

His eyes flickered with determination. Affection. “I’m learning you already.”

Lord help her, she couldn’t do anything but twine her fingers through his after that. She watched with a grapefruit in her throat as he kissed her knuckles gratefully, pulling her at his side toward the barn. Then . . . she was walking into a wine tasting holding Julian’s hand. Like a couple. He led her through a light-strung barn, through a gathering of about two dozen people, the scent of fermented grapes and straw heavy in the air. Guests stood in groups around candlelit high-top tables, their glasses of wine remaining noticeably full.

The waiter who’d obviously been hired to refill glasses and prod attendees to buy bottles to go looked stressed, unsure of what to do with himself. And his boss, the Navy SEAL turned Napa vintner, was too busy staring deep into Natalie’s eyes to advise him.

“Oh boy,” Hallie muttered.

“Uh-huh. Ask me how glad I was when your Uber pulled up.”

“Maybe we should help.” Julian slid a full glass of red wine in front of her, looked at it pointedly. She picked it up and took a sip, bitterness oozing down her throat. “Dear God,” she croaked. “There’s no way to salvage this.”

“None,” Julian agreed.

Someone a few tables over called Hallie’s name—a recurring client—and she waved, smiling and exchanging some predictions about what would be blooming soon. When she turned back to Julian, he was watching her closely, that deep groove taking up real estate between his brows. All she could do was stare in return, sighing shakily when he rested a big hand on her hip, tugging her closer. Closer. Until she was in the circle of his heat, head tilted back. "You're dangerous like this," she murmured.

That thumb dug into her hip bone, ever so slightly. "Like what?"

Tingles ran all the way down to her toes, hair follicles prickling on the crown of her head. "Are you going to pretend like you're not trying to seduce me?"

His focus fell to her mouth. "Oh, I am one hundred percent trying to seduce you."

A long, hot clenching took place between her thighs, tummy muscles coiling, skin temperature skyrocketing. With a trembling laugh, she glanced over her shoulder and quickly scanned the room. "At least three of my regular clients are here. It wouldn't be very professional to be seduced where they can see me."

Was he looking at the pulse in her neck? It started beating faster, as if preening under the attention. "Then I suggest we go for a walk."

She pursed her lips at him and hummed. "I don't know about that. The last time we went for a walk in a vineyard, I only came back disappointed."

The corner of his mouth jumped with humor, but his eyes were serious. "Not this time, Hallie."

A promise. A confident one.

"What does that mean, exactly?" Hallie asked softly, haltingly.

He hesitated a moment, tongue tucked into his cheek. Then he dropped his mouth to her ear and said, "It means, this time I'm not finishing on your thighs."

*Holy mother of God.*

Images bombarded her mind. Those wires in Julian's neck straining, hands roaming desperately in the darkness, her knees in his big hands.

If she didn't know any better, she would have thought that one sip of terrible wine had gone to her head, the giddy lift of lust was so magnificent. Letting herself get carried off on Julian's current could be a really bad idea. Not only did she have a secret—that *she* was his secret admirer—but there was no evidence that a relationship would work. In fact, it was a total long shot. People couldn't change so drastically, could they?

But weren't moments like this why she'd finagled her way into fixing the guesthouse garden in the first place? She'd wanted her dose of magic with Julian Vos. Now that she knew him, now that she'd fallen for the real man, being happy with a single moment was impossible. She didn't have to think about that tonight, though. She could just let herself be taken for the ride. The one she'd dreamed about since high school. The one that was so much more powerful now that she'd gotten to know him, this man who bought awnings for failing wineshops. Or jumped in to host children's story time and saved her from being arrested.

Lost in her thoughts, she swayed forward involuntarily, and her breasts grazed his upper abdomen, the suggestive rasp of their clothing making her want to moan. Rub against him like a cat. Especially when his eyes went smoky, lids heavy.

"Hallie," he half growled. "Take the walk with me."

With the word "yes" on the tip of her tongue, her conscience made a last-minute attempt to throw up a barrier, talk her out of taking something she needed and wanted. *Tell him the truth first, or you'll regret it.* But apparently she'd need more time to become a reasonable, non-reckless person. Because all she said was "Yes."

# Chapter Eighteen

If he didn't kiss her soon, the world was going to end. Julian was convinced of this beyond any shadow of a doubt. He was so starved for the taste he'd been denying himself that he hustled her out of the barn like they were escaping its imminent collapse. Nothing was collapsing, however, except his self-control where Hallie was concerned. How the fuck had he kept his distance from this woman? When he walked out of the barn and saw her teetering up the path, so familiar and so unforgivably unknown at the same time, he'd wanted to crawl to her on his hands and knees.

This was not the way he'd planned for the evening to go.

He was supposed to apologize. They were supposed to sit down and talk, sort through the obstacles between them and devise a mutual plan for moving forward together. As two adults with a common goal: a healthy, communicative relationship. Maybe if she hadn't worn that tight black dress, his chances for success would have been more realistic. Maybe if she didn't make him feel animalistic, he wouldn't be dragging her out into the darkness right now, his cock halfway to erect, a bead of sweat trickling down his spine.

And maybe if he didn't feel himself falling irreversibly in love with her, he might have already dragged her into the shadows by now and satisfied his craving for her perfect mouth. But he felt what was happening. Acutely. Thus, he couldn't ignore the sore weight of his heart where it sat in his chest, wondering why it hadn't been used until now. Couldn't ignore the way his throat seemed to be jammed through with pins every time she blinked at him.

Jesus Christ. Love was pain, apparently.

Love was being stripped down to the bones. Being more than willing to beg for more.

And because he wanted more than just one night, because he wanted to try his fucking hardest for more than a sweaty encounter with this woman, he slowed his step and breathed deeply in through his nose, out through his mouth.

"Everything you're thinking is right there on your face," she said to his left, echoing the words he'd said to her earlier. Because she was absolutely incredible. And he'd been denying himself due to his fear of the unknown. He was in the exact right place when they were together, and he couldn't fight that feeling anymore. More important, he needed to make sure she felt right being with him, too. As if they were standing in the exact same spot in this big fucking universe, not a single inch apart, physically or emotionally.

Was that utterly terrifying? Yeah. It was. As he'd known from the beginning, this woman threw him off-center, dashed his plans, and flaunted time like it was a suggestion. She could very well drive him completely insane. But while holding her hand and leading her into the vineyard, between the rows of fragrant nighttime vines, no other choices existed. Tomorrow no other choices would exist. Or the day or the year after that. There was only being with Hallie. He'd have to let something other than himself determine the course of his time going forward.

Chance. Possibilities he didn't control.

That realization was so heavy, so hard for a man like him to grasp, that he slowed to a stop about a hundred yards into one of the rows. As if they'd been made specifically to lock together, she walked right into his arms, her nose flattening against the side of his neck in such an endearing way, such a trustful way, it took him a moment to speak.

"Being in the vines reminded me of the fire. Until we went picking together. Now when I look out at them, I just think of you," he said, watching, fascinated by the way one of her curls looped around his finger. "Were you in St. Helena when it happened?"

His stomach was already plummeting like an elevator with a snapped cable in anticipation of her answer. He'd barely be able to stand it if she'd been scared, let alone in danger. Especially knowing he had been in town at the time.

"My grandmother and I drove south. We stayed in a motel and watched the news for five days straight." She pulled back and searched his face. "You stayed behind."

He nodded, hearing the distant crackling of burning wood. "My father and I did what we could to prepare. Evacuated everyone, moved equipment. But they said . . . fire officials told us we had six hours before the fire reached us. And it happened in one. One hour instead of six." He could still remember the way that stolen time had choked him, the way denial unzipped him straight down the middle. Time was supposed to be absolute. A foundation for everything. For the first time, it had betrayed him.

"My sister was in one of the larger sheds when it happened—she'd been loading wine stock into a truck. Just an ember carrying on the wind, they said. The whole thing was up in flames in a matter of minutes. I was acres away when it started. By the time I'd run to the building, it was engulfed. We were the only ones here, so no one heard her screaming. I almost didn't get her out." He didn't want to think about that, so he moved on briskly. "I'd never had an—"

"Wait. Go back." Was she *shaking*? "How did you get her out?"

"I went in," he explained.

"You went into a burning building to rescue your sister. I'm just clarifying."

"I . . . Yes. She needed help."

"You saved her life and she still brought you to this terrible wine tasting," Hallie murmured, shaking her head. Despite the joke, however, she appeared almost shaken by the story. "I interrupted what you were going to say. You'd never had a what?"

He rarely said the term out loud, but this was Hallie. "An anxiety episode. As a child, I had them, but not since then. Not as an adult. My schedules didn't make sense in the context of the fire. We were supposed to have six hours, and, suddenly, we're driving through smoke just hoping to escape with our lives. Time wasn't safe anymore. My sister wasn't safe. I didn't do well with it." He paused to gather his thoughts, wiping the perspiration from his palms down the sides of his pants. "I hated that feeling. That locked-up feeling. And you might think the fire would have acted as some kind of immersion therapy and I'd loosen my grip on time, realizing it can't be controlled, but I doubled down instead. I lost time. Completely. I just sort of went numb, Hallie. For days. My family was trying to salvage the winery, and mentally, I wasn't there. I did nothing to help them. All I could do was sit in a dark room and write lesson plans. Lectures. I remember almost nothing from the days after the fire.

"That's why I've been trying so hard to stay away from you. Anything that threatens this control I have . . . I've been seeing it as the enemy. When it gets ahold of me, I don't recover quickly like Garth. It's something to avoid at all costs. But I can't do that with you anymore, because you're worth burning for. You're worth turning and driving straight into the fire."

"Whoa," she whispered, the gray of her eyes swimming and starlit. "I don't know which part of that to address first. The part that maybe you're a hero for saving your sister, but you can only focus on a dark moment or—or . . ."

He stripped off his jacket and tossed it behind her onto the ground, only sparing a fleeting thought for the dry cleaning. "The part when I said I'd drive through fire for you?"

She nodded, her eyes locked on his fingers where they were unknotting his tie, then shoving the balled-up material into the right front pocket of his dress pants. "Yeah, that part."

"What about it?" he asked.

Her eyes lifted hesitantly. "What if I said I would do the same for you?"

This is what it meant to be choked up. To have his sanity in the hands of another person to do with what they wanted. "I'd be fucking grateful." He caught her by the hips and dragged her close, hissing a breath when her belly finally, finally met his aching length. "But I'd also lose my mind if you were ever in that kind of danger, so please don't ever say that out loud again."

"It was your analogy," Hallie teased, going up on her toes, a slow raking of tits and belly and hips up the front of his primed body, and he groaned loudly, there in the middle of the vineyard. "Thank you for telling me that."

Oh Jesus, he couldn't take her whispered gratitude on top of his dick being so hard. Who had sent this woman to kill him? He was hungry and desperate and ready to give up years of his life to get his hands on those breasts. "I'll tell you anything you want, just let me kiss that goddamn mouth. Let me get on top of you."

With a small sound of shock—did she not understand he was dying?—Hallie lurched higher onto her toes and gave up her mouth, letting him come from above and wreck it, broken and starved and needy, his hands trying to clutch and smooth every part of her at once, experience every inch. They tunneled through her hair and raked down her back, yanking her by the ass into the cradle of his lap, both of them gasping into the kiss over the miraculous friction they created. The chafe they kept alive with rubs and pushes and grinds.

"Tell me we're fucking tonight, Hallie," he gritted out, teeth pressed to her ear.

"Was your mouth always this dirty?" she gasped.

"No." He urged her down onto the ground, and she went, landing flat on her back on top of his spread-out jacket, her curls bouncing out in ninety directions, a sight that made his hands shake, it was so *her*. "And you can blame my colorful vocabulary on the fact that you've been bent over on your knees outside of my office window for weeks." He let his weight settle on top of her incredible curves, slowly, his breath escaping like air from a tire puncture, his balls throbbing like a son of a bitch. "*Weeks*."

"That is the standard flower-planting position."

He reached down, gathered the hem of her dress in his hand,

and worked it up to her hips, immediately rocking into the space between her thighs, deprived at never having been there before. Being like this, with her, was where he belonged. And God, the way she moaned and arched her back, covered in moonlight and a flush, was the closest he'd ever come to magic. "Flowers are the last thing on my mind when you're on all fours," he gritted out, rocking again, gratification thick in his stomach when she pressed her knees open, grabbed the sides of his waistband, and pulled, urged, lifted. "I'm thinking of your bare ass slapping against my stomach."

"G-great," she stammered in between hot rakes of their open mouths. "I'll never be able to do my job again without blushing."

"Speaking of this blush." Christ, he could barely make out his own words, they were so slurred with lust, muffled into her neck as he traced a line downward with his tongue, over the smooth patch behind her ear, the curve of her collarbone, the sweet-smelling hollow of her throat. "How far down does it go?"

"I don't know," she breathed. "I've never checked."

"We better find out." Julian watched her face closely as he licked a path over the hills of her cleavage, needing to know they were together in this. Continuing. "Hallie. Are you wearing that goddamn polka dot bra?"

"I . . . Yes. How did you—"

Groaning, he kissed her stiff nipples through the material of her dress, the fact that she'd worn that tormenting underwear turning his dick to stone. "Let me take it off and suck them, sweetheart."

She struggled to pull in a breath. "Oh, wow. Key moment to pull out the endearment."

He opened his mouth over the stiff bud, raking his lips side to side, groaning when it swelled, grew sharper. "I've been calling you that in my head for much longer."

"Just pull my top down already," she said in a rushing laugh that got his chest so heavily involved in the moment, even more than it already was, he had to press his face between her breasts and steady himself with her rapid-fire heartbeat. Inhaling through his nose and out through his mouth until the squeeze turned bearable. Mostly. "Julian . . ."

"I know." He had no idea what that exchange meant, only that Hallie's use of his name anchored him even more, made his mouth eager for the taste of her tongue again. And he gave in to it, traveling back up to her mouth for more kissing, more wild drawing of suction and wetness, then back down to her heaving tits. At some point, they'd started working down the neckline of her dress together, or maybe the drag of his chest up and down had done it, because her breasts were almost free of her bodice and polka dot bra, so big and lush and sweet, he whispered a prayer before his first lick across her bare nipples. "First part of you I saw up close," he muttered thickly. "Last thing I want to see before I die."

She giggled, and Julian accepted that he'd be going to hell someday, because Hallie giggling while he sucked her nipples, the polka dot bra pushing them up for his attention, his hands molding those pretty mounds thoroughly, was the hottest moment of his life. Nothing would ever top it. Although he was proven wrong a few seconds later when she started to whimper, her fingernails digging into his scalp, hips restless on the ground.

*"Julian."*

"That getting you wet?"

She nodded jaggedly, bottom lip clamped between her teeth.

"You going to let me check?" His fingertips were already trailing down her inner thigh, massaging the inside of her knee, then tracing up, up, toward the heat. "I want you more than ready, Hallie. I'll play with them until the zipper of my pants is your worst enemy."

"Oh my God."

The way she kind of melted into the ground and writhed her hips every time he said something dirty made it clear she loved it. And Julian loved it, too, the freedom to say whatever came to his mind, wanting her to know what he was thinking, down to the letter. He'd never cared before. Never spoken much at all during the act. Now he couldn't seem to keep his mouth shut, craving connection with her on every level available. Verbal, physical, emotional.

His fingers found her then, massaging through the thin nylon of her panties, dampness soaking through to meet him. *Yes. Jesus Christ, yes.* So much of it that he dropped his face between her tits and moaned, parting the folds of her flesh with a gently sawing knuckle and teasing her clit. When her hips reared up off the ground and she sobbed, he moved on instinct, capturing her mouth in a rough kiss, knuckling that sensitive little bud over and over again. The wild way she gave herself over to the kiss made him wonder if . . . was she already close?

Julian paused with his mouth on top of hers. They inhaled and exhaled together. Fast. Faster. Anticipation so real he could feel it pressing down on his spine. "You come easy, don't you, Hallie?" Looking her in the eye, he pulled down her panties, just below her pussy, trapped around the tops of her thighs. "I remember in the kitchen how sweet you got off. How quick." He parted her folds with his thumb, stroked the full length of her sex, and watched her eyes roll into the back of her head. "You're not just beautiful and sexy and—Jesus—the fucking *curves*." With a nip and tug of her earlobe, Julian pushed his middle finger inside of her. "You are a horny little thing, aren't you?"

"*Julian*."

She was saying his name, but he could only sort of hear it through the ringing in his ears. Tight. God, she was *really* tight. And the way her thighs jerked in around his hand, like the sensation of his finger was foreign? No . . . But when he looked down into her face and saw she was holding her breath, visibly waiting for him to catch up, he knew. "Hallie, you're a virgin."

A brief silence passed. "Yes."

Why wasn't he shocked? He should have been, right? This vital, spontaneous woman had somehow made it to age twenty-nine without exploring a sensual side of herself that was very much alive and well. The woman was practically vibrating beneath him, every single part of her engaged in what they were doing. Maybe he was just too overcome with hunger for Hallie to dwell on something so useless as surprise. His focus remained locked on the fact that she had needs *right now*. She'd decided to let him handle them and that was good enough.

If anything, he just needed to be extra sure. Before he took her virginity.

*I'm her first*.

Did the crowding of pride in his throat make him a caveman?

No. No, who wouldn't be fucking proud that a woman like Hallie had decided he was worthy of her first time? A man who didn't treasure this position didn't deserve it—and that was the last time he thought of men in general and Hallie in the same context, because his teeth were snapping at her neck as a result. *Mine.*

*Calm the hell down.*

Julian tried to inhale a steadying breath, but it brought her scent along with it and only succeeded in making him salivate. Press his finger a little deeper inside of her, just to watch the pulse jump at the base of her neck. "Hallie." Lord, he sounded like the big bad wolf. "Be one hundred percent honest with me now. Are you sure about this?"

Fingers flexing on his shoulders, she nodded vigorously. "Yes. Positive."

*Thank God.* "Why do you sound relieved?"

"I thought you were going to be responsible and call a stop to everything."

"That *would* be the responsible thing to do," he agreed, even while biting a path down the center of her body, nipping at her tits, her belly, her thighs, before bringing the flat of his tongue up firmly between the folds of her sex. "Your first time should be in a soft bed. Somewhere familiar. Comfortable." He pressed the V of his fingers over her flesh and strip of blond hair, opening her up to him, and he could only wish for sunlight to see her better. To memorize every ripple and shadow. "And here I am, getting ready to fuck you on the hard ground. Flat on your back with your dress up around your waist. Aren't I, sweetheart?"

Before she could answer, he drew the tip of his tongue up the center of her pussy and left it poised on top of her clit for long seconds, before wiggling it roughly. And God help him, she came. The proof of it met his tongue unexpectedly, and he didn't think, just followed instinct by lapping at her, pushing her thighs as wide as he could get them, and going for broke, licking that swollen pleasure source until she whimpered at him to stop.

*"Please!"*

Out of his fucking mind, horny beyond belief, he rose up over her flushed body while fumbling with his belt, his wallet, and the condom, ripping the foil packet open. She tried to help him, their hands knocking together, their mouths seeking each other for wet, illicit kisses that went straight to his head. Both of them.

"I'm putting on a condom, but I'm going to blow where it's so deep and tight, it'll feel like I'm wearing nothing—"

"Oh God, oh God."

"If I don't get inside you soon—"

"Don't even joke like that."

And so they were laughing in pure pain when he pressed his cock into her, the sound of amusement dying on a long, guttural groan from Julian. "Oh my fucking *God,*" he barked into her neck, easing his hips closer, closer, meeting the resistance of untried flesh and stopping, panting, inwardly calling himself a bastard for taking something so perfect, but her fingers fisted in the elastic sides of his briefs and pulled him deep, *so motherfucking deep,* her mouth moaning, hips lifting, the insides of her knees grazing his rib cage, her eyelids fluttering.

*Fuck oh fuck.* That was when he started to spin out.

Out of control. He was out of control.

He thought he could do this, throw himself headfirst into everything Hallie made him feel, but he'd been foolish to underestimate the magnitude of it. With her flesh stretching around him, her gaze locked on his for comfort, affection and gratitude and—God forgive him—possessiveness almost buckled his heart. There was no schedule to fall back on. No pen and paper to take notes. There was nothing to do but lean into what she made him feel, damn the outcome or consequences. He didn't have any tools available to build a dam. With each stroke of her fingers on his face, every kiss of his jaw and shoulders, she was stripping him of every last one of them.

"Hallie," he growled into her neck, starting to move, fisting her hair, and starting to fuck her. He couldn't do anything else with her clutching at him like that, mewling every time he went deep. Was her virginity obvious? Yes. God yes. He could barely get in and out, she was so fucking snug. But it was equally obvious that she was enjoying herself. Enjoying him. Her eyes were glazed over, her lips chanting his name, and those silky soft thighs, they hugged him like they never wanted him to leave. Or stop. In fact, they urged him faster, and he went, burying his tongue in her sweet mouth and kicking his hips into a gallop. "You've been doing such bad things to my dick, sweetheart. Just bouncing around with those curls in your tight shorts, not a care in the world, huh? Well, you've got to deal with me now. You've got to let those beautiful tits out and deal with me, don't you?"

"Yes," she gasped, her flesh tightening up around him, her hips impatient. A cue, permission to go harder, faster, and he did, pressing their moaning mouths together and increasing his pace, a shudder racking him in the exact moment she learned her power. Learned that she could flex her pussy and turn him into an animal. "You like that," she whispered.

"Yes, yes, I fucking like it," he panted hoarsely. "I *love* it. Again."

And really, it was a reckless request, because he forgot his own name after that. Forgot it was her first time and they weren't all *that* far from a public gathering. When she constricted her already too-tight flesh around him, her eyes flashing with excitement over his desperate response, that was it. His fingers dug into the earth, and he went blind, fucking to relieve the ache between his thighs. Fucking to claim her as his own—no help for that. No rationalizing it.

"Mine, sweetheart, *mine,*" he grunted in her ear, scoring his teeth down the side of her neck.

*Who am I?* He had no idea, only that this was right where he was supposed to be. With her. Even as his head spun and panic over the unknown threatened, he couldn't stop. There would never be any stopping. She was salvation and homecoming and lust and woman.

"Hallie. *Hallie.*"

"Yes."

What was he asking? No idea. But she knew. She knew and her body understood, her back arching so her clit could rub against his thrusting cock, this incredible virgin who'd learned her own body in advance and he praised her for it, bathing her neck with his tongue and scooping his hands beneath her ass, anchoring them so he could angle down and stroke where she needed, exultant when she whimpered brokenly in response and shook into another orgasm, her pussy clamping around him, making it impossible for him to do anything but pump deep and follow, the two of them shaking in the dirt together, mouths frantic, hands squeezing, trying to get through to the other side.

Relief like Julian felt shouldn't even exist. It was too potent. Too powerful. How would he go about his daily life ever again knowing this collision of power and weakness was available to him? To them?

He tried not to collapse on top of her and failed, his body utterly replete of tension. But she welcomed him, their tongues moving together lazily in each other's mouths, her hands molding his ass like clay inside his loosened pants. With . . . a sort of ownership that he couldn't bestow fast enough. "I'm yours, too," he said, still regaining his breath. Would he ever catch it again? "In case I forgot to mention that."

"I read between the lines," she murmured drowsily.

There was nothing to do but kiss her, savor the catch in her throat. For him. When she needed to breathe he pulled back, studying her, still unable to break the connection of their bodies, though he needed to soon. "I love you like this. Drowsy and pinned to the ground where you can't make trouble."

Those tiny, feminine muscles jumped along with the corner of her mouth. "Are you sure?"

"I take it back," he said in a gruff rush, his shaft swelling back to life. In a matter of minutes, he'd be capable of taking her again. Unbelievably, he *needed* to. More than he could remember needing anything. Even with his sweat still drying from the last time. This was love. This was infatuation. There was no way out, and he wasn't looking for an exit. No, he was sealing all of them shut. But was he going to fuck her again on the hard ground in the rapidly dropping temperature instead of caring for her like she deserved? Also no. As much as this was going to kill him. With a wince, Julian pulled out, took care of the condom. "Come home with me," he said, watching as she fixed her dress, covering love-bitten breasts and thighs chafed from the material of his pants. *Mine.* "Let me do this better."

"Wait." She blinked at him. "There's a better?"

His hearty laugh echoed across the vineyard.

When they reached the lighted area surrounding the barn, he took stock of Hallie's appearance, pulling pieces of straw and mulch from her hair, dusting dirt off her calves and elbows. She did the same for him, though he'd sustained far less damage. He pulled her close and whispered in the shadow of the barn about how she should wear her hair to cover the love bite on her neck, their fingers tangling together, mouths unable to stop connecting, lips brushing, kisses deepening.

Finally, they managed to muster some decent behavior, holding hands on their way back into the barn, which was now . . . empty.

They stopped short.

Well, not entirely empty.

Natalie and the SEAL—August, right?—were toe to toe, their noses inches apart. But this time, they weren't flirting. No, he knew his sister's "pissed off" posture when he saw it.

"Uh-oh," Hallie murmured.

"I was only making a suggestion," Natalie said, very succinctly, up at the hulking military man. "I grew up on a vineyard—fermentation is in my blood."

"Only problem with that, baby, is I didn't ask."

"Well, you should have asked someone. Because your wine tastes like demon piss."

"Didn't stop you from drinking a gallon of it," he pointed out calmly.

"Maybe I needed to be drunk to consider sleeping with you!"

The man grinned. Or bared his teeth. Hard to tell from this distance. "Offer is still open, Natalie. As long as you promise to stop talking."

With that, Natalie threw wine in August's face.

Julian shot forward, no idea how the SEAL was going to react. But he worried for nothing, because the man didn't even flinch. Instead, he licked the wine off his own chin and winked at her. "Tastes fine to me."

"I hate you."

"The feeling is mutual."

Angling her face toward the rafters, she shrieked through her teeth. "I can't believe the things I was going to let you *do* to me."

That gave August pause. He gave Natalie a very distinct once-over that Julian immediately wished he could erase from his brain. "Just out of curiosity," August started, "those things were . . . ?"

"All right." Julian cleared his throat. "I'll stop you both there."

"Where have you been?" Natalie cried out, throwing up her hands at her brother's approach. "You left me here with this *Neanderthal* and—" She spied Hallie over his shoulder, and her lips twitched with humor. "Oh. I see. Well, at least one of us got laid."

The back of Julian's neck heated. "Time to go, Nat."

She'd already started in his direction, but her steps slowed now. "You haven't called me that since we were in high school."

Natalie shook herself and kept walking, past Julian and out of the barn, to where Hallie waited. She didn't turn around once, so she didn't see August's regretful expression, but Julian did. It significantly turned down the volume on what he'd been *planning* to say, though not completely. "Talk to my sister like that again and I'll break your jaw."

August's eyebrows shot up, as if unexpectedly impressed, and Julian left the barn. He found Natalie and Hallie leaning up against the side of his rental where he'd parked it along the main road. Hallie was making Natalie laugh, but he still spied a fair amount of tension bracketing his sister's mouth.

"Hey . . ." Hallie rubbed his sister's shoulder and came toward him, tightening everything south of his chin. God, she was beautiful. "You should go take care of your sister. Anyway, I've never left the dogs overnight. I'm not sure if it would be a popular move."

"Jesus," he muttered.

"What?"

"When you spend nights at my house, you'll have to bring them, won't you?"

She peered up at him. "Worth it?"

"Bring a whole circus, Hallie."

Even after everything they'd done tonight, a breathless sort of surprise danced across her features. "It wouldn't be that far off." Worry cut through the surprise, but she tried to hide it with a smile. "Are you sure you're ready for that?"

"Yes."

That's what he said. And he damn well meant it. Because he was ready for Hallie in his life. In fact, her being there felt long past due. If there was a whisper of self-doubt lingering, drifting to the present from that night four years ago, he was more than willing to ignore it in favor of kissing his girlfriend good night.

# Chapter Nineteen

Hallie stood in the moonlight reading through her final secret admirer letter.

And, yes, this would definitely be the last one. She was coming clean.

After the wine tasting, she'd gone straight home and confessed everything to a piece of lined notebook paper and walked right back out the door with it, refusing to give herself a chance to back out. But *God*, did her actions sound stupid in black-and-white.

*Dear Julian,*

*This is Hallie. I'm the one who has been writing you the letters. You're welcome to hire a handwriting analysis expert, but I think once you've read through the full contents, you'll agree no sane person would own up to something so completely asinine unless it was true.*

*I had a massive crush on you in high school. Like, planning weddings in homeroom massive. Meeting you as an adult, it seemed obvious that I'd imagined the spark between us. Or that we'd grown too far in opposite directions to ever meet in the middle. Now I realize that love between adults means embracing flaws as well as the sparkly stuff.*

*You are a river that flows in one direction. There is some turbulence under the surface, but your current keeps you moving, positive you're going the right way. Meanwhile I'm a swirling eddy, unable to choose a course. But whirlpools have a surface, too. They have an underneath. I just wanted to expose it to you and see if we could relate. I wanted to relate to you, because everything I said in those letters was true. I do admire you. I always have. You're so much more than you give yourself credit for. You're thoughtful and heroic and fair. The kind of person who wants to be better and sees their own faults is someone I want to spend time with. They'll complement mine if we want it bad enough.*

*I'm sorry I lied to you. I hope I haven't ruined everything, because while I thought I was in love with high school Julian, I didn't <u>know</u> him. I know the man, though. And now I understand the difference between love and infatuation. I've felt both for you, fifteen years apart. Please forgive me. I'm trying to change.*

*Hallie*

That last line had been erased and rewritten several times. Something about that vow didn't sit quite right with Hallie. She *was* trying to make decisions with more confidence and to take a moment to think before making potentially disastrous ones. She'd even sat down and started a color-coded diagram of her plans for the library garden this morning. But there would always be an element of chaos inside of her. It had been there since she could remember, and even her grandmother hadn't been able to contain it. Not entirely.

Did she want to change for a man?

Nope.

Except he'd already started to change for *her.*

*It's come to my attention that I am far more wrong for you than the other way around, Hallie. You're nothing short of breathtaking. Unique and beautiful and bold. And I'm a goddamn idiot if I ever made you feel otherwise.*

*Let me learn.*

Did it qualify as changing for a man if the man was rearranging himself at the same time? Or was that simply the nature of compromise?

There was only one way to find out, and that was . . . trying. Giving their relationship a chance, up close and personal. No more hiding behind letters. No more hiding, period. They were vulnerable around each other. Had been since the beginning. And that was scary for people like them, but there was also a breath of possibility whispering in her ear, telling her that complete vulnerability could be glorious. It could be totally right. With Julian.

A chance to grow alongside someone, to adjust together until they met in the middle.

Emotionally, they had places to go. Physically?

They had that part down. Real well.

She'd dropped her defenses in the vineyard tonight like a bad habit.

Thinking about what they'd done, about breathless words spoken in chokes and rushes, not even the cold breeze could cool her cheeks. In all of her fantasies, she'd never imagined intimacy like Julian had shown her tonight. That desperate, down-in-the-dirt slaking of needs. She'd never expected to relinquish herself so totally to lust. To sensation. Or to have the wild feelings in her chest play such a part in what her body craved.

Standing there on the darkness of the path, she wanted him again. Not just the release of tension he'd give her, but the press of his weight. The scent of salt and wine and cologne, their fingers intertwining, his hips twisting and bucking between her thighs. She'd never been more honest in her life than she'd been underneath him, no critical thoughts for herself or second guesses. Just letting go. Just flying.

Hallie squinted into the distance toward Vos Vineyard and could just make out the silver outline of the guesthouse. She could go there now. Knock on his door and hand deliver the letter. Maybe she owed him that. Especially after he'd shown up tonight at the tasting with flowers and an apology. She could do the same, couldn't she? Face the music in person? And the last thing she wanted was to start down the road toward a relationship with a lie. She felt the increasing strain of that deception with every passing moment.

Hallie took a few steps in the direction of the guesthouse, her bravery slipping away like pebbles falling from a hole in her pocket. Eventually she stopped, the breeze blowing curls across her line of vision. Julian might read the letter and need time to process everything. To really consider her words. Would she be putting him on the spot by standing over his shoulder while he read it? Wouldn't it be better to end this journey how it started—with a letter? At least he'd have space to think. To consider what he wanted.

Decision made, Hallie tucked the letter as securely as possible into the designated stump crack and jogged up the path, trying to put as much distance as possible between her and the confession before she changed her mind and took it back. What if the admirer just sort of . . . vanished? Stopped writing? Julian would never know what she'd done.

*Nope. You're not getting off that easy.*

In a matter of hours, her craziest idea yet would be revealed to Julian and she'd just have to hope . . .

She'd have to hope he still wanted the circus.

After returning home from her letter-drop mission, Hallie had slept fitfully, the dogs seeming to judge her from the end of the bed. She'd woken up to find she'd overslept well into the afternoon, her stomach gathering like wool at the numbers on the clock. Julian would be getting ready for his run. Mere minutes from discovering her secret.

She got up and walked the dogs. Fed them.

Brewed coffee and sat in her backyard among the periwinkle hydrangeas, legs curled up beneath her on the patio furniture. Her fingers drummed on the side of her mug, a rapid-fire heartbeat in her chest. Julian must have found the letter by now. He was probably back home reading through it for the eighth time, wondering how he'd mistaken psychosis for charm. Any second now, her phone would ring and he would very curtly attempt to end things—and while she wouldn't blame him, she *would* try to change his mind.

That was one item she'd managed to resolve in the middle of her sleepless night.

Would she fight him if he tried to break up with her?

Yes. Of course. She was worth a little vexing, right? She was a slightly frazzled, often muddied gardener who could laugh easily, even while carrying around a lake of hurt inside of her. There was often no rhyme or reason to her professional ideas, but didn't they turn out beautiful enough? Likewise, when she did something ridiculous like steal cheese or begin a secret-admirer-letter-writing campaign, didn't she mean well?

Yes.

She liked her place. She loved her people.

She just needed to find a better way to channel her inherited impulses. She would, too, because sitting there in her backyard and waiting for the man she loved to discover her lies was torturous, and she never wanted to feel that way again.

When noon rolled around and there was no call or front-door arrival from Julian, Hallie set down her stone-cold cup of coffee and dialed Lavinia.

"Afternoon, love," Lavinia sang, the cash register dinging in the background. "How was the tasting last night?"

She heard a distant echo of Julian groaning her name. "Great," she responded throatily. "It was great. Listen . . . has Julian jogged past the shop yet?"

"Yes, ma'am. He was early today, actually." Someone ordered a box of assorted donuts. "Coming right up," Lavinia said, before dropping her voice. "Your man ran past the window shirtless at eleven fifteen. I remember the exact time, because that was the moment I forgot my wedding vows. Pretended to adjust the angle of the specials board on the sidewalk, but really I was watching the professor's sweaty back muscles flex in the sunshine. There's no reason you should have all the fun."

"Couldn't agree more." She paused in the middle of her pacing. "He was . . . shirtless?"

"Utterly. Beautifully. That will be thirteen fifty."

"You ogled my boyfriend, and I'm supposed to pay you?"

"I was talking to the customer. And who are you calling 'boyfriend'?" Her tone grew more and more excited. "Is that official, then?"

"Well . . ."

Lavinia groaned. "Fuck sake, woman. What now?"

"I confessed everything. In a final, no-holds-barred secret admirer letter. If he went jogging almost an hour ago, he should have found it by now. In which case, I might no longer be his girlfriend. At least during the estrangement period wherein I wiggle my way back into his good graces and we all have a big laugh about this at Thanksgiving."

"You've thought this through, which is unusual."

Pacing again, Hallie pressed a palm to her churning stomach. "I deserve that."

Her friend told the customer to have a good day. "Well, I might be able to shed some light on why your momentary boyfriend hasn't called yet cursing you to eternal damnation." She paused, sounding a little smug. "He took a different route."

Hallie skidded to a stop. "What do you mean he took a different route?"

"On his run. He didn't turn down the usual path."

"Let me get this straight. He was shirtless *and* he deviated? He shirtless deviated?"

"That is correct. Which leads me to my next question . . ." In the background, a door slapped shut and Hallie heard the flicker of a lighter. "How good was the sex?"

Halle sputtered. "What?"

"Babe. I have experience in these man matters. I left London to find a husband because I had effectively exhausted the search, if you know what I mean. No *stones* left unturned."

"Well, that needs to be on a T-shirt."

"Point is," Lavinia plowed on, undeterred, "I know a man who's been laid and laid well when I spot one. He stirred my pheromones from two blocks away."

"Okay, you're planning to leave *Julian's* stones unturned, right?"

"Oh, shut up. I'm a happily married woman. Just having a peek." Hallie heard the crackle of the end of Lavinia's cigarette as she inhaled. "Again, my point. You inspired him not only to run about town like a lion who just mated the lioness. But you inspired him to take a different path."

Pleasure warred with distress just below Hallie's collarbone. "But he won't find my letter that way."

"You'll have to tell him in person."

Not two seconds later, Hallie's doorbell rang.

Of course, the dogs lost their minds.

It wasn't very often that someone rang her doorbell. Even UPS had wised up and started dropping off packages unannounced to avoid the canine drama that ensued at the press of a button.

This time, however, as the dog sirens went off around her, they were no match for the explosives going off in her belly.

Julian.

Somehow she knew Julian stood on her stoop.

She confirmed it a moment later when she looked through the peephole, getting a magnified eyeful of Adam's apple and stubble that made her fingers twitch, her inner thighs growing ticklish at the memory of having his five o'clock shadow there.

"Julian?" she asked, unnecessarily. Stalling, perhaps, in an attempt to find out if he'd doubled back, gone his typical route, and found the letter?

"Yeah. It's me." He chuckled warmly, a sound that reached through the door and made her tingly. "Sorry for setting off the alarm."

Having recognized Julian's voice, the boys' tone had changed from defensive to excited. Why did that make her heart swell to the size of a balloon? They liked him. She loved him.

And he definitely, definitely hadn't found the letter.

Which meant she'd have to tell him in person. As in, right now. Before what was happening between them got any more serious. *Oh man oh man oh man.* Should she open with a joke? Unlocking the door, she cracked it an inch and found the most devastatingly handsome man in existence staring down at her. "Just remember that no matter what happens when you come inside, I have a lint roller."

"Consider me warned."

Biting her lip, she opened the door the remaining distance and stepped back, gesturing for him to come inside. He had to duck slightly to get beneath the doorframe, like a giant being welcomed into a dollhouse—and that theme continued as he stepped closer to Hallie, looking over her head and slowly scanning her cottage from left to right.

"It's exactly what I thought it would look like," he said, finally, voice pitched low. "Colorful and homey . . . and slightly cluttered."

Her mouth fell open on a gasp. "Are you serious? I just performed the biggest clean of my lifetime!"

Julian was laughing, lines fanning out around his eyes. "That wasn't a criticism." The smile on his mouth dropped in degrees, and he reached up to thread his fingers through her hair. "How could it be when it reminds me of you?"

The organ in her chest flopped over with all the grace of a cinder block. "Y-you're calling me cluttered, and I'm expected to find that romantic?"

He grazed their lips together, those long fingers spearing farther into her hair until he cradled her scalp, controlling the angle of her neck. Gently, he tugged, pulling her head back, and then—*oh Lord*—he ran his open mouth up the front of her throat. "If the clutter is yours, I want it," he whispered against her mouth. "If you're late, I don't care. Just fucking show up."

Hallie's knees, ankles, and hips nearly gave out, all at the same time. Especially when his grip tightened in her hair, angling her one way and his mouth another, devouring her like a meal. The kiss was leashed, but Hallie could feel the physical vibrations and knew it cost him a heaping dose of willpower to hold back. And she didn't want that. With his stubble rasping against her chin and his minty tongue licking into her mouth, she wanted more of what they'd done last night. Badly. But he ended the kiss with a growl before she could shed her robe and demand to be taken, his forehead pressing down on hers.

"I took your virginity on the ground last night, Hallie."

"Objection. I *gave* you my virginity on the ground last night, Julian."

"Fair enough." He seemed to be performing a serious study of the curls on the top of her head, that deep valley present between his brows. "But I didn't use as much care as I would have . . ."

"As you would have normally?"

"What do you mean 'normally'?" He frowned. "That implies that there is even the remotest comparison between you and anyone else."

*Oh.*

Okay, then.

"So I'm abnormal now?" she breathed, rearranging her entire definition of romance.

Apparently it was not wine and roses. It was this man telling her she was cluttered, perpetually late, and unusual.

"Definitely that." He took a long sampling of Hallie's mouth, until she was weaving drunkenly on her feet. "I meant to say, I didn't use as much care as I would have liked." The heel of his hand scrubbed down her spine, fisting the material of her robe. "If I hadn't let what I feel for you build until it was out of control."

Hallie stared deliriously up at the ceiling, her brilliant, beautiful lover speaking a uniquely blunt version of poetry into her ear. And she was supposed to tell him about the letters? That they'd come from her? Right now? She was just supposed to shatter this perfect bond of intimacy and honesty they'd formed? This sense that everything was right in the world when they were skin to skin, mouth to mouth?

*But you haven't been honest. Not entirely.*

Sure, every word of those letters had come straight from the heart. But she'd misrepresented herself. Let him believe he was writing to a perfect stranger. And worse, when he'd quoted her exact words, she'd let the opportunity to be truthful pass. Well, she couldn't regret it more than she did in this moment, when he held her so tightly, she had to limit her breaths.

"I loved what we did last night," she whispered, because at least it was the truth. And, since it felt so good to tell him the truth, she gave him more. "I want to do it again."

"We will," he said quickly, snaking a forearm beneath her butt and drawing Hallie onto her toes, aligning their laps, tilting his hips, their breaths accelerating like twin engines between them. "We damn well will, Hallie. But I'm taking you out first."

"You are?" She felt him thicken between them. "You have a plan, don't you?"

He bit off a curse and eased his hips back, holding hers away in a crushing grip. "Yes. I'm setting the tone." His mouth swooped down and caught her lips, delivering a dizzying onslaught of strokes from his tongue. "And the tone is, you're my girlfriend, not a girl I hook up with in a field and send home in an Uber, all right? I couldn't sleep last night. It felt like I'd left everything undone with you."

Last night.

When she'd been dropping off her confession letter at the stump.

*Tell him.*

He was being so honest, and she needed to do the same. But would telling him the truth only ruin everything? At the very least, she could bank a few more kisses before dropping the bomb.

"I didn't feel undone," she said, dazed from the prolonged contact, the shape of him, the heat they were generating. "I felt . . . done."

His rich laugh against her mouth sent a warm shiver down her spine. "Damn."

"Damn?"

"I don't want to leave you." He wound a curl around his index finger and let it spring free, watching it happen in fascination. "But there is a luncheon this afternoon in Calistoga. It's the twentieth anniversary of my father forming the Napa Valley Association of Vintners."

"I thought your father was in Italy."

"He is. Natalie and I are accepting the honor on his behalf, I'm making a speech . . ." That trench between his eyebrows now was accompanied by two more. "I told my mother I would."

"What's bothering you about doing it?"

A gruff sound came from his throat. He took his time, as if trying to pinpoint the exact source of his irritation. "Napa likes reminders of tradition. My father and grandfather were a huge part of establishing St. Helena as a wine destination—I'm not denying that. They're not the ones who kept it running when it barely had a pulse, though."

She searched his eyes. "You're talking about your mother."

"Hmm. She should be recognized, just as much as Dalton. More, possibly, at this stage." For a moment, he remained deep in thought, then cleared his throat. Looked at her, expression suddenly formal. "Would you come with us?"

"To the luncheon?"

"Yes."

"I . . . Are you sure?"

He brushed his thumb across her bottom lip, appearing riveted by the crease that ran down the middle. "If I've learned anything since we met for a second time, Hallie, it's that I'm much, much happier when you're with me."

*Oh. Mama.* He meant every word of that, too, didn't he? His honesty was so arresting, all she could do for long moments was stare. Obviously, after that admission, she was going to the luncheon come hell or high water. If she could be there to help him through a difficult task, she wanted that responsibility.

That privilege.

She did a mental inventory of her closet. "How long do I have to get ready?"

Visibly eager to calculate time, Julian looked at his watch. "Twenty-one minutes."

"Oh my God," she said, pushing away from him.

Todd picked up on her nervous energy and started to howl.

"Can you choose something out of my closet while I take a shower?" She shouted the second half of the question through her en suite bathroom door. "Whatever is appropriate for the dress code."

A moment later, there was a thud on the floor of her bedroom. "Hallie, are you aware that half of your possessions have been stuffed into this closet?"

Quickly, she flipped on the shower spray. "What? I can't hear you."

Muffled grumbling.

With a smile on her face, she pinned up her hair, showered, dried off, and applied some quick makeup. Her favorite black bra was hanging on the back of the door in the bathroom, and she put it on, wrapping a towel around the rest of her. She hesitated with her hand on the knob, wondering if it was too soon to walk around in front of him in a towel. With time constraints being what they were, did she have a choice? Blowing out a breath, she pushed into the bedroom. And there was Julian Vos, sitting on her bed, with a flower-print cocktail dress draped across his lap, as if he'd walked right out of her fantasies. Tall and dark and serious against the girlish white comforter.

"I have no idea if . . ."

He trailed off, the lump in his throat moving up and down, fingers curling into fists on the edge of her bed.

"You have no idea if what?" she asked.

"If this dress passes as business casual." He watched her move to the dresser and tug open her top drawer, selecting a pair of thin, nude-colored hipsters that would work for the outfit he'd picked. "I just want to see you in it."

Hallie gasped.

That last part was said against her bare shoulder.

When did he cross the room?

"I love that dress," she said with an effort. "I—it's a good choice."

His hand closed around the knot of her towel, gripped, and twisted, his mouth skating down the slope of her neck. "Can I see you without this on?"

Self-consciousness tried to ruin the party. Of course it did. She'd never been totally naked in front of a man before. Not in the light, especially. And while she loved her body, she loved it clothed more than she loved it unclothed. When she could control what and how much people saw of her thighs and stomach and butt. Could control how material sat against her curves. If he removed the towel, everything would be on display, down to her last dimple.

"Hallie, you can say no."

"It's stupid to be nervous. After last night . . ."

"It's not stupid." He kissed the area behind her ear, biting the spot gently. "Does it blow my mind that you're hesitant to show me your naked body when I would swim across a lake of fire for it? A little."

Her face warmed. "You might be picturing something else, though."

She felt him frown against her shoulder. "Would it help if you knew what I'm picturing?"

"I don't know. Maybe?"

His mouth settled in the hair above her ear. "I think you're soft. No, I *know* you're soft. I think you work hard in the sun and the dirt . . . and it shows in your hands and calves and shoulders. But the fact that you're a woman is also very . . . fucking . . . obvious. You have these incredible tits." He slid his hand up the front of her towel and slowly squeezed each mound, bringing her nipples to attention. "You've got hips. The kind that let me be a little extra rough last night." Her vision started to double, then triple, the perfume bottles on top of her dresser multiplying into an army. "I can still feel my sweaty stomach sliding up and down on top of your belly. I already love every inch of it. I probably left some chafing behind to prove it, huh?"

She managed a dazed nod.

"You show me when you're ready, sweetheart." His hand dropped, fingertips trailing up the inside of her thigh. Toward her wetness. *This* she wasn't afraid for him to know. To see and feel. They were past the point of pretending they didn't turn each other on, and, right now, she was so far over the borderline of turned on, she needed a passport. "In the meantime, can I leave you with a final thought?"

"Yes," she whispered.

His huge hand closed around her sex. The whole thing. He just swallowed it up in his grip and held it. Hard. "I know every little jiggle of this body. They've taken turns making my cock hard. One by one by fucking one." He clutched firmly enough to make her whimper. "Your curves shake when I'm packing this thing tight. I know it for a fact now. The parts you're nervous to show me are actually what make me hard, Hallie." Slowly, so slowly, he parted her flesh with his middle finger and dragged that digit through her soaked valley. "You think about that until tonight."

Secret admirer who?

Involuntarily, the letters were pushed to the back of her mind. To be thought about again . . . tomorrow.

Definitely tomorrow.

# Chapter Twenty

When Julian woke up that morning, he thought his biggest challenge would be the speech he was about to deliver. He'd put together some acknowledgments for the association recognizing Dalton Vos, their founding member—people Julian didn't know, who greatly admired his father. He was accustomed to that. To smiling and agreeing with admirers who spoke of Dalton's ingenuity, his revolutionary techniques and dedication to quality.

But as an adult man who knew a lot more now about responsibility, it had grown harder to grin and bear the compliments about his father. On the way through the lobby of the resort-winery, he'd shaken hands with winemakers and critics who spoke Dalton's name as if they were conferring about a saint.

But it turned out trying to navigate the current moods of the three extremely different women in his life was even more difficult. His mother sat to his left, a smile glued so securely to her face, she looked almost maniacal. Natalie was already on her second helping of Cabernet and appeared to be looking very intently for the meaning of life in the bottom of the glass.

And then there was Hallie.

She was on his right, her eyes on the speaker at the front of the ballroom. But there was a very distinct pinkness scaling the back of her neck, probably because *his* eyes were most definitely not on the speaker. Nowhere in the vicinity whatsoever. They were on those little curls at the nape of her neck, and she obviously felt him staring. Before they'd left her cottage, she'd worked her hair up into some sort of twist on the top of her head, and he'd never seen those extra-small ringlets of blonde up close before. If they were not sitting at the very front of a watchful audience, he would press his face to the spot from which they sprung and inhale the hell out of her.

To say she looked good in the dress he'd picked would be an unforgivable understatement. Did she realize the pink and green flowers splashed across the front of her dress corresponded with the exact parts his hands were dying to touch? Although he suspected the flowers could be in any location and he would want to touch that exact place, because every inch of her consumed and fascinated him.

Julian's fingers twitched in his lap, and he tamped down the urge to wind one of those curls around the same finger he'd touched her with earlier. Christ, they were going to call him up onstage any minute to make a speech and he had a semi—because of *ringlets*—so he needed to stop thinking of Hallie in that towel. With no panties on.

Feeling as if he had some sort of fever, Julian removed his suit jacket and hung it on the back of Hallie's chair, liking the way it looked there a little too much. A man didn't hang his jacket on the back of a woman's chair unless they were together, and now the room knew—and that satisfied something in Julian he'd never known existed.

*Mine.*

He'd said that to her last night in the vineyard, and it rang in his head now until he forced a swallow and tore his eyes from the nape of her flushed neck.

*Later.*

Julian let out a slow breath and turned his attention to Natalie and Corinne. His sister was now building a fort out of sugar packets and cocktail napkins. And he could see her nervous actions weren't lost on Hallie, who sent him a look of concern over her shoulder. Nor had they gone unnoticed by his mother, whose pasted-on smile had dimmed somewhat during the introductory speech. And if this moment, this few seconds in time, were taking place a month ago, he might have been thinking of nothing but the pacing of his prepared words. The schedule of the luncheon and how it fit into his day, the routine he would need to complete upon arriving back at the guesthouse later.

But this string of seconds wasn't happening a month ago. They were right now.

And he wouldn't trade this moment for any other. Background noise and movement in the ballroom blurred everything except for the women surrounding him. He reached for Hallie's hand beneath the table; then, deciding it wasn't enough to have only that one connection with her, he moved his chair closer until her scent was stronger and inhaled deeply.

All moments were not equal.

Every second was not a grain of sand in an hourglass.

Time was bigger than him.

Maybe time wasn't something that could be controlled at all; it was about making time matter with the people he cared about.

The speaker called Julian's name from the podium, and he

stood, took a few steps before realizing he was still holding on to Hallie's hand. He'd nearly dragged her off the seat.

"Sorry." He bent his head over her knuckles and kissed them, viewing the rapid intake of her breath and parting of her lips with the clarity of a man who'd just thrown out the script. Or had it been thrown out for him—he wasn't totally sure, and, ironically, he didn't have time to figure it out.

Julian accepted a plaque from the speaker. They stood shoulder to shoulder and posed for a flurry of photographs before he found himself in front of the microphone. He angled it higher to accommodate his height and set the plaque down on the podium. That's when he realized the note cards containing bullet points for his speech were in the pocket of the jacket hanging on the back of Hallie's chair. That really should have thrown him off, but he only found himself looking down at the table of women with a sense of . . . freedom.

*The hell with the speech.*

"Thank you very much for this honor. My father is grateful to the NVAV for recognizing his early contribution to the association after twenty years of success. He sends his appreciation from Italy." Julian paused, traced a finger over the gold engraving. "I'm not going to accept this recognition on his behalf, though. I'm going to accept it on behalf of my mother."

Some murmuring started around the ballroom, heads ducking toward each other, whispers ensuing behind hands. Julian didn't really see any of it, because he was busy watching Hallie and Natalie and Corinne. People. His people.

Corinne appeared to be shell-shocked, but there was a distinct sheen in her eyes that, in turn, created an odd prickle in his throat. Natalie's house of sugar packets had lost the battle with gravity, and finally, Hallie—God, he was so glad she was there—was smiling at him, her knuckles white in her lap. She was outshining the entire room, so beautiful he stumbled over his words and simply stared. What the hell had he been about to say?

*Focus.*

"My mother picked up the pieces after the fire four years ago," he continued. "It might not be her family name on the label, but her fingerprints are on every bottle that leaves the vineyard, I can promise you that. Along with the hard work of our manager, Manuel, and the grounds crew that cultivate the grapes as if their last name were Vos, too. The vineyard only thrives because of them, because of Corinne Vos, and as much as we appreciate this honor, she should be acknowledged here today. And every day. Thank you."

"I'M JUST SAYING, it would have added to the drama if you'd thrown the plaque across the ballroom into that wineglass pyramid," Natalie said from the other side of the table, all while signaling the waiter for another round of drinks. Instead of staying for the free luncheon, they'd sensed the chill in the air and decided to find a local restaurant instead. "You offended the wine gods today, bro. They are going to demand a sacrifice as payment. Anyone know any virgins?"

At that, Hallie promptly choked on her Sauvignon Blanc.

Doing his best to remain expressionless, Julian squeezed her leg under the table. "Not a single one—you?"

"Not since our mother made me go to band camp in tenth grade. And I'm pretty sure the virgins were no longer innocent once it ended." His sister fell back in her seat a little. "Band camp: an orgy with flutes."

"Lower your voice, Natalie," Corinne hissed, but there was a sparkle in her eyes that hadn't been there prior to the luncheon. "And that was a very reputable band program. You must be exaggerating."

"We secretly called it *bang* camp, Mother."

Corinne spat out her sip of wine, only managing to catch the tail end of spray with her napkin. "Jesus Christ," she choked out. "Please spare me the knowledge that you participated in any kind of . . . banging."

"Unless it was drum related," Hallie qualified, making Natalie laugh.

Julian tugged her closer in the booth until their thighs were pressed together, her shoulder tucked beneath his armpit, curls close enough to count. *There.*

"What you said today, Julian . . ." Corinne said abruptly, some light color staining her cheeks. "You didn't have to do that. My work at the winery has been hard, but it was never a burden. It's very rewarding."

"Rewarding work can still be acknowledged," Julian said.

"Yes." His mother shifted in her seat. "But I didn't *need* it to be pointed out publicly."

Julian shook his head. "No, of course not."

"That being said, it was very . . . nice." She reached for the breadbasket, then seemingly decided against it. Fussed with her hair instead. "I didn't mind it."

Natalie buried her face in a cloth napkin. "Your son makes a dramatic speech in your honor in front of the foofiest winos in Napa and all you can say is 'It was nice.'"

"I believe I said '*very* nice.'"

"Why are we the way that we are?" Natalie mused at the ceiling.

Corinne rolled her eyes at Natalie's dramatics. "Would you rather we hugged constantly and had things like movie night?"

"I don't know," Natalie muttered. "Maybe? Just to experiment."

Surprisingly, his mother didn't seem inclined to drop the subject of togetherness right away. "Well, I'd need my children to stick around awhile for that. If they are so inclined." She folded her hands on the table, her gaze fixing on Julian. "Julian, your fresh set of eyes on the vineyard is already making a difference. We have a plan—and I can't remember the last time I could say that. I hope we can put your father's harsh words where they belong. In the past. Forgotten. You aren't merely welcome to help manage the winery . . . I would really like that. I hope it's not temporary."

Julian could feel Hallie's questioning eyes on the side of his face. She was likely wondering what exactly his father had said to him. After the fire. After he'd pulled Natalie out of the shed where she'd been cornered by flames. That's when the second half of the anxiety hit, making up for lost time, the adrenaline wearing off and the numbness stealing in. Rendering him useless to everyone when they needed him most.

It had all happened, right there in front of his family.

*You've always been a fucking head case, haven't you? Jesus Christ. Look at you. Pull yourself together. Stick to teaching and just . . . stay away from what I've built, all right? Stay away from the vineyard.*

Yes, he now was determined to help revitalize the winery with or without the approval of his father, but would that niggle of doubt in his abilities ever truly go away? Maybe. Maybe not. But his independent mother was openly asking for help. She really needed it—and he *wanted* to give it. Wanted to bring the land of his legacy back from the brink of failure and help it thrive. For so long, he hadn't allowed himself to miss the place. The process. But just like Natalie said to the SEAL last night, fermentation was in his blood.

And yeah, last but certainly far from least, *Hallie was here.*

"I'm not going anywhere," he said, looking down at the woman herself.

Letting her know. *I'm staying. We're doing this.*

*God,* she was beautiful. He couldn't stop staring—

Natalie coughed into her fist, effectively breaking the spell between them. "Let's circle back to my days in bang camp."

Julian shook his head at Natalie. "Let's not. It was bad enough watching my sister's attempts at flirting this week. Not once but twice."

Natalie sat up straighter. "*Attempts?*"

Julian's mouth twitched. "I'll let the end result speak for itself."

"Oh you're the *expert,* are you?" His sister sputtered a moment, before her attention zipped to Hallie. "Since my brother seems to be implying that he's an expert at flirting, please tell us about his masterful technique."

Hallie dove in without a single hesitation, flattening a hand to her chest. "Well, first, he forgot we knew each other in high school. That *really* got the ball rolling. But then . . ." She fanned her face. "He criticized my gardening technique and called me chaotic. That really sealed the deal."

Memories stomped to the forefront of his mind, his stomach roiling. He turned to Hallie to apologize, but she spoke again before he could get there.

"Unfortunately, he foiled my plan to ignore him, when he bought three cases of wine from my favorite shop on Grapevine Way. Corked. They've been in danger of closing down for a while and it was my grandmother's favorite place. I told him that, never knowing he would have business cards made for Lorna and finagle you all into passing them out at Wine Down. *And then* have a brand-new awning installed, giving the place a much-needed face-lift that would triple her business overnight."

Julian realized his jaw was in his lap and snapped his mouth shut. "You knew?"

"I knew."

He grunted, finding it difficult to look at her in public with that shy gratitude on her gorgeous face. He didn't need credit for his deeds, but the proof that they'd served their purpose and made her happy? God, he'd choose her smile over oxygen, right here and now. Any day of the week. And if she thought she was happy now, tonight could not come fast enough. "Why didn't you say anything?"

"I was holding out for Corked's new line of merch, of course."

"T-shirts and corkscrews would be a good start," he said gruffly.

When did he get close enough to kiss her? With a hard clearing of his throat, Julian put an appropriate distance between them. But that distance didn't last very long, because his sister, wine drunk as usual, said something next that made Hallie scoot closer. "Don't forget about how he masterminded children's story time at Wine Down, Hallie." She dropped her voice to a baritone. "'I don't like it when Hallie is in distress. I will explode if I don't fix it for her.'"

All right. Now he was starting to sweat. "Enough, Natalie."

"Did you really . . . you said that?"

"Perhaps some version of it," he answered briskly. "Are we ready to order?"

"I'll have one of you, please," Hallie said, for his ears alone. In a way that was clearly meant to be spoken *inside* of her head, not out.

A hard object flipped in Julian's chest, and he pressed his mouth to her temple, inhaling the paradise scent of her hair. Skin. *Hallie.* "You've already got me, sweetheart."

# Chapter Twenty-One

Okay. Change of plans.

Come clean. In real life. Face-to-face.

Hallie could *not* let him find that letter.

That approach was too impersonal after he'd eaten lunch with one arm around her waist, that thumb occasionally digging into her hip like a promise. Not after she'd caught him looking at her so often between appetizers and dessert, as if he were seeing her over and over again for the first time. Not when they were kissing against the front door of her cottage, her keys having clattered to the ground five minutes earlier, neither of them making a move to pick them up.

His knuckles had traced her cheekbones as if they were made of porcelain. When they broke for air and locked eyes, they were in their very own solar system, the real world light-years away. His hard frame pressed her against the door securely, his hands familiarizing themselves with her breasts and hips and even her knees—he seemed particularly interested in those. Squeezing and circling his thumb around the cap. Dragging one of them high around his hip and keeping it there while he worked her up and down against the wooden barrier, his lower body rolling, surging. Bringing her up onto her toes over and over again with hoarse gasps.

God, she had goose bumps everywhere.

An escalating warmth between her legs.

She was a body of sensations and nerve endings and needs. And the more Julian kissed her, feeding her his tongue with licks she felt down to her toes, the sexier she became in her own skin. How could she feel anything but incredibly desirable when every reverent scrape of his fingertips on her waist made her breasts feel fuller, more tempting. He was so aroused, he seemed to be in pain, and now his hands were climbing the backs of her thighs to palm her butt, his huge body crowding her into the doorway with a guttural sound. *Oh Lord.*

"D-do you want to come in for coffee?" she half laughed, half moaned.

"Hallie, I need to take you to bed," he growled, momentarily breaking their frantic kiss. "This is not a joke."

His teeth raked down her neck, his mouth racing back up into her hair, messing it up. Messing every part of her up, inside and out. But especially her conscience—how could she bring this man inside and make love to him knowing full well she had a secret that might make him second-guess the decision to be with her in the first place?

*Tell him. Tell him now.* "Julian—"

"The problem is, I can't stop thinking about you having an orgasm." That confession was spoken directly on top of her mouth, her lips moving with his, as if they were forming the words together. "It was a problem before last night. But now . . . Hallie. Now?" His fingers moved between her thighs, massaging her through the thin material of her panties. Pulling the undergarment down hastily to the tops of her thighs and rubbing slowly, slowly—right *there*—with the heel of his hand. "Now I can't go a full minute without feeling the way this thing fucking *gripped* me at the end." His middle finger pressed deep, her mouth falling open on a silent moan. *God, oh God.* "I'm going to put you on my lap tonight. Your bra is going to be off. Gone. Burned, for all I care. And you're going to ride cock." Another finger joined the first, pumping in and out slowly, her breathy whimpers caught by nips of his lips. "I want to know how you feel from every single angle by tomorrow morning."

Maybe . . . she should reveal herself as the secret admirer in the morning, then?

Breaths rasping together, he shoved her panties down another inch, fingers pushing deep, their bodies rattling the door in an attempt to get closer.

Wow, they really needed to get inside.

Her house was surrounded by trees and her nearest neighbor wasn't close enough to witness her getting mauled on her porch, but it wasn't unusual for Lavinia to drop by for a visit. Also, the mailman happening upon them was a very real possibility.

"Inside," she sobbed when his teeth sunk into her earlobe.

"Yes." He stooped down to pick up her keys, shoving one of them into the lock, cursing. Picking another one. And then finally they were stumbling into the dark of the cottage, the dogs going absolutely nuts at their heels, their barks happy at first, before turning sort of outraged over being ignored. "Hold on," Julian said, drawing back and reaching into his pocket. He took out a balled-up napkin and unfolded it, revealing pieces of steak he hadn't finished at lunch. "Here, boys."

Hallie blinked as he laid down the strips of beef on the floor, replaced the napkin in his pocket, and captured her hand once again. "Did you plan that doggy bag diversion?"

"Yes. Believe me, I wanted to finish the whole steak." His gaze raked over her face. "But I wanted a distraction more."

"Diabolical," she whispered. "We should get out of here before they finish. We have about four seconds."

"Jesus."

Julian started to drag her toward the bedroom, but she tugged him toward her backyard instead. Maybe since she couldn't give him total honesty—not tonight, not when everything was so utterly perfect—she could give him this intimacy. Her personal garden. Her most private, intimate place. Even more so than the bedroom. On the way outside, she flipped the light switch and held her breath. Watching his face transform with awe when he stepped out through the screen door made Hallie's pulse go haywire.

"This is where I spend most of my time," she said, trying to see the space through his eyes. Wondering if it looked as magical to Julian as it always felt to her. Or if he viewed the towering greenery, jewel-toned lights, and wildflowers as an unplanned hodgepodge.

He circled the yard with narrowed eyes, as though taking the time to make a sound judgment. Hallie had a premonition that she would remember this moment for a long time, maybe forever. Julian Vos touring her backyard with a serious expression, professorial hands clasped behind his back, surrounded by rioting blooms and hanging vines while removing his coat, the sunset loving his bristly jaw and playing over the hill-and-shadow patterns of his muscles.

"What do you do out here with your time?"

Now she understood. When she'd informed him this was where she spent most of her time, that wire in his brain had lit up. The one that dissected minutes and hours and years, turned them into something scientific. "I have my meals out here. I read and garden and talk on the phone and play with the dogs." She thought of the way he'd been exposed at lunch, his behind-the-scenes care of her revealed—and her lips started to tingle. "I think of you."

His steps slowed. "Is that so?"

She gave a brief hum.

Jaw ticking, he went back to surveying the backyard, but he was moving in her direction now. With such brisk purpose, she couldn't breathe. *Touch me.*

"If I'd known you were in this perfect, hidden garden thinking of me, Hallie," he said, frowning at her mouth. "I'm afraid I would have ripped your door off the hinges to get to you."

"I wouldn't have minded."

Admissions. Truth. She would give him as much as she could to make up for the one thing she was too scared to tell him. *Yet.* They were finding middle ground. He'd taken a few steps into her chaos, and she'd started serious planning of the library job. Booking more appointments, committing, doing her best to arrive on time. And it felt good. She couldn't screw this up by revealing how absolutely harebrained she'd been.

What if the revelation was his tipping point and he walked away?

They looked at each other for so long, the sky darkened a degree with the onset of evening, turning from pink to burnt orange, the bourbon of his eyes rich and smoky. She was tempted to give him more truth but could only bring herself to act on the impulse with her body. She could open herself up and be vulnerable in this way—and, God, she wanted to. Needed to. Didn't want to hold back a single thing from this man.

That's how she found herself stepping forward, kissing the underside of his chin, her fingers working to unbuckle his belt.

Immediately, he started to breathe hard, his nostrils flaring, but he never stopped looking her in the eye. Not until she eased the zipper down past his thickened shaft and reached into his pants, stroking the full length of him through the opening. Then his lids locked down like shutters, squeezing tight. "*Hallie,*" he choked. "What are you . . . oh Christ. Oh shit."

She wasn't sure what led her to kneel. To guide him to her mouth and take him inside so eagerly. Maybe because she'd fantasized about this countless times, although, in her fantasies, they were usually in one of his lecture halls at Stanford—a fact which she'd take to the grave. Or maybe she just wanted to do good with a mouth that was holding on to a lie. She closed her eyes and worshiped the smooth steel of him, her hand growing more and more confident in its newfound skill as it pumped top to bottom, increasing the hard swell of him with every fisted stroke.

"Can't . . ." he heaved, fingers tangling in her curls. "Can't be your first time sucking . . . ?" Moaning around him, she nodded, and his breath caught, followed by the taste of warm salt in her mouth. "*Fuck.* I shouldn't have asked. I shouldn't have—I'm going to finish. Stop. You have to stop."

Oh, right. Like that was going to happen. Did he have any idea what it was like to watch the straitlaced professor of her dreams lose the grip on his self-control, to know she was the cause? At some point, he must have plowed a hand through his usually perfect hair, because it stood on end in places. His jaw was clamped down, throat flexed, and the flesh in her mouth was painfully erect. She remembered him like this last night. At the end. How he'd been at his stiffest right before the fall, and she cherished this knowledge about him now. His telltale signs. His weakness—her. *I'm his weakness.* There was so much strength and power in that knowledge that her confidence ticked up another notch, and she popped him out of her mouth. While maintaining her hold on his erection, she found his balls with her lips and blew a gentle raspberry onto one of them, before drawing it into her mouth on a groan.

"No, no, no, no. Hallie. Get up. No more of that. Goddamn, sweetheart." His fingers twisted in her hair involuntarily, a violent shudder passing through his powerful body. "Wait. Don't stop stroking," he heaved thickly. "Hard. While you're sucking them . . . *shit.*"

Using his hold on her curls, Julian hauled her face away, and as she gulped down oxygen, she savored the sight in front of her. The shine she'd left behind on his aroused flesh, the hair she'd never seen on his upper thighs and low on his muscular belly. All of him. All of him was so startlingly raw and beautiful. But then he was dropping to his knees and slamming their mouths together, angling her head to the right and invading her mouth with an animal sound.

Lust inundated Hallie, burning and wild, and she kissed him back, distantly aware of Julian searching for something in his wallet. Protection. Putting it on in a hurry while they raked every corner of each other's mouth with long strokes, hips pressing, grinding.

He must have finished applying the condom—thank God,

thank God—because he gripped her jaw and tilted her face up to meet his scrutiny. "How long have you been wanting to fuck me with this pretty mouth?"

"A long time," she admitted haltingly, barely recognizing her own voice.

She could see he wanted to question that too-revealing piece of truth further—and maybe he would later—but right now, the urgency was so great. The fire on high. "As long as we're working fantasies out of our system, how about you turn around and bury those knees in the dirt?"

*Lord. Oh Lord.* "Yes."

As soon as the word slipped out of her mouth, the next move was taken out of her hands. Julian turned her around and used his big body to press her forward. "Slide them around," he panted in her ear. "Get them filthy."

Hallie's eyes nearly crossed, her heart beating so fast and furious, she could feel it in her throat. Never in her life had she felt as sexy as she did while twisting her knees down into the garden soil, Julian's mouth raking up and down her neck, encouraging her with groans, his hands working the dress up her thighs.

"Are you ready to show me this body, Hallie?" His voice was a scrape of flint. "All of it?"

Knowing she wouldn't be able to speak above a wheeze, she nodded vigorously.

"No, I need the words." He palmed her backside through the dress, his hand dragging up her spine to tangle in her hair, drawing her head back in a way that made her feel utterly and welcomingly possessed. "I need you to say, *Julian, get me naked. Look at every hot inch of me.*"

The ground spun in front of her face, her inner thigh muscles turning to the consistency of microwaved butter, the slow slicking of liquid heat making it uncomfortable to be wearing underwear at all. *Just say it. Say it.* "Julian, get me naked. Look at every hot inch of me."

"That's my girl," he praised, jerking the panties down to her knees, then off. Tossed away. Bent forward on hands and knees, she battled to breathe through the rough lowering of her dress zipper, the soft material being stripped down her body, over her right arm, then left, the entire thing sent in the direction of her panties. *Oh God. Oh God.* Nothing but a bra left. And did it even matter at this point? She was bent over, knees covered in dirt, wearing nothing but moonlight, and nothing, not a single thing, was left to his imagination. "Jesus, Hallie." In one deft movement, he shucked her bra and dropped his clothed chest down onto her bare back, his hands sliding up her rib cage to take firm hold of her breasts. "You have no idea how gorgeous you are, do you? I'm stalling right now. I'm stalling, because I know as soon as I put it in, I'm going to come, you're so fucking *beautiful*. I can't deal with how tight you are on top of everything else. God, this *ass*." The last part was said through his teeth, followed by a shaky exhale in her ear. "You're going to get so comfortable with me looking and touching and tasting every part of your naked body that you'll learn to bend over with your butt in the air, just like this, and ask me to eat it whole."

With that, he thrust into her from behind, and she screamed behind her teeth at the perfection of it. How he filled and stretched her, how the blast of sensation chased away the lingering soreness from her first time. And then there was nothing save the way he groaned in her ear, thrusting into her slowly, slowly at first, then with more and more force, the expensive material of his shirt rasping up and down her back.

"You like that?"

"*Yes.*"

He collected her hips in a bruising grip, straightened in his kneeling position, and seemed to indulge himself for several sweaty moments, pounding into her quickly, hard enough that the heels of her hands slid forward in the grass, her knees burrowing deeper into the earth. She could feel the willpower it took for him to slow down. The way he bit off a frustrated sound and dug his fingertips into her waist, easing his thrusts into deep grinds that made lights twinkle in front of her eyes, her intimate muscles seizing around him like an omen. Welcoming him, wetter each time, a throb escalating in the deep recesses of her womanhood.

His tongue licked up her spine, his fingers dropping down between her legs, pressing and rubbing right where she needed it. And she wanted to tell him faster, faster, but her vocal cords seemed to have been rendered useless, so she reached for his hand instead and moved it in the right rhythm. He hummed into his next lick of her back and kept the pace she'd asked for, and his grateful acceptance of her expressed needs turned her on more than anything. So much that she couldn't stem the compulsion to reward him with pulsing constrictions of her inner walls, one after the other, until he gave a strangled yell and drove deeper, faster, with rough smacks of his lap against her backside.

"Look at that fucking shake," he growled through his teeth. "God, I love it."

Whatever self-consciousness of her body or her flaws that remained had already fled, and now beauty and exhilaration and boldness bloomed where it had once been. "I want to see you shirtless," she panted, positive he wasn't going to hear her, but the confession blew out of her nonetheless. Where had that come from? She sounded almost irritated.

"What's that, Hallie?" he said into her neck, never ceasing the rough forward momentum of his hips. "Shirtless?"

*Why are you like this?* "You j-jogged through town shirtless today. In front of people. And I . . . I mean, *I* haven't even seen you that way and . . ."

He slowed to a stop, and without his movements inside of her, she could marvel over how truly large and hard he was. How much space he occupied. "Are you . . ." He labored to breathe. "You're not jealous."

"I think I'm a little jealous," she muttered haltingly.

A heavy beat passed, full with the sound of crickets and mountain breeze and short, punctuated breaths. Then, with a pained grunt, he pulled out of Hallie and gently rolled her over onto her back . . . where she had a front-row seat to his disbelief. But he didn't question her. He didn't tell her she was nuts or debate how she should be feeling. Instead, he just found her mouth with his own, winding their tongues together while unbuttoning his dress shirt. He tugged it off hastily, ripping the remaining buttons free, sending them arcing into the grass. She kissed him with her glazed eyes open, watching all of it, seeing how tightly he closed his own while devastating her with the skilled journey of his tongue, deep and smooth.

Then he was shirtless, looming above her in the moonlight with a heaving chest. And wow, oh wow. She'd expected the lean lines of a runner's body, and there *was* definition where she thought to find it, but in between, the roundness of muscle and man and flesh was incredible. Human. His natural body type was not that of a runner. No, the huskiness, the thickness shone through regardless of his strict regimen. It was there in the fullness of his stomach and the meaty breadth of his shoulders. If he stopped running, he probably wouldn't fit into his suits before long, and why that should turn her on so much, she had no idea.

"Christ, Hallie. The way you're looking at me . . ." He shook his head slowly, laughter strained. "Just come and get it, already, you gorgeous woman."

As she rose to her knees and went forward, straddling his lap, she couldn't remember a single time she'd been anything but this—desired and cherished and locked in swelling heat with this man. With her butt cheeks clutched in his hands, he guided her down onto his shaft, his eyes turning glassy as she went, jaw falling open on a moan. She felt her power and flexed it, holding on to his bare shoulders and rolling her hips. On the very first one, his head fell back, teeth digging into his bottom lip, his left hand fumbling to become an anchor in the dirt, his right thumb finding the bud at the juncture of her thighs, moving in that fast, firm rhythm she'd shown him, and yes, yes, she'd be rewarding him for paying attention.

"Oh shit. Oh Jesus. Don't stop," he gritted out, strumming her, lifting his hips to meet the increasingly frantic bucks of hers. Their mouths collided in fast, wet kisses, and in between, he scrutinized her movements, her body, with a gaze that could have melted steel. "Hallie, I've got about thirty seconds of watching your tits bounce while you grind that tight thing down on my cock, all right? Please, sweetheart. Come on my fucking lap. *Christ, come on.*"

He didn't have to encourage her, it was already happening, but the way he looked at her, the way he spoke to her in that desperate rasp, propelled her closer to the edge. "More," she said through numb lips. And without her elaborating, his thumb pressed tight to her clit and rubbed deeply, deeply enough that she wailed his name, the dam finally bursting inside of her.

Hallie wrapped herself around him as the tumult washed over her, nerve endings snapping like blue fire, the terrible, wonderful pulling and releasing of her core, so intense it was almost too much to stand, but the rush . . . God, the rush on the tail end of it was blistering and beautiful and left her awestruck. Left her clinging to Julian's bucking body, before he went very still beneath her. Then he barked a curse and started to shudder, over and over again. Both of his hands were on her backside now, yanking her up and back in disjointed pulls and pushes, with a sharp, involuntary slap of his palm that she liked very much, thank you.

And then they both tumbled sideways into the grass, struggling for air, the sunset having faded to serene blue above them. Drowsy eyes met through the tall blades of green, and they smiled, tangling their fingers together between them, gravitating closer, closer until their naked bodies were pressed tightly against each other.

It would have been perfect if it weren't for the one black spot of deception that grew inkier and denser between them as her skin cooled.

But Hallie was the only one who could see it. And now that she'd allowed even more time to elapse with the secret between them, she started to get scared. What if he stopped looking at her like a goddess . . . and more like a girl who wrote intoxicated love letters in the back of an Uber?

Maybe they just needed a little more time to establish their relationship, to prove it could last before she threw a new test into its path?

Yes. That had to be for the best, didn't it?

She'd take back the confession letter and tell him later, once they were more solid.

However long it took to gain the courage, she *would* tell him.

Later that night, when they were asleep in her bed, Julian's arm curled around her waist, she carefully slipped free of his embrace, left a pile of treats for the dogs, and slipped out into the night.

# Chapter Twenty-Two

Julian woke up in stages, which was unusual for him.

Normally, his alarm sounded and he went from a dead sleep to fully awake, already on the clock, mentally prepared to dig into his schedule. For the last couple of weeks, he'd woken up praying he could adhere to *some* semblance of structure, though he'd started to find it hopeless these past few days. Now, in Hallie's bed, he regained consciousness totally devoid of any motivation to do anything but lie there in her warmth, in this room that smelled like flowers and detergent and dogs and sex. Because, yes, he'd gotten painfully hard watching her go through her nighttime routine of putting on lotions and short, silky pajamas and blowing kisses to the dogs. The mattress had creaked for another half hour before they fell into an exhausted spooning position, her amazing butt tucked into his lap like it was made for him.

Thank Christ he'd pulled his head out of his ass before doing something stupid, like going back to Stanford and leaving Hallie behind in St. Helena.

He loved teaching. A lot. He would look into sporadic guest speaking engagements, and, truth be told, he was even more eager to lecture about the meaning of time now that he had a new perspective. Before, he'd been concerned with passing on information. Facts. Now he wondered if he might make a difference in the lives of the students who came to listen to him. Maybe he could prevent them from making the same mistakes as him, taking for granted that the important things in his life would still be there when he was ready. More time would never yield itself unless he made it.

It didn't even require as much effort as he thought to picture himself here, in St. Helena, using his time to make his mother's days easier. His father might not be happy about it, but Dalton wasn't here. Julian was prepared to embrace the sense of ownership of the land that bore his name.

His sister's future remained to be seen, but he could help there, too, when she was ready to ask for it.

Then there was Hallie.

His heart woke up in his chest, firing so suddenly, he sucked in a breath.

Automatically, his hand smoothed across to her side of the bed, hoping for curls. Or skin. That smooth skin of hers that made him feel like sandpaper, roughing up and reddening her, leaving imprints of fingertips and teeth behind. He'd catalogue the damage right now. Kiss every mark he'd left behind . . .

His eyes opened, head turning.

No Hallie at all. No blond curls on her big, fluffy yellow pillow.

Where was she?

He sat up and listened, heard nothing except the dogs snoring in various places around the bedroom. Todd had taken edge-of-the-bed honors while the other two were sprawled on the dog beds in the corner. Other than that, there was no audible movement in the cottage. No lights on, either. Though maybe she'd gone into the en suite bathroom and left the light off so she wouldn't wake him up?

"Hallie," Julian called, annoyed by the finger of cold that traced up the back of his neck. There was no reason to be worried or alarmed. It's not like she'd disappeared into thin air.

Still, when there was no response from the other side of the bathroom door, he threw off the covers, his feet already carrying him across the angled area rug. He checked in the bathroom just to be sure, then left the bedroom with added purpose in his step. Kitchen or backyard. She'd be in one of those two places. They didn't discuss her sleeping habits, but didn't it stand to reason that Hallie's should be irregular?

A fond smile curved his mouth.

Had her off-the-wall, unscheduled lifestyle really annoyed him before? Because now the challenge of pinning her down excited the shit out of him. Like he'd said yesterday afternoon, she could show up late as long as she kept showing up. Period. Right about now, he liked the idea of carrying Hallie to bed and showing her there was no set schedule in terms of when he needed her. It was all the time. Every minute of every day . . .

Where the hell was she, though?

The living room sat eerily silent, the other, smaller bathroom empty. No one in the kitchen. No sign of anyone having passed through to get a drink of water or fix a snack. And the lights were off in the backyard. He went to check, anyway, opening the glass double doors and doing a turn around the unoccupied garden.

"*Hallie.*"

She'd gone out. At . . .

He turned on a light to check his watch, before remembering it was on the nightstand. Glancing back over his shoulder toward the kitchen, he spied the time on the microwave.

*2:40 A.M.*

She'd left the house at 2:40 A.M. There was no reasonable explanation for that. Not even for Hallie. People didn't go for walks in the middle of the night, and if she did, she would have taken the dogs, right? Nothing in town was open. Not even the bars. She had a friend . . . Lavinia? But he had no phone number for her, and anyway, regardless of where she'd gone or with whom, why wouldn't she wake him up? What the fuck was going on?

She couldn't have been . . . taken against her will somewhere, right?

The idea of that was ludicrous.

Was she a sleepwalker and failed to tell him?

What was that sound?

He listened for several long seconds before realizing it was his own wheezing.

*Fuck. Fuck. Okay, take a breath.*

But he couldn't. And in some weird, parallel universe, he could hear sirens and smell the cloying scent of smoke. There was no fire. No one was in danger. But he couldn't convince himself of that. Because Hallie could be somewhere out on the road in her pajamas or trapped somewhere. Was she trapped?

Now the dogs had gotten up to follow him around the house, their tails wagging, heads butting up against his knees. When did his pulse start ricocheting around the inside of his skull? He could hear the pumping of blood in his veins like there was a microphone inside of his chest. The kitchen, which he couldn't even remember entering, was smaller suddenly, and he couldn't remember the way back to the bedroom.

"*Hallie*," he called, a lot more sharply this time—and the dogs started to bark.

Goddammit, he didn't feel good. The closing of his throat and blurring of the immediate area, the stiffness in his fingers—he remembered it well. Too well. He'd spent four years trying to avoid this happening again, this helplessness running into him like a cruise liner splintering a rowboat. And before that, before the fire, he'd worked his whole life around not ending up here. So he wouldn't. He wouldn't.

"It's fine," he told the dogs, but his voice sounded unnatural, his gait stiff as he moved through the dark living room to the front door, throwing it open, only vaguely aware that he wore nothing but briefs. The blast of cold night air on Julian's skin alerted him to the fact that he was sweating. A lot. It poured down his chest and the sides of his face.

*Panic attack. Acknowledge what it is.*

He could hear Dr. Patel's voice drifting forward from the past. From those sessions a hundred years ago, when they'd worked on emergency coping strategies.

*Name the objects around you.*

Couch, picture frame, dogs. Howling dogs.

Then what?

He couldn't remember what the hell was supposed to come next, because Hallie was missing. This wasn't a dream, it was too vivid. Nausea didn't come in sleep like this. Nor did his jaw lock up, his hands useless and fumbling as he tried to get outside to go find her.

"Hallie," he shouted, walking stiff-legged down the path toward the street, searching right and left for her figure in the darkness. No truck. It wasn't parked in the driveway. Why didn't he think to look for that? Why hadn't he tried calling her? His brain wasn't functioning the way it was supposed to, and that scared the shit out of him. "Dammit," he huffed, rubbing at the concrete pouring down his throat. "Dammit . . ."

He needed to get back into the house to try calling her.

Focus. Focus.

The sound of tires on gravel stopped Julian short, just before he walked into the cottage. He spun around quickly, too quickly, to find Hallie running across the lawn, white as a ghost. Relief almost knocked him out cold, his hand gripping the doorframe to keep him on his feet. *She's okay, she's okay, she's okay.*

But she wasn't? Not really.

Her mouth was moving, but no sound was coming out.

He didn't like that, didn't like seeing her upset, and he needed to find out where the hell she'd been. If she'd gone out in the middle of the night, something had to be very wrong.

"Is there a fire?" he slurred.

"What? No." She stumbled back, hands on her cheeks. "Oh God."

"You're shaking," he forced out, jaw refusing to loosen.

"I'm okay, I'm okay." Despite her assurances, she started to sob, and the sound dug into his gut like a shovel. "Let's get you into the house. Everything is fine, I promise."

*You've always been a fucking head case.*

The final blow landed in the form of humiliation. His legs weren't working correctly and he sounded like an idiot and he was scaring her. Scaring Hallie. That fact scored his insides like a razor blade. On top of the unsteady feeling in his limbs and dulled cognizance, he was already anticipating the numbness that would follow. He wouldn't be able to comfort her then.

Wouldn't be able to do anything. He couldn't let Hallie see him like that. The way his father had witnessed him in the back bedroom of the main house. When Julian couldn't mentally surface enough to help. To act. To be a useful member of the family in the most trying of times.

*Stay away from the vineyard.*

In her effort to get Julian back on his feet, the corner of something white peeked out of the pocket of Hallie's windbreaker. He stared at it through the blur, through the blazing-hot mortification, not sure why it was triggering something in his memory. Something about the color and shape was familiar. If he wasn't so disoriented, he might have asked to see the object in her pocket, but in this state, where nothing seemed normal or typical, he reached for it without asking and drew it out.

And stared down at a . . . letter from his secret admirer?

What was Hallie doing with it?

"Where . . ." He shook his head hard, trying to clear the debris. "Is this where you went? To go get this letter? Why?"

Now Hallie's breathing matched his own. Scattered and wheezing and not making sense, as they were both sitting down on the steps of her porch, though he couldn't remember when they'd taken a seat. "I'm sorry," she said, hiccupping. "I'm so sorry."

The truth hit him like the spray from an ice-cold hose.

Hallie had left in the middle of the night to get this letter.

Which meant she'd known it was there . . . and didn't want him to find it.

Didn't want him to read the contents. Because she already knew what they were?

With a swallow stuck in his throat, Julian tore open the envelope and read the letter, his concentration returning to him in that moment, like the blunt swing of a bat. It was hard to decide in that moment how he felt.

"I pictured you as the admirer the whole time," he said, sounding foggy, words running together. "Should have listened to my gut, I guess . . ."

Hallie reared back, stricken. He tried to reach out and stroke her face, but his arm wouldn't lift. Was he angry? No. Not exactly. He really didn't know how to be angry with this woman. Was it humanly possible to be anything but grateful that she'd returned his feelings so strongly that she'd written letters to him? Grateful that she'd found a way to reach him when he'd had his head up his ass?

No, despite the fact that she'd lied, he'd honestly be a fool to be mad about this. Their connection, however it came about, was a gift. But now, the residual fear he'd woken up with—fear that she was hurt or in danger—threatened to choke him.

Julian lurched to his feet and entered the house, dead set on getting out of there immediately. It had happened again. Right in front of her. He'd just shown the woman he loved his greatest weakness. One that he'd done everything in his power to hide, to deal with, to overcome. And if he had to look at her sympathy for another second, he was going to die.

"Julian, can you please stop walking away from me? Say something, please?" She was panicking, crying, shredding the letter in her hands, and there was nothing he could do about it. Comfort her? He wasn't capable. Not in this state—and not when he already knew what was coming next. At least she was safe. *Thank God* she was safe. "I'm sorry. I thought you would find it earlier today. The letter. I wanted you to know everything, but then . . .

Please, everything was just so perfect, so perfect that I couldn't mess it up."

No, he'd been the one to do that.

The sweat was still clinging to his skin like an accusation.

His stomach burned. He couldn't even look her in the eye. It only added to the humiliation that he couldn't get his voice to work.

On legs he couldn't even feel, he went back to the bedroom and dressed, shoving his watch, his phone, his keys into his pockets.

"No, Julian. No. Where are you going?"

All he could do was walk past her out of the house, away from what had just happened. Just like he'd done four years ago. But this time—and he could feel this in the marrow of his bones—the price was much higher.

# Chapter Twenty-Three

Hallie walked down one of the residential blocks adjacent to Grapevine Way, hoping once again to avoid seeing . . . well, anyone really. Even Lavinia and Lorna. Talking and smiling like a normal person only made her feel fraudulent and exhausted.

Two weeks had passed since she came home and found Julian in her front yard looking like death. How long was she going to be dazed and sick to her stomach?

When would the hole in her chest suture itself closed?

She was beginning to think the answer was . . . indefinitely. Recovering from the consequences of being reckless and irresponsible didn't seem like an option. She'd be living with the reverberations of that night for a long time. Maybe forever. At least as long as she'd be living with this broken heart.

If she could go back in time and just be honest with Julian, instead of sneaking off in the middle of the night like a moron, she would jump inside the time machine and buckle up. Because he might have wanted nothing to do with her after she revealed the truth about the letters, but at least she could have spared him the fear and anxiety that had embodied him, sealed him up in a vacuum pack where she couldn't reach him for long, agonizing minutes. The fact that she'd been responsible for that . . . like he'd feared she'd be all along? It was unbearable.

The tendons in Hallie's chest and throat knit together and pulled. Her body had been maneuvering in all sorts of new, torturous ways for the last two weeks. Food made her queasy, but she forced herself to eat, anyway, because the emptiness inside of her was already winning and she couldn't give it another victory by withholding sustenance. All day long, she walked around feeling sick, her skin hot and cold at the same time. She was too embarrassed and guilty and regretful to face her own reflection in the mirror.

And she totally deserved this.

Her actions had caught up with her in an irreversible way. Julian had been right to drive away and never look back. She'd called him three times since that night to apologize again, but he'd never answered the phone. Not once. Three days later, she'd gone to the guesthouse and knocked on the door. No response. She'd planted the flowers she'd brought in the back of her truck and gone. There was a chance he'd gone into that same numb state he'd told her about. The one he'd landed in after the fire, the low that followed his panic attack.

But, God, didn't that explanation make everything worse?

After a week passed with no returned calls, she'd woken up with grim acceptance. Julian wouldn't be calling. Or showing up at her cottage. He'd dealt with her messy disorganized lifestyle, her doggy circus, a citizen's arrest, and chocolate-fueled toddlers in a wine tent, but this lie and its consequences were insurmountable. She'd lost him.

She'd truly lost the man she loved. Not just loved, but admired and cared about and needed. She *needed* him. Not for self-worth or success. Just because, when they were together, the air felt clear. Her heart beat differently. Someone saw her, she saw them in return, and they both said, yes, despite the flaws in this plan, let's execute it. Because she was worth it to him.

Right up until she wasn't.

Hallie reached the end of the block and hesitated before turning down Grapevine Way. She had no choice but to buy milk. After a cup of black coffee this morning and cereal mixed with water, she'd forced herself into real clothing and out the door.

*Please don't let me run into anyone.*

Lavinia had hounded her for a few days, then allowed her to suffer in peace, leaving the occasional box of donuts and wine on her doorstep. Hallie was grateful to her friend for not including a note that said *I told you so,* which would have been well within her rights. She'd canceled her jobs for a few days before resuming them. But she couldn't bring herself to go to the library. She'd driven by once, intending to cultivate the soil and prepare it for planting, but she couldn't get out of the truck.

*Who am I to take on a job this size?*

Did she really think she could landscape a town landmark? The woman who'd been stupidly impressed by her color-coding system of pink, light pink, and lightest pink? Because now she just wanted to laugh. *I am such a fraud. Look at the destruction I cause.*

With a permanent knot in her throat, Hallie put her head down and barreled into the small convenience store, hurtling herself toward the refrigerated aisle. She was being ridiculous, of course. The world wasn't going to end if she ran into someone she knew. She'd gone through months of grieving for her grandmother, so she knew it was possible to act normal under bad circumstances. The reason she didn't want to see or interact with anyone this time had more to do with self-loathing.

*I can't believe you did that.*

*I can't believe you hurt him that way.*

Hallie opened the glass door and took out a half gallon of milk, closing it again with a *schnick.* She move back up the aisle as quickly as she'd come, doubling back once to snag an unplanned jar of peanut butter—but she stopped on a dime about ten feet from the self-checkout register. Really? *Really?* She should have driven to the next town over to buy milk and impromptu peanut butter. Why did this town have to be so small?

Not one but two people that she knew were inside this shop. At eight o'clock in the morning on a Thursday, no less. What were the chances?

Natalie was leaning her hip against a shelf on the other side of the store, frowning down at the ingredients on the back of a cracker box. Despite liking Julian's sister so much, the woman was literally one of the very last people Hallie wanted to see. Not after what she'd done to Julian, dredging up traumatic memories from a fire. And then there was Owen. He was inside the store, too, hunkered down in front of the candy display selecting a pack of gum. He'd called her a few days ago asking where she'd been and she'd texted back claiming to have a cold. She couldn't avoid him forever, but was a few years of being antisocial and drowning her sorrow in Golden Grahams so much to ask?

"Hallie!" Owen said brightly, straightening so quickly, he almost knocked over the cardboard candy display. He steadied it with a sheepish eye roll before coming in her direction. Stopping a few feet away and raking his palms up and down the sides of his jeans. Grass-stained ones he obviously used for gardening. Over his shoulder, Natalie turned her head and surveyed the two of them sharply, her expression unreadable.

*Drop the milk and run.*

That's what Hallie wanted to do, but she didn't deserve to avoid this awkward situation. She'd made her bed and now she had to lie in it.

"Wow, must have been a hell of a cold," Owen chuckled, before catching himself. "Dammit, I . . . I didn't mean that how it sounded. You always look beautiful. I can just tell you've been sick, you know? Been through a few sleepless nights. No offense."

Behind Owen, Natalie was listening intently.

*God save me.*

"No offense taken." She forced a smile and sidled toward the register. "I'm sorry, I have to get home and walk the dogs—"

"Hey, I was thinking." Owen moved with her. "Why don't you take another few days to recover, then come with me to the home and garden show in Sacramento this weekend? I figured we could get an early start on Saturday and make a day out of it."

Natalie crossed her arms and got more comfortable in her lean against the shelves, as if to say, *Oh, I'm staying for the whole-ass show now.* Hallie gulped. And she couldn't help but search Julian's sister's face for some sign as to how Julian was doing. Was he totally recovered from his flashback? Was he writing again? Angry? Had he maybe even gone back to Stanford?

That last possibility had heat burning the backs of her eyes.

Oh God, she wasn't ready to be in town. She should have stayed home.

Cereal with water was fine. More than she deserved.

"Um, Owen . . . I don't think I can make it."

He drew back, his smile tightening in a way she hadn't seen

before. "I've given you a lot of space, Hallie. Either put me out of my misery or . . . try." The tips of his ears were turning red as a tomato. "I'm just asking you to try and see if we could be something. If we could work."

"I know. I know that."

Hallie was sweating under the fluorescent lights, black coffee burning laps around her stomach. Natalie, arms still crossed, was tapping a finger against her opposite elbow, shadows in her eyes. How many people had Hallie affected with her impulsiveness? First, her grandmother had rearranged her priorities to help manage Hallie's. Lavinia had been dragged along into her nonsense, although she *did* seem to enjoy the mayhem on occasion, even if she disapproved. Hallie's clients were always exasperated with her lack of reliability. She'd somehow managed to convince Julian she was worth all of the trouble she caused, but she'd blown even that. Lost him. Lost the man who made her heart tick correctly.

And now she stood, staring back at Owen. Here she was, once again presented with the consequences of acting on impulse, avoiding plans and sowing discontent, instead of just definitively saying *I'm not interested* in the beginning.

She couldn't do this for the rest of her life.

"I'll go with you," she said, her lips barely moving. "But just as friends, Owen. We're only ever going to be friends. If that's acceptable to you, I'll go. Otherwise, I understand if you'd rather go alone or with someone else."

Her fellow gardener and longtime friend looked down at his feet. "Sort of had a feeling that would be your eventual answer."

Briefly, she laid a hand on his arm. "I'm sorry if it's not the one you want. But it's not going to change."

"Well." He blew out a disappointed breath. "Thanks for being honest. I'll give you a call about Saturday. Sound good?"

"Sounds great," she called to Owen on his way out the door.

Now she only had to face Natalie.

"This was not worth a half gallon of milk," Hallie mused out loud.

Natalie smirked, pushing off the shelves to saunter in Hallie's direction. A full ten seconds passed without Julian's sister saying anything. She squinted at Hallie, instead, circling around the back of her, a cop interviewing a perpetrator.

Finally, she said, "What the hell was that?"

Hallie started. "What the hell was what?"

"That awkward redhead asking you out. Doesn't he know you're seeing my brother?"

*Huh?* All right, that was the last thing she'd expected the other woman to say. "Um . . . are you still living in the guesthouse with Julian?"

"Yes."

"And he didn't tell you that we broke up?"

Saying those words out loud made Hallie's eyes fill up with tears, so she tilted her head back and blinked up at the ceiling.

"Uh, I know he said some kind of bullshit about you both needing space. And then he locked himself in his office to finish his book. He hasn't come out for two weeks. Unless he emerges when I'm passed out, which is more and more often these days."

"You need to handle that."

"I know. I have a plan. I just need a little more courage before I enact it." A shadow danced across Natalie's features; then she was back to being steely-eyed. "Look, I don't know what happened between you two, but feelings don't just—poof—go away.

Not the kind you have for each other. Now, my ex-fiancé and I? Yeah, in hindsight, the success of that relationship was riding on money and image. I can see that now. You and Julian, though . . ." She gave Hallie a pleading look. "Don't be each other's one who got away. You can fix it."

"I wrote him secret admirer letters and deceived him about it."

"*That was you?*" Natalie sputtered. Gaped. "Why the hell did you do that, you crazy idiot?"

Hallie groaned. "It all sounds ridiculous now."

"Well, *yeah*."

"It started off with me wanting to get this . . . crush off my chest. But then, talking to him made me feel so much better about where I am. Who I am. Our discussions made my thoughts clearer. So I wrote my feelings to him in letters, hoping . . . to know myself *and* him better in the process. I didn't think it all the way through, and that's the problem. I *never* do. He was right to leave and stop taking my calls. He should forget all about me."

Natalie scrutinized her for a breath, then patted her awkwardly on the shoulder. "All right, let's not get dramatic."

"This is nothing if not dramatic!" Julian's sister was starting to look sympathetic, probably because of the tears that insisted on escaping her eyes, but Hallie didn't want that sympathy. Not until she'd suffered for at least another decade. "I should go."

"Wait." Natalie stepped into her path, visibly uncomfortable with Hallie's overwrought emotions. "Listen, I . . . get this. My brother barely talked to me for four years after rescuing me from a fire. It had the nerve to scare our stoic asses. We never learned how to express ourselves in a healthy way, so we lean on avoidance." She gestured to herself. "See? Hello, I'm three thousand miles from the broken pieces of my life right now. Nice to meet you."

Despite her misery, Hallie gave a watery laugh. "I see where you're coming from, but . . ." *He's better off without me.* "We're better off apart."

Hallie got the distinct impression that Natalie wanted to stomp a foot. "No, you're not. Me and that arrogant Navy SEAL, August whatever, are better off apart." She paused, looked far away for a moment, before shaking herself. "You and Julian are suffering right now, and one of you needs to stop being stubborn and fix it. Yes, I realize this is a pot-meet-kettle situation, but I'm not the one who wrote fake love letters, so I'm claiming the moral high ground for the purposes of this situation. If you go on a date with that dorky redhead, even as friends, I'm going to slash your tires."

"You really would, wouldn't you?"

"I carry a switchblade in my purse."

Hallie shook her head. "Dammit. I really like you."

She watched in confused awe as a flush took over Natalie's cheeks. "Oh. Well." She scratched at the dark wing of her eyebrow. "Who doesn't, right?"

They looked at each other in silence.

"It was bad, Natalie. What happened with us." A memory of him sweating in the doorway of her bedroom popped up. She had to breathe through it. "I can't even bring myself to tell you how badly I messed up. You'd slash my tires *and* break my windows."

"Maybe." Natalie sighed, searching for the right words. "Julian gets lost in his head sometimes, Hallie. Just give him a little while to find his way out."

She nodded as if agreeing to that, even though she wasn't.

If anything, the conversation with Natalie made her even more determined to move on and not allow herself to look back and hope.

She'd wreaked more than enough havoc on the universe already.

# Chapter Twenty-Four

Julian typed *THE END* in his manuscript, and his hands fell away from the keyboard. The outline of those two words thinned until they were swallowed up in white, disappearing completely. All that was left in the absence of typing was the electronic hum of his computer, the low ringing in his ears that had been there for . . . however long it had been since it happened again. He jolted at the reminder of why he'd locked himself in this room in the first place, desperate to have his distraction back.

All he had now was silence.

A bunch of words on the screen. Clammy sweat on his skin. Still. Or again. He didn't know.

Where was the almighty satisfaction that came from finishing a novel? It would sweep in any second now, surely. The triumph, the relief, the sense of satisfaction. He'd been chasing those things, needing them. Requiring *something* to be louder than the noise in his head. But there was nothing. There was nothing but his stiff joints and aching molars and bloodshot eyes, and that was fucking unacceptable.

He cleared his throat, but a hoarse sound came out instead.

He dug his fingertips into his eye sockets. Jesus, it hurt to lift his arms, his joints sore from being locked up so tight. He probably hadn't noticed, because none of it could compete with the spikes raking through his insides, and it was so much worse now that he'd stopped typing.

The light on his desk had gone out God knew when. The blinds were pulled down tight, but he could see around the edges that it was bright out. Birds were chirping, and dust motes danced in the slivers of light that he hadn't managed to keep out.

Dread weighed down his shoulders so severely that they were beginning to protest the strain, and he knew why. He knew what he was dreading, but as soon as he acknowledged it, the final stage of numbness would wear off. So he fought to keep that final veil from lifting. Fought against the outline of her head and the sound of her voice with clenched teeth and every drop of willpower he had.

Julian's hand shot out unexpectedly and sent the wireless keyboard flying across the room. He'd just finished a book. Wasn't something supposed to happen now? Wasn't there supposed to be more than an empty room and stale air and the cursor that was *still blinking*?

Wexler had done exactly what he was supposed to do. He'd braved the elements, he'd fought the enemy, solved the riddles left by his comrades from the past, and triumphed. Returned the artifact to its rightful owner. Now the hero stood in a valley, looking out, and there was no fulfillment. Only emptiness. Wexler was alone. He was alone, and he was . . .

Flawless. He didn't have a single thing wrong with him. Apart from being briefly captured by his rival, he'd made no mistakes. Not one throughout the single book. He'd been rigorous and brave and uncompromising. And Julian found that he could not care less that Wexler had won. Of course this protagonist without a single bad characteristic won in the end. He hadn't stumbled once. Hadn't questioned himself or been doubted. Hadn't recognized his own shortcomings and done anything to fix them. He'd just won. Wasn't that the dream? Didn't people want to read about someone they aspired to be? Julian did.

Normally.

But the ending left him totally empty.

Julian had been writing the man he *wanted* to be. A brave man. But there was no satisfaction in winning without the losses that came first. There was no bravery when victory was a given.

A hero with serious flaws and even weaknesses . . . could still be a hero. A person could only be brave if failing was a possibility.

And that night of the fire . . . did he fail? He'd always thought yes: *Yes, I let myself get overwhelmed, I let the screws tighten until my exterior cracked.* In reality, though, he was still here. He'd come back. The people he loved were safe. Time marched on, and he would do it all over again, even knowing the outcome. He'd run into the fire knowing the anxiety would crush him afterward, and maybe . . . maybe Wexler needed some of that. Fear. Fear of failing. Fear of weaknesses. Didn't that only make being strong more rewarding?

The screen of his computer faded to black from inactivity, and Julian surged to his feet, noting the time on the clock. Seven forty in the morning. He would sleep until noon, shower until ten after twelve . . .

Why?

*Why* schedule himself so ruthlessly? It didn't seem as necessary as it had before. Nothing seemed necessary, except for . . .

His focus drifted, and he found himself walking down the front steps of the house. He moved without conscious thought, knowing on some level he was moving toward the garden, but not being really sure why. Not until he stood in front of it.

The absolute . . . masterpiece of it.

The air was sucked straight out of his lungs.

She'd finished the garden.

It was a riot of color, just like her. It was wild and joyful and without structure, but, standing back as he was, it made sense. Blooms filled spaces and locked together like joints. They reached for the sky in some spots, crawling on the ground in others, creating a pattern that he hadn't been able to detect until now. When it was a finished work.

The journey hadn't been pretty, but the result was fucking spectacular.

Like this garden, she was chaos. But she was *good,* and he'd known this. He'd reached for her with both hands and asked to keep her, mayhem and all—but he hadn't accepted his *own* flaws yet. He'd recognized hers as beautiful while believing his were still hideous, and *that's* where he'd gone wrong.

He hadn't been fully right, fully ready for her. Not when he couldn't accept his own imperfections . . . and realize those imperfections were what made victory worthwhile.

And she was the victory. Hallie.

Her name in his head tore away that final layer of numbness, and, as he'd known it would, the panic ripped through him like a knife. The sound of her voice begging him not to leave, the soft but persistent pull of her hands on his elbow. The letter. The words from her letter.

*The kind of person who wants to be better and sees their own faults is someone I want to spend time with. They'll complement mine if we want it bad enough.*

Not really seeing the ground in front of him, he lurched toward the house. And then he started to run. Car keys. He just needed to get his car keys. Christ, he needed to see her *now.*

*I'm sorry I lied to you. I hope I haven't ruined everything, because while I thought I was in love with high school Julian, I didn't* <u>*know*</u> *him. I know the man, though. And now I understand the difference between love and infatuation. I've felt both for you, fifteen years apart. Please forgive me. I'm trying to change.*

They didn't even talk about her letter.

She'd had a crush on him in high school? He wanted every detail. He wanted to know everything. He wanted to laugh about it with her in her magical little garden and make up for being a stupid teenager and not knowing her and loving her for fifteen years. Where the fuck had his head *been* for fifteen years?

His mind was wide open now, free of the imprisonment of minutes and hours. They were nothing if he didn't spend them with her, that's all he knew.

Natalie emerged from her bedroom as he ran by, eye mask pushed up on her forehead. "Julian. You're out."

"Where are my keys?" He pointed at the console table that ran between the living room and the kitchen. If he didn't see a Hallie Smile immediately, he was going to split down the fucking middle. "They were right here."

"Uh, they *were* there. Now they're in my purse. I returned my rental, and I've been driving your car for weeks."

"Weeks." The clamp around his windpipe tightened. "What are you talking about?"

"You've been writing nonstop for two and a half weeks. You

showered once or twice. Ate a sandwich every once in a while. Slept here and there. I stayed out of your way so I didn't interrupt your"—air quotes—"'process.' But I'm not handing over the keys until you clean yourself up. I believe the scientific term for your condition is 'nasty.'"

Julian had only half heard everything Natalie said after "two and a half weeks." *Two and a half weeks?* No. Not again. *Please tell me I didn't do this again.* There were foggy memories of leaving the office, falling numbly into bed, watching through the grit in his eyes as his hands prepared food, words appearing on the screen. It was a blur, but he couldn't possibly have been away from Hallie that long.

He wouldn't survive it.

*You* have *barely survived it.*

His body was in horrible pain from being in a sitting position too long, but the cavern in his chest was the worst pain of all. And it stretched wider and wider now, as he realized all the important conversations that were never had. The forgiveness he'd never given. The time he'd wasted on a book that had been on the wrong trajectory since the beginning. When he could have been with her.

"Take a shower before you go see her."

"I can't. Two and a half weeks."

Natalie yawned, reaching into her room for her purse and dropping it outside the door. "Yeah—and you might want to catch her before she leaves for the home and garden show with the redhead. They are just friends, but, you know, I still don't think he's deleting his wedding playlist anytime soon."

His intestines just sort of melted into his socks. This was peak misery. How he felt didn't mean jack shit right now, though. He'd walked out on Hallie while she was crying, too bogged down in his own self-disgust that he'd neglected to take care of her. To reassure her that he wasn't upset over the secret she'd been keeping. He was *grateful* for it. Those letters were the first step in the journey to where he was now. To seeing the world differently. Seeing himself differently.

"How is she?" He rifled through his sister's purse for the car keys. Fuck the shower. "I didn't mean to leave her so long. She must hate me."

"Hate you? No." Natalie's tone of voice turned Julian around. "Julian, I don't know what happened between you two, but she's taking the blame. If she hates anyone, she hates herself."

No. No, no, no.

A pounding started in the dead center of his forehead, his stomach pitching, nausea picking up speed like a rogue wave. Driving to her house and apologizing wasn't enough. No, she needed more. A lot more. The most unique, loving woman on the planet had been writing him love letters, and he needed to show her what they'd meant to him. What *she* meant to him.

Everything.

Would she want him when he had the ability to go silent for weeks?

"The last time this happened, I . . . couldn't be there when my family needed me. Now I've done the same thing to her. She's been hurting for weeks, and I've been lost in my own head. Brought down by this fucking weakness. I was just . . ." He searched for the right explanation. "I woke up alone, and she was gone. I thought she was hurt. Or worse. And then I couldn't calm myself down . . ."

"Julian." He found Natalie looking at him with a thoughtful frown. "This has only happened to you twice," she said slowly.

"Once when I was in danger. And again, when you thought something might have happened to Hallie."

All he could think about now was getting to her. Holding her. "I don't follow."

Natalie didn't speak right away, her eyes turning slightly damp. "You're a protector. A solver of problems. Always have been, since we were kids. If your supposed weakness is caring too much about the people you love, to the point of *panic,* then that is a *strength,* not a weakness. It's just one that needs to be managed correctly."

His sister's words finally broke through. Was she right?

Did the worst of his panic stem from people he loved being in danger?

"When I check out like this, I leave everyone to pick up the pieces alone. I couldn't help with damage control after the fire. I've left Hallie for two and a half *weeks.* My God—"

"I don't have a way to solve that part, Julian. But there *is* a way to cope with it. I know there is." She tilted her head slightly, her expression sympathetic and understanding. "Maybe it's time to stop trying to do that on your own."

"Yeah." His voice was raw. "Okay. I know you're right." As soon as he didn't feel like dying for being away from his girl so long, he'd make the calls. He'd schedule the necessary appointments to get healthier. For himself. For everyone. But right now? None of that was happening without Hallie being healed first. "Natalie, please. I need your help."

HALLIE SAT IN her backyard, leaning up against the fence, surrounded by dozing dogs. She had a sketchpad in her lap, a pencil still rolling back and forth where it had fallen from her fingers. She'd finished it. The idea for the library garden was complete—and it was glorious. A plan that didn't necessarily look like one. A Hallie-style buffet of sunflowers and dogwood and native wildflowers. Shaded benches and water babbling over stones and a swing hanging from the oak tree. It was a plan Rebecca would have been proud of.

Hallie was proud of it, too.

Weird how the worst scenarios coming true could pull everything into perspective. She'd been thriving on distractions and disorder so that she wouldn't have to decide who to be. But the truth was, she'd already been the exact right person. She just needed to stop waving and shouting and listen. Feel. Center herself now in the stillness and sunshine. She was a survivor. A friend. Someone who brought the color in unconventional ways, but tried her best. She had a broken heart in more ways than one, but she was still standing, and that made her strong. She was stronger than she ever knew possible.

A car horn blared from the front yard.

Hallie's nose wrinkled. Who was that? Owen had stood her up via text this morning, claiming a work emergency—and anyway, it was late afternoon now and they'd missed the whole home and garden show.

The horn went off again, and the dogs all got up at once, howling at the sky and trotting in circles. "Okay, guys." Hallie used the fence to stand on legs that were half-asleep from sitting too long. "No need to get worked up."

Hallie padded through the house on bare feet, moving aside a curtain in the front window to determine who was causing the ruckus.

Lavinia?

Her best friend spied her peeking through the curtains and rolled down the passenger-side window. "Get in, loser."

Sketchpad still in hand, Hallie unlocked the front door of her house and went down the path, accompanied by three very harried canines. "What is happening here?"

"Get in the car."

"But . . . What? Why? Is something wrong?"

"No. Well, yes. But hopefully not much longer." Lavinia snapped her fingers and pointed at the passenger seat. "Get in this bloody Prius, Hallie Welch. I'm a terrible secret keeper, and I've got about five minutes before it just bursts out of me."

Hallie herded the dogs back toward the house, sputtering, "At least let me put on some shoes and lock the door!"

"You're pushing it!" Lavinia shouted, honking the horn.

Less than a minute later, Hallie was diving into the car in her flip-flops, still holding her sketchpad. She'd forgotten her phone and was pretty sure she'd locked herself out of the house, but at least the honking had ceased.

"What is going on?" She scrutinized Lavinia, but the donut maker remained stubbornly tight-lipped. Literally. She was pressing her lips together so tightly, they were turning white. And that's when Hallie noticed the necklaces.

Lavinia usually wore a simple chain with a small onyx pendant. Today, there were so many layers of jewelry around Lavinia's neck, Hallie couldn't even figure out how many necklaces she was wearing. Silvers and golds and chunky wooden costume pieces.

"Why are you—"

Lavinia cut her off with a middle finger, shaking her head.

All right. She was a hostage. Going sixty miles an hour in a

Prius, possibly being mocked for her taste in jewelry, and there was nothing she could do about it, apparently. Hallie leaned back in the seat, fingers wrapped around her sketchbook, staring out through the windshield and trying to determine where Lavinia was taking her. It only took about three minutes for their destination to become obvious.

Hallie lurched forward, very nearly reaching for the steering wheel to prevent Lavinia from turning down the well-manicured road that led to Vos Vineyard. "Oh God. No. Lavinia." For a beat, she seriously contemplated throwing open the passenger door and casting herself out of the moving vehicle. "I know you think you're helping, but he doesn't want to see me."

"Almost there," Lavinia gasped. "Almost there. Don't look at me. I can do this."

"You're scaring me."

The brakes screeched, and Lavinia shut off the car, making a shooing motion at Hallie. "Get out. Go. I'm right behind you."

"I'm not getting out . . ."

Hallie's protest died on her lips when three people climbed out of the Jeep beside them . . . laden with necklaces. Like, dozens upon dozens of mismatched ones. Hallie looked down at her own collection, displayed in the V of her white T-shirt, and felt a tug in her rib cage. For the last few days, she'd tried to whittle down her selection to one necklace, but she could never manage it. She liked them all. They represented different parts of her personality and experiences. The pearls were an ode to her romantic side, the gold cross a reminder that she'd been a good granddaughter—the best one she could manage. The pink choker with the bright, pretty flowers once represented the part of her that liked to avoid unwanted conversations, but now it was a reminder to stop using flowers as a distraction and have the tough talks. Especially with herself.

Although, she missed talking to Julian most of all.

The necklaces blurred together, thanks to the moisture in her eyes, and when she looked up and out the windshield again, it took a moment for the figure in front of the Prius to come into focus.

Natalie. Covered in necklaces.

"Seriously, what is going on?"

Lavinia got out of the Prius and lit a cigarette. "She's in the mood to be stubborn. You get one side, I'll take the other."

Natalie nodded and put on her sunglasses. "Let's do this."

Hallie watched in horror as both women converged on the passenger side, clearly intending to drag her out of the car. She was so stunned and confused that she didn't manage to lock the door in time, and truly, she didn't stand a chance. Each woman reached for an arm and pulled Hallie from the vehicle despite her protests, the sketchbook dangling from her right hand uselessly. "Please!" Hallie dug in her heels. "I don't know what this is, but . . ."

But what?

She wanted to avoid confronting her mistakes in person? She wanted to hide in her house for another two and a half weeks eating cereal?

No. If she'd learned anything from her time with Julian, it was that growing meant getting through the hard stuff, and coming out stronger on the other side. The sketchpad was proof she could confront her fears and tackle things she never thought herself capable of. So she could do this, too.

Whatever "this" was.

Hallie stopped struggling and walked between Natalie and Lavinia like a normal woman without avoidance issues. Obviously her friends had staged some kind of Hallie-themed cheer-up session, and they were welcome to try. Julian probably wouldn't even *be* there.

That assumption popped like a tire rolling over glass when she heard his voice ahead.

He was . . . shouting?

*"Anywhere you want,"* boomed his deep voice, just as they rounded the corner of the welcome center. There was Julian. In jeans and a T-shirt. Messier than she'd ever seen him. Standing in the back of a flatbed truck that appeared to be transporting an entire nursery worth of flowers and shrubs and various wooden trellises.

A large crowd of people had congregated around the truck, and Hallie immediately recognized several faces. Lorna was there. Owen. Several of her clients. August, the SEAL turned vintner. Jerome. The waitstaff from Othello. Mrs. Cross, who owned the coffee shop across the street from Corked. Mrs. Vos. Two giant groups of tourists holding half-empty disposable wineglasses. Julian was handing down random pallets of flowers and potted shrubbery to the assembled mass, his hands almost black with soil.

He wore dozens of necklaces around his neck.

"Find a place for them. Anywhere in the vineyard. And plant them."

"Anywhere?" Jerome asked, skeptically.

"Yes." Hallie watched in disbelief as Julian swiped a filthy hand through his hair, leaving it standing on end. "No rules. Anywhere it feels right."

What was this?

Hallie was still piecing it all together, but her legs were rapidly turning into cake batter. Was this a dream? Or had Julian organized a planting party at his family vineyard . . . in her honor? What else could the necklaces symbolize? Why else would he be instructing people to use the signature Hallie Welch method of having no method at all?

Julian's head turned sharply to the right, meeting Hallie's gaze.

They could hear the thump of her heart on Jupiter.

Looking into his eyes again, even from this distance, was so powerful that she almost turned and ran for the car. But then Julian was jumping down from the back of the truck and striding toward her, not debonaire and determined as he'd been the night of August's wine tasting. No, this was a haunted version of Julian that was hanging on by a thread.

"Hallie," he rasped, stopping a few feet away. Natalie and Lavinia let her go suddenly, which was not a good thing, because apparently they'd been propping her up in the face of this reunion. Hallie's knees buckled, and Julian shot forward, catching her in his arms before she could hit the dirt. "Okay, I've got you," he said gruffly, eyes racing over her face. "It's okay. My legs want to give out, too, from seeing you again."

She allowed him to steady her, but she couldn't find the breath to say a word.

People were fanning out into the vineyard with bright, beautiful flowers in their hands, preparing to plant them at random—at Julian's behest—and that meant something. It meant such a wonderful something that she couldn't articulate it out loud just yet. But maybe . . . had he found it in his heart to forgive her?

"Hallie . . ." Julian's big hands closed around her arms, fingers flexing. Head bowed forward, he released an unsteady breath. "I'm sorry. I'm so sorry."

Surprise jerked her chin up a notch.

What? Had she heard him correctly?

"You're sorry?"

"I know that's not enough after disappearing for seventeen days, but it's just a start—"

"You have no reason to be sorry," she blurted, still reeling in her disbelief that he was taking responsibility for *anything* that went wrong. "*I'm* sorry, Julian. I lied by omission. I let you believe you were writing back to someone else when I had every opportunity to be truthful. I pushed you into feeling a way you never wanted to feel again because I couldn't help making a mess, like always, and I won't let you claim responsibility for any of it."

She tried to pull away from Julian, but he gathered her close, instead, bringing their foreheads together. "Hallie, listen to me. You don't make messes. You follow your heart, and your heart is so beautiful, I can't believe it was mine." He seemed to brace himself. "Put me out of my misery and tell me it's still mine. Please."

She forgot how to speak. All she could do was stare. Was she dreaming this?

"It's all right, I can wait," he said, swallowing audibly. "I have so much I want to tell you. I finished my book and it's terrible."

Hallie was already shaking her head. "I'm sure that's not true."

"No, it's one hundred percent true. But I needed to finish the first horrible draft in order to know how to fix it. No one gets anything worthwhile right on the first try. That's why we evolve. That's why we change. I never would have learned that without you. Without those letters." He paused, visibly searching for the right words. "Bumpier journeys lead to better destinations. You. Me. We're the best destination of all."

Hallie's eyes started to burn, heart in a slingshot. "How can you feel that way about me after I made you panic like that?"

"Hallie." His filthy fingers sank into her hair, his eyes imploring her to understand. "I panicked like that *because* I love you." He didn't even pause long enough to let those incredible words sink in. "For so long, I thought I needed this strict control to keep the anxiety at bay, and maybe in a way, I do need structure. I'm going to find out. But that true panic only happens when someone I love is threatened. I realize that now. When I woke up and couldn't find you . . . all I could think was the worst. Hallie." He cradled her face in adoring hands. "If something happened to you, it would end me. But that fear is only an indication that my heart belongs to you, all right? It's right here. Please just take it."

Her breath left her in a great rush. But not all of it. She held on to just enough to whisper the words that had been etched on her soul in different handwriting and for different reasons over the course of fifteen years. "I love you, too," she whispered. "One bumpy ride, reporting for duty, if you're sure. If you're—"

"If I'm sure?" Foreheads pressed together, they breathed hard against each other's mouths for long moments. "All time is not created equal. I know that now. Time with you is the most substantial of all. I'll probably never be able to stop counting the minutes that we're apart, but the ones when we're together, I'm leaving room for anything. Whatever happens. Gopher holes, rainstorms . . ."

"Robberies, drunken love letters . . ."

"Drunken? The first one?" She confirmed with a nod, and he laughed. "It did have a noticeably different tone." His hands dropped from her hair, capturing her wrists and bringing them up to encircle his neck. Bodies meeting and molding together, they moved left to right in a slow dance to the sound of their heartbeats. "Promise you'll keep writing me letters."

Was she floating? "I'll write them for as long as you want."

He looked her in the eye. "That's going to be pretty damn long, Hallie Welch." His mouth slanted over hers and coaxed her into a dizzying kiss. "I'm going to write you back, too. One for every day I missed out on for fifteen years."

This was what swooning felt like. "That's a lot of letters," she managed.

His grin spread against her mouth. "We've got time."

LATER THAT NIGHT, after all of the flowers had been planted, the laughter fading into the starlit, fragrant Napa night, Hallie and Julian stood in front of the closed library, side by side.

She handed him her sketchbook and he looked it over with serious professor eyes.

"I don't know where to start," she admitted.

And he seemed to know exactly what she meant. Because he nodded once and returned to his car in that brisk, determined way of his. He opened the back door, the top half of his body disappearing into the vehicle. The muscles of his back flexed and her fingers stretched in response, missing the texture of his skin—but all thoughts of debauchery fled when she spotted the object Julian was hauling out of the car. It had been covered in a blanket before, and she'd assumed it was more supplies he'd purchased at the nursery. But no.

It was her grandmother's table.

The one that had sat outside of Corked since the fifties.

It was right there, thrown over Julian's shoulder, as he carried it across the street. The world seemed to tilt beneath Hallie, on all sides, her throat squeezing so tight it was a wonder she was still breathing. She said his name but no words came out. All she could do was run her fingers over the intricate swirls, the chipped white paint. Julian was already back at the car, taking the wrought-iron chairs from the trunk. He carried one in each hand and set them down beside the table, looking at her, chest rising and falling.

"Lorna needs triple the amount of outdoor seating now. We went ahead and ordered new tables. Chairs. None of them matched this one, though. Nothing could ever match it." He leaned over and rested his lips on the crown of her head. "Maybe it's time to give it a new home."

"I knew my plans were missing something." Through her tears, she smiled down at the familiar dips and plumes of the wrought-iron pattern. "It needed that piece of her. You brought me the heart."

His arms encircled her, wrapping her in warmth. "I'd have brought you mine, but I already gave you the whole damn thing, Hallie."

After the day he'd planned at the winery, she'd assumed her own heart was fully healed. But there must have been one missing component, because a final stitch threaded into place now and it beat like a lion's. Who could have anything less than a fiercely functioning heart when there was someone in the world who would do this for her?

Julian held out his hand, and they walked into the library courtyard together.

And they stayed late into the evening getting messy in the dirt, planting flowers and smiling at each other in the moonlight. Because their journey was only getting started.

THE END

**How does a down-on-her-luck Napa heiress end up married to an infuriating former Navy SEAL turned clueless winemaker? Read on for a sneak peek at Natalie's story . . .**

# Chapter One

For as long as August Cates could remember, his dick had ruined everything.

In seventh grade, he'd gotten a hard-on during a pep rally while standing in front of the entire school in football pants. Since his classmates couldn't openly call him Woody in the presence of their teachers, they'd called him Tom Hanks, instead. It stuck all through high school. To this day, he cringed at the very mention of *Toy Story.*

*Trust your gut, son.*

His navy commander father had always said that to him. In fact, that was pretty much all he'd ever said, by way of advice. Everything else constituted a direct order. Problem was, August tended to need a little more instruction. A diagram, if possible. He wasn't a get-it-right-on-the-first-try type of man. Which is probably why he'd mistaken his "gut" for his dick.

Meaning, he'd translated his father's advice into . . .

*Trust your dick, son.*

August straightened the wineglass in front of him in order to forgo adjusting the appendage in question. The glass sat on a silver tray, seconds from being carried to the panel of judges.

Currently, the three smug elitists were sipping a Cabernet offering that had been entered into the Bouquets and Beginners competition by another local vintner. The crowd of Napa Valley wine snobs leaned forward in their folding chairs to hear the critique from one judge in particular.

Natalie Vos.

The daughter of a legendary winemaker.

Vos Vineyard heiress and all-around plague on his fucking sanity.

August watched her full lips perch on the edge of the glass. They were painted a kind of lush plum color today. They matched the silk blouse she wore tucked into a leather skirt and he swore to God, he could feel the crush of that leather in his palms. Could feel his fingertips raking down her bare legs to remove those high heels with spikes on the toes. Not for the first time—no, incredibly far from the first time—he mentally kicked himself in the ass for sabotaging his chances of taking Natalie Vos to bed. She wouldn't touch him now through a hazmat suit and she'd told him as much umpteen times.

His chances of winning this contest didn't bode well.

Not only because he and Natalie Vos were enemies, but because his wine sucked big sweaty donkey balls. Everyone knew it. Hell, August knew it. The only one to call him out on it, however, was preparing to deliver her verdict to the audience.

"Color is rich, if a bit light. Notes of tobacco in front. Citrus aftertaste. Veering toward acidic, but . . ." She held the wine up to the sun and studied it through the glass. "Overall very enjoyable. Admirable for a two-year-old winery."

Murmurs and golf claps all around from the audience.

The winemaker thanked the judges. He actually bowed to

Natalie while retrieving his glass and August couldn't stifle the eye roll to save his life. Unfortunately, Natalie caught the action and raised a perfect black brow, signaling August forward for his turn at the judging table, like a princess summons a commoner—and didn't that fit their roles to a T?

August didn't belong in this sunny five-star resort and spa courtyard on a Saturday afternoon ferrying wine on a silver tray to these wealthy birdbrains who overinflated the importance of wine so much it felt like satire. He didn't belong in sophisticated St. Helena. Wasn't cut out to select the best bunch of grapes at the grocery store, let alone cultivate their soil and grow them from scratch to make his very own brand of wine.

*I tried, Sammy.*

He'd really fucking tried. This contest had a grand prize of ten thousand dollars and that money was August's last hope to keep the operation alive. If given another chance, he would be more hands-on during the fermentation process. He'd learned the hard way that "set it and forget it" didn't work for shit with wine. It required constant tasting, correcting, and rebalancing to prevent spoilage. He might do better with another season to prove himself.

For that, he needed money. And he had a better chance of getting Natalie in the sack than winning this competition—which was to say, he had no chance whatsoever—because yeah. His wine blew chunks. He'd be lucky if they managed to let it rest on their palates for three seconds, let alone declare him the winner. But August would try to the bitter end, so he would never look back and wonder if he could have done more to bring this secondhand dream to life.

August strode to the judges' table and set the glasses of wine in front of Natalie with a lot less ceremony than his competitors, sniffed, and stepped back, crossing his arms. Disdain stared back at him in the form of the two most annoyingly beautiful eyes he'd ever seen. Sort of a whiskey gold, ringed in a darker brown. He could still remember the moment the expression in those eyes had gone from *take-me-to-bed-daddy* to *please-drink-poison.*

Witch.

This was her domain, however. Not his. At six foot three with a body still honed for the battles of his past life as a SEAL, he fit into this panorama about as well as Rambo at a bake sale. The shirt he'd been asked to wear for the competition didn't fit, so it hung from the back pocket of his jeans. Maybe he could use it to clean up the wine when they spit it out.

"August Cates of Zelnick Cellar," Natalie said smoothly, handing glasses of wine to her fellow judges. Outwardly, she appeared cool as ever, her unflappable New York demeanor on full display, but he could see her breath coming faster as she geared herself up to drink what amounted to sludge in a glass. Of the three judges, Natalie was the only one who knew what was coming, because she'd tasted his wine once before—and promptly compared it to demon piss. Also known as the night he'd blown his one and only chance to sweat up the sheets with Princess Vos herself.

Since that ill-fated evening, their relationship had been nothing short of contentious. If they happened to see each other on Grapevine Way or at a local wine event, she liked to discreetly scratch her eyebrow with a middle finger, while August usually inquired how many glasses of wine she'd plowed through since nine A.M.

In theory, he hated her. They hated each other.

Dammit, though, he couldn't seem to *actually* do it. Not all the way.

It all went back to August mistaking his gut for his dick as a youngster.

As in, *trust your dick, son.*

And that part of his anatomy might as well be married to Natalie Vos. Married with seven kids and living in the Viennese countryside wearing matching play clothes fashioned out of curtains, à la *The Sound of Music.* If it were up to August's downstairs brain, he would have apologized the night of their first argument and asked for another shot to supply her with wall-to-wall orgasms. But it was too late now. He had no choice but to return the loathing she radiated at him, because his upstairs brain knew all too well why their relationship would never have gone past a single night.

Natalie Vos had privilege and polish—not to mention money—coming out of her ears.

At thirty-five, August was broker than a fingerless mime.

He'd dumped all of his life savings into opening a winery, with no experience or guidance, and losing this contest would be the death blow to Zelnick Cellar.

August's chest tightened like he was being strapped to a gurney, but he refused to break eye contact with the heiress. The growing ache below his throat must have been visible on his face because, slowly, Natalie's smug expression melted away and she frowned at him. Leaned in and whispered for his ears alone, "What's going on with you? Are you missing WrestleMania to be here or something?"

"I wouldn't miss WrestleMania for my own funeral," he snorted. "Just taste the wine, compare it to moldy garbage, and get it over with, princess."

"Actually, I was going to ordain it as something like . . . rat bathwater." She gestured at him with fluttery fingers. "Seriously, what's up? You have more asshole energy than usual."

He sighed, looking out at the rows of expectant spectators who were either in tennis whites or leisure wear that probably cost more than his truck. "Maybe because I'm trapped in an episode of *Succession*." Time to change the channel. Not that he had a choice. "Do your worst, Natalie."

She wrinkled her nose at his wine. "But you're already so good at being the worst."

August huffed a laugh. "Too bad they're not giving out a prize for sharpest fangs. You'd be unmatched."

"Are you comparing me to a vampire? Because your *wine* is the one that sucks."

"Just down the whole glass without tasting it, like you usually do."

Was that hurt that flashed in her eyes before she hid it?

Certainly not. "You are an—" she started.

"Ready to begin, Miss Vos?" asked one of the other judges, a silver-haired man in his fifties who wrote for *Wine Enthusiast* magazine.

"Y-yes. Ready." She shook herself and pulled back, regaining her poise and sliding her fingers around the stem of the wineglass containing August's most recent Cabernet. A groove remained between her brows as she swirled the glass clockwise and lifted it to her nose to inhale the bouquet. The other judges were already coughing, looking at each other in confusion. Had they accidentally been served vinegar?

They spat it out into the provided silver buckets almost in tandem.

Natalie, however, seemed determined to hold off as long as possible.

Her face turned red, tears forming in her eyes.

But to his shock, the swallow went down her throat, followed by a gasp for air.

"I'm afraid . . ." began one of the judges, visibly flustered. The crowd whispered behind August. "I'm afraid something must have gone terribly wrong during your process."

"Yes . . ." The other judge laughed behind his wrist. "Or a step was left out entirely."

The rows of people behind him chuckled and Natalie's attention strayed in that direction. She opened her mouth to say something and closed it again. Normally, she wouldn't hesitate to cut him off at the knees, so what was this? Pity? She'd chosen *this* moment? This moment, when he needed to walk out of here with some semblance of pride, to go easy on him?

Nah. Not having it.

He didn't need this spoiled, trust-fund brat to pull her punches. He'd seen shit during combat that people on this well-manicured lawn couldn't even fathom in their wildest dreams. He'd jumped out of planes into pitch-black skies. Existed on pure stubbornness for weeks on end in the desert. Suffered losses that still felt as though they'd happened yesterday.

*And yet you couldn't even make decent wine.*

He'd failed Sam.

Again.

A fact that hurt a damn sight more than this rich girl judging him harshly in front of these people he'd probably never see again after today. In fact, he needed Natalie to just drop the hammer already, so he could show her how little he cared about her opinion. It was his friend's dream never being realized that should hurt. Not her verdict.

August propped his hands on the judging table, seeing nothing but the beautiful, black-haired dream haunter, watching her golden eyes go wide at his audacity. "You're not waiting for a bribe, are you? Not with a last name like Vos." He winked at her, leaned down until only Natalie could hear the way he dropped his voice. "Unless you're hoping for a different kind of bribe, princess, because that can be arranged."

She threw wine in his face.

For the second time.

Honestly, he couldn't even blame her.

He was lashing out over his failure and Natalie was a convenient target. But he wasn't going to apologize. What good would it do? She already hated him and he'd just found a way to strengthen that feeling. The best thing he could do to make up the insult to Natalie was to leave town—and that's exactly what he planned to do. He'd been given no choice.

With wine dripping from his five o'clock shadow, August pushed off the table, swiped a sleeve over his damp face, and stormed across the lawn to the parking lot, failure like a thorn stuck dead in the center of his chest. He was almost to his truck when a familiar voice called out behind him. Natalie. Was she actually *following* him after the shit he'd said?

"Wait!"

Fully expecting to turn around and find a twelve-gauge shotgun leveled at his head, August turned on a booted heel and watched warily as the gorgeous witch approached. Why did he have the ridiculous urge to move at a fast clip back in her direction and catch her up in a kiss? She'd break his fucking jaw if he tried, but God help him, his dick/gut insisted it was the right thing to do. "Yeah? You got something else you want to throw in my face?"

"My fist. Among other, sharper objects. But . . ." She jerked a shoulder, appearing to search for the right words. "Look, we're not friends, August. I get that. I insulted your wine the night we were going to hook up and you've resented me ever since, but what you said back there? Implying my last name makes me superior? You're wrong." She took a step closer, her heels leaving the grass and stepping onto the asphalt of the parking lot. "You don't know *anything* about me."

He chuckled. "Go ahead, tell me all about your pain and suffering, rich girl."

She threw him a withering sigh. "I didn't say I've suffered. But I haven't exactly coasted along on my last name, as you seem to believe. I've only been back in St. Helena for a few months. The last name Vos means nothing in New York."

August leaned against the hood of his truck and crossed his arms. "I bet the money that comes with it does."

She gave August a look. One that suggested he was truly in the dark—and he didn't like that. Didn't like the possibility that he was wrong about this woman. Mainly because it was too late to change his actions now. He'd always have to wonder what the hell he could have done differently about Natalie Vos. But at least he could walk away from this phase of his life knowing he did his best for Sam. That's all he had.

"Did you ever want to get to know me? Or was it just . . ." Her attention dropped fleetingly to his zipper, then away, but it was enough to make him feel like he was back in that middle school pep rally trying not to get excited. "Just about sex?"

What the hell was he supposed to say?

That he'd seen her across the room at that stupid Wine Down event and felt like he'd had an arrow shot into his chest by a flying baby? That his palms sweat because of a woman for the first time ever that night? He'd already been on that Viennese countryside holding a picnic basket in one hand, an acoustic guitar in the other. God, she was so beautiful and interesting and fucking hilarious. Where had she been all his life?

Oh, but then somehow it all went to shit. He'd let his pride get in the way of . . . what? What would have happened if he'd just taken her verbal disapproval of his wine on the chin and moved forward? What if he hadn't equated it to disapproval of his best friend's aspirations? Was there any use wondering about any of this shit now?

No.

He'd run out of capital. The winery was an unmitigated disaster. He was the laughingstock of St. Helena and he'd dragged his best friend's name with him through the mud.

*Time to go, man.*

"Oh, Natalie." He slapped a hand over his chest. "Obviously I wanted to twirl you around on a mountaintop in Vienna while our children frolicked and harmonized in curtain clothes. Didn't you know?"

She blinked a few times and her expression flattened as she stepped back into the grass. August had to fist his hands to prevent himself from reaching for her.

"Well," she said, her voice sounding a little rusty. *Dammit.* "Have a lovely evening at home with your *Sound of Music* references and cozy nest of wine rats. I hope you're paying them a living wage."

"It won't be my home much longer." He threw a hand toward the event that was still in full swing behind them, the judges taking pictures with the audience members, more wine being served on silver trays. "This contest was it for me. I'm moving on."

She laughed as if he was joking, sobering slightly when he just stared back. "Wow. You really can't take a little constructive criticism, can you?"

August scoffed. "Is that what it was? Constructive?"

"I thought SEALs were supposed to be tough. You're letting winemaking take you down?"

"I don't have a bottomless bank account like some people in this town. In case it wasn't clear, I'm talking about you."

For some reason, that made her laugh. A beat of silence passed, then, "You've got me all figured out, August. Congratulations." She turned on the toe of her high heel and breezed away, moving that leather skirt side to side in the world's cruelest parting shot. "My sincere condolences to the town where you end up next," she called back over her shoulder. "Especially to the women."

"You wouldn't be saying that if you dropped the disgusted act and came home with me." For some reason, every step she took in the opposite direction made his stomach lurch with more and more severity. "It's not too late, Natalie."

She stopped walking and he held his breath, not fully aware until this very moment how badly he actually wanted her. Maybe even needed. The continued flow of his blood seemed to hinge on her response. "You're right, it's not too late," she said, turning, chewing her lip, eyes vulnerable in a manner that stuck a swallow in his throat. *I'll never be mean to her again.* "It's *way* too late," she concluded with a pinkie wave, her expression going from defenseless to venomous. "Go to hell, August Cates."

His stomach bottomed out, leaving him almost too winded for a reply. "Hell, huh? Your old stomping grounds, right?"

"Yup!" She didn't even bother turning around. "That's where I met your mom. She said she'd rather live in hell than drink your wine."

A crank turned in his rib cage as she moved out of earshot. Too far to hear him over the event music that had started up. Definitely too far to touch, so why were his fingers itching for her skin? His chances with Natalie were subzero now. Just like his chance at succeeding as a vintner. With a final long look at the one who got away, August cursed, climbed into his truck, and tore out of the parking lot, ignoring the strong sense of leaving something undone.

# Chapter Two

Natalie searched blindly in the dark for the button on her sound machine, cranking the symphony of rain and bullfrogs to the maximum level. Julian and Hallie tried to be quiet. They really did. But springs only creak at four o'clock in the morning for one reason—and creak they did. Natalie covered her face with a pillow for good measure and rolled back into the sheets, employing what she called the State Capitals Method. On the occasions her brother and his new girlfriend decided to make love down the hallway in the guesthouse they all shared, Natalie avoided that troubling imagery by naming state capitals.

Montgomery, Juneau, Phoenix . . .

*Creak creak creak.*

That was it.

Natalie sat up in bed and pushed off her sleep mask, giving the wine dizziness a moment to dissipate. No more excuses. It was time to bite the bullet and go talk to her mother. It was time to get the hell out of Napa. She'd been licking her wounds far too long, and while she was happy beyond words for Julian to have found the love of his life, she didn't need to witness it in surround sound.

She threw off the covers and stood, her hip bumping into the nightstand and knocking over an empty wineglass. One of *four*—as if she needed another sign that she'd turned into a lush in the name of avoiding her problems.

Life had ground to a standstill.

Looking out the window of the back bedroom, she could see the main house where she'd grown up and Corinne, her mother, currently lived. That was her destination in the morning. Asking her mother for money was going to sting like a thousand wasps, but what choice did she have? If she was going to return to New York and open her own investment firm, she needed capital.

Her mother wasn't going to make it easy. No, she was probably waiting right now in front of a roaring fire, dressed in all her finery, having sensed Natalie was on the verge of humbling herself. Sure, they'd had a few softer moments since Natalie's return to St. Helena, but just under the surface, she'd always be The Embarrassment to Corinne.

Natalie tossed her eye mask in the direction of the sad, empty wineglass quartet and plodded into the en suite bathroom. Might as well get the talk over with early, right? That way if Corinne said no to Natalie's proposal, at least she'd have the whole day to wallow. And this was Napa, so wallowing could be made very fashionable. She'd find a wine tasting and charm everyone in attendance. People who had no idea she'd been asked to step down as a partner of her finance firm for a wildly massive trade blunder that cost, oh, a cool billion.

Nor would they know she'd been kicked to the curb by her fiancé, who was too embarrassed to meet her at the altar.

Back in New York? Pariah.

In St. Helena? Royalty.

Snort. Natalie shed her sleep shirt and stepped beneath the hot shower spray. And if she thought her brother doing the deed constituted an unwanted image, it had nothing on the memory of August Cates yesterday afternoon in all his beefcake glory.

*I don't have a bottomless bank account like some people in this town.*

If only.

Natalie didn't have anything to complain about. She was living in a beautiful guesthouse on the grounds of a vineyard, for God's sake. But she'd been living off her savings for over a month now and she couldn't open a lemonade stand, let alone launch a firm, with the amount left over. She had privilege, but financial freedom presented a challenge. One she would hopefully overcome this morning. All it would cost was her pride.

The fact that August Cates planned to leave St. Helena imminently had nothing to do with her sudden urgency to leave, too. Nothing whatsoever. That big, incompetent buffoon and his decisions had no bearing on her life. So why the pit in her stomach? It had been there since he approached the table to have his wine judged yesterday. The man had a chip the size of Denver on his shoulder, but he always had kind of a . . . softness in his eyes. A relaxed, observant quality that said *I've seen everything. I can handle anything.*

But it was missing yesterday.

And it caught Natalie off guard how much it threw her.

He'd looked resigned. Closed off.

Now, drying her hair in front of the foggy bathroom mirror, she couldn't pretend that hole in her belly wasn't yawning wider. Where would August go? What would he do now that winemaking was off the table?

Who *was* August Cates?

Part of her—part she would never admit to out loud—had always wondered if she would find out eventually. In a weak moment. Or by accident.

Had she been looking forward to that?

Natalie turned off the dryer with a snappy movement, ran the brush one final time through her long, black hair, and left the bathroom, crossing to her closet. She put on a sleeveless black sweater dress and leather loafers, added a swipe of nude lipstick and some gold earrings. By the time she was finished, she could see through the guest room window that lights were on in the main house and she took a long breath, banishing the jitters.

All Corinne could say was no, Natalie reminded herself on the way up the path that ran alongside the fragrant vineyard. The sun hadn't risen yet, but the barest rim of gold outlined Mount St. Helena. She could almost feel the grapes waking up and turning toward the promise of warmth from above. Part of her truly loved this place. It was impossible not to. The smell of fertile earth, the tradition, the magic, the intricate process. Thousands of years ago, some industrious—and probably bored—people had buried bottles of grape juice underground for the winter and invented wine, which proved Natalie's theory: where there is a will to get drunk, dammit, there is a way.

She paused at the bottom of the porch steps leading to the estate. Old-world charm oozed from every inch of her childhood home. Greenery spilled over flower boxes beneath every window, rocking chairs urged people to sit and relax, and the trickle of the pool's water feature could be heard from the front of the house, even though it was located behind. A gorgeous estate that never failed to make winery visitors swoon. The place was incredible. But she had more affection for the guesthouse than the manor where she'd lived from birth to college. And right now, all it represented was the obstacle ahead.

A moment later, she knocked on the door and heard the sound of footsteps approaching on the other side. The peephole darkened, the lock turned—and then she was looking at Corinne.

"Seriously?" Natalie sighed, giving her stately mother a once-over, taking in the smoothed black-gray hair and perfect posture. Even her wrinkles were artful, allowed onto her face by invitation only. "You're fully dressed at five o'clock in the morning?"

"I could say the same about you," Corinne replied without missing a beat.

"True," Natalie said, sliding into the house without an invitation. "But I don't live here. Do you even own a bathrobe?"

"Did you come here to discuss sleepwear?"

"Nope. Humor me."

Corinne closed the door firmly, then locked it. "Of course I own a robe. Normally, I would be wearing it until at least seven, but I have virtual meetings this morning." In an uncharacteristic move, her mother let a smile peek through before it was quickly quelled. "Your brother has negotiated a deal making us the official wine of several wedding venues down the California coast. He is really helping turn things around for us."

"Yeah, he is." Natalie couldn't help but feel a spark of pride in her brother. After all, he'd overcome his own baggage pertaining to this place and landed on the other side much better off. At the same time, however, Natalie couldn't ignore the wistfulness drifting through her breast. God, just once, she'd love someone to talk about her like Corinne spoke about Julian. Like she was vital. Valued. Wanted *and* needed. "It's hard to tell him no when he's speaking in his stern professor voice. Takes people right back to seventh grade."

"Whatever he's doing, it's working." Corinne squared her shoulders and came farther into the foyer, gesturing for Natalie to precede her into the living space and to the right, overlooking the rambling vineyard, the mountains beyond. They took seats on opposite ends of the hard couch that had been there since Natalie's childhood and almost never used. Voses didn't *gather.*

They kept moving.

So in the interest of family tradition, Natalie turned toward Corinne and folded her hands on one knee. "Mother." If she'd learned one thing from phase one in the finance industry, it was to look a person in the eye when asking for money, and she did so now. "I know you will agree—it's time for me to go back to New York. I've been in contact with Claudia, one of my previous analysts, and she's agreed to come on board with my new company. We're going to be small, more of a boutique firm, but both of us have enough connections to facilitate steady growth. With a couple of smart plays—"

"Wow." Corinne framed her jaw with a thumb and index finger. "You've been making important phone calls in between wine binges. I had no idea."

Clang. A ding in the armor.

Okay.

She'd expected that and was prepared for it. *Just keep going.*

Natalie kept her features composed in an attempt to disguise how fast her heart was now beating. Why was it that she could make million-dollar trades without her pulse skipping, but one barb from Corinne and she might as well be dangling from the side of a skyscraper by a pinkie, cold sweat breaking out beneath her dress? Parents. *Man*, they messed up their kids.

"Yes, I have been making calls," Natalie replied calmly. She didn't deny the wine binges, because, yeah. She'd definitely done that. "Claudia is working on lining up an investor right now, but before anyone in their right mind gives us money, we'll need to register a new business name. We need an office and some skin in the investment game, however light." She tried not to be obvious about taking a bracing breath. "Bottom line, I need capital."

Not even the slightest reaction from her mother. She'd seen this coming and it burned, even though they'd both been aware this talk was on the horizon.

"Surely you saved *some* money," Corinne said smoothly, a gray-black eyebrow lifting gracefully toward her hairline. "You were a partner in a very lucrative investment fund."

"Yes. I was. Unfortunately, there is a certain lifestyle that has to be maintained for people to trust financiers with their money."

"That is a fancy way of saying you lived above your means."

"Perhaps. Yes." Oh boy, keeping her irritation at bay was going to be even harder than she thought. Corinne had come locked and loaded for this conversation. "The excess is necessary, however. Parties and designer clothing and vacations and expensive rounds of golf with clients. Morrison and I had an apartment on Park Avenue. Not to mention, we'd put down a nonrefundable deposit on our wedding venue."

That last part burned. Of course it did.

She'd been offloaded by a man who claimed to love her.

But for some reason, Morrison's face didn't materialize. No, instead she saw August. Wondered what he would say about a six-figure deposit on Tribeca Rooftop. He would look so out of place among the wedding guests. He'd probably show up in jeans, a ball cap, and that faded gray navy T-shirt. He would crush her ex in an arm-wrestling match, too. Why did that make her feel better enough to continue?

"In short, yes, I do have some money. If I was simply going back to New York, I could afford to find an apartment and live comfortably for a few months. But that is not what I want to do." The kick of adrenaline in her bloodstream felt good. It had been a long time. Or maybe while getting lit to mourn the loss of everything she'd worked for, she'd accidentally numbed her ambition, too. Right now, in this moment, she had it back. She was the woman who used to look down at rows of analysts from her glass office and feel prepared to kick ass and take names. "I want to return better than ever. I want them to realize they made a mistake . . ."

"You want to rub it in their faces," Corinne supplied.

"Maybe a little," Natalie admitted. "I might have made one huge mistake, but I know if Morrison Talbot the third had made that bad call, instead of me, excuses would have been made. He probably would have been given a promotion for being a risk taker. They met in secret and voted to oust me. My partners. My *fiancé*." She closed her eyes briefly to beat back the memory of her shock. Betrayal. "If you were me, Mother, you would want a shot to go back and prove yourself."

Corinne stared at her for several beats. "Perhaps I would."

Natalie released a breath.

"Unfortunately, I don't have the money to loan you," Corinne continued, her face deepening ever so slightly with color. "As you are aware, the vineyard has been declining in profitability.

With your brother's unexpected help, we're turning it around, but it could be years before we're back in the black. All I have is this house, Natalie."

"My trust fund," Natalie said firmly, forcing it out into the open. "I'm asking for my trust fund to be released."

"My, times have changed," Corinne said with a laugh. "When you graduated from Cornell, what was it that you said at your post-ceremony dinner? You would never take a dime from us as long as you lived?"

"I'm thirty years old now. Please don't throw something in my face that I said when I was twenty-two."

Corinne sighed, refolded her hands in her lap. "You are well aware of the terms of your trust fund, Natalie. Your father might be racing cars in Italy and parading around with women half his age like a fool, but he set forth the language of the trust and as far as the bank is concerned, he's still in control."

Natalie lunged to her feet. "The language in that contract is archaic. How can it even be legal in this day and age? There has to be something you can do."

Her mother let a breath seep out. "Naturally, I agree with you. But your father would have to sign off on the change."

"I am *not* going groveling to that man. Not after he just blew us off and pretends like we don't exist. Not when he left you to do damage control after the fire four years ago."

Corinne's attention shot to the vineyard, which was lightening in the path of the sun. "I wasn't aware you cared."

"Of course I care. *You* asked *me* to leave."

"I most certainly did not," her mother scoffed.

Really. She didn't even remember? Natalie would digest that later. Getting into the semantics of the last time she'd been in

St. Helena wouldn't do her cause any good now. "We'll have to agree to disagree on that."

Corinne appeared poised to argue, but visibly changed course. "My hands are tied, Natalie. The terms of the trust are set in stone. The recipient must be gainfully employed *and* married for the money to be released. I realize that sounds like something out of Regency England, not modern-day California, but your father is old-school Italian. His parents' marriage was arranged. It's glamorous to him. It's tradition."

"It's sexist."

"Normally I would agree, but the terms of Julian's trust are the same. When the contract was set forth, your father had some grand vision in his mind. You and Julian with your flourishing families taking over the winery. Grandchildren everywhere. Success." She made an absent gesture. "When you both left without any intention of joining the family business, it broke something inside of him. The fire was the final straw. I'm not making excuses for him, I'm just trying to give you a different perspective."

Natalie lowered herself back down to the couch and implored her mother with a look. "Please, there has to be something we can do. I can't stay here forever."

"Oh, I'm so sorry that staying in your family home feels like exile."

"You try waking up every morning to the sound of Julian and Hallie trying and failing to stifle their sex noises down the hall."

"Jesus Christ."

"They call for him, too, sometimes when they think I'm not home."

With a withering eye roll, Corinne pushed to her feet and strode to the front window. "You would think your father's hasty departure would bruise the loyalty of his local friends and associates, but I assure you, it has not. They still have him up on a pedestal—and that includes Ingram Meyer."

"Who?"

"Ingram Meyer, an old friend of your father's. He's the loan officer at the St. Helena Credit Union, but more importantly, he's the trustee of yours and Julian's trust funds. Believe me, he will follow your father's instructions to the letter."

Natalie's jaw had to be touching the floor. "Some man I've never heard of—or met—holds my future in his hands?"

"I'm sorry, Natalie. The bottom line is that . . . short of convincing your father to amend the terms, there is nothing I can do."

"I wouldn't ask you to do that," Natalie sighed. "Not after how he left."

Corinne was silent a moment. "Thank you."

That was it. The end of the conversation. There was nothing more to be said. Currently, Natalie was the furthest thing from gainfully employed. And even further from being married. The patriarchy wins again. She'd have to return to New York with her tail between her legs and ask for a low-level position at one of the firms she once called rivals. They would eat up her humility with a spoon and she'd . . . take it on the chin. Pulling together enough money to open her own business would probably take a decade, because God knew nobody would invest in her after a billion-dollar mistake. But she would do it. She'd do it on her own.

"Okay." Resigned, hollow, Natalie stood on shaky legs and smoothed the skirt of her dress. "Good luck with your meetings this morning."

Corinne said nothing as Natalie left the house, closing the

door behind her and descending the steps with her chin up. This morning, she would head into town, get her hair and nails done. At the very least, she could look good when she landed back in New York, right?

But everything changed on the way to get that balayage—and like some weird nursery rhyme from hell, it involved a cat, a rat . . . and a SEAL.

# About the Author

#1 *New York Times* bestselling author Tessa Bailey can solve all problems except her own, so she focuses her efforts on fictional stubborn blue-collar men and loyal, lovable heroines. She lives on Long Island, avoids the sun and social interactions, then wonders why no one has called. Dubbed the "Michelangelo of dirty talk" by *Entertainment Weekly*, Tessa writes with spice, spirit, swoon, and a guaranteed happily ever after. Catch her on TikTok @authortessabailey or check out tessabailey.com for a complete list of her books.

MORE ROM-COMS FROM #1 *NEW YORK TIMES* BESTSELLING AUTHOR AND TIKTOK FAVORITE

# TESSA BAILEY

**SECRETLY YOURS**

The first in a steamy new duology about a starchy professor and the bubbly neighbor he clashes with at every turn...

**IT HAPPENED ONE SUMMER**

The *Schitt's Creek*–inspired TikTok sensation about a Hollywood "It Girl" who's cut off from her wealthy family and exiled to a small Pacific Northwest beach town . . . where she butts heads with a surly, sexy local who thinks she doesn't belong.

**HOOK, LINE, AND SINKER**

A former player accidentally falls for his best friend while trying to help her land a different man. . .

**FIX HER UP**

A bad-boy professional baseball player falls for the girl next door . . . who also happens to be his best friend's little sister.

**LOVE HER OR LOSE HER**

A young married couple signs up for relationship boot camp in order to rehab their rocky romance and finds a second chance at love!

**TOOLS OF ENGAGEMENT**

Two enemies team up to flip a house . . . and the sparks between them might burn the place down or ignite a passion that neither can ignore!

MORROW